MASTERS OF KINGS

SWORDFATHERS
BOOK ONE

DANIEL SHIELDS

LINDENFYRE PRESS

FULCGRUM

FORSBEME
WANDERING WATERS
ANGERED SEA
RAVENTYN
NEW VALOIS
MIDDLE RIVER
STONEBANN
RIVER OF PLENTY
SATINWIND

N
W   E
S

Swordfamilies

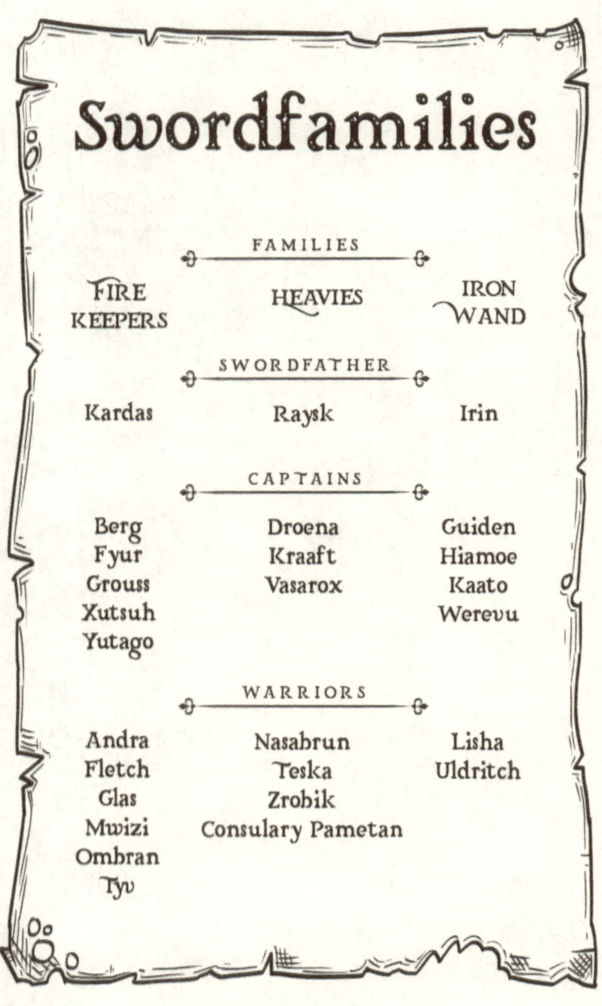

Swordfamilies

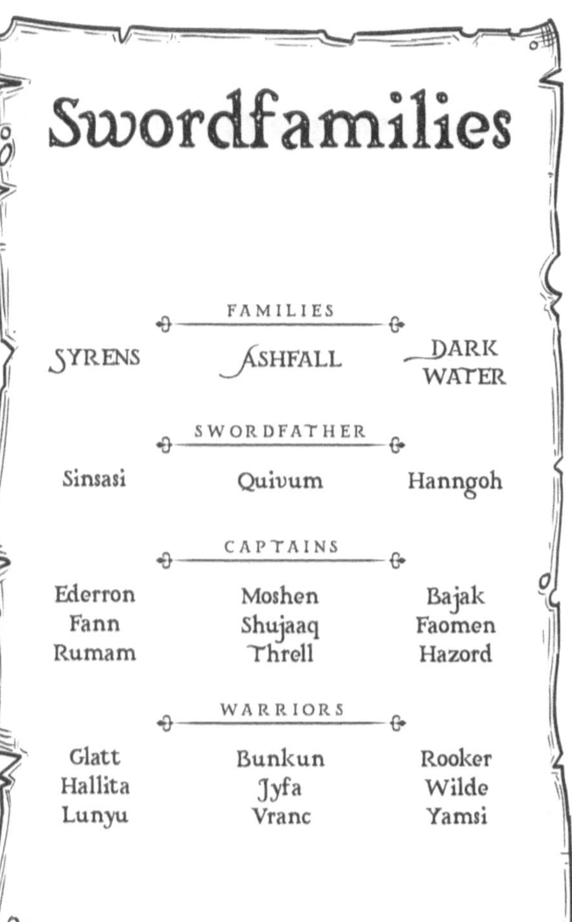

Emerald Crown

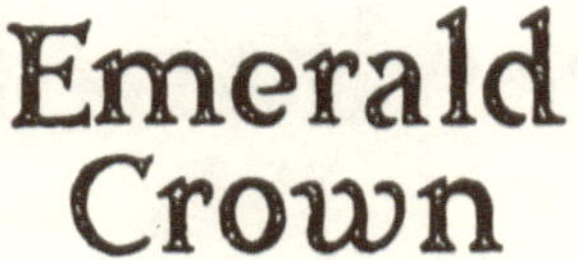

King Fallov   Queen Minacia
Counselor Voden   Counselor Melyq

Prince Opvolk   Princess Silny

Prince Bruun   Princess Modawa

Prince Tajnum   Princess Tajna

CHAPTER ONE

FIRE KEEPERS

"They can't kill our dragons. Only we can kill our dragons!" Kardas bellowed. He slammed his fist down on the arm of his oaken chair. "How many is that since the last triple eclipse?"

"Five," replied a woman sitting on a half-empty cask of strong ale. "That we know of, anyway."

Kardas leaned back and frowned hard. A naked blade lay across his lap. An unsheathed sword usually served as a threat that its owner was eager to wield it. Not this sword. Thick lines of dark rust streaked the dull steel. The point was blunt from bearing its master's weight as a cane. The most unyielding foes the blade now clashed against were cobblestone paths. For longer than he would admit, Kardas had used his ruined sword only for walking, not warring.

"Are you certain the dragon was dead, Andra?" he asked the woman perched on the cask.

"See for yourself," she replied.

Brilliant sunlight flooded the dark room as Andra pulled aside a rough cloth. She revealed a window that framed a turbulent river. Snow on the peaks of the Pader

Mountains had begun melting in the springtime warmth. The snowmelt raced down mountainsides to swell many streams that joined the river called Wandering Waters.

"Why is the river boiling?" Glas asked in an unusually high tone.

"Upstream from the dragon there were chunks of ice bigger than a man. That water should be so cold right now that it could nearly freeze the fish," Andra replied. "Instead, they're cooking in it."

Kardas curled his fingers around the grip of his sword. He pressed its point onto a dimpled patch of wood floor that had been rubbed bone white. Rising for a better look through the window, the hilt bore much of his weight and the white patch in the floor garnered another dimple.

The Wandering Waters roared as its surface churned in a rolling boil. Schools of dead fish were swept downriver by the current. Wilted cattails lay on the banks like dying men on a battlefield.

Without taking a single step toward the window, the Swordfather had seen enough. Kardas relieved his cane of its burden and sank back into his chair.

"Wretched poachers," he mumbled. "Where in the refuge did you find the dragon?" He absently poked the sword into a pile of glass shards mounded on the floor near his feet.

"She was upstream lying on the riverbank next to her nest," Andra replied. "Foxes devoured her eggs and the hatchlings. She can't have been dead long. A white cloud rose where her blood poured into the river." She turned to address Glas. "That's why the Wandering Waters is boiling."

The tallest and widest man in the room absently pounded a war hammer into the palm of his hand. He moved the steel hammer as if it was made of dried reeds. "What about the body? What was missing from it? That'll tell us who killed our dragon."

Andra shook her head. "That's what I don't understand, Berg," she replied, her eyebrows raised in confusion. "She looked as if her neck had been laid on a chopping block. Her head was hanging on by the scales. They didn't take anything as a trophy. All of her spikes were still there. Those could have been ground into powder and fetched a fat pouch of gold scythes. She had her eyes, too. The eggs were left for the scavengers." Andra bit her lip. "The strangest thing was the wings were cut off and laid over her body. As if the dragon was sleeping in a bed."

Shards crackled as Kardas kept poking the point of his sword in the mound of glass. Many pieces were caked in dried blood. "This isn't the work of poachers. They didn't kill to harvest from the body or rob the nest. They did it for one reason only." He sounded very tired. "To send a message."

"Inked in the blood of our own dragons," Andra added ruefully.

A cold rage spread through Kardas like the first frost of autumn.

"The Ashfall family has groused about our dragons burning their crops," Glas offered.

Kardas didn't hear the boy's words. "The dragons in our refuge are the moat that protects our Swordfamily. Killing our dragons drains that moat. We kill those wondrous beasts only to squelch illness and keep the herd in good health. Whoever's doing this aims to kill us, soon or late." He stared at the glass pile near his feet.

The large group of Fire Keepers in the room fell silent. Their voices were replaced by the boiling growl from the

Wandering Waters and the tavern's raucous din below. To Kardas's ears, the river sounded like ominous thunder rolling through dark clouds.

The thick door to the room rattled as someone battered the far side. Half the Fire Keepers in the room flinched.

Berg readied his war hammer and yanked the door open. The man on the other side raised his hands in mock self-defense.

"It's the crown's counselor, Melyq," Berg said with an air of indifference. He turned and stomped away from the visitor.

"Berg, that's no way for a captain to greet a friend from the royal court," Kardas said in an apologetic tone. He leaned on his sword to stand and welcome their visitor. "Please join us, Royal Counselor Melyq."

Melyq passed scores of Fire Keeper captains and warriors as he walked the length of the room. His steps were quiet as falling snow. The counselor's eyes swept over the Swordfamily. Their faces were neither welcoming nor hostile.

He stood directly before Kardas and said, "Swordfather." Then he began to kneel.

"Stop that!" Kardas exclaimed. "I *put* the bloody pile of glass there so our guests would *stop* kneeling. Now I *have* a bloody pile of glass there because they *keep* kneeling!"

Melyq froze as his knee met a shard. The piece was peppered with dark splotches of dried blood. The counselor rose with a small tear where his velvet trousers had pressed against the sharp glass. A single drop of blood beaded on his skin.

"What must I do to keep you all from kneeling? Smash a hole through the floor? Pour hot coals on it?"

The two men laughed together and clasped each other's forearms.

Kardas stood head and shoulders above Melyq. Or he would have, were he not leaning on his sword. The Fire Keepers' Swordfather had a short beard that hung over his thick neck and little more. His brown hair was engaged in a fighting retreat against the rapidly advancing gray. Tired eyes made his wrinkled visage equal parts humble, genuine, and wise. The simple cloak he wore was made of coarse cloth. It was threadbare in many places. A dragon fang hung from the flax string that circled his neck.

Melyq wore fragile, thin cloth embellished with intricate goldwork. His puffy hands told of a life spent wielding a quill rather than a sword. The softness pervaded his body from his feet to his face. His lips were plump sausages cooked nearly to bursting. One of his wrists bulged against a bracelet shaped like a snake eating its own tail. The snake had yellow fangs, blue eyes, and green skin.

Kardas sank back into his old chair. His bones creaked more than the chair as it resumed bearing the Swordfather's weight.

"All who serve in the royal court may count the Fire Keepers among their friends." Kardas laid his sword across his lap.

Fiddling with his bracelet, Melyq frowned. "Regretfully, I must inform you that I am no longer a member of the royal court."

Many brows furrowed in response to this statement.

"I'm truly sorry to hear that, Melyq," Kardas replied in a kindly tone. "Whether you're in the court or seated on the throne hall's back benches, the Fire Keepers will always lend you aid. You have only to ask."

Melyq clasped his hands together. "Ah, the situation is

not what you think. Through the grace of the thundering horde of gods, I remain very much involved in royal affairs. It is the court itself that has changed. After much discussion, the king and queen have formally recognized the rift that has existed for some time. The royal court has been rent in twain. That is, there are two courts now and I serve in the queen's court as her counselor."

Kardas shifted in his chair.

Andra folded her arms. "A queen's court and a king's court? Do the three princes and three princesses get their own courts, too?" she asked with disdain. "What's next, a fool's court?"

"As you are no doubt aware, relations between the king and queen are...strained. The crown thought it best to separate their affairs for the time being. Despite this new approach, they remain dedicated to governing the kingdom with their customary masterful leadership. The two courts act as emissaries, go-betweens that carry messages from one throne to the other."

"Thrones do not grant power." Kardas stroked his short beard. "The king and queen are just as powerful seated on their thrones as they are on their chamber pots. You come before me on the queen's behalf?"

Melyq nodded.

"What favor would Queen Minacia ask of us?"

Melyq's eyes darted over the Fire Keepers. "The matter that I wish to discuss is quite sensitive. Perhaps we could speak where fewer ears listen?"

Kardas broke into a wan smile. "It is said that the city walls have ears. But we are well outside of Fulccrum's walls and you are in the company of friends. Whatever you would say to me, you can speak before my family."

A shallow nod was Melyq's reply, his hands now

clasped behind his back. "Lord Wrand, Sentinel of the Lava Sea, is one of the crown's few friends east of the Pader Mountains. He has sent a chest of gold and gems to Fulccrum to pay homage to our Emerald Crown."

"A lord sending tribute to our feuding king and queen in the capital city does not seem to require the Fire Keepers' skills," Kardas said in a patient voice.

The noise from the boiling river grew louder, as did the tavern's merriment below.

Beads of sweat formed on Melyq's upper lip.

"Lord Wrand's tribute was requested by King Fallov. It's only half the amount that the queen deems acceptable. She needs the Fire Keepers to procure the chest before it arrives in Fulccrum. You will then bring me the chest discreetly. After it goes missing, Lord Wrand will have no choice but to fill another chest with riches and send it to the crown. The two chests, together, will satisfy the queen's desire for Lord Wrand to show the Emerald Crown proper respect."

Berg eyed his war hammer. "Why do you need us for this little errand?"

"We require the aid of those who rule the shadows," Melyq began. He winced and gritted his teeth as he sucked in a quick breath.

Laughter served as Kardas's immediate reply. "Shadows, you say. I beg to differ, because our endeavors are much alike. Your crown takes coin the same as my family. When a Swordfamily takes coin, you call it *theft*. When the crown takes coin, you call it *tax*. Hahr! Different words for the same deed!"

Melyq took a deep breath. "Apologies, Swordfather. I meant no offense. I simply chose the wrong words. The queen needs help from people who can be trusted. No one can know who takes the chest or where it goes."

Kardas's shoulders slumped and his eyes widened. "That's quite a request. Now I'll ask Berg's question again. Why come to the Fire Keepers with this? It sounds like something more suited to the Heavies. We've had peace among the six families and the Emerald Crown long enough for my sword to rust. I don't want to step on another family's toes with a sabaton." He ran his fingers over the dragon fang resting on his chest.

"There's more," Melyq said as beads of sweat sprang from his brow. "You cannot kill or harm any of Lord Wrand's men."

The Fire Keepers gathered in the room erupted in protest. Their deafening cries eclipsed the noise from both the river and tavern. Kardas remained still as carved granite. He waited patiently before silencing his family by raising a hand.

"I see why you're here and not in their cavern. If the Heavies did this, there would doubtless be more than a few corpses left in their wake. They do enjoy their work," Kardas said. "What of Iron Wand? Why not them?"

Melyq scoffed. "That family should be named 'Smoke and Looking Glasses.' We want to steal from Lord Wrand, not entertain his men with a foolish magic show. The other families are similarly ill-suited to this undertaking. This will require creativity that I believe only the Fire Keepers possess. And I need a Swordfather that I can trust. Deliver the chest to me unopened and you will be rewarded handsomely from the queen's own coffers."

The oaken chair groaned as Kardas leaned forward. His beard tucked against his neck as he looked down. The Fire Keepers stared at their leader. He examined the broadside of his sword and picked at a splotch of dirt near the rounded point.

"Lord Wrand's chest will be delivered to you cloaked in secrecy. But we've been able to raise much gold through our taxes—I mean theft." Kardas spoke slowly and deliberately. "We have little need for the queen's treasure. We'd much prefer that you pay for our services with your debt."

A single bead of sweat on Melyq's forehead dribbled down to join its brethren above his lip. After a pause, he spoke slowly. "I accept, Swordfather."

"Where is this chest now?"

"On a wain in the Crimson Realm approaching the Paders. A five-day ride from Fulccrum on a courser. Perchance thrice as long for Wrand's team pulling the wain."

"Very well." Kardas ran his fingers through his thick beard. "To do this, we require one thing from you. In the east chambers of the castle on the third floor there's a room in the corner farthest from the stairs. The room is almost always locked, which is odd because the only thing inside it are old portraits. My family stumbled upon them while searching for something at the king's request. Before we take the chest, you must provide us with a portrait."

"Any of them?" Melyq asked.

"We'd prefer the one that bears a strong likeness to the eldest royal child, the prince," Kardas replied.

"The man who resembles Prince Opvolk, the Prince of the Eclipse? I believe I know the painting you mean," Melyq said. He gave Kardas a shallow bow and whispered, "I am in your debt, my Blade."

The queen's counselor spun and strode away, disappearing through the door. He left behind a trail of wet spots where the sweat from his face had dripped.

The Swordfather announced that everyone in the room was to assemble by the funeral pyre outside except for

Andra, Berg, and Glas. The Fire Keepers obeyed, departing through a door behind Kardas that opened to stairs on the back side of the tavern.

Only the four remained on the second floor.

Andra scoffed, "Two royal courts? They can't even rule their own throne hall. This is what happens when power is gifted by blood instead of earned by strength!" She kicked over the cask of ale that had been her seat.

"Unearned gifts make men soft and weak," Berg agreed. He turned to Kardas. "Do you think Melyq was here on the queen's orders? Do you trust him?"

"Trust him? Hahr! The lies dripped from his mouth like venom from a snake's hollow fang!" Kardas shook his head. "Lies are like men. The older they get, the bigger they grow and the worse they age. Soon this one will rot."

"Melyq moves like quicksilver on a looking glass. Fast and invisible. We're blind to whatever truth he's veiled with his lies. It's like playing chess against him, but we can't see his pieces," Andra protested. "If the king hears of this, he'll be wroth. Why do it, my Blade?"

"It's a risk, but that's how we throw our dice." Kardas coughed into his hand. "I expect that we'll soon need many friends on the royal court, however many royal courts there are. King Fallov and I have been close for a great many eclipses. But the queen is no friend of mine and Melyq is the queen's man. If Melyq asks a favor of us, I would gladly put him in our debt."

Andra flashed a knowing grin. "Another strand in your web of debts, eh?"

Beginning near the hilt, Kardas slid his finger along his sword's dull edge.

"You must weave a web of debt." The wrinkles around the Swordfather's eyes grew deeper as he spoke. "Each thread in your web must be a debt disguised as a gift. The favors you grant draw your prey closer and bind them tighter. All Swordfathers spin their own webs. It's a matter of survival. They're a greater defense than our dragons, or the Heavies' strength, or the Syrens' beauty."

When his finger reached the blade's point, he began to trace the other edge back to the hilt.

"You either lie in wait at the center of your web of debt, or get snared in the threads where your enemies lie in wait for *you*." Kardas paused and locked eyes with each of his three Fire Keepers in turn. "You must weave strong and straight. Elsewise your tangled web may wrap around your own neck. If your web becomes a noose, when it tightens you'll cry for the sweet relief of a headsman's blade."

Kardas spoke from hard won experience.

Berg shouldered his war hammer and grinned. "You wield debts like the victor at the Melee of the Risen Knight swings his sword."

"Hahr!" Kardas laughed, his cheeks swelling as he grinned. "The threads of my web are stronger than any steel clutched in a knight's hand. Weak debts make weak webs that tear like rotted cloth."

"To think, all those debts spreading out from that spot, right there." Glas pointed at his Swordfather's chair. "It's like the hub of a wagon wheel holding all the spokes."

"'Tis a humble throne of debt." Kardas petted the arms of his chair. Then he sighed. "And now we mourn our dear friend."

The Swordfather curled his fingers around the hilt of his sword. The pommel shined brightly, having been polished by his palm. The leather wrapped around the grip was loose and frayed. One of its cross-guards was broken. The sword again became Kardas's cane with its point pressed inside the bone white patch on the floor. As he rose, his cloak snagged on a notch in the blade where it had met with stronger steel.

"Whatever his intentions, I suspect that Melyq has done this without the queen's knowing. He has more flaws than my sword, but stupidity is not among them," Kardas said breathlessly. "If he spoke any truth, he knows why she's angered and what she wants. By asking this in secret, he makes a gamble but takes no risk. He offered us the queen's gold knowing we'd want his debt instead. If we succeed, he presents the chest to the queen and wins her favor because she gets all the gold that she wanted from Wrand. If we fail, the lord's wain was raided by a gang of outlaws and we are very much on our own. Even if he doesn't win, he still doesn't lose."

Atop a cask full of brown ale, a cat slept on its side. The feline was so large that her fur spilled over the edge of the cask head. Her gray and white coat was unnaturally bright, as if each hair had been polished to a shine. Her body was covered in long fur except for the shorter hairs on her neck, shoulders, and the two little wings on her back. Spikes made of fur lined her backbone and nubs poked up in front of her ears. More tiny nubs stuck out from the end of her tail.

"Furwing, get over here," Andra called.

The cat slowly raised her head. She yawned with her pink tongue so curled that the tip pointed at the back of her throat. Standing on all fours, she stretched with her hind legs tall and her front legs straight forward. Properly invigorated, the cat flapped her tiny wings a few times. She padded across the room to rub against Andra's legs.

"Your cat hasn't caught many rats lately," Glas said. "All

that dragon milk she drank as a kitten must have dulled her feline side."

Furwing hissed at him.

"Long may she purr," Andra said in a brassy tone.

The sounds of Fire Keepers milling around the funeral pyre below drifted in through the window. Among them were fragments of gallows humor commingled with lavish praise for the dead.

"Andra, you'll lead our raid on Lord Wrand's chest," Kardas said. He didn't give her a chance to refuse. "You must find out which kind of horses are drawing the wain that carries the chest. Learn their colors and exactly what the wain looks like. Every detail of the chest and what the drivers wear are of great import." Kardas closed his eyes as he parsed the job in his mind. "They'll be on the road for a fortnight traveling slow, so our warriors will have time to spy that out. I know enough about Lord Wrand to know that his guards are always in full armor with great helms over their faces, so they won't be able to see much."

"How can you know that?" Andra interrupted, incredulous.

"Wrand's been cautious ever since he was ambushed just a few leagues from his own castle walls." Kardas winked at her. "Send our best warriors and learn all of those things with much quickness. After that's done, come to me and I'll tell you how we'll win Melyq's prize at Six Corners." When Andra opened her mouth to object, the Swordfather pressed his index finger against her lips. "After we get that chest to Melyq, you'll be made a captain." He pulled his finger away.

Berg grinned wide. The floor shook as he slammed his war hammer against it in celebration.

"One more thing," Kardas said. He pulled out a piece of

cloth stained with dark red splotches. He covered his mouth with it and coughed hard. "Before you deliver the chest to Melyq, open it. If there's gold, count it. If there's anything other than gold, tell me exactly what it is."

Glas began to protest that Melyq wanted the chest closed.

Kardas parried his objection before the warrior finished. "I know what Melyq said. But he'll never know that we've taken a look because you'll pick the lock." Kardas put his hand on Glas's shoulder. "After it's open and we discover what's so precious to Melyq, you'll lock it up again. This is a big job; don't disappoint your family. Come now, we have a funeral to attend."

The four Fire Keepers left through the rear door. Berg went down the stairs first to stay ahead of, and below, Kardas.

Thick gray clouds had quickly gathered to blot out the sunlight. The sign on the building the Swordfamily had occupied read "Lye Tavern." Its faded wood was cracked and rotted so badly that the words were difficult to read.

Between the Lye Tavern and Wandering Waters a dead man lay on his back. The body rested on a stack of flat rocks. Beneath him, the rocks were covered in black scorch marks and a dusting of ash. On the ground, ringed around the rocks, were gold coins. A warrior neared the funeral pyre and tossed another coin at its base. He whispered, "May the thundering horde keep you," and shuffled away.

The man's muscles were taut and defined, as though they'd been carved from ironwood. A dragon skull was positioned over his head. Its jaws were opened wide to expose the dead man's face. Tanned dragon hide covered his body.

"Our first captain to die in many eclipses," Berg said. He

leaned close to the departed Fire Keeper. "Hard to believe that Fyur died fetching some frozen book. He could swing a greatsword faster than most men can slash a dagger. He once dueled a man and shoved his sword so far down the fool's throat that the man crapped a steel blade as he died. Fyur didn't deserve this. He deserved an honorable death in a glorious battle."

"He runs with the thundering horde of gods now," Glas mumbled.

Berg glowered at him. "Gods are for people who beg for help because they're weak. That's not our fallen captain. That's not Fyur. He mounts the Cloud Dragon to join his strength to the Keepers Beyond."

"At least Dark Water was able to pull him from the sea so he can be burned properly," Andra said, her voice filled with sorrow. She pressed her hand on a pyre stone. "I've never understood why the townsfolk bury men in the ground. What do they think a body is? A seed? They plant a body and a stone grows from its head?" She wiped the bud of a tear from her eye. "Sow the dead and reap the stone? Mayhaps they believe a graveyard is a garden."

A grove of spreading chestnut trees painted the far riverbank with dark shadows.

Andra set her bleary eyes on the flowers near the swollen river banks. Blooms beyond count swayed in the gentle breeze. They were made of yellow, white, and purple petals in a medley of shapes. There were snowdrops, crocuses, and daffodils. As her eyes flitted between the clusters, they lingered on a large group of pale blue flowers. Tears streamed from her eyes.

"Do you see those flowers?" Andra asked Glas, her voice breaking. She pointed at the blue flowers. "The farmers call them forget-me-nots."

Glas nodded and turned his attention to the boiling Wandering Waters. "The townsfolk dubbed that river the headsman's privy, because of all the headless bodies that've been found in it. That river must flow through the thundering hells before it gets here. It carried headless men down to the port and now it's boiling. Surely it's cursed."

Berg ignored the warrior. "Fyur had such a liking for that ink he put in his skin." He glanced over the fallen captain's body. Most of Fyur's tattoos were concealed as he lay on the funeral pyre, but the ink on his neck still showed. "I never understood it, but he asked a favor. Said that if he went before me, I should pour a bottle of skin ink down his gullet. So I did." Berg folded his arms. "He wanted even more lines and dots inked on his body after he died, too. He must've lain on the blue ice in the undercroft for the better part of an eclipse before they finished drawing on him." Berg furrowed his brow. "Seems needless. All of him will be the same color soon."

"Cold comfort that his dragon made it back alive," Glas said. "If only Hoqqes could speak. She hasn't been the same since she returned. Something's not right."

Berg grabbed Glas by the elbow and pulled him away from the body. "Stand back," he barked.

Two women approached Fyur. They wore hoods and black dragon wings wrapped around their bodies. Each of them held a long iron pole straight up. A bowl filled with red liquid was suspended from a chain between the two poles. The two women stopped with the bowl directly above the open dragon jaws around Fyur's face. The dead captain's mouth was agape.

The inside of Fyur's mouth was stained black from the ink that Berg had poured into it.

The Fire Keepers watched in solemn silence.

Another woman, clad in red dragon wings, held a small torch in one hand and a dragon fang in the other. She thrust the fang under the bowl and tipped the bottom up. The red liquid poured from the bowl into Fyur's open mouth. A thin tendril of smoke rose past his lips.

Glas's eyes narrowed as he watched the smoke.

"Aged dragon blood," Berg whispered to him.

The woman in red placed the dragon fang on Fyur's forehead. For a fleeting moment she held the torch, no bigger than her hand, over his mouth. Then she dropped it. Flame shot from his mouth, up through the dragon skull's open jaws.

All three women said in unison, "The Family Beyond will find our fallen."

The Fire Keepers responded with their chant: "Born to burn! Born to burn! Born to burn!"

Points of flame ate through spots in Fyur's tattooed skin. They quickly grew larger and merged together. In the same time it took to draw a few breaths, the funeral pyre devoured the body and loosed a pillar of black smoke.

Fire Keepers that had closed around their fallen comrade took several steps away from the blistering heat.

"Fyur, may you rest in the peace that eluded you in life," Andra whispered after the chanting died down. "Climb the mountains of gold before you now. The highest summits will be yours forever." She paused for a long moment. "As will my heart."

"More like than not, he's lounging on a golden mountain. Looking out over shining lakes of silver." Glas nodded, as if agreeing with himself. "The thundering horde is circling it all, guarding the riches and our Family Beyond for when it's our time."

"I'll be the one giving the eulogies one day," Berg muttered.

Servers rushed from the tavern carrying trays covered in cups. Fire Keepers swarmed to them, grabbing the drinks. Not one of them took a sip as they awaited the signal from their Swordfather.

"Fire Keepers!" Kardas began and his family cheered. "We are brothers and sisters and we are here, together, to mourn our beloved captain." The sword that served as his cane wobbled as he leaned on it. "We will grieve him today, tomorrow, and forever more. Most importantly, we'll mourn him late into this night and the morrow's morning!"

A cheer rolled over the family like a wave.

"Fyur died in service to our family and way of life. Remember always, Family First!"

The Swordfamily cheered their agreement.

"Thrones are merely soft chairs. We are the true kings and queens of this realm. Our thrones are the saddles mounted on the backs of our mighty dragons!"

The Fire Keepers pumped their fists in the air as they roared.

"Royalty passes by blood. Our power passes by strength! We're born paupers, but we die lording over the crown!"

The Fire Keepers erupted into frenzied cheers. Kardas leaned on his sword for a couple of breaths and gathered his strength.

"Join me in a toast," he yelled as he rose to his full height. A captain handed him a cup that Kardas held high. The scores of Fire Keepers who surrounded him raised their own drinks. "Fyur, you were my friend, my family, and my Fire Keeper. Burn in peace. He goes before us and we shall follow! What do we cry?"

"Born to burn! Born to burn! Born to burn!" The crowd's chant was so loud that small children nearby covered their ears and fled. Every cup held in salute was quickly drained.

The flames that had engulfed Fyur began to shrink. The scorching dragon blood reduced his body to motes fragile as gossamer. Tall flowers on the riverbank bent sideways as a strong breeze carried away his ashes.

He was buried in the wind.

The air became chill and the Swordfamily drifted away into the dim twilight and the tavern. As the family scattered, two Fire Keepers remained at the foot of Fyur's pyre, as if anchored to the earth.

Kardas leaned hard on his sword. "We've long enjoyed quietude in Fulccrum. The six families have not troubled one another." He gripped Andra's shoulder, steadying himself. His sword alone was not enough to keep him upright. "It was a good peace."

Hazy smoke lingered over the empty funeral pyre.

"There is balance in Fulccrum and I mean to keep it," Kardas said. His voice sounded hollow. "Balance is best. It's agreement and peace. The six great Swordfamilies have thrived under it. But it is so, so fragile." He shuddered as he drew a deep sigh. "For the families to enjoy harmony, there need be peace in the Emerald Crown's throne hall."

Kardas pulled himself up so his lips were close to Andra's ear.

"I fear that pax familia is in its death throes. Families will fall."

CHAPTER TWO
IRON WAND

"I've used a dagger as a wand. Sometimes to cast, sometimes to cut, sometimes to do both at the same time," Guiden said coolly. "Using a broken arrow to cast spells isn't all that strange to me. It's not the worst wand, but it's certainly not the Wailing Wand."

The steel arrowhead spun as he rolled the shaft between two fingers. Then he stabbed the wand into the air, as if casting a spell.

Lisha kept her eyes on the wand. "I'm from outside the city. I mean *far* outside Fulccrum. Past the roads where weeds grow tall in wagon wheel ruts. Out there you have to cast with whatever you can find. But I'm through playing games. I'm here to master magic. They say Iron Wand has the best spellcasters in this realm and a library bursting with grimoires." She lowered her voice. "It's said that when one Iron Wand kills another in a duel, the victor brings the vanquished back from the dead."

A noise that sounded suspiciously like a stifled laugh escaped from Guiden. He stood in silence for long heartbeats. Then he handed the wand back to Lisha.

"I abandoned my lord and life to come here," she pressed. "Show me your secrets."

Long, lean, and blond were the three words that came to Lisha's mind as she looked over Guiden. With his thin lips and emotionless mask, she couldn't read him at all. The nearly black cloak that hid most of his body matched the darkness of the catacombs that stretched behind him. The only thing that held the darkness at bay was a single torch burning in a sconce.

"Very well, you may enter. I'll show you some of the catacombs." He pulled the torch from the wall and pointed it down a tunnel. "This way."

The walls and barrel ceiling were made of crumbling gray bricks. The clay mortar that held them together was encrusted with thick moss. Water wept through cracks, streaking the stone with dark mold and light minerals.

Pieces of fallen brick crackled under their feet as the two made their way down the tunnel. Where their feet didn't land on stone fragments, they splashed in puddles of stagnant water.

As a child, Lisha had once hidden in a graveyard to ensure she wouldn't be found until the next morning. Walking through the tunnel, its sickly scent evoked her long-suppressed memory of sharing the bottom of an open grave for a night.

"Why do you hide in caves?" Lisha asked, luring her thoughts away from her youth. She clutched her wand tight and kept its arrowhead at the ready.

"These are catacombs, not caves," Guiden patiently corrected her. "They were built by ancient settlers who worshipped long forgotten gods, eons before Fulccrum had its first city walls. Generations later, it was used as a prison. When the air down here became so bad that even the rats were dying, it was abandoned and sealed with rock. The door you came through is where the first Iron Wands cast the spell that shattered a boulder into pebbles. That spell opened our way inside. We've remained here ever since to enjoy the...solitude. Iron Wand occupies many catacombs that straddle the city wall. Some are in Raventyn and the others are outside the city."

A wooden door held together by rusted iron stood before them. Some of it had been burned away completely, and the charred wood that remained was blacker than the iron. Guiden pushed on the door, to no effect. Then he kicked the door hard, wrenching it from the bottom hinge. The ruined door stubbornly hung from its top hinge to continue blocking the way inside.

Guiden drove his shoulder into the door. The hinge squealed in protest as the door finally swung open and spit a cloud of dust into the air. His torchlight flooded the room to reveal nearly nothing. Lisha squinted as she struggled to discern the room beyond the door.

"This is our athenaeum," Guiden said.

Lisha responded with a blank look.

"Our library, a repository of books. It's our place of learning."

With a squeeze of Lisha's shoulder, Guiden bid her to follow. They entered the room together and walked along the walls. Heaps of burned wood lay mounded in side-by-side lines. The ruins of a few sets of shelves were barely recognizable from their shape. Most had been reduced to little more than ash.

Lisha knelt and picked up a book that had withstood the flames better than the others. Before the fire it must have been a weighty tome. Now the pages sounded like dry leaves clapping in the wind as she opened the scorched front cover. She pulled out a page that was black as pitch.

"What happened here?" Lisha yelled as she waved the ruined page in Guiden's face. The paper disintegrated into ash.

"One of our mages went mad. She's no longer with the family. Or the living," Guiden replied. "She conducted experiments with quicksilver for far too long."

A grunt of disgust was Lisha's reply. She slammed the book to the floor. Where it landed, black paper motes swarmed like flies around a rotting corpse.

"I came here to unlock the secrets of magic. To master the arcane art of spellcasting. Your books are supposed to recount the story of Iron Wand!" Lisha spat in disgust. "And they do. These tomes tell a story of ruin and decay better than a skillfully penned chronicle. My research in your library has taught me everything I need to know about the Iron Wand's dedication to sorcery."

She kicked a pile of charred books, unleashing more clouds of angry ash.

"I want to be a true mage," she growled. "Where are your books, your grimoires? How will I learn the words needed to cast lethal magic?"

Guiden smirked. "The most dangerous words aren't spells...they're *promises*."

Lisha clenched her jaw tight. "Don't you have mentors or some way to train acolytes?"

That same noise like a stifled laugh escaped Guiden once again. "We have salvaged some books imbued with an uncanny resistance to fire. And our Swordfather does acquire grimoires from time to time." A grimace flickered across his face. "But magic training here has never been formal. There is no school. There are no teachers. One becomes a mage with the Iron Wand through apprenticeship and dueling." His eyes narrowed as he spoke. "You fight to learn and learn to fight."

"Some say that pain is the best teacher," Lisha replied. "Show me where you duel. It had better be more impressive than the old granary at my home where I used to practice. I set up a suit of armor as a target. It took some time, but eventually I dented its chest."

Guiden's torch burned between the two. Lisha could see her reflection in the Iron Wand's eyes. Her own eyes and silky hair were the same dark brown. Her pale face still had the tautness of youth. A finely woven traveling cloak concealed everything below her neck. A garment of its quality cost a bulging pouch of silver crowns, after an afternoon of haggling.

Only the drip of water from the ceiling made a sound as they traveled through another passageway. Guiden placed his torch in an empty sconce, as the way ahead was lit by torches and candles.

Doors made of rough-hewn wood lined this stretch of tunnel. All of them were closed tight. Some had small, barred windows at chest height. Darkness on the other side concealed anything within the rooms.

At the point where four tunnels joined together, Guiden turned left. They followed a winding passage before descending two flights of stairs. After more nearly identical tunnels and climbing another flight of stairs, he stopped.

An empty archway stood at the top of the stairs. A pile of jagged iron that had held together a door now lay beneath the keystone. Next to Lisha's feet were the door pull and a crude lock. The remaining iron was more rust than metal. Thick splinters of rotted wood littered the wet stone floor.

"This is Iron Wand's arena. Where we duel."

Guiden remained near the ruined door. Lisha stepped over the pile of rotten wood and rusted iron.

She marched to the cavernous room's middle. The walls were the same crude brick and mortar as the tunnels. They formed a wide circle with a high ceiling. A dozen sconces lined the walls but only three held lit torches.

Lisha's robes shook as she trembled with rage.

Dark black marks peppered the arena where fiery spells had missed their targets. They reminded Lisha of the spot where lightning had struck her lord's castle tower. Many stones in the floor had cracks shaped like a spiderweb. As if a giant hammer had smashed them.

A thick film of dust lay on most everything. Black cobwebs dangled from the ceiling. Against the wall stood several suits of armor, each with a white X painted over the breastplate. Crude archery targets peppered with burns were placed near the armor. Rotting tapestries hung from the walls. Troughs for water, all of them dry, were near the door.

Lisha turned to face Guiden. Between them, the dust was so deep that she could see the path that her cloak had cleared as it dragged behind her.

"This isn't an arena. It's a graveyard," she said, her voice trembling. "This is where you've buried the magic of your forebears under dust."

"All of us are born, grow, age, and die. Those are the four seasons of life," Guiden replied. "Families are made of people and are trapped in the same seasons. In our family's spring, it grew with strength. Then, some time ago, we fought with the Fire Keepers. Ever since, we seem to be frozen in our winter."

"Your family may simply lack the right spark to grow."

"We didn't ask you to come here."

"I don't wait for people to ask," Lisha shot back. She clenched her wand in one hand and pressed the arrowhead against the palm of her other hand. A tiny rivulet of blood trickled to the dust-covered floor. "I traveled for leagues and leagues to find a library where books are burned instead of read and a training arena where the only thing that practices its craft are the spiders."

Bronze torchlight danced across Lisha's face as she waited for an answer.

Guiden sighed. "We do conduct some...experiments. Our Swordfather has made work in the laboratory the family's priority. She is desirous of powers that we can only achieve through experiments that some would call dangerous."

"Your father is a *she*?"

"Swordfather is what we call our leader whether they're a man or woman."

"Interesting." Lisha put her hands on her hips. "Is your laboratory a ruin, too?"

"Not presently."

"Take me there."

"As you wish."

"I don't wish, I demand," Lisha finished. Sensing the immediate danger of having gone too far, she showed the whisper of a smile as a peace offering.

Guiden beckoned her to follow.

The two marched past so many doors and sconces that Lisha began to wonder whether she was being led to a dungeon cell rather than the laboratory.

"Are you sure you know the way?" she asked with an edge in her voice.

"I told you," Guiden began impatiently. "The laboratory

can be perilous. That was no jest. It's been rebuilt twice that I know of. After the last time it blew up, the townsfolk rioted for a fortnight when the Hall of Joining collapsed into the crater. No one ever ventures there and to this day they believe the ruins are cursed. They're probably right, even our family avoids it."

"Why did they care so much about a hall caving in?"

"Their beloved Lord Mayor was getting married in it at the time."

"I see."

"He was Fulccrum's last Lord Mayor. Several of our family were burned at the stake for that...unforeseen happening. The land near the old lab has been shrouded in mist and darkness ever since. The ground there is always coated in rime and the air is frigid, even at the height of summer. The commoners call it Mages' Mist. Those who dwell in Raventyn are still quite bitter about it. Iron Wand rebuilt the laboratory in the catacombs outside of Fulccrum's city walls. That way, the next time the lab becomes a ball of fire, it'll do less damage to the rest of our dwelling. Also, the townsfolk won't seek vengeance for some trivial death."

Lisha noticed that Guiden's tone did not show any sympathy whatsoever for the beloved late Lord Mayor.

Wordlessly, the couple continued for a time before they passed through four heavy doors set close together. Unlike most of the other doors, these were made of sturdy oak and their iron was strong. In the short distance between the doors, the hallway twisted in the shape of a horseshoe. Guiden led the way and latched each door tight behind Lisha.

After they walked through the final wooden door, the two were confronted by a thick wall made of large stones.

"This wall is a lesson learned from the last fireball." Guiden tapped his fist against the stone. "The door to the previous lab was incinerated and flames shot deep into the catacombs. When another misfortune befalls our laboratory, this stone will bear the brunt instead of the doors."

Lisha's eyes grew wide as she suddenly understood the reason for the hallway curved like a snake and the doors latched behind her.

They walked several paces along the wall to arrive at the laboratory.

The room was filled with smoke and bursting with activity. Steam rose from glass jars brimming with strange bubbling liquids. Coiled glass pipes drew liquid from one jar and dropped it into another. A mage put a circular glass up to his eye as he tracked bubbles flowing through a pipe. The glass he held made his eye look impossibly large.

Shelves holding bottles and jars and boxes lined a wall. Some were labeled with symbols unfamiliar to Lisha. One clear jar had a lid on it that was sealed with a fat layer of wax. The liquid inside shined like silver.

Guiden pointed at the sealed jar. "That's quicksilver. There are two kinds. One will drive you to madness; the other is harmless." Guiden tapped the jar with his finger. "This is what drove the mage to burn the athenaeum."

"Quicksilver drove her to reduce a library to ash?"

"She also disagreed with the teachings in certain books."

Stacks of small wooden barrels were placed around the room.

Flames rose from bowls on trestle tables. Half a dozen mages tended to the fires. They sprinkled in powders or poured in liquids, scribbling on pieces of parchment after the flames grew or shrank or changed color.

Guiden and Lisha approached a table where the mages busied themselves. "Dark Water found a giant fish that has slippery brown water inside of it. We learned that the water burns hot. These mages are trying to make it burn even hotter." Guiden pointed at a bowl where the brown liquid burned with a purple flame. A mage tending to the bowl sprinkled in a white powder. The flame changed color to royal blue. The mage scrawled something on a piece of parchment. Lisha stepped back from the table as the heat became unbearable.

"Dark Water? That's a strange name. You said something about Fire Keepers earlier, too. What're you talking about?"

"Ah yes, of course the names of Swordfamilies mean nothing to someone from the hinterland. Dark Water is the family that controls the port, docks, and rivers of Fulccrum. They pretend to be pirates. The Fire Keepers remain wardens of the dragons, despite our fervent efforts many eclipses ago."

"You keep saying Swordfather. And family. Do you mean *crime* family?" Lisha finally mustered the courage to admit her ignorance.

"The word 'crime' implies that we're breaking serious laws. I think of Iron Wand as a family that substitutes its own laws for the crown's amusing requests," Guiden said. He tugged at her sleeve and they continued their stroll through the lab.

"When I first learned of Iron Wand, I thought it was merely a fellowship. Perchance a guild. Some mages honing their skills," Lisha said. "But you're guildsters."

Guiden shrugged. "There are six families. The Syrens fancy themselves the most beautiful people in the realm. Their battles are fought between their opponents' thighs.

The Heavies are brutes that enjoy crushing skulls." He pursed his lips. "Then there's Ashfall. They spend their time in a smoke-filled den distancing their minds from reality."

"Iron Wand, Dark Water, Fire Keepers, Syrens, Heavies, and Ashfall?"

"The six great Swordfamilies of Fulccrum. You've been attentive. Good. That's an important skill for an aspiring mage."

Screaming behind them made Lisha spin on her heels and thrust out her wand. A mage sprinted away from a bowl of burning liquid. The flames had wrapped themselves tightly around his arm. He swung it wildly in a desperate attempt to put out the fire. One mage tackled him to the ground. Another grabbed a small wooden barrel from a stack and slammed it on the burning arm. The wooden barrel shattered into pieces and water splashed over the stricken mage's arm.

Guiden grabbed Lisha's hand and pulled her away from the commotion. They arrived at a nook in a corner of the lab, away from the mage's charred arm.

"This is one of my fellow captains," Guiden said quickly, eager to redirect Lisha's attention.

A squat man sat on a stack of loose bricks. His skin was the same color as newly turned earth. The man's chin and neck were nearly indistinguishable. His narrow eyes had rolled so far back in his head that only the whites could be seen. He mumbled words that Lisha didn't recognize.

"Captain Hiamoe's experiments use things that we acquire from Ashfall to enhance spellcasting."

The captain began mumbling as Guiden spoke.

"What kind of things?" Lisha asked. "Spices?"

"Spices add flavor to food. Hiamoe's using drugs. They make you think things that you otherwise would never think. He believes they can be used to make our spells more powerful." Guiden scratched his neck. "Most of his experiments seem to simply make his eyes roll to the back of his head."

"I see," Lisha said with contempt. Her right eye twitched. "Ashfall? You mentioned they like smoke."

"That family's expertise is…they are purveyors of drugs."

Hiamoe's mumbling reached a fever pitch. Cold sweat poured from his forehead and dripped from his fleshy jowls.

Lisha held her wand like a dagger. "I did not cross leagues and leagues to be ignored by a sleeping, drug-addled fool!"

She stabbed her arrow down onto the back of Hiamoe's hand. Half the arrowhead sank beneath his thin skin. Guiden quickly grabbed her by both arms and pulled her back.

"Wake up, you dullard! I came here to become a mage! I warn you, do not stand in my way!" Lisha shrieked as she struggled to free herself from Guiden's grip. "This family is nothing but limp wands!"

The captain's stream of muttered nonsense slowed. His eyes fluttered as his pupils rolled down to where they could see past his nose. Hiamoe drew a deep breath and shook his head. He smacked his lips and eyed the dark blood that trickled from the arrowhead stuck in his hand.

He glared at Lisha, his gaze more pointed than a foil.

"How dare you interrupt me? Can't you see that I'm busy?" Hiamoe yelled. He pulled the arrowhead out of his hand and threw it at her feet. His head tipped up and his eyes rolled away. Moments later, his stream of unintelligible muttering resumed. Blood dripped from the cut on his hand.

Lisha finally pulled herself away from Guiden. "Take me to your Swordfather," she demanded, picking up her wand. "I want to see this Swordfailure before I leave you and your family in these catacombs where you belong. Buried and forgotten."

Hiamoe's blood dribbled from Lisha's wand.

"Very well," Guiden said, ignoring the insult. "I'll take you to her. But you must give me your wand."

She handed the broken arrow to him, grudgingly.

He paused for a moment. "When you meet her, don't be surprised if you hear screaming in the distance." He locked eyes with Lisha. "And you must quiet that temper of yours. If you berate my Swordfather, those will be the last words that you ever speak."

The pair retraced their steps and rounded the thick wall of stone that protected the door to the laboratory. Traversing the long passageway that led back to the Iron Wand's lair was done in silence. Lisha winced every time a drop of cold water fell on her head. She tried to map the catacombs in her mind, but the number of turns and doors they passed through left her feeling as though she'd been spun around inside a maze.

Arriving at a door much larger than the others, Guiden knocked. Unlike most doors in the catacombs, this one was new and well built. The planks of wood were wide and flush. Not a speck of rust befouled the iron.

"Remember what I said about the screaming," Guiden whispered as he leaned against the wood.

The hinges didn't whisper a sound as the door swung open.

Behind a desk made of shiny granite sat a woman clad in brilliant white robes. She was flanked by a pair of torches in sconces on the wall behind her. A stack of books sat atop a pedestal and a gold flagon rested on the books. Trinkets and instruments that Lisha didn't recognize were arrayed on the desk.

The number of years this Swordfather had seen was a riddle. The youthfulness she radiated was marred by tell-tale signs of bitter aging. Her taut, dark skin would have given the impression of a young girl, had it not been striped with wrinkles. Except for a single streak of black, her hair was the pure white color of wind-driven snow. She had full lips and the color of her eyes seemed to change each time Lisha looked at her.

"Swordfather Irin, I present this seeker," Guiden announced.

The woman stood and motioned for her visitors to enter. "Welcome. Please, sit," she said in a melodic voice. Before the pair had seated themselves, she poured red wine from the flagon into chalices on her desk. "This is a Kabern smuggled from the east side of the Pader Mountains. It's my favorite vintner."

Guiden quickly grabbed his chalice by the stem. Lisha didn't reach for hers.

"Swordfather," Guiden began, but Irin interrupted him.

"I do wish that you'd use some other appellation. Swordmother or Wandfather or the like. I've never held a sword and my prospects of fatherhood are grim at best."

"But, Swordfather, it's tradition."

"Yes, slavishly following tradition is always the best course of action. I have a name. It's Irin. I respond to that as well." She turned her attention from Guiden to the newcomer. "Tell me of yourself, honored guest." She sipped the blood red wine.

Lisha cleared her throat. Hiamoe's blood felt sticky on

her hand. "I've come here from what Guiden calls the hinterlands. We call it the Land of Dancing Water."

"The far side of the Pader Mountains?" Guiden asked with surprise in his voice.

"Yes, I crossed the Paders to get here. My trek was slowed by all the stonecutters in the passes. Our lands have pools of boiling hot water. Scalding water spurts from the ground in places. Some of them spray more times in a day than you can count. Others only blow once or twice between eclipses."

"Triple eclipses, when three moons blot out the sun?" Guiden asked.

"No, that doesn't happen back home," Lisha replied. "Where I lived only one or two moons stopped the sunlight."

"The eclipses here are much different. We mostly see triple eclipses over Fulccrum. They're so common that we simply call them eclipses. Everyone understands that we mean all three moons hiding the sun, one right after the other. They happen twice a year."

Irin swirled the wine in her chalice. "Dancing Water? I know this place. The Lava Sea isn't far from it. Who is your lord?"

"Who *was* my lord," Lisha corrected. "I'm not going back. Vlymner *was* my lord." She finally took her chalice from the desk. "He also happened to be my father." Wine dribbled down her chin as she drank greedily. "He's very loyal to the Crimson Crown."

"I see," Irin said without emotion. She set down her chalice. "I rose to become the Iron Wand's Swordfather recently. If Guiden showed you our catacombs you may have noticed that our family is undergoing, how shall we say, a metamorphosis."

"Looks more like your family underwent an inferno." Lisha set her empty chalice on the desk and wiped her chin with the back of her hand. "What's that supposed to be?"

Lisha pointed at a wooden ball on the desk. The ball was large enough that she would need both hands to hold it. Squares covered the ball, alternating between a light and dark color. Small, familiar figures stood on the squares. Some of the figures were black and plainly made of iron. Other figures had been painted white.

"That's chess played on a sphere instead of a board. Think of it as a chessboard wrapped around a ball," Irin replied.

"I've only seen it on a square board. I've played many times against my father's advisors." Lisha leaned forward in her chair. "How do the pieces stay on the board? Why aren't they falling off?"

Spinning the ball around, Irin plucked a king off the chess sphere. She handed it to Lisha. "It's made of iron. Feel it." Lisha ran her fingers over its rough surface. "I'm in the middle of a game so I'll need that back." The Swordfather took the piece from Lisha and placed it on the same square that it had occupied. "Lodestone is underneath the chessboard's wood shell. It pulls on anything made of iron. Werevu made it. He's also a captain and one of our most clever mages. He thought it would make the game more interesting."

"Uldritch the Unwise has sharper wits, but he spends most of his time gazing into the night sky," Guiden added.

"This kind of chess must be much harder. The pieces aren't confined the way they are on a square," Lisha said. "They can go almost anywhere, so you have to consider the far side of the board, er, sphere. There's hidden danger."

Irin smiled.

Without invitation, Lisha stood and moved to the chess sphere. Her eyes darted over the squares as she slowly spun it around. She tilted the sphere on its pedestal to get a good look at the pieces on the bottom. Satisfied, she returned to her chair.

"What do you think?" Irin asked.

"White. Mate in five," Lisha replied.

Irin smirked at Guiden. "I told you I would win."

He grunted and crossed his arms.

In a corner behind the desk sat a dragon's skull mounted on a pedestal. The maw was open and pointed straight up. Lying on the floor beneath the skull were two halves of a crystal ball. Dim purple light pulsed from the halves. Lisha guessed that before it fell, the crystal ball had rested between the dragon's jaws against the dagger-like fangs.

"So that's why your mages are playing with fire. You're trying to melt that broken crystal ball back together," Lisha said.

Guiden raised an eyebrow and spoke slowly. "That is one reason for some of our experiments, yes. If the crystal ball was made whole, we could resume our scrying."

A single purple pulse shined brighter than the others.

"I sense genuine potential in this one," Irin said, eyeing the dark red wine in her chalice. "I have recently acquired a grimoire that I anticipate will be helpful in restoring the Iron Wand to its rightful place of prominence in Fulccrum." She patted the ancient tome on her desk. Its tarnished bronze lock was fastened tight. It was the largest book Lisha had ever seen. "Join the Iron Wand and together we will divine its secrets to make this family revered once more."

Lisha eyed the grimoire as she considered the Swordfather's offer.

The crystal ball radiated purple light.

"Revered...and feared," Lisha replied, her gaze still fixed on the grimoire.

A heartbeat later, faint screams in many different voices echoed somewhere in the distance.

CHAPTER THREE

FIRE KEEPERS

"This would be easy if it weren't for all the impossible things we have to do," Glas whined.

"Steady yourself, Swordbrother," Andra said in a patient voice. She patted him on the shoulder. "We've pulled this one plenty of times. We call it burn 'em and turn 'em." She sighed. "It's not the job I'm worried about. It's the man who asked for it. If Melyq owes us a debt, he's like to repay us in poison."

"Another throw of the dice, I s'pose." Glas frowned. "I hope this job doesn't go bad like Fyur's did. I don't trust Dark Water or their tale about how he died. They're lords of the seas, right? How could Fyur drown unless they let it happen? Even the sharks fear Dark Water."

Andra said nothing.

The two warriors sat next to each other at the front of a wain that had been carefully built and decorated. Dull black paint coated the length of it. The color was even, except for a dent where the wood was exposed on the tailboard. The spokes on the wheels all had the same curves and appearance, except for one spoke on the left rear wheel. It was a straight rod painted in light gray.

Every detail of Andra's wain matched the one that Lord Wrand's men were pulling to Fulccrum with a chest full of gold. The only outward difference between the two wains was that behind the Fire Keepers sat a pile of chopped wood instead of a black chest.

Two draught horses were harnessed to the wain. Andra loosely held their reins.

The Fire Keeper who had stolen the horses chose them carefully. They were nearly identical in appearance. Both had dark crests and brown bodies with light splotches over their flanks. Streaks of white adorned their muzzles. One horse was slightly bigger than the other. The larger horse had been purposefully hitched to the wain's right side, in front of Andra.

Andra and Glas wore identical cloaks made of red fox furs. The insides of the cloaks were lined with rough, gray cloth.

"The hardest part for you will be that lock," Andra said. "Remember, Glas, that's what you're here for."

"Yes, yes. I have my tools," Glas shot back. "Whatever they locked it with can't be harder to pick than the lock on the chest that holds the eldest princess's privy clothes."

Andra sneered at him. "I don't want to know."

Glas smiled. "Someone has to make sure they've been washed and put away with the delicate lace properly folded and..."

Andra slapped him before he could finish. "Your mind is a stinking chamber pot filled to the brim."

Glas laughed.

Nestled in a small clearing surrounded by tall pines, the

pair waited in silence for a time. They listened to the many hooves falling on the dirt road a short distance away.

A rouncey galloped toward them with lather foaming from its neck. It came to a halt within arm's reach of Andra. The rider pulled back his hood to reveal a shock of blond hair sitting atop a square face. "It's time," he said breathlessly.

"Is everything put in motion, Fletch? Will Berg start from the other road?"

The rider nodded in answer, breathing heavily.

"What about the dragon blood for the piles of green leaves down the way? Did you send a rider to have them spill the blood?"

A second nod from Fletch answered that question.

"And our 'bandits,' Mwizi and Tyv, they're on time?"

"Yes, yes, yes," Fletch growled, having caught his breath. "The warriors have been dispatched. All is ready!"

"Don't get cross with me. It's not that I don't trust you, it's just that I don't trust anybody."

Andra and Glas pulled up their hoods at the same time. Their faces were almost completely hidden beneath the red fox fur.

"Somewhere inside that chest filled with gold is the treasure I've been seeking for eclipses," Andra said. "Making captain."

She snapped the reins hard. The wain jerked forward and left the nook of trees where they had waited for word from Fletch. They emerged from the dense trees to join a narrow road. The bare dirt they traveled on was still damp from the last rain, softening the normally jarring ride.

"Shouldn't we be going faster?" Glas asked.

"No. We need Berg to get there before us. He's the lead wain."

The acrid scent of burning leaves filled their nostrils. Andra permitted herself a tiny smile as she breathed in the dark smoke that comes from wet leaves.

"What's in the back?" Glas asked. "Beneath the wood."

"In our chest?" Andra turned and glanced at the back of the wain. "Some lava rocks. They're small, rough, and light. Kardas wants the king's men to see them. It's rock that's common in Lord Wrand's lands. That way, the king will think the gold was stolen by Wrand's own men, not some strange riders just outside Fulccrum." Andra shrugged. "Don't know if it'll work but it's better than putting a dragon skull in there. The lock is solid and they'll have hells of a time getting it open. That should give us enough time to duck into the woods."

Glas began to ask another question but Andra hushed him.

"We're getting close to Six Corners," she whispered. Both draught horses pulling the wain whinnied and shook their heads. Andra pulled on the reins, steadying her beasts of burden.

As they approached the crossing, the thick forest by the road yielded to a stretch of grassland. Through the darkening smoke, Andra could see where three roads crossed in the distance. The roads that came together were all straight. Around the crossing, weathered signs adorned with crudely etched names pointed travelers to destinations near and far. The tallest sign simply read "Six Corners."

Two of the three roads were narrow, barely wide enough for two wagons. Large stones littered these roads, even in the ruts. The wagons that traversed them were slow and plodding. These were minor roads mostly traveled by farmers and the devout seeking to worship the thundering gods in the capital city.

The third road was wide and smooth. Known as the Shamrock Road, it joined Fulccrum with many of the largest cities in the Emerald Realm. Most days it was traveled by swarms of wagons lumbering in and out of the capital. Andra thanked the thundering horde of gods as she saw that today the number of commoners flowing through Six Corners was less than usual.

Andra searched for her fellow Fire Keepers. Instead, she saw three wains traveling down the Shamrock Road. Each one of these wains carried some wooden boxes and a single guard wearing boiled leather armor. They were followed by a motley collection of commoners on foot and riders that looked more tired than their horses. Closer to the city walked groups of poor folk intent on joining the Kingdom Guard.

Through the gathering smoke, Andra finally saw what she hoped to see. A wain identical to hers traveled down one of the narrow roads. On that wain sat a driver and another person. They both wore red fox fur cloaks with the hoods drawn up. Although Andra couldn't see the driver's face, she knew it was Berg. A Fire Keeper warrior, Ombran, sat next to him on the front bench. In their wagon bed sat a chest with the same appearance as Lord Wrand's chest.

"They better hurry. Our prey is coming up fast," Glas said, his eyes on Berg's wain.

Two of Lord Wrand's men, also clad in red fox fur cloaks, drove a wain down the Shamrock Road toward Fulccrum. Their wain looked the same as the Fire Keepers' two replicas driven by Andra and Berg.

Four knights guarded Wrand's wain. Two knights rode in front of it and two were behind. Each was mounted on a powerful destrier. They wore full steel plate armor and great helms that covered their faces. The only openings in the helms were small slits for their eyes. The knights held high the standard of Lord Wrand, a crimson wave of lava against a field of navy blue.

Berg's wain reached the Shamrock Road with little time to spare. He turned his team of horses to the right, toward Fulccrum. Behind Berg's wain trotted a couple of rounceys carrying travelers caked in dust. The dirty travelers were followed by Lord Wrand's wain.

Andra pulled gently on the reins, slowing her team. A cart passed them. It was loaded with clucking chickens bound for Old Town Square Market. Where the narrow road she followed met with the Shamrock Road, Andra turned left. Her wain trailed well behind Wrand's men.

"Only four knights? I would've expected more if they're carrying what Melyq told us," Andra said under her breath. One of her draught horses whinnied shrilly.

The three wains rolled along in a line.

Berg's wagon led the way. He pulled on the reins to slow his team.

Lord Wrand's wagon traveled in the middle. The knights rode close to their charge. They couldn't see two nearby riders mounted on swift coursers because of the great helms they wore. The pair of riders wore drab clothes made of shabby hides. Each had a sheathed sword on their hip.

Andra and Glas brought up the rear. Andra snapped the reins, pressing her team for a faster pace.

Dense forest returned to the Shamrock Road's edge as the trio of wains traveled away from Six Corners.

Smoke now enveloped the road and its travelers like a dense fog in early morning. The confused travelers covered their mouths and shook as they coughed. They surveyed the road for any sign of fire. Out of sight, and upwind, Fire Keepers poured watered-down dragon blood on piles of green leaves that smoldered instead of burned.

Only a single rider now remained between Berg's wain and the mark behind him. The Fire Keeper captain pulled hard on the reins. His team slowed and the lone rider sped past.

Andra and Glas made themselves tense and ready. Andra's knuckles turned white as she clenched the reins tight.

The horses pulling Lord Wrand's chest neared the rear of Berg's wain.

"Driver! You there!" a knight near the front of Wrand's wain called. "Pick up the pace before I run you through with me sword!"

Berg didn't respond. He yanked hard on the reins and his wain came to a shuddering halt.

"Whoa!" cried Lord Wrand's driver, pulling on his reins. The horses clenched down on their bits. They whinnied in protest and slammed into the back of Berg's wagon. A knight's horse reared and almost threw its rider to the ground.

Alarmed, the knights unsheathed their swords as they fought for control of their mounts.

The two nearby riders clad in shabby hides were the Fire Keeper warriors Mwizi and Tyv. They unsheathed their own swords and, using the broadside of their blades, smacked the back of the knights' helmets. A thundering clang shook the knights' helms and heads. Wrand's men tried to steady their horses and find their attackers.

At the same moment, Berg whipped both of his draught horses hard and yelled, "Hyah!" His team launched into a fast trot, speeding away from Lord Wrand's men. Mwizi and Tyv held their swords high as they squeezed their fast coursers to pursue Berg's wain.

The four knights followed their two attackers and, in the dense smoke, what looked like their lord's wain and chest. Their heavy destriers were slow to close the distance.

Lord Wrand's driver snapped the reins to chase after his guards.

Andra guided her wain alongside the undefended mark as it moved slowly. Glas jumped into the back of Wrand's wain. He used a hand to steady himself by leaning on the chest that held their prize. With his other hand, he pulled a cudgel made of ironwood from beneath his cloak. His hands were shaky, but deft. Two quick strokes fell, first for the passenger and then for the driver. Glas's victims were out cold.

The two wains, Andra and Lord Wrand's, traveled side-by-side on a long stretch of road with forest close on both sides. The smoke and shadows plunged the wains into a darkness deep as a moonless night. The few travelers that had candle lanterns on hand lit them.

Crawling into her wain's bed, Andra still clutched the reins. She hooked them around her foot and whispered a prayer to the thundering gods for the horses to keep their course. Then she began to heave the chopped wood onto Lord Wrand's chest.

Glas steadied Wrand's horses to keep the wains together as they continued down the road to Fulccrum. With quick hands when they were needed, he kept the unconscious passengers from falling onto the dirt road and under the wain's wheels.

With aching arms, Andra tossed the last piece of wood. Now emptied, the Fire Keepers' replica chest filled with lava rock was plain to see in the bed of her wain. Wrand's chest was now buried under the wood.

Farther down the road, Wrand's knights charged at Mwizi and Tyv as the two harassed Berg's wain. The knights' slow destriers brought them close enough to slash at their attackers. The two Fire Keepers posing as bandits baited their pursuers for the better part of a league before they squeezed their swift mounts hard, leaned forward, and disappeared into the smoky darkness.

The four knights slowed and fell into position around Berg's wain.

"Driver!" called a knight in the rear. "Did those bandits get at our chest?"

Berg slowly pulled back his hood and turned to face the knight. "Many thanks to you noble knights, sirs. We're mighty glad you scared off those nasty thieves. But I do not know you." His face was devoid of emotion.

The knight ripped his great helm off in a single motion. "Halt! Open that chest! *Now!*" he roared at the Fire Keepers.

Berg stopped his wain. Ombran climbed into the bed. He slowly worked to unlock the black chest, trying seven keys that didn't work. The knight kept yelling at him to hurry, and the chest was unlocked with the eighth key. He wedged his fingers under the lid and heaved it open.

Reaching deep into the chest, Ombran pulled out a portrait of a dour-looking man. The aged man's fierce visage was dark as obsidian except for great patches that were white as snow. The black hair of his long beard was streaked with white.

"We carry a gift for the oldest prince," Ombran explained. "This painting is of a dear blood relation to Prince Opvolk, I'm told."

The knight's eyes grew wide. He barked a command at the other three knights to turn back and ride hard.

Smoke wafting between the knights and Andra's wain gathered thick enough that the knights couldn't see her work. Behind that dark curtain, her wain rolled along next to Lord Wrand's. Glas struggled to guide the horses pulling Wrand's wain as he grabbed the driver under the arms and hoisted him over to Andra. She hugged the driver around the waist and pulled him onto her wain. His body was limp as she placed him on the bench and put the reins around his hands. With sweat dripping from their brows, the two Fire Keepers hoisted the passenger onto Andra's wain.

After the passenger was leaning against the driver's shoulder, Andra jumped onto Lord Wrand's wain. She and Glas spun around their cloaks so the gray cloth showed on the outside and the red fox fur was hidden on the inside.

Lord Wrand's horses whinnied shrilly when Andra pulled back hard on their reins. Instead of obeying the command to slow, the horses sped into a brisk trot.

"They must be spooked," Glas said, his voice wavering.

"The horses pulling the false wain stopped," Andra fumed. She looked back at the wain holding Wrand's drivers and the fake chest filled with rock. "The knights will see us first."

Pulling the gray hoods over their heads, they both looked down and rolled forward in silence. Andra tried another tug on the reins to slow the draught horses, but they only responded with more whinnying.

Andra kept her head down. She could feel Glas trembling as the board they sat on shook. Drops of water fell from his face. With his hood up, Andra didn't know if they were sweat or tears.

"Halt! You there, driver!" bellowed the knight with no

helm. "Your wain is much the same that we were guarding! Did you steal it?"

Recognizing the knight's familiar voice, the horses came to a stop.

Andra drew her hood back. "No, we didn' steal yer wagon, me good sir," she lied. "But we did see 'nother wain just like this one not long ago. It's back behind us. The driver was slumped over, as if he was sleepin'. This bad dark coulda made him real sleepy."

Both horses whinnied in turn.

"How can your wagon look like ours? That just can't be!"

Andra shrugged. "Maybe we bought it from tha same wheelwright? Mighta been a lazy workman and made a bunch o' 'em all tha same. We didn't order it special or nothin'. We just haulin' wood into tha city, see?" She pointed at the wood piled high over the chest in the bed.

The knight narrowed his eyes.

Andra's mind raced to beat his order to search the wain.

"We takin' it all tha way to Emerald Ezzy down by tha docks. A hundred men hung from tha tree it was cut from. All at once and all murderers, the lot o' 'em. Was so many they looked like moss hangin' from tha branches. They say tha wood's cursed real bad." She spoke in the simple tongue of the poor folk from the New Valois district. She spat a thick wad of phlegm. "I don't believe 'em any more than when my fatha told me he loved me. But Ezzy pays real good for tha things she thinks got ghosts in 'em."

The knight glared at her, then the pile of wood. Glas's hood concealed some of his trembling. Andra dropped one hand from the reins and slowly started to feel for the dagger tucked inside her belt.

"Sailors that've been through Fulccrum say Ezzy's half

witch," said a knight who still wore a helm. "The other half is crazy. They say she can throw a kiss that'll curse your manhood. We can come back. Those horses can't go anywhere fast with that load."

Travelers cursing the darkness traipsed by the stopped wain.

The helmless knight hesitated. Then he yelled, "Come!" Kicking his destrier hard, he and the other three knights galloped away from their own stolen wain. They raced over the Shamrock Road back in the direction of their own drivers and the fake chest.

Glas leaned over the side of the wain and heaved out everything in his stomach. Strands of snot joined his wretched waterfall.

Andra petted the horse in front of her as the team trotted ahead. She gave it encouragement as she searched the forest for a sign.

The horses had quieted and were wholly obedient when Andra saw a single tree branch shaking wildly a short distance down the Shamrock Road. When she pulled on the reins, her team responded to the command by slowing. As she neared the shaking branch, the brush underneath the tree parted. She guided the team off the smoke-filled road and into the dense forest. After the tail board crossed from road to forest, Mwizi and Tyv dragged the brush back together and the wain disappeared from the road completely.

Andra stopped when they were so deep in the forest that she couldn't hear the noise of passing travelers on the road to Fulccrum.

"You did it!" Mwizi said. "You're a fine warrior, er, I mean captain!" She gave Andra a deep, but mocking, bow.

"These horses must be as daft as those knights. They

wouldn't listen to me," Andra shot back. "We were a whisker away from rotting in an angry lord's dungeon. There better be a king's ransom in there for what I just went through." She ran her fingers through her hair. Her cheeks looked like bellows as she sighed. "Glas, can you get it open?"

He finished using his cloak to wipe his dripping face. His answer was a silent nod, but his hands trembled so much that Andra doubted that he could hold the lockpicks steady.

"Here, this'll steady your hands," Tyv said as he handed Glas a wineskin. "Might wash some of that nasty taste out of your mouth, too."

The skin was half empty before Glas took his next breath.

Practiced fingers held thin pieces of metal. With his ear close to the black chest, listening for telltale sounds, he turned and twisted the inner workings of the lock. He moved the lockpicks like a master artisan painting his magnum opus. With a final spin and pull, a loud click sounded from deep within the strong metal.

Glas lifted the lid no more than the width of his hand.

"Are you sure we stole the right wain?" he asked as he peered into the chest.

Mwizi, Tyv, and Andra exchanged nervous glances.

"Yes, of course I'm sure. Look at it," Andra replied, waving at their stolen wain. "It looks exactly like the scouts told us, right down to the spoke they fixed."

"Isn't there supposed to be gold in here? That's what Melyq told us, right?" Glas became paler than when he was vomiting.

Tyv flung the lid wide open and the Fire Keepers leaned over the chest. Black velvet lined the inside. Resting on the bottom of the chest was a neatly arranged pile of bones. The largest bones were at the bottom, underneath the smaller ones. A skull sat atop the small skeletal pyramid. The bones were charred.

"The only gold in this chest are those couple of teeth in the skull," Tyv said.

"Close it and lock it," Andra ordered Glas. "We need to get this to Melyq before nightfall." She stole another glance at the bones. "Kardas must know of this."

Glas slowly closed the lid and used his picks to lock the chest.

"That's so strange," Mwizi whispered. "Why would Melyq want a pile of charred bones?"

CHAPTER FOUR
HEAVIES

"I'm feeling bloodthirsty," Raysk thundered. "And I must slake that thirst."

He sat on a coarse boulder. His face and scalp were covered in dark red scars. He could grow neither a beard on his chin nor locks on his crown. Nearly all the scars were made by hands that held no blades. His bulging arms looked as if they might burst open. The stitches on the hides that he wore as trousers were pulled taut; the girth of his legs threatened to rip them apart. His hulking body made the boulder look small.

"You would go to war with the Swordfamilies to quench your thirst for blood? We don't need to start a war to do that. We can find some knights to slaughter if it's blood you want," Droena said. Though she was much leaner than Raysk, her muscles were just as firm. The most pronounced difference between Droena and her Swordfather was the elegant beauty of her face. Her Swordfather's visage was a swarm of scars whereas the only red on Droena's face were her lips.

Raysk scowled at her. "You know our rules. You can't

address your Swordfather without showing me your Heavies' strength." He wagged an index finger at her in reproach.

A large pedestal of iron shaped like a fist stood in front of Raysk. On it sat an anvil that weighed almost as much as the boulder the Heavies' Swordfather sat upon.

Droena made no attempt to conceal her annoyance. "This is why we don't stand in front of the pedestal when we talk to you. It's a foolish tradition begun by fools. Why must we hold an anvil just to speak with our Swordfather?" She neared the pedestal, where she waited for several long and futile moments.

A reply to her question was not forthcoming.

The captain surrendered to her Swordfather's whim. She grabbed the anvil's horn and heel, then lifted it to her chest. She grunted from the effort. Deep gouges in the ground beneath her marked where other Heavies had dropped the anvil.

"Pleased?" she asked between deep breaths.

"You're not supposed to grunt. True Heavies make it look effortless."

She ignored the slight. "A war between the families is needless. You know the tales from the last war. Much of our family was lost. Swordfathers fell like wheat before a scythe. It's bad for business, it's bad for the Swordfather, and it's bad for the family."

The anvil shook in her hands.

Raysk punched a fist into his palm. "We have no choice. I'm not stupid and I'm no more bloodthirsty than usual. Peace has made our family strong. It's made us rich. If peace was an option, might be that I'd choose it. But the quiet between our families requires a strong crown. When the king and queen are united and powerful, it's not worth the effort to corrupt them." He scratched at the darkest scar that followed his pronounced jawline. "A weak crown makes a weak peace. Without the crown weighing on us all, the families will fight. If the Heavies don't move first, another family will."

"If we spill the first blood, we must spill it by the cask," Droena said. "All of the families have grown strong during this peace." Sweat dripped from her face to splatter on the anvil. The wet metal shined.

They spoke in a sprawling cavern that served as the Heavies' fortress. It lay underground near the city of Fulccrum, a short ride from the Colosseum in the Stonebann district. Long caves wound through the rocky ground to open at the foot of small cliffs not far from the city walls. Torches in sconces mounted to stalagmites striped the cavern with light and shadow.

Two Heavies sparred. Metal striking metal with great force sounded through the cavern. The noise their weapons made wasn't the shrill ring of two swords clashing. The clacking noise was low-pitched and short-lived. These Heavies sparred with anvils. Holding their iron weapons high, they slashed and thrust the horns to attack. Sweat and fresh blood dripped from the horns. The black iron shined like a still lake at night.

Another pair of Heavies trained near a large pile of rocks. Each rock was bigger than a man's head. One Heavy knelt by the pile as another stood a short distance away with a war hammer resting on his shoulder. The Heavy by the pile picked up a rock and threw it. The war hammer came off the other Heavy's shoulder. He swung the weapon with both hands and smashed its head into the pitched rock. A shower of gravel and dust exploded in the air when the steel head slammed against the stone. Both Heavies laughed.

Raysk clasped his hands. "This talk demands more than the two of us. You may lower the anvil."

Droena imprisoned her rage. With gritted teeth, she silently set the anvil back on the pedestal.

"Why'd you make me do that if you're going to hold a war council?" She closed her fists tight and opened them wide to stretch her aching fingers.

"War is upon us. Everyone in this family must follow my orders with unwavering obedience. Captains like you are the ones who must not question me, or tolerate questions from the warriors that you command. You didn't refuse to lift the anvil. That's good, because that was a test."

Droena remained silent.

"Vasarox and Kraaft," Raysk called to the Heavies smashing stones with the war hammer. "Join us at the war table."

"You mean the drinking table?" Vasarox asked.

"It's the same table, right?" Kraaft added, pointing his war hammer at the table.

Raysk growled at them.

A dozen casks full of ale sitting on end in a circle served as the table where they gathered. Droena took her place opposite from her Swordfather.

A woman sat to the left of Raysk. She had curly black hair, green eyes, a slim face, and a missing hand.

Vasarox took his customary place on the right side of the Heavies' Swordfather.

Warriors brought everyone at the table a horn full of strong, dark brown ale.

"Why do you wear steel armor all the time?" Vasarox asked Kraaft.

"Because you never know when you'll need to kill someone," Kraaft replied casually. His heavy brow rested on dark eyes. His long beard had the same straw hair that had fled from his now shiny scalp. "Why *don't* you wear steel armor all the time?"

"Because I like looking at my arms and I want everyone else to look at them, too," Vasarox replied. He had a soft, round face and bristly black hair. His skin was the color of leaves lying on the ground beneath an oak in late autumn. His brown eyes were nearly as dark as his pupils and they hungered for mischief. He wore a sleeveless jerkin made of worn leather.

Vasarox flexed hard, forcing the veins to pop from his rippling flesh.

"I'll drink to that," Kraaft said, draining his horn with relish. "Then again, I'll drink to anything!" He wiped his mouth with the back of his steel gauntlet, which succeeded only in spreading the ale on his lips to the rest of his face.

"Them?" Droena asked, nodding toward the Heavies sparring with anvils. "What about Zrobik? Should he have a seat with us?"

Iron sounded as Zrobik thrust his anvil forward, only for its horn to be met by his opponent's parry. Sweat sprinkled from the young man. He was slender for someone who could wield an anvil like a blade. Every muscle in his arms tensed like a drawn bow as he managed the iron's weight. He was naked above the waist. Droena noticed that on his back was a large, crude drawing of a horse inked into his skin.

"No," Raysk replied in a growl. "Zrobik will be tasked with other duties, once we find something worthy of our family's efforts. To have a future with the Heavies, he'll need to be successful. Same as you, back when you were a warrior. If he fails at any of them, he will swim in the stream."

Droena didn't ask about the many other warriors and captains milling about the cavern. Some were brawling, but most were engaged in contests of strength. Half a dozen competed to see who could throw a stone shaped like a box the farthest. The stone had been stolen from the battlement atop a tower in the Emerald Crown's castle. On a dare, a warrior pulled it from a high tower and evaded, or overpowered, the Kingdom Guard to present his trophy to Raysk in the cavern. Much ale had been drunk earlier that night.

"We will soon be at war with the families," Raysk announced. "This is our first war council. It will not be our last. We'll go to the rushes."

As he finished speaking, Raysk looked straight at Vasarox. The captain sat within arm's reach of his Swordfather. With the two so close, Droena could see that Vasarox was nearly the equal of Raysk's hulking size.

Kraaft took a deep draught of ale from his horn. Then he commanded a warrior to bring more ale.

"You want to fight over that trinket?" Vasarox grumbled. "It's useless, not even a real sword. It's one of those... what are they called?"

"A ceremonial sword," the woman with one hand answered.

"Yes, Consulary Pametan, that's it," Vasarox agreed. "Those are fancy words to say it's of no use. Why do you want it? Swordfamilies can be crushed just as easily with or without that sword."

"The other families don't know it yet, but the war has already begun. If we don't seize the sword first, another family will." Raysk dragged his fingernails over a patch of scars on his cheek. "Someone must needs retrieve it from the tomb of Auzken and bring it to me."

Pametan leaned forward. She cast a long, narrow shadow

over the casks. "We must seize the Bleeding Blade as the critical first move. It sends the message that the final night has fallen on our long peace. One family will again rule the others. The family that possesses the sword has the advantage. Any who would dare challenge us will have to take it by force." She settled back as she spoke. "Vasarox, you should not be so dismissive of the Bleeding Blade. There are strategic advantages to possessing the sword. It weeps more blood when it senses Swordfamily death and battle in the offing."

Droena slammed her fist on a cask. "Very well. If you want that damnable thing, I'll fetch it."

"No. This is a job for the man who sits at Raysk's right hand," Vasarox said, glaring at Droena. The skin at the corners of his mouth made small crescents as he frowned deeply. "I will seize the Bleeding Blade."

Droena looked inside her horn. It was empty. She raised it to her lips and feigned taking a drink.

"A Swordfamily is a stock of men and women to be used as tools by their master craftsman, the Swordfather," Raysk mused. "Vasarox will bring me the blade."

The warriors on the far side of the cavern began using their anvils to joust. Two Heavies sprinted toward each other, the horn of their weapon aimed like the point of a lance. As they clashed, one sent the other reeling to the ground. Cheers rolled through the cave, loud enough to knock loose motes from the stalactites above.

"Might makes right, and we are flush with might. But I'll need to outthink them, too," Raysk said. He picked at a light scar on his neck that was nearly the color of his skin. "I must know if a family is ahead of me. If the Bleeding Blade is missing from Auzken's tomb, another family seeks to seize power. If it's gone, I'll call a Council of Sheathed

Swords and challenge the cowards that stole it from me to come forward."

Steel armor clinked as Kraaft crossed his arms over his chest. "This is good. I tire of crushing stones. I'd rather be crushing skulls." He gazed upon his war hammer like it was his best lover.

"Allies aren't needed, but they would be welcomed," Pametan added. "This war should be won before the next triple eclipse. The Fire Keepers are the only family with enough strength to pose a real threat to us. No doubt Ashfall is furious with them since their dragons keep burning those mind-melting plants in the refuge. An alliance with Quivum's drug peddlers may benefit both families. We could also use friends at the royal court."

Vasarox raised an eyebrow.

Dozens of Heavies sparred with greatswords around the cavern. The ringing of their blades sounded like a stream of gold coins poured onto stone. Other Heavies hammered away at castle gates made of wrought iron. The latticed bars snapped like twigs as the steel hammers fell again and again. Another group of warriors chopped at stone statues that the Heavies had stolen from castles as souvenirs to remember their jobs. Each warrior struck the stone harder and harder until the sword broke and the onlookers cheered.

"You can never have too many swords at the ready. That's even more true when the other side has dragons," Droena said.

Raysk eyed his empty horn. "Another family by our side would shorten the war, and the only cost would be sharing a sliver of power when it's done," he said in a disinterested tone.

"I agree with Pametan. We should turn Ashfall against the Fire Keepers." Kraaft shrugged.

"Ashfall? Quivum's frog lickers?" Droena said dismissively. "They're more likely to weigh on our strength than add to it."

He grinned, but Raysk's mask of scars made his expression more like a pained grimace. He nodded at Consulary Pametan. "You're my consulary, my advisor. Now advise my captains."

"Ashfall has attributes that make a partnership desirable. They supply drugs to some of the royal children, which is a chink in the Emerald Crown's armor that we could exploit," Pametan reported. "Also, our longstanding use of that family's enhancements makes easier the path to alliance."

Having quickly tired of a voice other than his own, Raysk leaned back and interrupted. "That will do for now. We shall speak of the families another time. For the nonce, my thoughts are with the crown. Counselor Melyq has offered an opportunity to win favor with the royal court."

Droena opened her mouth to correct him, but Raysk spoke before her.

"Or the *queen's* court. The crown is obsessed with names and titles. Your majesty, grace, sir, medam, what they call their courts. To me, it matters not. A king by any other name would be as weak," Raysk sneered. "Melyq has asked us to drop some bones in the Fire Keepers' refuge. Why he wants this done, I cannot say."

"Pametan, what whispers have you heard?" Vasarox asked.

"Nothing that would tell me why Melyq has made his request." Pametan shrugged. "Talk in the castle is dominated by the growing threat east of the Paders. Most all is fear and rumor. There's talk of summoning the king's nephew from the Crimson Crown's realm as a precaution."

"As I say, Melyq didn't reveal his purpose to me," Raysk added.

"The rumors and the request may be two halves of the same deceit," Droena guessed.

"Two halves?" Pametan asked. "If this is Melyq's scheming, I'd wager a stack of gold scythes that this deception has more pieces to it than a full suit of armor."

As he stood, Raysk signaled the meeting was at an end. "The counselor's plan is not important; his debt to the Heavies is. After all, the crown is weak but not powerless. Droena, you and Kraaft will drop the bones."

"Why not send a warrior, like Teska?" Kraaft protested.

"I won't trust this to warriors. You'll work under cover of darkness and get it done before daybreak."

Droena opened her mouth to ask a question. She thought better of it and remained silent. Kraaft smirked.

"Come to me before you leave. I have Melyq's bones. And I'll tell you how to fool the dragon."

CHAPTER FIVE
EMERALD CROWN

"I'm destined to fight two wars at once. Battles without the castle walls and battles within," King Fallov muttered, waving his hand back and forth. "If I'm vanquished in one, a second defeat will surely follow with much quickness." The king dragged his palm down his face. "I wouldn't put it past the queen to let the Crimson Crown burn our realm just to spite me."

Before the king was a table large enough to hold a great feast, though not a single course had ever graced it. On this table was a map of the territories held by the Emerald Crown and the Crimson Crown. The attention to every minute detail was a powerful testament to the artisans' skill and care.

The Pader Mountains meandered through the middle of the table, dividing the land in two. Rocks harvested from the Paders themselves were carefully chiseled to copy the mountain range's peaks and passes. They towered above everything else on the map.

To the Paders' west, the Emerald Crown ruled the land. The crown's seat of power was a tall castle that shadowed large swaths of Fulccrum in the late evening sun. The castle's ramparts and towers on the map had miniscule lines on them to show individual stones. The city of Fulccrum itself was a maze of winding streets and paths slicing through a crowd of buildings. It had all been carved with tiny blades that made daggers look like greatswords by comparison.

The city sprawled along the shore where it met the Angered Sea. Tiny sabatons made of copper were mounted on pedestals on either side of the port. Inside were ships adorned with white sails hardly larger than insects. They floated at anchor in the pale blue waters painted on the table top.

On the east side of the Paders, toward the north, the Crimson Crown held dominion. Though, in truth, their castle stood taller than the Emerald Crown's, the artisans had crafted the Crimson Crown's seat of power slightly smaller than the castle in Fulccrum. Every other aspect of their realm was shown truthfully. Even the geysers on Lord Vlymner's Land of Dancing Water were depicted in wood painted sky blue.

"My king, war with the Crimson Crown is not a foregone conclusion," said a woman with bright blue eyes. "Our forces can plug the mountain passes. Even if they mustered every mammophant in the Crimson Realm to march against us, they still must cross the Paders. We need only guard the widest passes, which are few and far between. We have the advantage of concentrating our strength at those points." She pointed at the lowest paths between a handful of mountains as she spoke.

The king strolled around the table, sliding his hand along its edge. In his other hand, he held a gold scepter resplendent with jewels. He regarded the woman coolly.

She wore gilded armor as opulent as it was curved. The armor's many-colored gems and high polish gave the impression of fragility. Though this armor had never seen battle, there were scars hidden beneath its steel. Voden had thick arms, thicker legs, and sapphire eyes. Her flaxen hair nearly disappeared where it lay against the gold.

"Counselor Voden, you're assuming that the Emerald Crown's forces are united as one. In a short time, instead of a Kingdom Guard we may have a king's guard and a queen's guard. Tomorrow our forces may be fighting each other with more zeal than if they were defending Fulccrum against an invader from a foreign land."

A pool of red paint in the east marked the Lava Sea. When King Fallov's eyes fell upon it, his thoughts drifted to his favorite nephew. After a dragon had slammed its tail into the boy's face, the royal healer had been summoned to replace some missing teeth with gold. Shortly thereafter, the king had sent the young lad to learn obedience under the tutelage of Lord Wrand, whose lands abutted that fiery sea.

Gripping the scepter tight in both hands, the king slammed its head on the peak of a Pader Mountain. He brought it down hard against the stone, again and again, with the motion of a spinning windmill. Prized jewels flew from the scepter's head like loosed arrows. Two diamonds clinked against the plackart of Voden's armor that covered her belly.

The scepter's soft metal yielded to the hard mountain stone to become a scraped and misshapen ruin. After his temper cooled, King Fallov held a lump of gold pockmarked with empty gemstone settings. The piece of Pader Mountain rock that withstood the punishment remained unscathed. He held the broken scepter in limp fingers. A ruby and an emerald that had been mounted on the scepter now lay in a field where the Fire Keepers' herd roamed.

"Soon, I fear, the chasm opening between the queen and I will spread wide enough to swallow up our castle, city, and finally the realm. It will all disappear in the void that's growing between us." The king leaned heavily on the Crimson Crown's lands. "At least the prospect of the reds overrunning us may keep some of our unruly lords in line."

Voden tugged at a lock of her pale hair. "You underestimate your power. Since your family's reign began, the realm has known neither war nor hunger. The people are your strength. Act for their betterment and they'll act for yours."

The king pulled himself up to his full height, a head taller than his counselor. His dark brown hair was as long as Voden's. When the discord between the king and queen had begun in earnest, one of the few things they had both agreed on was that neither would wear emerald, their family color. The mantle Fallov wore now was royal blue with silver trim. Beneath his bulging robes was a form that had once been flush with muscle. The eclipses had been unkind and the king's body withered such that the servants who saw him naked wondered if their king was eating enough.

"My father seized the Emerald Kingdom in a single, bloodless stroke of genius," Fallov said. His brown eyes focused on nothing as he spoke. "Other than that insolent prince who mouthed off to my mother, of course. But he was hung from the gallows, not beheaded, so no blood was spilled." The king shrugged. "What is it the commoners call our throne? Ah, that's right, the Unbloodied Throne. Before Father set his plan in motion, he had all the pieces precisely where they needed to be. The Whenyards had no way out.

Their time was at an end. Sending them to exile instead of slaughter was another triumph. The commoners neither loved nor hated the Whenyards. Fixing that family's young so that none of them could ever breed and sending them away made the whole affair far more palatable to the realm."

Fallov laughed as if hearing an unspoken jest. "Without my mother, none of that would have been possible. Her scheming was at least the equal of Father's. Their minds worked together like moons eclipsing the sun. Their arguments sharpened each other's wits like they were hammering hot steel fresh from the forge."

Tossing the ruined scepter on the Crimson Crown's lands, Fallov rounded the table and came to stand near Fulccrum. The king dragged his finger along the Middle River, where it ran closest to the city center.

"I fear that my only chance to hold the Unbloodied Throne is to make the Middle River run red with blood." He pressed the castle's tiny drawbridge. The fine strings on either side of it became slack and tight as the king raised and lowered it. "If I do manage to hold onto the throne with white knuckles, my family will remain hopelessly divided. Even if we survive this night, my house will see little of the dawn."

"We will find a way," Voden whispered.

Fallov sighed. "Mayhaps the queen and I can talk through our problems in an honest fashion and reconcile our differences."

Voden and the king burst into laughter.

The king's mirth carried on long enough that he became short of breath. "Ah, I can't rule my castle or even my court, let alone the realm." He wiped tears from the corners of his eyes.

"Speaking of the court, or should I say courts, it's time to hold them," Voden said, sneering as she spoke the word "courts." "After you've heard the last audience, we must discuss the matter of more coin for the Kingdom Guard. They can keep peace inside the city with the amounts we've set aside for them. But if the threat from outside the realm emerges, we must devote far more gold to our forces."

"Yes, yes, I know. The Crimson Crown will need to wait, but we must return to this discussion soon. For the nonce, I'll fight my more immediate wars."

His blue robes rolled like heavy seas as the king departed the war room with his counselor in tow. They descended a stone spiral staircase inside the circular tower. At the bottom, after following a winding series of hallways lined with torches and empty suits of armor, the two arrived in the throne hall. Both courts had already assembled, including the queen.

The throne hall, or thrones hall as some called it after the royal court split, was long and wide with a high cathedral ceiling. Pillars sculpted from green marble stretched from the floor to the ceiling, each ringed with torches mounted in gold sconces. A plush green rug with gold trim ran from the great oaken double doors all the way to the dais that held the thrones. Tapestries depicting random acts of valor hung from the stone walls.

Toward the back, near the doors, rough wooden benches had been placed for commoners waiting to state their grievances. Among those commoners, wearing the same threadbare clothes and grim expressions, were warriors who served as the ears at court for each of their respective Swordfamilies.

Chairs with fine cushions were placed closer to the

thrones. Only lords and other dignitaries were permitted to sit in them.

Before the rift between the king and queen, the dais upon which the thrones stood had been decorated all in emerald green. The royal couple sat on thrones made of gold and upholstered with the finest green silk. Hundreds of flawless emeralds had adorned the thrones. They had flashed like green stars when torchlight shined on them.

After the rift in the royal court, the king and queen each refused to let the other wear the family's emerald green color. As a result, the only green on the dais was the banner emblazoned with a crown that hung from the mezzanine above the thrones.

The queen had decorated her side of the dais in a mustard shade of yellow. Her satin dress, the cloth of her throne, and her three daughters' dresses all matched. The color paired well with the queen's dark skin and brown eyes. She had gone so far as to remove every emerald from her jewelry, including her crown. She replaced them with yellow sapphires. She would have preferred yellow diamonds, but in the Emerald Realm diamonds of that hue were even more rare than honest men.

Each of their three daughters, the princesses, took their places on the side of the dais farthest from their father. Their mother lounged on the throne behind them. Next to her stood Counselor Melyq.

The king had responded in kind to the queen's choice of royal color by seizing a shade of blue. The choice was purposeful, and hopeful, since it blends with yellow to create green. His royal blue mantle matched the cloth on his own throne, the regalia of their three sons, and the blue sapphires that had replaced the emeralds on his crown.

The princes stood in front of the king, far from their mother.

Despite the rift in appearance on the dais, the crowns worn by the king and queen remained much the same. They were mountains made of gold and capped with silver snow. Each mountain was crafted in the unique shape of a Pader Mountain. On the front stood Mount Densmore, the tallest peak in the range. A small ruby was set on its summit as a constant reminder of the Crimson Crown on the far side. The bottoms of the crowns, that had been ringed in emeralds, were now decorated with either yellow or blue sapphires.

Counselor Voden assumed her customary place adjacent to the king's throne.

"His majesty, the king, and her majesty, the queen," a herald cried with a vein pulsing from his forehead. He blew on a busine and its loud sound hushed the crowd. "His majesty's court and her majesty's court are now in session."

The king raised his hand at the assembled subjects before he sat upon his throne. Waiting a few moments for the king to become comfortable, the standing audience in the throne hall took their seats as well.

Before the royal couple's civil war, the king and queen's thrones had the same appearance and height. When hostilities broke out, and the two chose different colors, they also commissioned new thrones. This resulted in the construction of a series of thrones, each one taller than the last, as both sovereigns desired to sit higher than their spouse. When one belligerent had a throne built with tall legs and a high seat, the other countered with an even taller throne and higher seat.

That battle was won by the king when the queen, who was slightly shorter, had a throne made with legs so long that she required a stepping stool to take her seat. The king, who had longer legs and could mount his throne unassisted, triumphed with the slightly higher throne.

The queen surrendered. To avenge this indignity she made certain that her next throne, with a slightly lower seat, had a higher back than the king's throne.

"Call the first petitioner," King Fallov said with an air of indifference.

Queen Minacia sat on her throne with her arms and legs crossed tight. She looked away from the king and toward the princesses standing before her.

"The crowns call before them their vassal, Lord Kellington," the herald cried.

The lord rose from his seat and approached the dais. Two dozen paces from the king and queen, the he halted and knelt.

"Lord Kellington, I welcome your return to Fulccrum," Queen Minacia said before her husband could open his mouth. The old lord wobbled as he rose. "It's been too long since you graced us with your presence. I trust that your dear wife has recovered from the unfortunate illness that vexed her so?"

"After downing enough potions to fill the Angered Sea, the illness has left her. Though I cannot truthfully say she is free from its clutches," Kellington answered.

"A terrible pity. I ask that you bring her with you the next time you visit the capital," the queen said.

"The day is long, but my patience is short. State your business, my vassal," King Fallov said brusquely. He drummed his fingers on the arm of his throne. "We have many grievances to hear."

Kellington cleared his throat. "Yes, my king. As you know, my lands are bordered on the east by the Paders. The mountains' bounty has been generous to me and my forefathers. We've mined good metal from them for generations. The streams that pour down them when the snow melts in the spring give us almost enough water that we could farm all summer even if it didn't rain."

The king did not cover his mouth as he yawned. "Yes, yes. Your lands are the envy of the realm. What of it?"

This lord was short and solid. Kellington embodied his family's motto: "We shape the mountains and the mountains shape us." His head was perched at the summit of a wide body that was flanked by shoulders shaped like ridges. The hair on his head was as white as snow above the tree line. His beard fell like a waterfall escaping from a crack in the rock.

"The grant the crown gave to my family tells of where our lands begin and end. Our boundaries to the north, west, and south are so familiar to us that I could read them aloud and my blind uncle could walk them using his hands to feel." Kellington ran his fingers through his beard as he spoke. "But the grant says little about what is ours to the east."

"Why should it?" asked the queen impatiently. "Does House Kellington propose to move mountains?" The queen's side of the dais laughed politely at her jest; the king's side remained silent as the grave.

The lord's eyes narrowed very slightly. "Of course not, my queen. Though if we could push the mountains over and crush the Crimson Crown, we would do it for our good king and queen!"

"Your loyalty is as admirable as it is welcome," King Fallov said with an edge in his voice. "You will now state your request forthwith."

Kellington pulled on his beard so hard that he winced.

Now he began to speak very fast. "Since there's no cost to the crown and the crown doesn't use the mountains at all, we want to mine farther into the mountains past our old grant and we don't want to pay any tax on whatever we mine, including any veins of gold."

Kellington hadn't finished but the king lurched forward and blurted out, "Gold? Did you say *gold*?"

"Yes, my king," Kellington replied as he continued to stare at his feet. "For generations we've mined the grant and paid the crown every piece of tribute that's been asked of us."

"Required of you," the king corrected.

"Aye, required. But now is different. The deeper we mine the mountain, the more dangerous the work. We've lost whole crews of miners inside our grant. We'll lose many more when we're pulling out new gold. If we have to pay tribute on the new gold, it won't be worth the risk."

The queen scoffed again. The king shifted on his throne.

"Tell me, Lord Kellington, are there any mountain passes that open into your land?" King Fallov asked.

Kellington's eyes lit up. "Why, yes, there're some passes that wind through four low gaps between the shorter Paders. Our sentries guard those gaps day and night."

"Of course," the king said dryly. "Tell me, how wide are these passes?"

"Some are wider than others, your majesty." Kellington resumed pulling on his beard. "For most, the wheels on a wain can barely fit. Smugglers that try to sneak past our sentries use big saddle bags and bring a line of mules through. Some have special wains with the wheels set real close together."

The king frowned. "Your request as stated is denied, Lord Kellington. The crown has been generous to your family. You've been granted many fine lands, as you, yourself, just told us." The king stroked the arm of his throne. "We will grant you permission to mine deeper. But anything that you take from the Paders will be subject to your grant. To be clear, that means you'll pay the same tax under the same terms as your original grant."

Before, Kellington had been nervous and anxious to please his sovereign. Now that the king had denied his request, the lord's demeanor changed. He began to shake with anger.

The queen remained disinterested. She devoted the time during this exchange to admiring a particularly large yellow sapphire on one of her bracelets.

"The crown has every confidence in your loyalty. But in my experience, more gold requires more guards. This is particularly true considering that you share a border with the Crimson Crown. We will station more Kingdom Guard at your mines to ensure their safety," the king said.

Kellington gave the king a sharp nod. He spun around and marched the throne hall's length to the double doors, trailing a wake of deafening silence.

The herald obediently waited for the king to signal the next grievance. Though the queen had won the hard-fought battle for her own court, the king retained responsibility to conduct the court as a prize of war.

Slight movement from the king's hand provided the anticipated order. "Now before their majesties for their consideration is the matter of Skail. He stands accused of murder," the herald proclaimed.

A small, slender man dressed in loose black clothes approached the thrones. He had black hair, eyes, and lips. Dried blood caked his temple. His arms were held tight by large guards. Two more guards stood behind the prisoner with their swords drawn and ready.

The guards on his arms pushed him down until his knee thudded against the green rug.

"Your majesty, this man has committed murder," a guard reported. "He broke into our most heavily guarded dungeon. He choked out five gaolers and snuck past the rest. Then he picked the lock to a cell and murdered the man inside."

The guard paused for a moment and opened a black bag. He pulled out a small dagger with a round blade that looked like a smooth, thin icicle made of metal.

"He used this dagger to kill the prisoner. Strangest weapon I ever did see. We think he stabbed it in the prisoner's ear. The only blood on the body was a few drops that dribbled out from there. The prisoner must've been sleeping when he was killed. Some of his blood was dried on the sack under his head."

"Who was the prisoner?" the queen asked as her eyes remained on the yellow sapphire.

"A murderer condemned to die by the headsman's blade."

"How was this murderer of a murderer caught?" the king asked, pointing at Skail.

"A guard that he had choked out woke up."

The king's eyes narrowed. "Why didn't you kill the guards?"

"Because nobody paid me to kill the guards," Skail replied without a hint of emotion in his voice.

"Why did you kill the prisoner?"

"Because a man paid me good coin to kill the prisoner."

"But his death by the crown's justice was drawing near. He was going to die."

"The man didn't want the crown's justice. He wanted the murderer to be murdered."

"Why did he want the prisoner dead?"

"I don't know. I didn't ask."

"What was his name?"

"I don't know. I didn't ask that either."

"Well, then, what *did* you ask the man?" sputtered the king.

"For all the gold in advance, of course."

The crowded throne hall erupted into peals of laughter. Moments later, the king silenced that laughter with a menacing look.

"Your majesty, my deed may not have been honest but my reasons were. I didn't kill that man from anger or hate or revenge. I did it for the coin. What I did wasn't wicked; it was work. I was merely plying my trade."

"This is an outrage..." the king began, his voice booming down the hall.

"Silence!" the queen screamed and, despite the ever-growing hatred between the spouses, the king fell silent. "Tell me, guard, who was the condemned prisoner that met his end by this man's hand?"

"My queen, the prisoner was a foul murderer. His victims were many, both women and men. The justiciar heard tales of the bodies and sentenced the prisoner to death by beheading. The acts were so heinous that the justiciar was of a mind to execute the prisoner with a garrote. Instead, he settled on the headsman using a dull and rusted blade."

A cold silence fell over the audience in the throne hall.

The queen smiled triumphantly. "Well there you have it, King Fallov. This man, what was his name?" She paused and thought. "Skail's act wasn't murder. It was mercy. His victim was already dead. What do you care if this mongrel killed the prisoner before your oaf hacked him in two? I say the crown releases him."

A red darker than the Crimson Crown's banners flushed the king's face. "That prisoner was to die by the king's justice. *My justice*. The justiciar decided that his punishment was beheading." His voice sounded like a heavy wagon wheel rolling over loose gravel.

"You men are always so concerned with your swords," the queen shot back.

"This man who calls himself Skail has committed murder. The punishment for murder in my kingdom is death."

"Your majesties," Melyq said, a moment before the queen launched her counterattack. "It's clear that you see this crime...differently... I beg your permission to confer with Counselor Voden so that we might find a resolution to the impasse."

Permission was granted through shallow nods of approval. The king and queen sat impatiently, each staring away from the other. Melyq and Voden stepped forward and met below the dais. They traded whispers in one another's ears.

"How many years have you seen, Skail?" Voden asked the prisoner.

"That's another question for which I don't have a ready answer."

Voden inspected the prisoner's face. She searched for lines, wrinkles, and other features that betrayed the man's age. Another round of whispers between the counselors followed, louder than the last.

"The king wants this man dead and the queen wants him freed. He looks to be thirty, or close enough that the difference matters not," Melyq said, addressing the queen. "A man such as this would be fortunate to see forty years and some eclipses, and truly charmed to see many more. We agree that from this day the prisoner will remain with the quick, at most, a score of years. The counselors suggest imprisoning him for ten of those years."

"Your sage advice is to throw him in the dungeons' bowels for twenty eclipses, eh?" The king grunted. "Don't kill him, don't free him, instead take half his life. Split the murderer, one could say. I thought you two had more wit than that."

The crown's indifference greeted their proposal, which the counselors took as assent. They returned to their respective thrones. The guards yanked Skail from the floor to begin serving his ten-year sentence. Most prisoners in the dungeons died before their beards grew a finger's width. Though the blade of the Emerald Crown's headsman would remain sheathed, the punishment the king and queen had handed Skail was a death sentence in all but name.

The king announced that he had grown weary and the next petitioner would be the last for the day. The waiting commoners on the back benches groaned. They had just been sentenced to return to court with their grievances another day.

After the herald received his signal from the king, a commoner was granted her audience before the crown. She limped from the back bench all the way to her place before the thrones.

The woman had crow's feet at the corners of her almond eyes. Her long, brown hair hosted many streaks of silver. She had a youthful, but tired, face. She wore a long, brown dress made of heavy cloth that only had a few patches. She wore simple jewelry bereft of jewels.

Clutching a kerchief, she dabbed at tears that gathered by her crow's feet.

"Your majesties," she began in a tremulous voice with her head bowed. "I beg your leave to remain on my feet. Were I to kneel, the humors that swell my throbbing knees are like to spill onto your fine rug."

"So granted," Voden responded.

"The criminals...the *monsters*...in our fair city have gone too far. I beg for your help, my crowns. Me and my husband run a shop down on the docks in Stonebann. It's called Emerald Ezzy's Curios and Oddments. We buy goods, sometimes from the cogs coming in from the Ring Islands. Supplies, weapons, treasures, things like that." She paused and blew into her kerchief. Her nose was almost as loud as the herald's busine. "Me and him had many happy years together. Everything was going so, so good. Then those she-demons got their claws in him. Those women in the evil pleasure houses where they take over the minds of men."

The oldest prince blurted out, "Syrens!" He immediately realized his blunder and closed his eyes. A smattering of suppressed laughter and polite coughs came from the crowd, but it was confined to the benches at the very back of the throne hall.

"Aye, them. They weren't the only ones, neither. Some others got him, too. It was them louts that're always smoking and snorting things. The ones that like to lose their minds. My husband fell prey to those scum, too."

Two princesses bit their lower lip and a prince began chewing on his tongue.

The crowd in the throne hall lost interest in the

woman's familiar tale of woe that had been told countless times by aggrieved spouses. They began to talk amongst themselves.

"You speak of Ashfall," Voden said.

"Yes, yes, this is all very upsetting. But men get trapped in the vise of their vices every single day. Of what concern is this to the crown?" the queen asked. She folded her arms across her ample chest.

"I beg for justice for them fiends that stole my husband," Ezzy sobbed loudly into her kerchief.

"You have our pity, but if the crown hunted every man seduced by the Syrens or that Ashfall has made a leech, we wouldn't have any Kingdom Guard left to protect the realm," the queen said in a distinct tone of disinterest.

Voden rested her hand on the king's shoulder and squeezed. She smiled at Ezzy.

"The Syrens and Ashfall stole more than my husband. One of them took a strange blade of great value," the woman said.

The sovereigns became alert.

Anticipating their next question, Ezzy continued hurriedly. "I know what you're thinkin' and I know the law. The crown gets the first chance to buy any rare things that come into the city. Me and my husband was going to bring the sword here to court the day he disappeared. When he left me, he took the sword with him. Those criminals didn't just steal my man, they stole what could have been property of the crown."

Unfurling a scroll of parchment, Melyq began searching for the particulars of the law that required importers to present exotic relics to the crown before selling them to subjects. The queen waved at Melyq, commanding him to roll up the scroll.

"Tell us of this sword," the king demanded.

"Never seen anything like it. Because I couldn't see it at all. I think it was a short sword. Much longer than a dagger, but shorter than what the Kingdom Guard carries. I can't be sure because we had to feel the blade to find its length. The blade, by the thundering horde of gods, the blade was sharp." She held up a hand to show the cut on her finger.

The murmuring in the hall yielded to silence. Everyone listened to the woman's words, even the commoners seated on the bench in the very back of the throne hall.

"Was this blade born of some dark magic?" the queen asked.

"I know not. May have been something like glass. But it wasn't cloudy like glass. It was very clear. Like a diamond with no color that don't flash when it's in light. When it was more than the length of a finger from my eye, I could not see it. Some master craftsman across the Angered Sea may've made it. The cog that carried it came from the smallest Ring Island. The crew called it the Shard of the Specter. As I say, I was going to bring it here to give the crown the first chance to buy it. When my husband took it, he stole it from me and our shop...and the Emerald Crown."

The queen spoke quietly so that only the king and the counselors could hear. "An invisible sword? I know where to find such a thing. Melyq, search his majesty's royal crotch at once."

Fallov moved to rise from his throne, but Voden's quick hand kept him on his seat.

"Dwell on that while I'm seated on my second favorite throne," the queen whispered, winking at her husband. She glared at Voden.

Voden leaned down to speak in the king's ear. "Do not

rise to the bait. Let it rot. In the throne hall, the king must be kingly."

A growl through clenched teeth was the king's response. Crimson again flashed across his cheeks.

"Please grant Ezzy's request," Voden whispered, even quieter than before. "As a favor to me."

The hair on the back of the king's neck stood up. "The crown thanks you for bringing this matter to our attention, Emerald Ezzy. A bounty of fifty gold scythes is placed upon your husband. To collect the full bounty, the crown requires that he's brought to us alive. We have questions for this man."

"Melyq, put a bounty on the sword of a hundred more scythes. Make it known that the crown will look favorably on whoever brings it to us," the queen added.

The king and queen nodded in agreement. It had been so long since they'd agreed on anything that the counselors and the herald were uncertain about what to do next.

"I promise to make up for my lying husband's great crime. When the three moons next make a wide triangle near the horizon, I'll set sail for the Crescent Isles and return with relics the likes of which none in the Emerald Kingdom has ever seen. That is, unless those whirlpool-loving, salt-brained..."

"That will be enough," the king interrupted. "Go to the Kingdom Guard for your district and describe this husband of yours to them."

"I thank you for your good justice, your majesties." Ezzy bowed her head.

Clutching her kerchief tight in her hand, the woman turned and limped down the throne hall. She stepped with one foot and dragged the other, leaving a trail in the green rug made of woven wool. Her limp became less pronounced the closer she came to the double doors. When she took her last few steps inside the throne hall, she didn't limp at all.

Before the herald could announce the court's close, Melyq descended from the dais and turned to face his sovereigns. He bowed to each in turn.

"My queen and king, begging your forgiveness, there is one more matter that must be addressed. I fear that I bear ill tidings for the royal family." Melyq wrung his hands as he spoke. "The whereabouts of your beloved nephew, Romlad, are unknown."

The queen did not react to this report. The king sat bolt upright.

"You'll recall that the boy was sent to recover from his wounds and learn the importance of discretion under Lord Wrand's tutelage."

"Of course we recall," the queen responded sharply. "That was after he tried to mount a dragon in the refuge. He's always been infatuated with those wretched creatures. I seem to recall that he needed two new teeth after that dragon's tail smashed him in the mouth." She paused for a moment.

"Forgive me, my queen, but Romlad lost three teeth from his encounter with the dragon, not two," Melyq corrected. "All of them were replaced with gold teeth. After the beating he took, he was lucky not to lose more."

The king nodded in agreement. "Why the boy kept sneaking away to meddle with the dragons, I'll never know. Lord Wrand's realm spares Romlad of such temptation. Never understood it. Everyone in the realm knows that mother dragons go mad at the sight and smell of yolk from a dragon egg. He's fortunate he didn't get worse from crushing the egg in that nest."

"Lord Wrand recently sent a messenger pigeon with the troubling news that Romlad has vanished from his lands."

As Melyq spoke, the king gripped the arms of his throne very hard.

"Wrand provided scant details, but he did say that his men are still searching for the boy. He begged your forgiveness and said that a chest full of gold scythes would be sent as atonement for his failure. His men did bring us a chest, but when it was opened, we found only lava rock."

Voden could barely contain her indignation. "Is this some cruel jest? Or has Lord Wrand lost his wits entirely?"

"The guards and wain drivers were questioned thoroughly," Melyq replied. "They mentioned some trouble with bandits near Six Corners. When the Kingdom Guard was sent to investigate, they found no trace of bandits or the like. The travelers and innkeepers spoke of nothing unusual. Lord Wrand's men must have been mistaken. Or mayhaps the lord trusted men who were not trustworthy."

"Dispatch search parties *now*! Scour the realm! If he's west of the Paders, we must find the boy!" the king roared. "Deploy the elite Kingdom Guards to the dragon refuge!"

CHAPTER SIX

HEAVIES

A thick blanket of bright stars spread across the dark and cloudless sky. Two moons, Dragon Without Wings and Night Scythe, glided through the lights that shimmered like guttering candles. The cool air of spring had come rushing down the distant mountains to wash over Droena. She found comfort in the cacophony of young insects surrounding her and the familiar sound of her leather boots parting the grass that had already grown tall. The torches that she and Kraaft held not only lit their way, but warmed them as well.

"Beautiful night for an ugly task," Droena whispered as she admired the points of light in the sky.

"Thundering horde of gods, I wish I had my steel armor on right now. At least it would break the gusts of wind," Kraaft grumbled. As soon as he finished speaking, the wind blew hard enough to bend the grass. "I feel naked wearing this boiled leather. Like a fool on a fool's errand." He elbowed Droena in the side. "You probably wish you were wearing that armor that matches your lips."

"The noise from you clanking around the refuge would

let any dragon or Kingdom Guard within shouting distance know that we're here," Droena shot back. "You're carrying a shield instead of wearing armor and we're both walking instead of on horseback for the same reason. To dodge the dragons. What good do you think a suit of armor would do against dragon fire? You'd cook like stew in a pot above a fire." She shrugged. "At least Raysk let us bring swords."

Shoulder to shoulder, the two walked across a boulder-strewn field. They navigated around the giant rocks that, in some places, were as thick as trees in an old forest. In other places, they crossed stretches of wide-open grassland streaked with babbling brooks. Kraaft swore each time the cold water seeped through his leather boots.

"The way is too long to go across the countryside. Dawn will break before we make it to where we're s'posed to drop the bones," Kraaft said under his breath.

"If we take a path, a search party could see us. Melyq said he'd order them to stay near the paths."

"Did he order the Fire Keepers' dragons to stay near the paths, too?" Kraaft growled.

She ignored him.

Slung over Droena's shoulder was a large leather sack. Its contents clicked and clacked with each step that she took. Kraaft held a small cloth bag in one hand and a thin chain in the other. At the end of the chain was a lamb with an iron collar around its neck. It walked behind the two Heavies.

In the distance, thick plumes of light gray smoke reflected the moonlight.

"I'd rather be sitting at a table emptying horns of ale right now." Droena moved the sack to her other shoulder. "Doesn't feel right."

"It's the lamb, isn't it?" Kraaft chuckled. "You don't

want the lamb to die? We eat lamb. Do you swallow your feelings every time you swallow a bite of lamb?"

The look Droena gave him was colder than the night.

"I eat lamb, but I don't throw it on a fire while it's still alive," she said.

"Ah, the cook throws it on the fire after it's dead. Much different." Kraaft tugged on the chain and the lamb quickened its steps. Droena didn't look back. "Melyq's debt is good pay for this little deed. If a job calls for killing, it's easier to kill a lamb than a man." He poked at the leather sack on Droena's back. "This man's already dead, so why turn it down? This isn't a job; it's a gift."

How can the sun rise in the north? Droena wondered. Then she realized that was impossible. She stopped and squinted at the light in the distance. The red glow disappeared to be replaced by more tendrils of gray smoke rising in the moonlight. "Dragon fire," she whispered.

The lamb bleated softly.

"It'd be far easier if we weren't on the refuge. How many dragons do you think are out here?" she asked.

"Too many, but we'll only need one of them to collect the other half of the pay."

Droena sighed. "My son loves lambs. He's always begging me to take him outside Stonebann to see a farm. He dotes on a little ball of wool. I worry for him, when the war comes. What the other families might do to him."

"Raysk will fight this war all the way through, down to the last Heavy. But don't worry about your son. The code of Sacred Kin protects our blood outside the Swordfamily, even if every family goes to the rushes."

The chill air made Droena shiver. "Vasarox told me about Auzken's tomb. The Bleeding Blade was gone."

"Aye. Another family moved first. We're not the only

Swordfamily that knows a weak crown makes a weak peace." Kraaft yanked on the chain again. The lamb bleated, louder this time. "Did Vasarox tell you anything else about it?"

Droena shook her head.

"Then he left out the best part. Auzken's body was lying in one of those big stone boxes important people get buried in. The lid was next to the body. It was smashed into gravel." A smile spread across Kraaft's face. "The box was filled with blood as black as pitch. He couldn't even see the body. It's said that Auzken was laid on a bed of gold, but Vasarox didn't see that either. He plunged both hands in the blood and groped around for the sword. He only felt the body. The blood stained his arms up to his elbows. The red is even darker than his skin. Raysk calls him Darker Hands now. We didn't start this war, but it's already begun."

"A tomb full of dark blood? That means..." Droena didn't finish her sentence. She remembered Pametan's words about why the sword bled. She glanced back at the lamb.

Kraaft followed her eyes. "Worry not about your son. The families have few codes, but we do obey them. There will always be honor among the Swordfamilies. Only those in the warring families are killed, never their kinfolk. If it were any other way, every family's mothers, fathers, sons, daughters, wives, and husbands would be slain in a war. Nobody can protect all their kinfolk. If we don't mind Sacred Kin, our victory prize would be the corpses of our own blood." He paused and huffed. "Unless your little son takes up arms against a Swordfamily, of course, then he'd be fair game." Kraaft laughed under his breath. "What's the biggest blade he could wield? A dagger?"

"He's older than that," Droena muttered.

Three more blasts of dragon fire lit up the night sky. They were close enough that the Heavies could hear the roaring flames rushing past the dragon's fangs. The scream of the dragon fodder pierced the night. The lamb froze. Kraaft pulled hard on the chain and the lamb toppled over with its rigid legs perfectly straight. He picked up the lamb and put it under one arm.

Carried through scattered boulders, open fields, and groves of trees, the lamb recovered and again followed behind the Heavies.

The dragon refuge was unfamiliar territory for Droena. She set down her leather sack and pulled a parchment from her belt. She turned away from Kraaft to hide her shaking hands as she unrolled it. The crude map from Melyq that she studied in the moonlight told her that the two were nearing their mark.

As the pair marched on, the moons shone with enough light for Droena to see dark patches in the open fields where the grass had been burned away. They looked like great scabs on the rolling grassland.

When the inky black of night first began to yield to pale blue, Droena announced that they had arrived.

Boulders taller than Kraaft circled a large patch of ground. The plants inside the ring grew low to the ground and in straight lines that ran parallel to each other. Purple leaves with jagged edges sprouted from spots on the stems. Droena walked through a wide gap between the boulders. Close to the center, she found a group of small pebbles in the shape of a circle no bigger than her fist.

She swept the pebbles away with her boot and dropped the leather sack where they had been. She grabbed the bottom of the sack and turned it upside down. The contents spilled onto the ground.

At Droena's feet was a pile of charred bones. She arranged the bones where she thought they might fall if a man was hit by the full brunt of a dragon's flame. Following Melyq's instructions, she placed the jawbone under the skull so that all three gold teeth were plain to see.

When the Heavies spoke to each other, their words were barely loud enough for the other to hear.

"Raysk will call the council?" Droena asked as she walked exactly six paces toward the center of the circle.

"He already has. When Vasarox returned and told him about the blade, Raysk was furious. Another family taking the blade means that we may have a strong challenger. It also means that their thinking is ahead of Raysk's. The war hasn't yet begun and some clever Swordfather is moving like a fox." Kraaft stomped on plants as he joined Droena. "In his rage, he broke a greatsword over his knee like it was a piece of dry wood. The blade ruined the cuisse that he wore when he broke it."

"He is quick to rage," she said. Then she hesitated for a moment. "Is it true what they say about him?"

"Many things are said about Raysk. The crazier the claim, the more like it is to be true."

"I'm a captain whose been around longer than many. But I still don't know if I believe it. What they say about Pametan, I mean."

Kraaft smiled. "Ah, that."

"Did he do that to her hand?"

"Yes. She freed him from The Need, and she did it on his orders. Her reward was losing her hand. Only time I've seen Raysk show remorse. He crushed her hand in a blind rage after she cut him. Anyway, she's still alive and with the family. She was a captain before it happened but she can't fight so good now."

"Why did he command her to make the cut?"

"It's the only way a man can escape the Syrens."

Droena began to ask another question.

Kraaft stopped her. "Let us speak of this another day. We have much work and little time."

She took the chain from him.

He set down his shield and opened the small cloth bag. Slowly, to avoid the sound of iron striking iron, Kraaft pulled out a hammer and a long stake.

"What if it was a family you'd never expect, like the Scabbards?" Droena dared a different question. She kept scanning the wide gaps between the boulders. She handed the chain back to him.

Kraaft cinched the chain to the stake and pressed its point against the ground. "The Scabbards know their place in Fulccrum. They're a lesser family. They make sure the six families don't kill each other when we're together. If they took the Bleeding Blade, the families' wrath would come down on them like they were drowning in the Lava Sea."

"They'll be guarding the Swordfathers at the council, right?"

"Yes, and that's why it'll be perfectly safe. When the families meet, anyway. As soon as they step away, it'll be war."

Kraaft placed the small bag that had carried the tools on the stake as he hammered. The cloth bag muffled the blows that drove the stake deep into the ground. When the stake would sink no farther, it was well hidden by purple leaves. When he yanked the chain, the stake didn't budge.

The lamb at the other end of the chain bleated softly. Droena didn't look at it.

"If we had a Fire Keeper here, they could summon a

dragon for us," she mused. Her eyes darted around the circle. "Those monsters obey them like whipped dogs."

"If a Fire Keeper saw us doing this, we would be a hot breakfast for their livestock." Kraaft put the hammer back in the bag and tucked it into his belt. "Dawn is breaking. Raysk ordered us to have this done before first light. It's past time we finish."

Kraaft pulled his leg back and kicked the lamb hard in its ribs.

The lamb's head whipped violently as it ran, pulling the chain tight as it strained against the iron collar. It bleated loud enough that a nearby flock of doves took to the sky. The bleating stopped only for the moment when the animal choked itself against the collar before sprinting the length of the chain in the opposite direction.

The two Heavies trotted outside the circle of boulders. They ducked behind a rock that Melyq had marked on the map.

"Melyq said the nearby nests are on the other side," Kraaft whispered.

"Get that shield ready," Droena hissed.

They waited for a short time. The lamb bleated less and its cries became softer.

The sky was still the same shade of pale blue when Kraaft's patience was exhausted. He slipped his arm through the leather straps on his shield. It showed no heraldry or symbol; its steel was naked. The pavise was tall and wide enough for both Heavies to crouch behind and protect their entire bodies. Kraaft's forearm braced hard against its width. He smashed the broadside of his sword against the shield.

Droena frowned at him as the clash of steel on steel rang through the retreating darkness.

The lamb sprinted at the end of its chain, bleating loudly as it circled.

Kraaft shrugged. "Maybe dragons like the taste of knights cooked in their own armor better than they do lamb." He grinned.

Droena drew her sword.

The lamb bled from the iron collar tearing at its skin. The white wool around its neck turned blood red. Tiring from its frenzy, its bleating became little more than a whisper. Its head hung low and it nibbled on a narrow purple leaf.

A few heartbeats later the dragon crept into the circle opposite from the Heavies. They watched in silence as it moved through a wide gap between the boulders. The lamb was unaware of the silent beast.

Larger than a destrier by half, the dragon stepped as lightly as a hungry cat stalking its prey. Its countless tiny scales moved like rolling swells over a deep sea. Their dark shade of purple was nearly black. Its leathery wings were folded tight against its flanks. A spiderweb of veins lined the wings. The tip of its tail bristled with spikes.

Eyes like polished gemstones flashed as the dragon surveyed its prey. Droena swore the beast smiled as the flesh around its fangs pulled back. Those bared teeth were shaped like the blade of a scythe. They were even sharper than the mane of spikes laid back against its neck. The slits that served as its nose flared as it drew in the lamb's scent.

The lamb finally sensed that a predator had neared. It became very still.

Droena's heart sank.

Thin smoke drifted from the dragon's nostrils. The Heavies pulled back behind the boulder as the dragon swung its head to peer in their direction. Suddenly, everything around the two became bathed in a bright orange glow. A roar like a monstrous bonfire made of bone-dry logs filled their ears. The Heavies pressed their backs firmly against the boulder. In the time it took to draw a breath of hot air, a second blast of dragon fire flowed around them. The boulder that sheltered them became warm to the touch.

As the Heavies remained motionless, silence descended.

A haze of smoke fouled the air. Sounds of the dragon's feet crushing leafy plants came from inside the circle of boulders. The Heavies curled around their boulder hesitantly, shield and swords held tight.

A patchwork of fires burned the crops. The dragon approached the lamb. It launched streaks of flame on either side of its prey. The flames from a blast made the chain that held the lamb glow bright red. The prey opened its mouth but made no sound.

"What's it doing?" Droena whispered.

"Playing with its food," Kraaft replied, even quieter.

Three tiny dragons, barely larger than the doomed lamb, pranced into the circle. They playfully jumped on the fires and bit at the flames. When they opened their mouths to breathe fire like their mother, only puffs of gray smoke poured out. Some of them rolled on the flames. Their legs flopped from side to side as they rubbed their backs in the heat.

As the sun crested the Paders' peaks to the east, the first warm morning air came with it. This whisper of heat after the cold night pushed a light breeze over the Heavies. It continued into the circle of boulders and scattered the smoke that had pooled within.

The large dragon's nostrils flared. The spikes that had lain against its neck now spread wide to become a menacing hood around its head. As it turned toward the Heavies, the dragon bared even more of its dagger-like fangs.

A blast of flame shot toward them and the Heavies retreated behind the boulder. The flame passed so close to Droena that it singed the tips of her hair.

Without a word, the two fled.

Abandoning the lamb and her young, the dragon leapt toward its newfound quarry. This prey moved much faster. The boulders between the hunter and the fleeing Heavies stood too close together for the dragon to pass. After trying to ram its way between the boulders, the dragon extended its hooked talons and clambered over a rock. It closed the distance to the Heavies with quick strides.

Kraaft spun around and slammed the bottom of his pavise into the ground. He knelt and braced his forearm against the steel. Droena tucked behind him and pressed her shoulder against Kraaft's back. Their swords were ready.

The dragon reared and spread its wings high over its head. The breadth of its full wingspan gave the beast a terrifying size as it stayed perched on its hind legs. Satisfied that the hiding animals posed no threat, the dragon dropped back onto all fours.

A shaft of blazing flame struck the pavise and split apart. The fire shot for so long that Droena's chest ached as she yearned to breathe. When it stopped, the shield began to glow a faint red. Droena's leather jerkin shook against her skin as the dragon threw back its head and roared.

Another blast of fire met the shield. Wisps of smoke rose from where Kraaft's forearm, clad in boiled leather, braced against the steel. Thick smoke surrounded the Heavies as they became an island in a sea of charred ruin.

The shield glowed bright red and radiated a terrible heat. Sweat poured from the captains and steam rose where the drops touched the ground.

The third blast of fire broke the stalemate. Kraaft screamed as he desperately pushed against the shield, but the leather straps that he held came loose with their ends aflame.

The shield sloughed to the ground. It folded into a heap of glowing metal.

Droena pulled Kraaft up by the collar. He grabbed at his burned arm.

The dragon pulled in a deep breath. Only a short distance of smoldering field separated it from the Heavies.

Droena threw her sword at the creature in a futile attempt to frighten it away. The dragon paused as gray smoke rolled from its mouth. A moment before it launched the fatal inferno, the sound of small dragons screeching erupted from the circle of boulders.

The large dragon froze.

In the gaps between the boulders, Droena saw the lamb running around the circle. A short length of red-hot chain dragged behind the crazed animal. Two small dragons shrieked in protest. The third gave chase to the lamb as it trailed thin smoke.

Gusting wind fanned the flames around Kraaft's ruined shield as the dragon spun away from the Heavies. It lunged toward its young in a movement that was more like a long jump than a flight. As it bounded again and glided into the circle, Droena was surprised to see that the dragon's wings were barely larger than its body. The dragon was so low in the air that its claws scraped the top of a boulder before it landed inside the circle.

A roar and terrible screech followed. Smoke rose where

the lamb's bleating stopped. Kraaft dropped his sword and the Heavies ran. The tall grass whipped at their legs as they put stride after stride between themselves and the family of feeding dragons.

"Thank the thundering gods its young cried out. That dragon cared more about them than roasting us!" Droena said breathlessly as she sprinted.

Smoke trailed Kraaft's forearm as he ran beside her. "It cared more about a little lamb than my strength. The dragons will pay for that *disrespect*."

CHAPTER SEVEN

FIRE KEEPERS

The late afternoon sun wandered in the sky, flooding the dragon refuge with brilliant light. Every boulder, tree, and stream looked radiant. Each towering sorcerwood cast a dark shadow like an eclipse. At the top of a knoll, Kardas, Berg, and Andra admired the view. Their horses enjoyed the break in the ride, grazing on the tallest blades of grass.

"The first time I saw the dragon refuge, I knew that I had to be a Fire Keeper," Andra said. She squinted against the sunlight as she surveyed the boulders sprinkled over a sea of grass. "Every chance I had, I'd sneak away to the city. I begged a captain to take me out here for weeks. After I'd finished a backbreaking day of work at home in the woods, I snuck away and found him at the DragInn. He brought me here. The three full moons lit up the countryside like it was early morning. The dragons and the danger all nestled amongst rolling hills of peace." She realized the futility of conveying the emotion of that moment. "Forsbeme is a lovely district, but it could never compare to this place."

"Was it Fyur?" Kardas asked. "The captain, that is?"

Andra said nothing. *To you, he was just a captain. To me, he was the bearer of a cherished love that I've lost forever.*

"He always had a liking for women that he could impress with the dragons," Berg said. "Might be the only reason he became a Fire Keeper."

Clenching her legs against her mount, Andra and her streaming tears rode forward at a brisk trot. Behind her, Kardas scowled at Berg.

Quickly riding up to Andra, Berg cleared his throat. "You did well on that Lord Wrand heist. Glad me and Ombran could throw off those knights for long enough."

She rode in silence for a few steps. "I wonder what we stole."

Berg was such a large man that he could use only the stoutest of hackneys as his mount. His chest pulled the threads of his jerkin tight. He held the reins with hands that were calloused from long years of wrestling dragons. The brown hair on his head was longer than that of his beard. Kardas said that when Berg was young, he slept with the dragons. His skin was almost as rough as dragon scales and Andra did not doubt her Swordfather's words.

The captain shrugged. "What does it matter? We got what we wanted."

Andra didn't respond.

"Melyq doesn't know that we opened the chest before we delivered the goods. We know something of the truth and collected a debt. To my mind, that's a job well done."

"This realm is built on a foundation of lies. Truth is poison and it will get you killed one of two ways, slowly or quickly," Kardas sighed. "We may never discover the truth, but you must always chart a careful course through this sea of lies. Andra, you will ascend to captain this day. You must embrace the true nature of our realm." His eyes sparkled as he spoke. "You're much more than a warrior now."

An azure colored dragon approached the trio from behind. It was about the size of the palfreys that Andra and Kardas rode. A fox squirmed between its jaws. The fur of its captured prey had been burned off, leaving only a few patches of singed stubble.

The scaly beast trotted between the Fire Keepers. As the dragon raised its neck, Kardas slid his hand over its head. In response to the show of affection, the dragon purred loudly. Andra watched its tail sway as the large dragon quickened its pace to speed ahead.

A second, smaller dragon trailed the first. This one also approached the riders from behind. When it reached Andra and Kardas, it matched the speed of their mounts. The little dragon was half the size of the one with the fox in its mouth. Most of its scales were azure like the larger dragon, but this one also had black stripes wrapped around its belly, tail, and neck. Its spikes were black as well.

The small dragon sniffed at Andra. Then it licked her calf and nuzzled against her leather boot. Its tongue flopped from the side of its mouth as it sprinted away, chasing after the larger dragon.

Furwing rested on the rump of Andra's mount. The cat hissed at the small dragon with the black stripes. Andra reached back and bumped her cat on the nose.

"Hasten to follow your mother, little one," Kardas called. "Young dragons must arrive on time for hot meals, or they'll choke on ash and bones instead of gorge on meat. The youngling dragons can only breathe smoke, so they must cleave tight to their fire-breathing mothers."

A second small dragon followed behind the youngling that had nuzzled Andra. This one was identical except it had white stripes and spikes, instead of black. It licked the bottom of Andra's boot and puffed gray smoke at her before racing to catch up to its family.

Furwing yawned and licked her own nose.

"Looks like you made a couple new friends," Berg said to Andra. "Must be a brother or sister of that other little one."

Farther down the winding path, the Fire Keepers found themselves surrounded by dragons frolicking over rolling hills. They had many different shapes, sizes, and colors. Most of them had a coat that was all the same color. Others wore stripes or spots over their bodies. A few dragons had scales so dark that they seemed to swallow the light.

The largest dragons were nearly twice the size of the Fire Keepers' horses. Some had wings bigger than their bodies. Others had no wings at all. The dragons that flew managed several flaps before they landed. After taking to the air, they only traveled a short distance.

Some dragons hunted, stalking with skill that big cats would envy. Others played, grappling with each other and rolling on the ground together. They shot small lines of flame as they romped. One dragon traipsed through a shallow pond and, having crossed to the other side, breathed fire on its own feet to dry off.

A few dragons lay on their backs with their feet in the air, basking in the warm sun.

Furwing, curled with her head against her tail on the rump of Andra's mount, dozed in the warmth. The furry wings on her back, so small not even a butterfly would envy them, flapped furiously as the napping cat dreamed of chasing a flying bird through the air.

The path that the Fire Keepers followed dipped through a wide brook. A dragon's nest sat underneath a tree so close that Andra could have reached out and touched it. A clutch of four eggs lay in the nest. Each one was a different color. Rather than the sticks that a bird would use to build its nest, the dragons piled rocks in the shape of a great bowl. Andra felt heat radiating from the eggs. They were warmer than the midday sun.

"Let us hasten our pace," Kardas said. He whipped the reins against his palfrey to order it into a gallop. Berg and Andra followed. After they had ridden far enough that the crests of six hills separated them from the nest, Kardas signaled for them to stop. "Most dragons prefer to build their nests on anything above the ground that can hold rock. Makes it harder for foxes and the like to get at the eggs. Others build their nests near water. Like the one that Andra found bleeding into the Wandering Waters." Kardas looked at a patch of scarred skin on the back of his hand. "Dragons are our kin. They are members of our family, same as if they were warriors, captains, or a Swordfather. But don't ever meddle with their young or linger near their nests. They'll burn you same as if you were a fox. They're more protective of their young than Melyq is of his secrets."

"And may the thundering horde of gods help you if their yolk spills," Berg said, his eyes wide. "They can smell better than any hound. The scent of that yolk, 'specially when it's fresh, will drive a dragon mad."

"Speaking of smell, what's that in the air?" Andra asked, drawing in a deep breath. She grimaced. A thin gray haze surrounded them. "It's smoke, but thu'gods it's foul."

"Who knows? The dragons burn things out here all the time. It's what they do," Berg replied dismissively.

The tops of some boulders were barely visible over a hill.

Kardas pressed his legs against the sides of his mount,

beckoning the others to follow. The source of the smoke came into view as the hill crested. Below, a large ring of boulders surrounded a burnt patch of land. The three rode down and through a wide gap between the boulders, where they dismounted.

The ground inside the circle of rocks was mostly black and dusted with ash. Gouges and scratches in the earth showed where the dragons had stepped. Some were deep and wide, but most were small, shallow, and close together.

Berg picked up a singed piece of a purple leaf. "Crops," he said. Then he put his hand over his mouth and coughed hard from the befouled air.

Taking the leaf from his captain, Kardas agreed. "Ashfall must have sowed its weeds here." Kardas crushed it in his hand. "They plant their filth in the refuge because they know the Kingdom Guard avoids our dragons. Then they whinge about the dragons burning their crops." He dropped the leaf.

"There's some bones over there," Andra said, pointing.

Small bones lay scattered in some burned grass just outside the ring of boulders. The three stood over it, pondering the skeleton's former owner. Berg picked up a thin, curved piece of bone with a small bit of cooked flesh on the end. He took a bite and chewed it thoughtfully.

Andra choked back a mouthful of bile as the captain savored his small meal.

"Lamb," Berg said through the side of his mouth. "Overdone, for sure, but it's definitely lamb. Maybe the DragInn will hire one of our dragons as a cook." He laughed at his own joke and then swallowed the chunk of lamb.

"What's a lamb doing out here?" Andra wondered after she had vanquished the bile.

"Might've wandered away from a farm," Berg suggested.

The Fire Keepers returned to the smoky patch of land within the boulders where their horses waited. Before Berg climbed onto his hackney, he noticed something sparkle on a small dark patch of ground outside the circle of boulders. He hustled over to the spot and beckoned the others to join him.

At their feet lay a bulbous mound of steel surrounded by burned grass. Andra touched the metal.

"It's warm," she said.

Berg wedged the toe of his leather boot under the steel and flipped it over. The underside had cooled in the shape of the dirt where it had melted.

"Nothing on it," Berg observed.

"There's a sword," Andra said, pointing at a nearby blade that had bent down a patch of long grass. She picked it up and glanced it over. "Don't recognize anything about this, either. Whoever carried it must have left in a hurry." She pursed her lips hard and returned her attention to the melted steel. "That must've been some armor or a shield."

"Maybe a greatsword. Ashfall trying to protect its crops?" Berg wondered.

"No," Kardas replied. "This field they planted is too small to die for." He gave the smoking grounds inside the circle a hard look. "Either of you see anything else?"

Both shook their heads.

"Somebody came onto the refuge and made our dragons angry. If only they could talk. I'd want to hear about this trouble." Kardas sighed. "A slaughtered lamb, melted metal, and an abandoned sword. Remember this."

The three resumed their journey. Andra's mind invented the possible events in the refuge not long ago.

Riding in silence for a time, they neared some mountains painted in the sun's warm yellow.

"When I first saw them, I thought they would be bigger," Andra said absently as a group of dragons raced past the Fire Keepers. "The dragons, I mean. In the old tales, knights ride dragons as big as Dark Water's ship. They soar through the sky, in the clouds even! Raining down fire on all who dare threaten them."

"Hahr! We don't live in a fairy tale!" Kardas laughed. "The dragons around us are friends to every Fire Keeper, but it wasn't always this way. Before our Swordfamily, even before a crown came to Fulccrum, wild dragons the likes of which you've heard covered this land thicker than fire fleas on a hellhound's back.

"They were huge and wild. Even the charms of a Syren couldn't tame them. Before we could make them obey like the horses we're riding now, the dragons had to be smaller. No knight, no mage, no king could impose their will on a grown dragon. The men and women whose descendants went on to become the first Fire Keepers bred the dragons to be smaller.

"The maniacs would crawl into dragon nests. More than one of them became a hot meal for the hatchlings! Hahr! The old nests used to be near as big as these hills. The Fire Keepers snuck into them when the dragons left to hunt. They smashed small holes in the bottom of the biggest eggs and stuffed cloth in the break so it wouldn't leak much. Made the dragon think it was just bad, not broken.

"The small eggs were left alone, the ones with the runts inside. Methinks that's why our dragons are so possessive of their young nowadays. When their big eggs kept going bad, the giant dragons worried over their offspring. The dragons today have that sense burned into their skulls.

"Our dragons are the progeny of the little dragons born from those little eggs. Now they're halfdragons with small wings that can't fly very high or far. Except for a few that can perch on the Paders' highest peaks and fly over the whole mountain range to the east. But that's only a few of them, like Fyur's old dragon Hoqqes."

Andra permitted her thoughts to wander to the orange and black dragon with a white face that had been her lover's. But only for a moment.

"They still have strong bodies and minds," Kardas continued. "Wild streaks in them, too, faint echoes of those giant monsters. We're their keepers and they're our friends. The dragons are also our weapons, like a sword or wand. A weapon is only as lethal as the man or woman who wields it. We are intertwined, dragon and Fire Keeper, our families and our fates."

Kardas put his hand on Andra's shoulder.

"It's not the size of the dragon in the fight; it's the size of the fight in the dragon."

Andra grinned.

A hundred paces ahead lay the carcass of a dead dragon. Without a word, the trio left the path together to ride close to the body. It had died recently. The scavengers in the refuge hadn't yet torn away any flesh. Its head was missing. The neck had been sliced clean through with a single stroke. A greatsword was buried in its belly up to the cross guard. The hilt was deformed from the hot blood that had spilled out. The spikes were gone and the rough lines on the flat stumps that remained told of the effort it took to saw them off.

"When we kill our dragons, it's to thin the herd so they don't get that malady where their scales fall off and they die," Berg said. "A poacher killed this one. Those bastards kill for coin."

"They took the head for a trophy. Probably selling it in the Old Town Square Market right now," Kardas said coolly. His chin trembled with rage. "The spikes will fetch a handsome price from a druggist, or worse, Ashfall. When we catch the men who did this, their last words will be terrible screams."

The Fire Keepers left the headless dragon to the scavengers and continued on their ride.

"My little brother keeps begging me to join our family," Andra said. "He won't stop no matter how many times I tell him that he can't join because we share blood. At least my sister's never asked me about the family." Her face darkened as her thoughts turned to Fyur's funeral. "I worry about them if there's a war. What could happen to them."

Berg shook his head. "They'll be safe. The families would never break the code of Sacred Kin. If a family ever broke that code, all the other families would come down on them with the wrath of the thundering horde."

Following a path through a long stretch of dark woods, the Fire Keepers entered a great clearing at the foot of the Pader Mountains. Inside it stood a strange castle. The walls were made of towers. Not a single stretch of stone was laid in a straight line. Instead, dozens of towers of different heights stood so close together that they touched. The lowest towers in the front were barely taller than a small tree. The highest towers near the back rose so far that only a strong archer could hope for their arrow to strike the top with lethal speed.

Scattered at the tower bases were the bodies of dead baby dragons. Some bodies looked perfectly normal, other than the unsettling stillness of death. On others, the flesh had rotted away and only the small bones remained.

Andra's eyes lingered on the dead.

"The weak hatchlings get pushed from the nest," Berg said, reading her face. "They're like birds in a lot of ways, even if they can't fly so good."

Heads of mother and father dragons looked down from the tops of many towers. Some carried a limp fox or a small deer in their mouths. When they dropped the animal, smoke billowed above the towers as if they were huge chimneys. A burst of squeaking from excited baby dragons was followed by a long silence as they devoured their meal.

A dragon smaller than the palfrey beneath Andra emerged from the forest. The brown dragon trotted to the base of a short tower. It squatted on its haunches and leapt into the air. Flapping hard, it landed atop the tower. After another jump and a few strong flaps from its wings, it mounted the next tallest tower. The dragon paused for a moment before repeating the effort and landing on an even taller tower.

"They use the towers like we use steps," Andra mused.

"Many towers have nests on them, too," Berg replied.

"Our fortress is their sanctuary," Kardas added. "This is the foundation of our family's power. A solid foundation it is."

Dragons flapped and wandered around the clearing. The many-colored dragons shined bright in the sunlight. Two dragons breathed pillars of flame in the air as if they were crossing swords. Young dragons rolled on the ground as they wrestled and played.

"Takes my breath away every time I see it," Andra whispered.

Kardas beamed with pride. "They like to nest in the

mountains, but getting up there is a chore, even for dragons with claws made for climbing. Here, it's easy for them to feed their young. It's safer for them to roost together, too."

Andra's eyes scaled the Pader Mountains at the back of the Castle of Towers. A score of dragons grasped the mountainside or laid low in a nest built on a ledge. Even over the long distance, Andra could see the rippling muscles on the dragons' legs as they climbed.

"All this is less than a half day's ride from Forsbeme," Berg said.

"My brother would like very much to see this place," Andra said, shaking her head.

"There are colonies of wild dragons all along the Paders, too," Kardas added. "Most are like our dragons, but much wilder. They've not been broken. They stay away from men and, unless they're burning farmers' cattle, men stay away from the wild dragons."

No moat surrounded the Castle of Towers. It had a single entrance, a huge archway wide enough for a dozen knights to ride through it abreast. No gate or drawbridge protected this opening.

The towers ringed the castle bailey that was empty except for a few wooden structures, including a small stable. The ground was covered with a thick film of ash. Pieces of bone littered the bailey as well, most with deep gouges made by sharp fangs.

The eastern tower that stood against the Paders and farthest from the archway was larger than all the rest. The Fire Keepers rode to this tall tower under the watchful eyes of the dragons above.

Their horses' hooves kicked up small puffs of ash as they trotted through the bailey.

"No moat, no gate, not even a wood door," Andra said. "I still don't think that's wise."

"Anyone who wants to throw their dice in this bailey, surrounded by our dragons, is welcome to try," Berg responded with a grin. "The dragons know their own kind. Fire Keepers and our friends get a nice quiet entrance to the Castle of Towers. Our enemies leave as ash."

The three stabled their horses.

Kardas put his arm around Andra's shoulders as they approached the door to the tallest tower. His other hand remained on his cane.

"You've done well, Andra. You've shown loyalty, determination, and when I've given you freedom on a job, you've shaped our plans like a skilled blacksmith shapes metal," Kardas said. Then he leaned in close to her ear and whispered, "You deserve this. I've no doubt that eclipses from now, you'll deserve even more."

Iron hinges squealed as the three Fire Keepers entered the eastern tower through a heavy oak door. Furwing padded close behind. Rushes lay on the floor around the large room, so close together they almost completely covered the rough stone underneath. Above, light graced the cobwebs that hung from the ceiling to make them shine bright as flags flying high over a festival.

In the room was a table made of ash wood. It was fashioned in the shape of a dragon's face. Deep lines carved in the top showed the detail of the dragon's eyes and fangs and spikes. Between the eyes was a chalice filled with red liquid. Tucked around the table were five chairs. Near the table stood a man and woman who looked similar.

The woman was petite and lean with narrow brown eyes. She had long, straight black hair and an olive complexion. Her modest curves and tight lips gave her presence far more gravity than her diminutive frame. She crossed her arms and exuded an air of casualness.

Differences between the man and woman were few. The two were married, not related by blood, but their uncannily similar looks led some people to ask if they were twins. As compared to his wife, he had broader shoulders, his eyes were wider set, and he stood a little taller. Leaning forward, he pressed his hands on the back of a chair.

"Kardas will make anybody a captain these days," the woman said. "You managed to make it through the refuge without getting eaten by a dragon, so you must be worthy."

"In the last war, some families lost half their captains," the man added. "We need to build up our reserves now. Like filling a granary before winter."

The man and woman came around the table to greet the newcomers. Andra whispered, "Yutago," as the woman embraced her. Then she grasped the man's hand and wrapped an arm around him as she said, "Xutsuh." He gave her a shallow kiss on the cheek.

"Today our family becomes stronger," Kardas said. "Heading into war, you cannot have too much strength."

Furwing found a nook and sat with her front legs tucked under her body.

"Your cat looks like a loaf of bread," Xutsuh laughed. "And I've seen bigger wings on a butterfly!"

Andra ignored Xutsuh and eyed the mats on the floor. "Looks like there are more rushes in here than there are Fire Keepers. If a war goes bad, there'll be plenty of places to sleep, though the stone might be softer than the rushes."

Berg slapped her on the back. "If we go to the rushes, the stone will be hard beneath the rush the first time you sleep on it. But after a few days or weeks, captains and warriors will fall. You can take their rush and put it on top of yours. Then it'll be nice and soft." He laughed and scratched his chin. "You don't sleep well on one rush because it's hard. If you're sleeping on two or more, you still won't sleep well because it means we're losing the war!"

"At least you won't be on the stone floor," Yutago added. "The ice in the undercroft below is like filling a cellar with the deepest winter. If you put your hand on this floor it's like to freeze."

Andra's thoughts lingered on those rushes as they crackled under her feet. When she thought of Fyur lying on the ice in the undercroft before his funeral, she bit her tongue.

Her seat at the table was a chair between the dragon's two horns atop its head. "Cut like a dragon's face and made of ash wood." Andra dragged her finger along a line carved in the table top. "Kardas, you've never been one for show, whether it's your threadbare cloak or that hovel you call a home."

"This table is special. It's where your old life will end and your new one will begin," Kardas smiled.

"We all took our vows to become captain before this dragon. It's Fire Keeper tradition." Xutsuh beamed a smile at her. "Fyur would be so proud of you. He will be missed by all, though I know that our grief is a shadow of yours." He took a deep breath. "The stronger your affection grows for another, the weaker your pain for him will become."

"That's what I'm hoping," Andra said, her eyes misty.

Their Swordfather patted her on the shoulder.

"Your captaincy vows will be different than the others," Kardas said as he took a chair opposite Andra, near the dragon's mouth. "Not because of the words, but because our Swordfamily may soon be tested. The key for us to win a war isn't destroying the other families. We must champion balance. To do that, we must support the Emerald Crown. A strong crown is the castle that shelters peace and prosperity for the Swordfamilies." He paused to make certain they heard those words.

As Kardas spoke, Berg's eyes lingered on the fang that hung from his Swordfather's neck.

Yutago leaned back in her chair and said, "You speak of balance for the families."

"But we must balance supporting the crown with preserving our strength," Xutsuh finished his wife's thought.

"The king is a good man and the queen is a good woman, even if they're not good to each other," Kardas said. "When King Fallov's father took the Unbloodied Throne, he did it with aid from the Fire Keepers. The king owes me a debt, and when the time is right, I will collect it. I will think on this. But we are here for a different purpose." His chest rattled as he drew a deep breath. "Captains, let us begin the ceremony."

Xutsuh, Yutago, and Berg extinguished all but a few torches. They returned to the dragon head table with the room dark as dusk. The light from the remaining fires danced in their eyes and cast shadows streaking over their faces.

Yutago held a bowl with burning liquid. She placed it in front of Andra. The flames rose all the way to Andra's lips.

"Andra Fire Keeper, we have summoned you here to take a great oath," Kardas said. "We offer you the post of captain within our honorable Swordfamily. Remember now the vows you spoke the day that you became a warrior. You swore to obey the code of Fulccrum Families. You took the Swordfamily name of the Fire Keepers. You will now renew those vows, as have all Fire Keeper captains before you. This code is the six great Swordfamilies' sacred law."

Berg placed a dragon claw next to the bowl of fire. The claw was long, curved, and sharp. Before he returned to his seat, he stole another look at the fang hanging from Kardas's neck.

"Family First. The Fire Keepers' needs come before everything else in your life," Berg said to Andra. "We come before the thundering horde of gods. We come before your blood family and your own life. When you are told to carry out a task that you know will mean your own death, you will do it. When you are told to do something that means you will be unfaithful to your blood family, you will do it. When you are told to do battle with the Emerald Crown, even if you're ordered to attack the Kingdom Guard, you will fight to the death." Berg paused for a moment. "Andra Fire Keeper, do you renew this vow?"

"Yes, I renew the vow. Know that my deeds will obey my words."

Xutsuh placed a dragon fang on top of the claw.

"Screaming Silence. If you are ever taken by another family or the crown, you will never tell them of our family's secrets. You must reveal nothing, as if you were ashes on a funeral pyre. You will never tell the crown about the other Swordfamilies, even if that other family has brought pain and death down upon us. This is called Screaming Silence to honor our forebears who held true to the code under torture. Fire Keepers have never spoken; we have only screamed." Xutsuh drew a deep breath. "Andra Fire Keeper, do you renew this vow?"

Andra repeated her response.

Yutago draped a piece of dragon wing on top of the fang on the table.

"Sacred Kin. You must not harm the blood family of any Swordfamily. Swordfathers, captains, and warriors have fathers, mothers, and children who are not Swordfamily. These kin must not be touched. Our debts are not their debts. Our wars are not their wars. They are sacred and you shall never act to harm Sacred Kin who has not taken up arms against us." The flames in the bowl grew hotter as Yutago paused before finishing. "Andra Fire Keeper, do you renew this vow?"

A third time, Andra spoke her words. After swearing to the code of Sacred Kin, her thoughts turned to her mother, brother, and sisters.

"Honor Thy Debt." The wrinkles on Kardas's face were so deep that they cast their own shadows as he spoke. "Never forget when a favor is done for you. And you will always collect the debt for a favor that you grant to another. That is what gives our Swordfamily its strength. Debts within debts within debts." As Kardas frowned, deep crescents formed at the corners of his mouth. "Make certain that you often lend and seldom owe."

"Yes, my Blade," Andra replied.

With his elbows planted firmly on the table and his hands clasped, Kardas leaned forward.

"These oaths are sacred and they must always be obeyed. They are vital as we prepare to lay a long peace to rest on its waiting pyre. The coming war will break Swordfathers, captains, and warriors. But it must never break our vows."

"Yes, my Blade," Andra said. "Family First. Screaming Silence. Sacred Kin. Honor Thy Debt."

"What do we cry?"

"Born to burn!" the captains yelled together.

"Andra Fire Keeper, you must sacrifice all on the altar of

Swordfamily. The Swordfamily's needs come before your own family and yourself. Do you willingly become a captain and renew the vows that you took as a warrior?" Kardas asked.

"Yes, my Blade."

"The piece of dragon wing that I set by you, put it in the flame." Yutago pointed at the fire above the bowl before Andra.

The bright red piece of dragon wing felt the way it looked, slick. It shook as Andra fought in vain to steady her hand. She held the piece above the bowl where the flames licked at it.

"A dragon must not burn. Its wing must not burn," Yutago said. She rose and took the piece of wing from Andra. "A dragon wraps its wings around its family to protect them. You must never harm kin outside the family just as the other Swordfamilies will never harm those of our blood."

"The dragon fang that I gave you, put it in the flame," Xutsuh said.

Andra stuck the fang inside the flames. The fire did nothing to the fang.

"A dragon must not burn. Its fangs must not burn," Xutsuh said. He took the fang from her. "Remember the vow of Screaming Silence. A dragon may scream, but it never speaks."

"The dragon claw that I gave you, put it in the flame," Berg said. Andra again repeated her task, the fire wrapping around the tip of the claw.

"Hold it there until I tell you to pull it out," Berg ordered.

The chalice in the center of the table was half filled with red liquid. Yutago picked it up and set it down by Andra.

"We mark this great occasion by drinking dragon's blood." Kardas held up his hand before Andra could protest. "A dragon's blood is hot as fire. Yutago and Xutsuh took it from the wound of a dragon. The blood is aged, but still too hot to drink by itself. We must cool the dragon blood."

"Pull the claw from the fire," Berg said. After she followed the instruction, he took it from her. Then he stabbed the claw point into the center of his palm. He did not wince. When he pulled the claw away, he curled his wounded hand into a fist. He held it above the chalice. A thin stream of blood fell from his fist into the red liquid. The dragon blood hissed. After the last few drops landed, Berg thrust the claw point back into the flame. He held it there until the fire burned the last of his blood from the claw's tip.

Yutago took the claw from Berg and repeated the same steps, adding her own blood to the chalice.

Her husband Xutsuh took it from her and poured his blood.

Kardas bled into the chalice. After he bathed the claw in the flames, he handed it to Andra.

None of the Fire Keepers had hinted at any pain. They were all silent and stone-faced as they poured their blood.

Sweat dripped from Andra's brow. Some of it fell due to the intense fire in the bowl before her. Most of it fell from the anticipation of stabbing herself.

She grasped the claw. It was so hot she could feel her palm reddening. When she tried to stab the center of her palm, her hands shook so hard that she poked her thumb instead. She shook her head, took a deep breath, and hit the middle of her palm, thrusting hard.

As the claw dug into her flesh, she winced. It felt like a

knife that grew to a dagger as she pressed. She ignored the pain, though her sweat fell in torrents.

A hand wrapped around the claw. She opened her eyes, not realizing that she had closed them.

"You're going to go straight through your hand if you don't stop," Xutsuh said, releasing his grip.

She pulled the claw back and made a fist. Streams of her blood poured into the cup that was now filled to the brim.

Kardas picked up the chalice. He raised it toward each Fire Keeper. Then he drank deeply, savoring the taste. The captains followed him, first Berg then Yutago then Xutsuh. Andra drank last.

The dragon blood tasted like courage.

Firelight from the bowl near Andra shined in Kardas's eyes. "With this final act, the blood of a Fire Keeper captain flows through you."

"My Blade, I am thankful that you've made me a captain. I owe you a great debt. My life as a captain is dedicated to earning this honor."

Kardas and Andra clasped their bleeding hands together. Their mixed blood fell onto the rushes below.

"I saved this family. Then I built it anew. But I didn't build it alone." Kardas clenched Andra's hand, squeezing so hard she bit her tongue to stay quiet. "I built it by choosing great people to lead. You will be a great captain and, together with your brethren, the foundation of our victories from this day forward." Their hands released.

Xutsuh and Yutago beamed at Andra. Berg's eyes remained fixed on the fang hanging from Kardas's neck.

"Before we take our leave, there are many secrets here in the Castle of Towers that I'll show you," Kardas said. "Becoming a captain means that you must be able to lead, even when our backs are here, against the Pader Mountains. To do that, you have to know our fortress better than the flesh of your best lover. All the secret passages, hidden rooms, even the tunnels that lead back into the Paders." Kardas looked at the bloodstained palm of his hand. The scar in the center of it was thick from the many ceremonies he had led. "All the families wield swords. We're the only family that wields dragon fire. Remember that when you see sharp blades flashing all around you." His eyes wandered to the part of the wall farthest from the tower door. He spoke breathlessly. "That's what gave me strength as the Heavies pinned me against the wall inside this very room."

CHAPTER EIGHT

SWORDFAMILIES

"The guards must be thorough when the guests are murderous thieves," Guiden explained as a man patted on his legs. "He's a Scabbard. Their Swordfamily serves the other six families of Fulccrum. One thing they do is protect us from each other. They do it here at the DragInn, and they'll ensure the Swordfathers' safety at the Council of Sheathed Swords. He's checking for daggers and the like."

The silent man searching Guiden was tall and wide with a dark beard that fell to his waist. His eyes were small and black. He wore a hauberk under a heavy black cloak and a nasal helmet made of rusty iron. He finished patting Guiden's body and moved over to perform the same task on Lisha. A sign above her scrawled in crude lettering read, "No war hammers, swords, dirks, daggers, dragons, wands, or anything else that would make the Scabbards angry."

"There are few places in the city where the families can mingle without worrying about a dagger in the back. This is one of them," Guiden said. Lisha scowled when the Scabbard's hands lingered on parts of her body where she clearly was not hiding a weapon. "The pat down is a nuisance that's necessary to make this place safe for us. Another nuisance is what you have to pay to get in."

He gave the Scabbard two silver crowns.

The Iron Wands stood just inside the entrance to the DragInn. A sprawling tavern occupied the room before them. The inn's rooms for lodging were on the floors above.

At the far side of the tavern was a long bar made of dark wood. Above it hung a pair of silver dragon wings spread wide. The innkeeper serving up drinks was as round as the casks of ale stacked behind him. The hair on his head was curly, black, and thick. His beard was black with a dusting of red. His eyes were narrow but jovial. He regarded the two new patrons with interest.

"Well, what does it look like I'm doing here? Waiting to die?" the innkeeper called to them. "What'll it be for you and your friend, Guiden?"

"Bring us some ale at my table if you would, Reddy," Guiden replied. "A flagon will save you steps this evening. I have a thirst. Bring the one made by that exceptional alewife. She brews ale the way my Swordfather casts spells."

Not a single torch burned inside the tavern. The fire in the hearth didn't burn either. It smoldered without any flame, filling the room with a smoky haze. The only light came from small wax candles carefully placed so that many nooks and tables in the room were shrouded in darkness. The smoke and low light were intentional. The DragInn's patrons were mostly captains and warriors who sought to mingle outside their own Swordfamilies. No family had a code against fraternizing with the other families, but those who entered the DragInn understood that drawing attention to their fellowships was unwise.

A minstrel stood in a shadowed corner, playing a lute and singing of heroes as old as they were great. No one in the tavern cared what he sang. Instead, the purpose of his crooning was to make it difficult for eager ears to steal words from private conversations.

The Iron Wands took a table close to the door. Almost every table had curtains hanging around it from the tops of posts. They were positioned such that patrons could pull the curtain to conceal themselves from others in the tavern. Guiden reached for the curtain but stopped short and left it open.

"This is my usual table," Guiden said. He pointed at the nearby door they had just passed through. "In case it becomes necessary to leave the DragInn with little fore-warning."

"The man at the door wasn't very gentle," Lisha said. She straightened her disheveled robes. "How are lackwits like that supposed to keep us safe? Let alone all the Sword-fathers when they gather?"

Guiden put an arm over the back of his chair. "The Scabbards know their place. The entire family came here from the Ring Islands. It's a place that few have seen and even fewer have survived to tell stories about. They're a strange and backward people. They're also loyal and violent. Intellect is not their strength, but they're smart enough to know that if they tried to become a great family, they would fail. Afterwards, every Scabbard would be dead or back on their island scraping moss off a rock for supper. Everyone benefits from their services, including them." Guiden searched the tavern for signs of his flagon. "There's never any trouble between the families when the Scabbards protect us. They're our Kingdom Guard. They sheathe the Swordfathers."

A small bell tied to the handle on the front door chimed as it opened. A short man with bulbous muscles stepped into the tavern. He wore a loincloth scarcely large enough to cover his loins and carried a small bag fat with coin. The Scabbard barely touched the new arrival before collecting his fee and waving him inside. There was almost no cloth beneath which to conceal a weapon. The man strode directly to the bar, where he joined a group of men and women who were similarly built and attired. They cried, "Hail, Heavy!" as he arrived.

The bar shook as a Heavy drank an entire tankard of ale in a single motion and slammed it down. Her brothers- and sisters-in-arms cheered loudly in response. "Thu'gods, that's good ale!" she roared, wiping her mouth with the back of her hand.

Lisha turned away from them in disgust. "Dullards and their unwashed herd of gods," she mumbled.

A young woman with pale skin and sunken eyes approached the Iron Wands. She wore dark blue robes with the hood pulled up. Her head remained still as her eyes darted all around the tavern. A clinking noise sounded from underneath her robes.

"Whatever the lad and lady favor, I got supplies for every cravin'. Powder of dragon spike, meltin' mind, and purple pleasure. But with that last one I got to warn you that your skin might turn purple for a time," she said. Then she opened her robes slightly to inspect the stock concealed in pockets underneath the rough cloth. "I even got some fresh picked mushrooms from the Phantom Forest. I think they're the reason so few people make it out alive, but the reel lasts for days. So at least they're reelin' when they meet the gods. Had some me-self and I saw things I bet your best spells couldn't conjure."

"Not tonight, Jyfa," Guiden said dismissively. "How come your robe isn't croaking?"

"You know the toad doesn't leave Quivum's side," Jyfa replied. Her robes clinked again, the sound of two glass bottles hitting each other. "You sure about not havin' any tonight? Way all the warriors in here talkin', could be a good long while before we can all get together again."

"Peddle Ashfall's goods elsewhere," Guiden replied.

Jyfa responded to the dismissal by simply moving to the next table and repeating her offerings.

Lisha gave him an incredulous look.

"I've partaken in Ashfall's indulgences from time to time. But unlike most of their patrons, I know when to stop."

"Some of our brethren seem to lack your willpower," Lisha said. "Like that captain in the laboratory."

"His name is Hiamoe Iron Wand. His approach to research may be, how shall we say, unorthodox. However, his findings have been interesting. He's experimented on quite a few townsfolk. Fed them some of Ashfall's drugs and then dazzled them with simple magic. For a time some of them became his thralls, obeying every command no matter how ludicrous. He ordered a man to fetch a dragon egg from a nest in the refuge. At night. The man didn't come back, but his bones were found by a nest so he must've tried."

Lisha's eyes again fell on the muscle-bound revelers at the bar. The man who had walked in after them gulped down a tankard and, like the Heavy before, declared the ale's deliciousness was worthy of the thundering gods' attention.

"The gods in this realm are a bore. The folk under the Crimson Crown have more interesting gods. Most of them have something to do with fire, probably owing to the Lava Sea and the boiling hot water spraying from the ground. I never cared for any of their gods and I paid them little mind. But they hold sway over the commoners."

The warriors where Jyfa now hawked her goods, several tables away, spoke with her eagerly. They handed her some silver crowns and copper townies. She took their coin and her hand disappeared under her dark blue robes. She held the drugs tight in her fist and discreetly passed them to the patrons, who trembled in anticipation.

Guiden leaned forward, almost halfway across the table. "What are you going to do, buy some Ashfall filth, feed it to some orphans, and start a religion? Sweep away the faceless rabble of gods they worship now and give them something more distinct to beg for help?"

Lisha shrugged. "Religion could be a useful tool," she mused. "We could dream up a bevy of stories to convince them that our mysticism is better than a herd of gods and scarce metals. Though it may be burdensome to replace the old gods."

"You might use the thundering herd of gods as a foundation," Guiden offered. "But a foundation for what?"

"What would you call a small religion with a few dozen zealots who would sacrifice anything?"

"A cult."

Now Lisha leaned forward over the table, too. "Exactly," she whispered. "Haven't you ever wanted to be a god, if only to a few? This is how we could do it..."

Amber ale splattered on the table as Reddy slammed down a flagon. He slid two tankards onto their table. Guiden did nothing to conceal his contempt for the innkeeper's timing. He slowly drew out a gold scythe and a silver crown. Then he tucked the silver crown back in his pocket.

"Thank ya kindly, Guiden." Reddy saluted him with the gold scythe. "Funny thin' about these big gold coins. I'm told they named 'em gold scythes to celebrate great harvests. I been thinkin' some, though. Seems to me the gold scythes celebrate harvestin' all right. But methinks the coins might be harvestin' us instead of us harvestin' the gold coins."

Reddy shrugged and left the Iron Wands. He ambled across the tavern. As he went, he took orders from patrons yelling at him from all directions.

"The top of me bar looks like an open treasure chest!" Reddy cried after he made his way past the barely covered group of Heavies yelling drinking songs. Waiting for him on the bar were some gold scythes, dozens of silver crowns, and copper townies from the Heavies. "I got me own mountains of gold, lakes of silver, and fields of copper! All I need now are some gods to keep it safe!" He set about pulling the coins into his many pockets and replacing them with tankards brimming with strong ale.

The Heavies kept howling and drinking. One of them waved her stone tankard as she belted out the noisy tune. The ale within sloshed and foamed like heavy seas.

Many of the women in the group, and even more of the men, had shed their loincloths and now carried on completely naked. Their cloths lay on the floor, trampled under their bare feet. Reddy had seen this performance many times. The Heavies' tight skin was a marvel. Nothing was loose or jiggly, except for some of the parts that had been covered by the loincloths. He often wondered if the Heavies were born or sculpted.

Reddy looked down at his own ample belly and sighed loudly.

When the Heavies' last song finally came to its end, the sound of clinking tankards rang out like bells. The minstrel scowled at them. Before they started their next drinking song, the Heavies yelled at each other almost as much as they hit each other. Reddy couldn't make out many words between the grunts, but some caught in his ear.

"The bloody Bleeding Blade was gone and only bloody blood was left in the bloody tomb so bloody war it is!" a Heavy declared. Then he burst into laughter.

Another Heavy, even deeper in his flagons than the first, roared, "He's goin' to call a council of swords that're sheathed?" The Heavy's eyes were half open and the words crawled from his mouth like a troll from a cave. A crude drawing of a horse was inked into his back. "Well I'm callin' a council, too! I call to order the Council of the Full Flagons!" he yelled.

All the Heavies cheered in agreement and raised their flagons high before they drank their ale low.

"You there, barkeep," a man shouted at Reddy. He was smaller than the Heavies, but not small against most townsfolk. Although he wore neither the armor nor the sigil, the innkeeper knew that the man was a Kingdom Guard. "Give me a flagon but fill it with water."

"Are you *mad*?" Reddy asked in bewilderment. "That's the most poisonous drink in here, worse than the beer or wine or even the fire wine. The stuff Ashfall's peddlin' would take longer to kill you than the water. Thunderin' hells, the rats in me cellar stay away from the water."

The Kingdom Guard slid a silver crown across the bar.

"A'ight then," Reddy replied, pocketing the silver. He knelt behind the bar and grabbed a bucket of water that he used to wipe down the bar and tables. He chose the water with the lightest shade of brown. Then he poured the bucket into a flagon, stood, and handed the drink to the Kingdom Guard.

Having collected the treasure left by the Heavies, the innkeeper returned his attention to the thirsty patrons at the tables. He efficiently filled a flagon with dark ale. With far more skill than a man of his size and age had any right to, he navigated the merrymakers and arrived at a table far from the two Iron Wand mages.

"Your dark, from the finest brewers under the Crimson Crown!" Reddy announced. He slid the flagon and two tankards onto the table.

A Heavy and Fire Keeper were seated there. They stopped their conversation mid-sentence as the drink arrived.

"You hungry? Try the salted veal. It's the best in Fulccrum! Better than what they got at Jugglin' Moons, Fat Ronalt's, or even the place all those high lords haunt, the New Line," Reddy said. When both warriors silently shook their heads, he pinched the silver and copper that waited for him from the table. When the innkeeper turned and stomped away, the Fire Keeper pulled their curtain.

"Thanks for the drink," the Heavy said. She wore modest clothes common of the townsfolk, not the revealing loincloths of her family at the bar.

"You paid the last time," Glas replied, drawing his hand away from the curtain.

The Heavy tipped the flagon of dark ale to fill both the tankards.

"You always manage to get the ale right to the top, Teska," Glas said.

"We do a lot of drinking in my family," she replied. "Since I'm a warrior, that means I do a lot of pouring."

The Heavy and the Fire Keeper clinked tankards and drank deeply. They sat together in contented silence for a time. The little space hidden behind curtains was their refuge from the brewing storm.

"There's been peace for so long that I thought maybe we were inside a wonder tale. Where all the characters are happy for as long as they live," Glas said, his voice full of longing. "You know, a happy ending and all that. The type of story that makes you forget about the rotten world around us. If only for a short time."

Teska looked down at the table. She was lean for a Heavy, but just as physically imposing as the rest of her family. She had a homely face but her skin was smooth as porcelain. Her dark eyes made a look from her almost magnetic.

"Not everyone you love is going to die with a smile on their face, lying in a warm bed at a ripe age, surrounded by their kin." Teska took a long drink of ale. "Lovers don't always die in each other's arms and peace can't last forever."

"We don't have to be part of this, you know. We could leave our families. I haven't been a Fire Keeper very long. I'm just a warrior. I could walk away and go back to working the forge as a blacksmith. No one would come looking for me. Well, Andra might. She's always been very kind to me but she also longs for Kardas's favor. We could be so *happy* together."

Glas took a draught from his flagon. He had red hair, a thin beard, and a clutch of freckles on each cheek. Bigger than most Fire Keepers, but smaller than a Heavy, his most prominent feature were his sad green eyes.

"We could leave it all behind, but who wants to toil in a field all day? What can a commoner do that's worth living life? For me, it's family or death. I couldn't spend my days shoveling cow droppings and praying to gods that deafen in my time of need. Let's hope for a short war. Better than hope, why don't you tell Kardas to surrender? Your dragons are so small that I could pick one up and throw it in one of those big sabatons by the port. At least that way those metal boots would get some use. The crown will never build the rest of that statue. Not even the ankles."

Glas gazed into her eyes. "Maybe so, but there's a strength in our dragons that has nothing to do with their size. Besides, we have the advantage of experience. Kardas has forgotten more strategy than most men learn in their entire lives."

Another silence descended on the two. This one less comfortable than the last. Glas closed his eyes and let the minstrel's melody distract him for a few verses. The brief reprieve ended when the minstrel began to sing of a prince and princess madly in love but trapped in separate, warring kingdoms.

"Why aren't you over there, by the bar with the other Heavies?" Glas asked.

Teska tore a slender piece of wood from the edge of the tabletop. She started breaking it into smaller pieces without realizing what she was doing. "I'll be spending plenty of time with my family very soon. I don't need to be with them now. Besides, it's still spring. I'll not be walking through the chill air in what they're wearing."

Glas slid his tankard on the table between his hands, batting it back and forth. "When are the Swordfathers going to meet?"

"Droena told me that Raysk called the council." Teska

had already halved the length of the sliver of wood. "It'll be each Swordfather, and they can bring an advisor. I don't know when it is, but we all know what's going to happen."

Dark ale slopped over the rim of Glas's tankard. He didn't notice, even when the ale splashed onto his fingers. "War is certain, wonderful. Tonight, we pour each other's ale. On the morrow, we pour each other's blood."

"To be fair, I'll be carrying a war hammer so I probably won't stab you. I'll crush your skull instead."

"That's no jest, Teska," Glas said. "Do you love me?"

"So much that I would think twice about crushing your skull."

"Keep thinking on that." Glas stopped sliding his tankard. Now he spun it around slowly. "And while you're thinking, I want you to remember something, too. Remember when you were on my family's dragon refuge. You were there to fetch an egg and take it to your family. You were probably doing it for the same louts over by the bar yelling like fools. If I hadn't stopped that dragon from breathing hell on you, tonight would be much less painful for me."

The sliver of wood now lay on the table in a tiny pile of ruin. Teska folded her arms and closed her eyes. "Our two families are going to be at each other's throats. Neither of us will be safe."

Glas cleared his throat. "We could do it. We could break the code," he whispered.

The Heavy warrior's eyes opened wide. "Which code?"

"Screaming Silence."

"You know that code isn't just when Kingdom Guard try to get us to talk, right? The silence is outside of our family in front of anyone. You, me, a Swordfather. It doesn't matter."

"Listen to me. If you don't live through this war, then I won't live long after it. Let's make a pact. Swear to me that if you know something that'll help me survive, you'll tell me. I'll do the same for you. We won't tell each other anything else. The chances that we both make it through the war are better that way. Codes and oaths be damned." Glas drank from his tankard until he emptied it.

Teska sat with her lips pursed for a long while. "Death isn't the worst thing that can happen to you. Do you remember what the penalty is for breaking the code of Screaming Silence, Glas Fire Keeper?"

"It is death, Teska Heavy."

"Not just death, but your Swordfather chooses how you die. The few Heavies who have dared to break the silence are killed in ways that I won't speak of, except to say that when Raysk executed them, they begged for death long before they died."

Glas shifted in his seat. "In the Fire Keepers, death comes more quickly. When it's done there's nothing left but a few bits of charred bone. It's painful, but it's quick."

Teska gave him a sad smile. She wiped the tiny pile of wood off the table. "I'll do it."

They both leaned over the table and shared a bitter-sweet kiss. When they separated, Glas lingered over the table longer than Teska.

"This may be our last chance to be together for a good bit of time," Teska observed.

"Let's go upstairs," Glas quickly replied as he pulled back the curtain.

The Heavy and the Fire Keeper left one after the other. Glas waited until Teska had paid for the room and walked up the stairs before he followed her.

"Put ya in a nice quiet room," Reddy said to Glas as he neared the stairs.

"It won't be quiet for long." Glas winked.

Behind the bar was a door that led to a deep cellar. Reddy opened it and descended into musty air laden with the scent of earth. He walked past casks filled with ales and common wines brought into Fulccrum from around the Emerald Realm. He found the cask filled with the DragInn's finest wine and filled a flagon.

Like a mother dragon fretting over her eggs, Reddy studied his precious casks to make certain they hadn't been disturbed. Satisfied with their condition, he returned to the bar, picked up two ornate chalices, and started toward the largest table at the inn.

As he passed the bar, he saw that another stack of coins had sprouted there. The Heavies were now even louder and wearing fewer loincloths. Reddy assured them that he would return soon, then bolted.

Upon his arrival at the large table in the darkest corner, Reddy heard the unmistakable moaning of pleasure that is only made one way. The tavern lacked windows, but that didn't stop the drawn curtains from trembling as if hit by a gust of wind.

Reddy cleared his throat as loud as he dared. When the curtain stopped moving he said, "Beggin' your pardon, my, uh, my..." He searched in vain for the right word.

"Patrons," offered the man with bright green eyes who pulled back the curtain. "We're just a couple patrons visiting your fine inn."

"Though we're a bit more coupled than your other guests," said the woman sitting on his lap. The man gave her a playful thrust. She fought hard to suppress another moan of delight.

She lost that fight.

"We ordered your finest wine ages ago. What've you been doing all this time, mashing the grapes?" the man groused.

Reddy cleared his throat as his face turned scarlet. "Apologies for...interruptin'...ya...two." He made the mistake of making eye contact with the woman and his wits abandoned him completely. "Ah, yes," he stammered, "and of course ya highness and ya and...it's just someone might...ya know that I rent rooms for this sort of thing, right? But, ah, you're more than welcome..."

His nonsensical words were reduced to nothing more than grunts and apologetic tones. Reddy set the chalices and the flagon filled with Kabern wine on the table. He picked up the waiting gold scythes with numb fingers. They were the cleanest coins in the DragInn. He didn't notice that his patrons had paid him far more than the price until after he returned to the bar and splashed some ale on his face to clear his wits.

The man with the woman pulled the curtains closed.

"Let's keep going, Opvolk," the woman whispered to her lover. "Please?"

"Ah, Reddy's probably right. We should go to our room upstairs," the man replied, putting his hands on her hips and lifting her up. "It's not as exciting after we've been found."

"I hope you're not getting bored," she replied as she dismounted and moved to sit across from him. "I'm not."

"I'll never get bored with you, Hallita," Opvolk replied. He tucked away his manhood and fastened the front of his trousers.

She filled their chalices with blood red wine.

Hallita smoothed her dress and crossed her legs. Her

sheer dress was almost completely transparent. It concealed nothing, except that which men most desperately wanted to see. The dress clung tight to her thin body, trapping those who looked upon her in a prison of anticipation. Her tawny skin was smooth and tight as the head of a drum. Her face was charming and friendly. She had bright eyes, yellow as a sunflower, and full lips that radiated warmth when she smiled.

"That's good, because if my Swordfamily learned that I bored you, they'd kick me out and make me join the Heavies." She shuddered in mock disgust.

"Is that what I am to you, merely another conquest for the Syrens?"

"Oh no, my sweet prince, this quest is mine alone." She reached under the table and squeezed his leg just above his knee. He playfully batted away her hand.

Opvolk was the fractured royal family's eldest prince. He was a large man with thick arms and legs. His sizeable muscles were a gift from the gods, not earned by working a field or forge. They had a slight softness from the prince spending his youth in a castle that had a servant for every task. His eyes were the same bright shade of green as the first leaves of spring. Like his two younger brothers, he had a square jaw and heavy brow.

The trait that set Opvolk apart from his family and everyone else in the realm was his skin. At birth, he was nearly as dark as his mother. While he was still an infant, patches of white began to appear on his left knee. The king and queen summoned healers, mages, and disciples of the thundering gods from throughout the realm, hoping to halt its spread. Those efforts were in vain. As a toddler, more light patches appeared around his left elbow. Over the years, still more appeared until the left side of his body was white as bone and the right side was dark as a raven. A jagged, unbroken line curved down the middle of his body to divide his skin and hair into two halves, one light and the other dark.

When he was a young child, the cruel remarks about the prince's skin were always whispered and never spoken near the king or queen. As Opvolk grew into his formidable size and keen mind, the prince changed and so did the remarks. They were no longer mean-spirited and no longer whispered. As a man, his unique skin was celebrated by the king, queen, and the Emerald Realm's subjects.

"I'm sorry for yelling your family's name at court," Opvolk said. He sipped some Kabern and savored it for a moment before swallowing. "It's your fault really. When that shopkeeper spoke of her husband getting seduced by the Syrens, my mind immediately went to the woman seducing me."

"You made the Syren in the throne hall blush. I think that's the first time that's ever happened to anyone in my family."

"A rare lapse in my otherwise sound judgment," Opvolk laughed. "I won't let it happen again."

The curtains that surrounded them rustled. "Powders, potions, and puffs of pleasure, I got them all right here for you," a voice on the other side said.

Hallita pulled back the curtain to reveal that the owner of the voice was the Ashfall warrior peddling her pleasures.

"Ah, good evenin' to you," Jyfa said, addressing Hallita. "I see you're wearin' that fine dress that's more like mist than silk. Please save some of the men for the rest of us womenfolk who don' got your...gifts."

Jyfa took a long step back when she noticed Hallita's companion.

"Well if it isn't the Prince of the Eclipse. You can have anythin' you want for nothin'. Not just because you're royalty, but because I make most of my coin sellin' my goods at your eclipse festivals. Just me and my friends at Ashfall sayin' thanks."

"Your generous offer is very kind, but as you can see, we're well provisioned," Opvolk said in a voice that every minstrel in the kingdom envied. He pressed a finger in the dragon spike powder that coated the table. He dragged his finger across it, plowing another clean line through the brown powder. He sniffed it and closed his eyes.

Jyfa gave them both a deep bow and took her leave.

Hallita pulled the curtains closed.

"The Emerald Realm will always adore you." Hallita's voice had a touch of envy. "The commoners will never forget that your body inspired the grandest festivals here in the city and long leagues away from Fulccrum. A festival every triple eclipse dedicated to the Prince of the Eclipse." Hallita took both of his hands, one white and one black, in her own. "The realm that used to ridicule your body now celebrates it. Twice a year." She stroked his hands. "A sun and a moon, heavenly bodies within my hands."

"You know that festival has been going on for generations. If they celebrate me, it's because they hope to make the crown throw bigger festivals," Opvolk said as he grudgingly pulled himself from the dragon spike powder's blissful effects. "If I keep talking like a fool at court, the townsfolk will mistake me for the lowest jester. Meaning no offense to that jester who cut off his own head while juggling axes."

Hallita squeezed his hands. She leaned forward so the plunging neckline of her thin dress exposed her cleavage to the prince. The flickering candlelight on her bare skin added an air of mystery to his view. She stopped leaning when her breasts rested on the table. Then she slowly slid them around in the dragon spike powder as she licked her lips.

She squeezed the prince's hands tight. The hairs on his hands stood up straight.

As she released his hands and leaned back in her chair, Opvolk's gaze fixed on the curves of her breasts. They were caked in dragon spike powder. Hallita's dress hid her nipples from Opvolk's view, but the powder that now clung to them made his groin feel like rushing water.

"Reddy was *definitely* right. We need to get a room," he groaned.

Hallita drank deeply from her chalice. "We both know that as soon as we go upstairs, there won't be any more talking. Tonight, we need to talk."

Opvolk groaned again, this time from frustration. "This is about the Swordfamilies squabbling, isn't it? The families have their little fiefdom and I have my kingdom. I don't see why a fight between those commoners means anything to me. I don't pay any mind when drunk sailors bludgeon each other to death on the docks. Why would I care when towns-folk who give themselves silly names do the same? They'll have their war, and if the Crimson Crown chooses to get bloodied, I'll have mine. Never the twain shall meet." He took a long draught from his chalice.

"Your family will be a part of our fight. There are Sword-fathers who would tear down the Emerald Crown. Others will want your house to rule for generations."

"What do you want?" Opvolk asked.

"I want to sneak around a crowded tavern to satisfy my princely appetites," Hallita said, winking at him. She slid her chair beside him and leaned in so close her lips were almost against his ear. "Then I want something even more exciting." The moisture from her whisper caressed his cheek. "I want to be your wife." Her hand brushed against the bulge in his trousers that had remained the same size since she dismounted. "I want to make love to you on the Emerald Throne."

Opvolk breathed so deep that his chest shuddered. Blood thundered through his veins. Hallita rubbed her breasts against his arm as she kissed his neck.

"What do you want?" she asked.

He took her chin in his hand and kissed her hard.

"I want to be king and make love on my throne. The lines of our princes and princesses will stretch from the throne to the doors. They will rule this realm for generations."

She ran a hand through the black side of his hair and squeezed his bulge with the other.

"Your parents would never allow us to wed."

"I don't intend to ask them for permission. My mother was a Syren."

"She wasn't just any Syren, she was our Swordfather. Minacia abdicated a position of great power to become a lowly queen," Hallita laughed. "She had enemies inside our family, but her allies outnumbered them. Even if she doesn't object to you and me, there's the other half of the crown to consider. The man who sits on *your* throne."

Opvolk dragged his thumb hard over the dragon spike powder on the table and pressed it against the bottom of his nose.

"Enough talk of days yet to dawn. Dragon spike powder makes me hard as a steel blade. We have a long night ahead of us."

"My love, I don't think that's the powder." Hallita

winked and nibbled his ear. "But about our night, you have the right of it, my Prince of the Eclipse."

Ten gold scythes clattered as Opvolk carelessly tossed them onto the large table. He pulled the curtain aside and the two walked straight to the stairs that led to the rooms above. As they passed through the tavern, every woman and man who saw Hallita stopped speaking and stared at her. The crowd of naked Heavies who stood on their loincloths, having begged everyone at the inn to gawk at their bodies, now made clumsy attempts to feign disinterest in the Syren's unequaled beauty.

Hallita and Opvolk made their way to the royal room. They walked past Reddy without a word. He simply nodded in their direction, keeping his head down so that he wouldn't ogle at the prince's lover.

The innkeeper scampered over to the large table where the two had sat. He picked up the ten gold scythes. He immediately spent them thrice over in his mind. He noticed that the table top was strangely dusty, as if it hadn't been wiped for many eclipses. Dipping a ragged cloth into the bucket of water he carried, he wiped the table clean. When he was done, the amount of dragon spike powder that he had ruined was worth far more than all the pieces of gold, silver, and copper in the DragInn at that very moment.

Reddy grabbed the chalices and flagon from the table. He tucked the half-empty flagon behind the bar, where it would remain until another wealthy patron ordered the expensive red wine.

At the other end of the room, he spied a regular patron wave his hand to order his usual drink. The innkeeper drew it from a large cask filled with the least expensive ale.

As he carried the cheap ale inside tankards, his ears were alert. He sensed anxiety coupled with abandon pulsing through his inn. Usually, the DragInn's patrons were subdued, careful to speak quietly and position themselves to hide their faces. Tonight, the mood was different. The Heavies, men and women alike, had shed their loincloths much earlier than normal. They sang bawdy songs at the bar. Many of the curtains that were usually closed were now opened wide. The patrons around him spoke loudly.

On this night, few hid in the shadows.

Reddy passed a table where a woman and a man spoke. The man was the Kingdom Guard who drank the only tankard in the DragInn filled with water. Just below the corner of his eye was a mole shaped like a tear. He said, "Mwizi, we've been so happy for so many years. If the worst happened and we met in battle, would you do it? Would you kill me?" The woman shook her head and asked the same question of her Kingdom Guard companion. With tears streaming down his face, and over his mole, he answered Mwizi's question by mouthing, "I love you."

Reddy found the regular who had summoned the cheapest ale. "Your drink, Faomen, my friend," he said as he took the realm's smallest coin, a copper townie, from the patron.

Before the patron could respond, yelling broke out near the bar. Three Heavies pushed each other hard. One of them threw a punch and they began to wrestle, knocking into the bar and other patrons trying to order a drink. The Heavies started shoving warriors from other families.

Scabbards clad in chainmail armor emerged from the shadows. Their swords were drawn and raised. As they descended on the fight, Reddy ran to quiet the scene before he had to mop up blood.

Faomen sipped from his tankard as he watched the fight grow.

"Didn't know we'd get a show tonight," Jyfa said, sitting across the table from him. "Of course, the thin's we sell the Heavies to make them stronger make them angrier, too." She rubbed her bloodshot eyes.

Their table was among the most exposed and least desirable. They sat near the middle of the tavern and there were no curtains. Every patron who cared to look their way had a clear view of them.

"The Heavies can't wait to fight all the other families, so while they wait, they'll fight each other," Faomen replied.

"I'll drink to that." They clinked tankards and drank.

Jyfa put her hands on her face and sighed. "Thought I'd make a killin' tonight with everyone buyin' up everythin'. Thu'gods know if we'll be able to come back here soon. I can sell in other spots but it won't be easy." She grabbed onto her fire red hair and yanked it. "The prince always wants me dragon spike powder, but I've sold him so much now he has more than me!" She pounded her fist on the table. "Captains be scarce tonight. They'd a thrown me a gold coin or two. Must be scared with this storm brewin'."

"I'm here and I'm a captain." Faomen put the leather pouch that held his coins on the table. He turned it inside out to show that the inside was bare. "Wish I could help you, love, but I'm fresh out of gold, silver, and copper. Would you sell to me if I paid in seaweed? I could trade you Dark Water's weed for some of Ashfall's weed." Faomen raised his eyebrows and Jyfa responded by taking a drink. "Just remembered, I may have a little something tucked away." He reached up underneath the thin, black cloth wrapped around his head. He pulled out a silver crown and slammed it down on the table triumphantly.

The Ashfall goods tucked underneath Jyfa's cloak

clinked together as she took the piece of silver off the table. "What'll it be, me Dark Water captain?"

Faomen scratched his stubbly beard while he thought. "Give me some of those leaves you have. Not the ones that scramble your mind. Give me the brown ones, the ones that make your heart race."

She patted her cloak before reaching up one of her sleeves. Faomen grinned as she produced a long bunch of brown leaves that were rolled together. The roll tapered at both ends. Faomen took it from her and lit an end in the candle burning on the table. He took a few deep puffs. Then he coughed as smoke scratched against the back of his throat.

"The war won't be that bad for us." Faomen took another drag from the rolled leaves. "My family, I mean. Dark Water's out in the port. We're small and we keep to the waves and rivers. Usually we're at sea hunting for sunken treasure."

Jyfa cocked her head to one side. "Oh, is that all you're doing out there?"

"Well, 'tis true that we usually sank the ship with the treasure in it. And sometimes we take the treasure before the ship sinks. 'Tis mighty hard to dive all the way down to the sea floor. If the ship were to sink in deep blue water, nobody gets the treasure. That'd be a waste of treasure! So we're right to take it before it gets wet."

The deep wrinkles on Faomen's leathery face made obvious the years that he had spent at sea. His skin was thicker than the sails hoisted on the ships his family used to stalk their prey. The loose and airy clothes that he wore kept him cool on the sea where there was even less shade than a desert. Every other tooth in his mouth was made of gold. His eyes were hazel. At all times, at least one of his ears had water in it.

"Dark Water will be safe. We don't cause no trouble. We'll be on our nice little ship anchored in the port. If the war gets nasty, we'll sail past where they're building that giant statue and into the Angered Sea. Maybe by the time we get back the statue will be finished! Hah!"

Faomen put the roll of leaves to his lips and drew in more smoke. This time, it felt smooth.

"You've no reason to worry, either." He pointed the lit end at Jyfa. "Ashfall sells all the families what they need to be happy." Foamen's eyes shifted to the bar. "Look at those animals."

He pointed the rolled leaves at the Heavies by the bar. The Scabbards had squelched the brawl. Both Heavies that had clashed now had one arm around the other. In their other hand, they both held a tankard.

Jyfa drummed her fingers on the table. Then she reached under her cloak, grabbed something, and tossed it into her mouth. She moved so fast that if Faomen had blinked, he would have missed it. Some heartbeats later, her pupils grew to twice the size they had been only moments before.

"Did I ever tell you why my family is named Dark Water?" Faomen asked between puffs. "On our ship, there's a plank out over the water. Wherever we drop the anchor, there's always a whirlpool below the plank. Strangest thing I ever seen. If it's not there the day we drop, it'll be there the next morn. I think it's our Swordfather's pet. It follows us around like it's on a chain.

"I saw it near the end of my ceremony to become a Dark Water captain. *Shark Queen* was anchored in the port and I walked out to the end of the plank. I looked straight down. Below me was this great monster of swirling white water. It spun around with roaring waves churning the port into an angry foam. The center was the worst part of all, made of smooth water like a giant arrowhead pointing to the bottom.

"My heart didn't beat for a long time. Chest was still. I knew that I was going to die whether I stayed on that plank or jumped. I fell down into that smooth water and it gripped me like a giant hand. Pulled me farther and farther into the depths. Everything went black. That's why we're Dark Water. The water gets real dark when you can't breathe. Anyway, the next thing I know, my Swordfather's poking his sword against my chest to wake me up. Good thing the whirlpool liked me. It kills the ones it judges unworthy. The crew thinks it's our Swordfather's spirit in the sea."

"Swords," Jyfa murmured. She said the word slowly and deliberately, as if it took tremendous effort. "The realm's been losin' swords the way small children lose they teeth."

Faomen put the rolled leaves against his lips and drew in a long breath. He tilted his head back and blew a thick cloud of smoke above their table. "Aye. Lots of swords missing these days. Bleeding Blade has been swordnapped. Emerald Ezzy says the Shard of the Specter was stolen by her husband. Thu'gods, it can't be seen so how does she know it's missing? Might be hidden someplace she never goes, like his side of their bed!"

He motioned for Jyfa to come closer.

"I'll let you in on a little secret, my sweet." Now he whispered as he spoke. "Shard of the Specter, I think I know where it is."

Jyfa's pupils shrank as her eyes opened wide. "So where is...?" she began.

"Faomen! Faomen!" Reddy yelled as he sprinted toward the couple. He shook his hands in the air to get their attention before he slammed into the table. "Faomen, ya have to put it out! Now!" he begged in a harsh whisper. "It's the Heavies, they're gettin' fearsome angry. They say they hate the smell of that smoke. Ya have to put it out!"

The rolled leaves dangled loosely from Faomen's lips. He turned to face the Heavies. The tavern had fallen silent.

"Please, just put it out. They're bored of beatin' on each other. They want to tear apart someone else," Reddy pled. "If the Scabbards hack 'em to pieces, they'll never come back! I'll go broke!"

Faomen took another drag from his rolled leaves. As the end burned, the leaves glowed a brilliant red. He drew the smoke deep into his chest. Then he turned the leaves around so the burning end was by his mouth. He smiled as he opened his mouth wide and stuck out his tongue. He breathed out the smoke as he plunged the burning end onto his tongue, making a dark cloud that smelled like burning flesh.

The rolled leaves stopped burning.

Faomen never stopped smiling.

Reddy looked over at the Heavies. He licked his lips as a bead of sweat trickled down his forehead. The Scabbards again emerged from the shadows with their hands on the hilts of their swords.

The naked Swordfamily turned away. Faomen noticed a horse inked on the back of a Heavy.

The Scabbards retreated to their shadows.

"Reddy!" a voice called. "We're done over here."

The innkeeper obediently trudged to where he was summoned. On his way, he passed a patron whose skin was a light shade of purple.

"You wanting another flagon?" Reddy asked Guiden.

Guiden shook his head. "No, my friend and I are finished for the night. I've spent more than enough time in Forsbeme. You can take it away." He handed the innkeeper the flagon from his table.

"I thought ya said that ya had a thirst? The Angered Sea could've dried up before ya two Iron Wands finished this," Reddy said. He scooped up the flagon and tankards, which still held much ale, and scurried away.

"Anyway, that's one way to use Ashfall to create a cult," Lisha said, returning her attention to Guiden. "As you've said, Iron Wand is the smallest family. We don't have strength in numbers. But if we had an army of unquestioning minions, that would be a weapon we could use on the battlefields to come."

Guiden regarded his fellow Iron Wand with great interest. "That plan is rife with risk. It could very well fail." He narrowed his eyes and clenched his jaw. "We can put this to Irin. Our Swordfather can decide whether your idea has merit."

"Very well." The small amount of ale that Lisha had pulled from the flagon had given her the false confidence she needed to ask a question. "I've told you my plan. Now I want you to tell me something."

Guiden cocked his head.

"Why does Irin's wand scream?"

He frowned.

"Tell me. I haven't been in the family for long, but I want to know. If you don't tell me, I have other ways to find out. I'd prefer to hear it from you."

"Yes, I have no doubt. You seem to be quite...inventive." Guiden cleared his throat. "Very well, then. I'll tell you." He took a deep breath. "Mages have long been feared in this realm. Over the years dozens of mages, men and women alike, were burned at the stake. The most powerful mages were tied to the same stake and set alight.

"That stake was made of eldritch wood. It was hard as rock from the Pader Mountains. Each time a mage was burned and their body no more than a pile of ash, the stake would remain unscathed. It's said that water itself would burn to cinders before flame could taste that wood. When the realm's zeal for mages' ashes subsided, the masters of magic who survived had the scorched stake made into a wand. Woodworkers couldn't cut it. Instead, stone carvers chiseled it into shape."

A thin shadow crept across Guiden's face.

"Legend has it that when a mage was burned, their spirit and magic were trapped inside the stake that held them to the fire." He paused for a moment. "When the stake trapped the mages' spirit and magic, it also absorbed their fury and pain. Only the mages' screams will ever escape from the wand."

"You mentioned a wand the first time that I met you. What did you call it?" Lisha asked.

"The Wailing Wand. That's our Swordfather's wand, the one crafted from the stake. It's terribly dangerous." Guiden turned over his hands to reveal scars on his palms. "I suffered these wounds while casting with lesser wands. Many skilled spellcasters have perished using the Wailing Wand." He closed his hands into tight fists. "Not all the screams you heard from Irin's wand were from mages who burned at the stake. The most terrible screams are from mages who tried to wield the Wailing Wand. Instead of casting a spell, they were consumed by the wand. Their bodies joined the ashes of mages past and their voices joined the wand's chorus of eternal screams."

"I would very much like to cast a spell with this wand," Lisha said.

"The Wailing Wand has a will of its own. Some mages have wielded it for years, only to be struck down by an elementary spell. When you cast with the Wailing Wand, each spell is a throw of the dice."

"What does it look like?"

Guiden smirked.

CHAPTER NINE
FIRE KEEPERS

Thick sheets of rain lashed at Andra as she rode through Raventyn near Middle River. She took the wide Gilded Granite Street to Fulccrum's largest gate, the East Gate. Dark clouds, all colored the same gray shade, hung low. The thundering gods had painted the entire sky with a single cheerless color this morn. The rain was relentless. Her traveling cloak soaked through mere paces from the city wall, as if made of loose straw. Her long hair matted against her back and chest. Every step her palfrey took on the drenched road was a battle with the stubborn mud cleaving to its hooves.

The long road that began outside the East Gate was the realm's main thoroughfare. It was called the Shamrock Road for the many green banners that commoners hung along it to show allegiance to their crown. Close to the capital, this road hosted inns, taverns, and merchants who mainly sold to farmers leaving Fulccrum with empty wains and full pouches of coin. The buildings were solid and simple, lacking the style and adornments of their counterparts inside the city walls. Even the signs were less ornate, with names and symbols crudely carved into wood.

Riding alone, Andra kept her hood up and head down to deflect the curious eyes of fellow travelers. She had woken early to spend the darkness before daybreak sharpening her sword with a whetstone and oil-cloth. She took comfort in having a blade on her hip so sharp that it could nearly cut through its own scabbard. The price she paid for that comfort was that while she honed the blade, her mind lingered on the unpleasant task awaiting her at the end of the ride.

I've dreaded this ride more than killing men that I respected.

The sun burning behind the clouds would move over a quarter of the sky before she arrived, providing ample time for both rain and dread to soak her through.

After Andra had traveled a short distance from Fulc-crum, the buildings that loomed over the road gave way to farms. Through the rain's pattering, Andra heard calves calling to their mothers. Chickens clucked frenetically as they fought for the scarce coverings that offered protection from the rain. Pigs grunted and squealed as they rolled in the fresh mud with reckless abandon. Stone walls lined the road to keep travelers away from crops and animals. The stones were stacked higher next to the road than near the farmhouses.

A few leagues away from Fulccrum, the farms shrank. Farther still, the tiny farms were separated by stretches of tall forest. Here, the flow of travelers headed toward Fulc-crum slowed to a trickle. At Six Corners, Andra jerked her palfrey's reins to the right. As she departed from the Sham-rock Road, and Six Corners disappeared behind her, the nearby forest trees stood even taller. The trees crept so close to the road that the branches above her wove together.

Spring growth on those branches spared her from some rain, but also dimmed the precious sunlight that had battled its way through the opaque sky.

The tree trunks in this forest are worse than iron bars in a dungeon cell.

The road split several times and became narrower with each turn that Andra made until it was little more than a path. A few more turns and the path disappeared entirely. She now guided her palfrey by following a thin line of sparse hoofprints that had been stamped into the forest floor.

She approached a rickety shelter nestled in a small clearing surrounded by pine trees. A tendril of thin smoke wafted from a crude chimney atop the simple hovel. Moss was heaped like snow on the roof. Its walls were made of logs from trees felled nearby. The stumps of those trees had shed all of their bark and were rife with holes where wood-eating bugs enjoyed a feast.

Andra tied her palfrey to a sturdy tree. She found a bucket collecting rain by the hovel. She placed it before her grateful horse. After feeding the mount some oats, she lashed her sheathed sword to the saddle.

With that, she had exhausted all of the excuses to delay her arrival. She took a few deep breaths and shuffled to the door. *At least there'll be a little less rain inside.* The rough-hewn door wasn't just rough; thick splinters poked out like spikes on a dragon's tail. Andra brushed some of them aside and slammed her fist on it.

From inside came the clatter of steel and excited voices. Andra waited as bulbous drops of rain harried her. She raised her fist again, grateful for the glove protecting her hand from the splinters. As she pounded on the door, it swung open.

In the doorway stood a young man. His eyes opened wide. "It's you," he said, his voice full of surprise.

"Who in the thundering hells is named 'you'?" a shrill voice called from behind him.

"Hello, Mistahn. It's good to see you again," Andra said. The owner of the shrill voice appeared behind him. "And you, too, Lecata. Sorry that I've been away for so long."

The knife in Mistahn's hand slipped and fell onto the hovel's dirt floor.

The three stood in silence for a long moment.

"If you're worried about defending yourself, I can get you a sword," Andra offered.

Mistahn threw his arms around her and hugged his older sister tight. She leaned into him and returned the embrace. After repeating the gesture with Lecata, Andra entered her childhood home.

The one-room hovel was festooned with dozens of furs hung from the walls. A few frayed rushes lay in random places on the dirt floor. Against the walls were piles of hay covered with cloths that served as beds.

On the far wall was the stone fireplace that produced the smoke that Andra had noticed when she arrived. The fire was hot, but not blazing. Above it hung a cooking pot filled with a simmering stew. Andra recognized its scent from her youth. The pot held a rabbit stew with carrots, barley, and chopped potatoes. A trestle table stood near the fire with a crude chair at each side.

Near a wall, large hooks made of iron hung from the ceiling. Beneath them was a sturdy table. On the table lay the carcass of a dead sheep. The animal's belly had been cut open. It looked underfed.

"You caught me in the middle of something," Mistahn

said. "I need to get the pelt off this sheep before mother gets back or she'll have my hide instead."

He approached the table and picked up a pair of leather gloves. He wiped the dirt off the knife that he had dropped. Grabbing the sheep's front legs, he cut around the knees and pulled off the lower part.

"I'm sure it's been awhile for you," he called over his back toward Andra. "Do you still remember how to skin an animal?"

Andra draped her sopping wet cloak on the back of a chair. She put her hands on her hips. "I've been skinning wild animals since Mother made me skin soiled baby cloth off your bum."

Mistahn cut down the length of the sheep's back legs, on their insides. "I trust that you thanked her for giving you such a great honor!" He peeled back the skin on the legs and sliced it off at the joint.

"Where'd you get that sheep?" Andra asked. "When I lived here we found deer and foxes and the like in the woods. You been tracking wild sheep on the game trails? Should I call you the sheepslayer?"

The knife in Mistahn's hand moved precisely between the skin and muscle as he began pulling the hide off the animal. He pulled and cut, beginning at its rump.

"Sometimes there's game around here, other times there's not," Mistahn replied. He grunted as he removed the sheepskin from the belly of the carcass. "On those farms closer to your big city, there's always game. They have so many animals behind their stone fences they're not like to notice if one is missing." He wheeled to face her with his knife in his hand. "Those farmers have plenty to eat. We have what's lying on this table." He pointed at the thin sheep with his knife.

"You shouldn't break the crown's law. You may look like that sheep if the Kingdom Guard catches you," Andra said.

"We'll start following the Emerald Crown's laws when you do," Lecata scoffed. "At least our game is just animals. Yours is men."

Returning his attention to the sheep, Mistahn took off the animal's head faster than Andra recalled ever doing it herself. He finished pulling off the sheepskin and laid it on a table with the wool facing down. He scooped chunks of salt out of a bowl and rubbed it against the sheepskin and the meat.

"I killed it today. The weather's cool enough that I'll have time to finish salting it tonight."

He hung the skinned carcass from a hook above. Then he wiped the sweat from his brow with his forearm. Removing the gloves, he set them away from the blood that trickled from the body.

Mistahn had a kind face with mischievous eyes. Despite being years younger than Andra, he was bigger than her. His beard was short and thin with scarcely enough whiskers to let anyone who saw him know that he wasn't a boy any longer. His long red hair was pulled together in a tail. He had round shoulders and a stout build. The dirt underneath his fingernails formed dark crescents.

Across his face was a mark that made his visage linger for days in the minds of those who gazed upon him. A streak of red, dark as Kabern wine, slashed across his face. As though a crimson blindfold had been cinched tight against his face and pulled away, leaving a stain where it had pressed against his skin. He had carried the mark since the day of his birth and rued it since the lads he had known in his youth teased him for it mercilessly.

"I'm glad that you're here. It's been too long," Mistahn

said. "But you're not here very often, and never without aim. I must needs ask what has brought you to our door this time."

"Glad tidings. Kardas has bestowed upon me a great gift." She crossed her arms. "I'm a Fire Keeper captain now."

Mistahn's mouth fell open and his eyes widened as if they might never close again. He threw his arms around her and laughed so hard that he almost choked.

"What? What's so funny?" Andra asked as she pried him off.

"You can do it now, right? You can pull me in? You're right below the Swordfather! You have his ear! You can force Kardas to let me join the Fire Keepers! I can be a warrior. I'm free!"

Lecata glared at their brother. "Pardon his manners. What he meant to say is that we congratulate you and we're very glad that you've graced us with your presence." Though her tone was not warm, she took her sister by the hand. "Come and join us. We were about to take our lunch. Doesn't taste like much, but you already knew that."

The trio sat together at the trestle table. Lecata had her back to the fire, so her face was shadowed. Mistahn faced the fire, making his birthmark redden in the bronze light. Andra sat on a side between the two. Half of her face was lit up from the flames, while the other half was dark.

Lecata was very much her brother's sister. Born within the same year, the two looked so similar that their mother wondered if the thundering gods had meant for them to be twins. The main difference between the two was that the red birthmark on her face was small and only on one cheek. Also, Lecata kept her fingernails clean.

Mistahn sat with his arms crossed and maintained an

uneasy silence. A few drops of rain leaked through the roof and pattered on the dirt floor that had become muddy in places.

"It was right there, right?" Andra asked Mistahn. She pointed at a spot on the dirt floor about an arm's length away. "From what I remember, that's where I buried it."

"Yes, that's where you buried my spoon long ago. The way you've treated me since, you might as well have buried me with it."

Lecata retrieved some wooden bowls and set them on the table. They were filled with rabbit stew fresh from the cooking pot.

"I remember thinking that was the funniest thing in the realm." Andra sipped a spoonful of stew.

"Everything I ate tasted like dirt for eclipses. It's one of my earliest memories," Mistahn growled. He chewed on a piece of rabbit as he shook his head.

Lecata didn't touch her own soup. "From the sound of it, you're not leaving that gang of bandits now, are you?" she asked, not bothering to mask the disdain in her voice. "Why do you do it? You kill people for gold."

"Sometimes it's just silver." Andra shrugged. She swallowed a bite of rabbit. "You kill animals for food. Killing is killing."

"It's not the same," Lecata shot back. "We kill to feed ourselves. You kill to fatten your pouches of coin."

Soup splattered from his bowl as Mistahn dropped his spoon. "Why won't you let me join the Fire Keepers?" he demanded.

"Because I don't want you to be a murderer. I hope that poaching sheep from a flock is the worst thing that you ever do. And you know that my Swordfather forbids it."

"I can kill, too. Better than you! I've killed most of the

animals in here." He pointed at the pelts on the walls. "Like that bear over there, that was me! Killing is killing, you said it yourself! I'm a killer, *just like you.*"

Andra chose to finish the carrot and potato sitting in her spoon before replying. "Killing men is different," she said slowly. "When you kill an animal, like that small bear you felled, they don't plead for their lives with tears in their eyes. They don't scream about their wives or husbands. Or ask you who will provide for their children." The chunks of rabbit in her bowl had sunk to the bottom. "It's an ugly business."

Lecata took a drink of cool water. "How many have you killed?" she asked.

"Enough that I've forgotten many of them," Andra replied in a voice almost as tired as her eyes.

"I've killed men before," Mistahn protested, his voice deeper than before. "I don't hang their skins on the walls. I give them as good a grave as I can dig. You see this dirt?" He held up his hands so that Andra could see his fingernails. "Not all of this dirt is from foraging."

Andra shook her head.

Jumping to his feet, Mistahn went over to a large wooden box with a broken lock. He moved fast and in a straight line, not bothering to avoid the rainwater dripping from the ceiling. Rummaging through the box quickly, he grabbed something and returned to the table just as fast.

"I want you to have this," he said. He placed a small piece of wood on the table. It was shaped as a cube with lines carved all around its sides. The top of the cube was wavy and a tiny piece stuck up.

Andra studied the carving. "Is this...?" she started.

"It's our home," Mistahn said. "It's where you grew up and where your family still lives today."

"Your *real* family," Lecata hastened to add.

Details in the little carving became apparent the longer Andra held it in her palm. The lines around the sides had been cut where the logs in the walls rested on top of each other. The roof was wavy and bulged over the walls, the way the moss outside hung from its edges. The tiny chimney stood atop the roof in the right place, carved a little wider and shorter than it should be. Andra guessed that was so the tiny detail wouldn't break off.

"It's nice," she said. "You spent a lot of time carving this, didn't you?"

"Cutting it was a welcome distraction from counting the mushrooms growing on the stumps outside," Mistahn replied. "Take it with you. Carry it for good luck. Think about us. Think about your family when you look at it. *Think about me*, trapped inside this dungeon cell of a shack."

She placed the carving on the table and sighed.

"Believe me when I tell you that you're better off here, Mistahn. The shame is worse than the pain when you kill a man that you don't hate."

"Then why do you do it?" Lecata pressed. "Is it the gold? Is it the feeling of power?"

"Tell us why you abandoned us here," Mistahn added. "Why do you condemn me to live out the life that you fled?"

The only sound in the hovel was the soup simmering over the fire and raindrops pattering against the roof.

"It's the gold, isn't it?" Lecata said. "That's the only reason anybody does anything in this realm. Gold, silver, copper. A man drowning at the bottom of the Angered Sea would probably wish for gold before he wished for air. The only thing the thundering gods do is guard a big pile of gold and the people worship them for it. We worship riches in this life and the next."

"We're here sleeping on beds of hay like animals. Andra probably has a nice soft bed waiting for her when she rides back." Mistahn stared at the rabbit stew cooling in front of him.

Andra frowned. "That's most people, but that's not me." She swallowed her soup. "It's not Kardas, either. You're right that many join families for the gold. Most Swordfathers live in palaces nicer than the Emerald Crown's castle. They have almost as many servants, too. Sometimes they host feasts that put the Festival of the Eclipse to shame. It's hard to imagine that kind of life exists less than a half a day's ride from here, but it does."

Her appetite vanished and Andra set her spoon down next to the wooden bowl. "Kardas is different. His house and his clothes are modest. When old wounds made it painful to walk, he didn't get some gold staff. He unsheathed his sword for the last time and used it as a cane." She rubbed her eyes. "I am Andra Fire Keeper because I love Kardas as my father. I will repay that debt with my loyalty every day that I draw breath."

Mistahn grunted. "It's nice that you've made a friend in the old man. But that doesn't help me here, deep in these woods. I spend my days hunting animals in farms and forest. I've peeled so many hides off their bodies that before I loose an arrow I can see the bare muscle underneath their fur." He pounded his fist on the table. "Then we drag the hides wherever we can sell them to buy whatever we need to stay alive. It's living in a dungeon made of wood and guarded by dead animals. That's what I did yesterday, today, all my days that have passed, and all my days yet to come." Mistahn's voice shook like a leaf in strong wind.

"Until my body yields my spirit. When it does, I'm going to spend my mornings, noons, and nights haunting you worse than one of your victims begging for mercy." Tears streamed from his eyes.

"This is why she doesn't come around anymore," Lecata mumbled, poking her spoon in the soup. "You do this every time. We just have to accept that her life is in Fulccrum now. Our lives are here."

Mistahn's shoulders slumped. He stared at his rabbit soup.

The door swung open and a short woman with a dead fox draped on each shoulder entered. Without looking at the table where the three sat, she threw the dead foxes on the table where Mistahn had cleaned the sheep. After hanging her drenched surcoat by the fire, she sat in the empty chair at the table.

Lecata fetched a bowl of simmering stew from the cookpot and wordlessly put it in front of their mother.

"What brings you into my home? Ill tidings? Fleeing Kingdom Guard?" she said as her greeting. She tore a chunk from a loaf of stale bread and swirled it in the stew. She tossed the stew-soaked morsel in her mouth. "You've tired of that soft city life? Or you're looking for the finest pelts in the Emerald Realm?" She said all of this without looking her daughter in the eye. "Or you've got orders from your Softfather to kill me or Lecata or Mistahn?"

Andra's mother was stunted and lean. Her face looked like it had been carved by a woodworker using only a dull axe. Everything that she wore was encrusted with dirt darker than the hovel's floor.

"Hail, Mother, well met," Andra replied. She mustered as much courtesy as she could, but it was precious little. The words sounded more like an insult than a greeting. "I didn't come here for any of those reasons. I came here to tell you something."

"Ah, so it's ill tidings then!" her mother said, ripping off another chunk of hard bread. "I'm holding my breath. I want to hear of your adventures. Did you bring any man pelts for us? If not, you'd best turn around and ride back to those evil lizards."

"I came here to tell you that the Fire Keepers made me a captain."

"A captain? What does that mean? Are you in charge of a boat now?"

"It means that I will serve my Swordfamily for the rest of my life."

"Serve them what? Stew? Meat and ale? Or mayhaps you'll serve them some other way to satisfy their needs?" her mother said, batting her eyes seductively in jest.

Andra pushed her bowl away. "You never make this easy. You won't accept my gold, you hurl insults at me every time I ride out here, thu'gods only know what you say about me while I'm away. You have my thanks for not skinning me alive and hanging my pelt from your walls, and little else. Every time I walk through that door I throw dice that turn to ash."

Her mother stood. "I had three daughters once. Your elder sister is many things, but she will never again be my daughter. You could be, if you left that make-believe family of yours. That's not a family; it's a farce. So long as you're one of them, you're not welcome in my home."

Andra pulled herself up to her full height. "I thank you for the fine stew." She nodded at Lecata and Mistahn. "Mother, I came here to tell you that all of my tomorrows are now writ in stone. I was merely a warrior before. Those men and women come and they go. I am a Fire Keeper for life. I had two families once. I hope to have them both again one day."

Her mother tore off another chunk of stale bread. She threw it in the stew.

Gathering her traveling cloak from the back of her chair, Andra noticed that it hadn't dried at all. It felt colder than the air as she put it on and pulled the hood over her head. She didn't look back as she opened the door and walked outside. The door swung noiselessly as she closed it.

The palfrey whinnied at her. She rewarded him with a few more oats. She climbed onto her horse and grimaced as her arse found that the saddle was as wet as her cloak.

Rain fell harder and heavier now.

The rain could fall thick as waves on the Angered Sea and I still wouldn't detest this ride as much as I did the one that brought me here.

"Andra!" Mistahn cried. He ran from the house, slamming the door behind him. He hadn't pulled anything over his jerkin before venturing into the rain. "Please don't leave me here! Please! There's nothing for me here but a lonely death after a lifetime of tedium. I watch mushrooms grow and count the leaves on trees. It's a miserable life here. Take me with you. I'm begging!"

Mistahn's face was drenched from the rain. Andra suspected that it hid more than a few tears.

"No!" Andra said so loud it was almost a scream. "I forbid it. Kardas forbids it. If my Swordfather were here, he'd tell you the same!"

"Do you remember," Mistahn started to say before he choked on the words. "Do you remember how you used to tell me those stories? You would tell the tales of maidens trapped in towers as if they were cells in a dungeon. Some knight would come along and rescue them from the tower."

Mistahn's chest shuddered. "You're my knight and this is my dungeon. Please, I'm begging you, rescue me. Make me a Fire Keeper."

"You already have my answer, Mistahn."

"Then I'll ask my other sister in Fulccrum for a place in *her* Swordfamily."

"War dawns inside Fulccrum. Your dreary life is preferable to an exciting death."

His shoulders slumped as he accepted defeat. "I ask only this from you. If you ever have need of me, you have only to ask. You know where I'll be and you know that I'll say yes." He raised his fist and opened it to show the small carving of their home that Andra had abandoned on the table. "Carry this with you. Remember me when you look upon it."

Andra took the carving and thrust it into a leather pouch.

Rain fell hard as Andra reached down and patted Mistahn on the shoulder. Then she squeezed her legs tight and her palfrey took its first slow steps back to Fulccrum.

Andra didn't look back. But she swore to herself that she wouldn't forget her brother's desperation in this moment.

After she had traveled leagues on the Shamrock Road, Andra reached into her pouch and squeezed the tiny carving of their home.

CHAPTER TEN
SWORDFAMILIES

"Knees bend before they break! Swords break before they bend!" Raysk began. "That's why the Emerald Crown watches over the realm, but the Swordfamilies rule it. They have the *crown*, but we have the *power*." He slammed his fist against the table as he spoke the last word. "This Council of Sheathed Swords is open."

He stood at a table with six sides. Shaped as a hexagon, the table had been commissioned by the six great families of Fulccrum many Swordfathers ago. The sides were exactly the same length to ensure that each family was allotted the same amount of space at the table. This shape solved the problem that arose with the previous round table. Swordfathers would begin to arrive at councils earlier and earlier to claim outsized portions of it. Arguments would begin even before the issues of the day had been broached.

Swordfathers were permitted to bring one advisor to the council, usually a captain or consulary. The seating was arranged by the ability of each Swordfather to tolerate the family seated next to them. For that reason, the Heavies sat opposite from the Fire Keepers.

Precisely eight steps behind each Swordfather stood a Scabbard captain. The only movement they made was to blink. Each one of them had one hand wrapped around the hilt of their sword.

The council took place at the top of a monument called the Gods' Blade. It was an obelisk that, even half a league away from Fulccrum, looked like the raised blade of a colossal sword. The first kings who ruled the realm built the monument with green marble. It stood a stone's throw from the castle in Fulccrum, provided that stone was thrown from the top of the monument.

The obelisk was slightly shorter than the castle's tallest tower. The early kings believed that while they must present this homage to the horde of gods that the commoners worshipped, the castle must stand taller. That way, the townsfolk would understand that although the gods were welcomed, the crown ruled.

Both the monument and castle stood in the New Valois district. After the last stone of the Gods' Blade was placed, the kings and queens who dwelled within the castle during the ensuing years questioned the wisdom of placing such a tall monument so close to the castle walls.

Inside the monument were many rooms, both great and small. The council room stood inside the tiny pyramid that formed the sword's point. Drapes made of white silk waved as a light breeze drifted through the large windows on all four walls that were nothing more than openings that stretched from floor to ceiling.

A blood red sun lingered over the Angered Sea to the west. Its light sent long shadows streaking across the council room. The Gods' Blade cast its own shadow to cut through the districts of New Valois and Raventyn. Its darkness shrouded Gilded Granite Street. The point fell upon the city wall by the East Gate.

Fulccrum was a realm unto itself. The Emerald Kingdom's capital city was divided into five districts, each one robust as a kingdom. Its port was the heart of trade over the vast Angered Sea, pulling in carracks and pumping them out over trade routes that bound together distant realms. Fulccrum's web of rivers and roads spread inland to unite the kingdom's far-flung corners.

The capital city's influence was more than practicalities. Every corner of the Emerald Realm celebrated the triple solar eclipses that Fulccrum witnessed twice a year. The festivals dedicated to the three moons passing between the sun and city had taken place for generations. As he grew and Prince Opvolk's skin reminded the commoners of the moons occulting the sun, the Prince of the Eclipse was also feted as divine favor from the thundering gods.

The city had grown like a tree, its thick rings showing its three ages like the stump of a felled oak. The first ring was the island of New Valois that held the city center. In Fulccrum's early days, the waters that separated the island from the mainland had protected the city like a great moat. Time passed and the capital city grew a middle ring on the continent. Lacking any natural protection, its rulers built a city wall, the ruins of which were now known as the old city wall. The city's third ring was made of newer buildings and gathering places like the Colosseum and festival grounds. The newest part of Fulccrum was protected by a city wall much taller and stronger than its predecessor.

On a clear day, the entire city and most of its landmarks could be seen through the yawning windows atop the Gods' Blade. The Colosseum loomed in the east with its stacked colonnades supporting the great stone structure. A patchwork of canvas roofs over the stalls in the Old Town Square Market looked like a crude tapestry. The darkness over the cluster of buildings where the Iron Wand laboratory had collapsed, Mages' Mist, was plain to see in the ruddy sunlight. The old city wall curved through the city's interior. The bases of the partially built statue at the port entrance were easy to spot, although only the huge sabatons rested on them.

Raysk took his seat with Consulary Pametan behind him. He felt more at ease in steel plate armor than he did in the soft clothes that he wore now, but Pametan had insisted that he wear attire more suited to the occasion. She did this because he had called the council, and grave issues were to be discussed.

Although he wore delicate clothes, Raysk did not opt for a delicate approach.

"The Heavies opened Auzken's tomb. The final resting place of my family's greatest Foreblade." Raysk took deep breaths between each sentence that he spoke. "Captain Vasarox did this to make certain that the Bleeding Blade still rested with the last Greatsword. The Heavy who ruled the Swordfamilies as the Blade of Blades. When Vasarox returned to me, he did so with dark arms and dark tidings. The sword was gone. In its place, Auzken's final resting place had filled with blood."

The Swordfathers listening to Raysk did not react to his words. They betrayed no emotion, nor did their advisors.

"That means at least one Swordfather in this room knows where the Bleeding Blade is." Raysk's eyes narrowed. "And it's not me."

Pametan swept her eyes over the Swordfathers as Raysk spoke, searching for any movement that would allow her to peek behind the guilty party's emotionless mask.

"Years ago, when the Swordfathers all stood together and sealed that blade in Auzken's tomb, they agreed what it would mean if it was ever stolen. It would be the beginning of a war between the six great Swordfamilies of Fulccrum."

Raysk drummed his fingers on the table. The act was a small crack in the dam that held back his rage.

"I'm a reasonable man. I conduct my business in the manner that befits my family. When that sword was taken from the tomb, whoever stole it committed an act of violence against not only my family, but all the families."

He pounded his fist on the table. The Scabbard behind Raysk gripped the hilt of his sword more tightly.

"Whoever did this must know that they have committed a great wrong. Not just against me and mine, but against any family who honors the solemn oath of our forebears. I ask the Swordfather who took the blade to be reasonable. To that person I say, state your intentions. You want war, tell me to my face *right here and now*. Do not cower in the shadows with the blood from that sword spilling at your trembling feet."

Raysk glared at the Swordfathers, a wordless challenge to those five families. Pametan marked their expressions.

After long moments, the Ashfall Swordfather cleared his throat.

"I, uh, I didn't take the sword and I don't know who did," he began. He was gaunt, pale, sweaty, and his eyes were bloodshot. Which was typical of him. "I do have a question though."

"Quivum," Raysk responded. "I welcome the Bladeslayer's words, even if some of my guests do not. To me, killing a Swordfather is a show of strength. It's no cause for shame, only glory. Go on now, ask your question."

A dark cloak rested on Quivum's shoulders, over his

white jerkin. Both of his hands trembled slightly, but not from fear. His greasy brown hair was matted against his head.

"Does it matter who has the sword? It's just a trinket of sorts. It's not very strong. The stories say the blade is dull. It's a ceremonial thing." His cloak shook as he spoke. "It doesn't give the Swordfather wielding it any advantage. I suppose the bloodletting would let you know when a battle's about to start or some Swordfather's going to duh-duh-die." He wiped the sweat from his forehead with his cloak. "It matters not."

Raysk regarded Quivum as if the Ashfall leader were a small child. "If you took the blade, I'm sure it wasn't to declare war. You stole it so you could drink the blood it spills."

"I hadn't th-th-thought of that," Quivum said as he scratched at his scraggly beard.

In the New Valois district, to the north, burned a giant blue flame atop a tall column. The flame stretched higher than the buildings around it, beckoning all who yearned for escape from the city without leaving the city walls. It marked the place where Ashfall peddled its goods at all hours.

"The weak ask. The strong take," Irin said plainly.

"Your own words, Swordfather Raysk, if I'm not mistaken," Guiden added. The Iron Wand captain was behind Irin. "A refrain familiar to us all."

"The Iron Wand is learned," Pametan hissed from behind Raysk. "No doubt you're able to divine which family has secreted the Bleeding Blade, what with your superior intellect and dusty grimoires."

Irin's hands rested on the council table. "I only guess when I know the truth." She curled her fingers together, as if she held a wand. "On this matter, I know not. But if you've taken offense, then you've misunderstood my words. I do not mean to suggest that whoever took the Bleeding Blade is strong because they stole it. Quite the opposite. The Swordfather harboring the blade is weak. Their theft did not make the peace they desire. Instead, it asks for war. I suggest that we decline their request. War among the families would turn our font of gold into a trickle. The consequences would be worse than a war between crowns."

Behind Kardas, Andra breathed heavily. The Scabbards wouldn't allow her Swordfather to bring his walking cane because no blades were allowed. She drew deep breaths, still recovering from the effort required to help him climb the many stairs to the council room. Despite her fatigue, she kept her eyes trained on the Syrens' Swordfather.

"Irin's right," Kardas began. "This theft is more farce than force. Possessing the Bleeding Blade meant something long ago. Now it has no more power than Auzken dead in his tomb. Whoever took it merely wants to stir trouble betwixt the families." He noticed smoke rising from the dragon refuge. The gray columns rose to the northeast, tall and dark enough to be seen over long leagues. "They want to rekindle old fights and make us remember wrongs that no longer matter. Elsewise, the Swordfather who holds the blade should throw it on the council table and make their claim as the Greatsword."

Irin and her captain, Guiden, nodded in agreement. The other Swordfathers and their advisors remained still.

"What do you make of this, Sinsasi?" Kardas asked. Andra leaned over his shoulder and whispered in his ear after he asked the question.

The Syrens' Swordfather had sea blue eyes and rose red

lips. Sinsasi's arrow-straight hair changed color from red to blonde depending on how the light shined on it. Daylight made it sparkle as if her strands were spun from gold. She wore the sheer dress that her family favored, hiding nothing except that which the person gazing upon her desired to see most. The only opaque clothing she wore were white silk gloves covering her hands and forearms up to the elbow.

Every Syren, women and men alike, wielded their beauty with the lethal skill of a master assassin. But their power was deeper than what the eye could see. Exposing nearly all of their skin was the bait they used to lure the unwary into an aura that transcended beauty. Syrens did not merely fan the flames of desire; their prey willingly surrendered control.

"These halcyon years have graced us with wealth that the Swordfathers who suffered the War of the Rusted Blades couldn't fathom," Sinsasi answered. "Why go to war over a blade that only inspires fear in the servants who have to wash the rushes and jerkins it bleeds on?"

Hallita stood behind Sinsasi. As a warrior, she was the lowest ranking family member at the council. Like the other advisors, she followed orders to listen intently and keep a keen eye on the other families. She mostly followed this order although occasionally her gaze wandered through a window to a tall castle tower. In that tower she could see the feather bed in Prince Opvolk's chamber where she had spent many exhausting nights.

"Tell me, Sinsasi," Pametan asked, "if you do not possess the Bleeding Blade, what about another blade? The Shard of the Specter?"

Raysk crossed his arms. After Sinsasi didn't reply, Pametan continued.

"We all had ears at the last royal court, or whatever our bickering sovereigns are calling their throne hall follies. Emerald Ezzy spoke of a sword. She called it the Shard of the Specter. She told the king and queen that her husband stole it for the Syrens."

The Swordfather of Dark Water had held his tongue through the council. Hanngoh had olive skin, narrow eyes, narrow lips, curly black hair, and a dusting of a beard. A salt-stained cloth was wrapped tight around the top of his head. A collection of earrings, each one with a story of its own, dangled from every part of his ears. Dazzling gems of different sizes and colors hung from the ropes of gold wrapped around his neck. He had more wrinkles than most men his age, a gift from his long days at sea spent behind his ship's wheel.

Hanngoh leaned forward. He put his elbows on the table and traced a circle on it with a finger. "Ezzy spoke like a child beggin' forgiveness from the thunderin' gods," he said slowly. "Talked o' the Syrens and Ashfall. She was goin' to speak of me Dark Water before the crown put a merciful end to her natterin'. I know this woman better than most. I sell to her for that shop she runs. She must be madder than a dragon drenched in yolk if she's brayin' about half o' the families in Fulccrum at a royal court."

He took a deep breath and leaned back in his chair. Then he put his feet on the table and crossed his legs. Mud dripped from the bottoms of Hanngoh's boots. Their brown leather was faded and wrinkled by the sun.

"I put no stock in her words and ya shouldn't either. She's a liar, and yer a bigger fool than our king if ya believe her." Hanngoh crossed his arms. "If ya don't believe me, ask yer thralls that were there. The ones by the throne hall doors. If any o' them had sharp wits, they could see her lies after they heard them."

In Fulccrum's port below the Gods' Blade, the Dark Water ship lay at anchor. The words "Shark Queen" were carved on the transom at her stern. The ship's hull was covered in countless shark's teeth. They were taken from sharks so massive that the fins on their backs looked like small sails when they were near the surface. A plank made from whale ribs stuck out from its starboard side. Beneath the plank spun a whirlpool. Sunlight glinted off the bronzed figurehead mounted to the prow of the ship. The other ships in the port docked or anchored as far away from *Shark Queen* as the protected waters would allow.

The Swordfathers and their advisors sat in silence for long enough that Hanngoh began to nod off.

"Do enlighten us," Guiden said for Iron Wand.

Dark Water's leader smacked his lips and shook his head. "There's more to Emerald Ezzy than hawkin' wares by me docks. Most o' what she sells can't be bought, only stolen. I'm not talkin' about breakin' into shops with locks so weak I could pick them with a fork and knife. If half o' what I've heard about Ezzy is true, she's part snake, part shadow, and runs her affairs like a Swordfather." Hanngoh stretched and put his hands behind his head. "That pageant play she gave the crown lacked only a wagon. Her last few steps before she left the throne hall were a confession. Those who know Ezzy know better than to trust her words." He pursed his lips. "She's a Swordfamily of one."

Hanngoh loosed a soft laugh. Andra's eyes lingered on him and, only for a moment, their eyes met.

Pametan whispered in Raysk's ear.

"I summoned you all here so that we could know who

among us is baiting the families into war." Raysk stood quickly, knocking over his chair. It slammed into Pametan's shin. "War is not my aim. I seek unity. There are forces at play that will shape the future of our families long after everyone in this room sleeps with Auzken." His hands closed into fists. "We all see the long war on the Emerald Crown's horizon. With the king and queen's eyes far away from the city, our families must rally together under a Greatsword."

Words of disagreement were uttered around the table. Heads shook.

Raysk looked at Pametan, then returned his attention to the council. "More important than the crown's foolery, I've received word of events to the east of far greater import. The Swordfamilies of Lysnap have banded together under a single Swordfather. A Greatsword. When the Emerald Crown falls, the Lysnapi Swordfamilies will come and they will be unified as *one.*"

The council erupted. Swordfathers roared and pounded on the table. Advisors shook their fists as spittle flew from their lips. Every Scabbard pulled a quarter of their sword from its sheath.

"Savages in the east!" screamed Sinsasi.

"Those Lysnapi barbarians have no code!" Hanngoh yelled.

"Their magic is darker than the Wanderer," Irin groaned with her palm hard against her forehead.

Quivum pulled something from inside his dark blue robes and quickly put it in his mouth. His pupils grew wide enough that they nearly covered his eyes.

Kardas folded his arms over his chest and sighed.

After the yelling subsided, an uneasy silence filled the room.

"Unity is imperative." Raysk scratched at a thick scar

under his chin. "We must all hang together, or the Lysnapi will hang us all separately."

"You would cow the families beneath a sword instead of joining together to defend ourselves," Sinsasi said. "I'm not accustomed to kneeling." As she spoke, the long white flags that flew over her family's Shrines of Solace to the south snapped in the gusts blowing through the Satinwind district. "You called this Council of Sheathed Swords, but it could be a feint. You're as like as any of us to hold Auzken's sword."

"If I had the Bleeding Blade, I would thrust it into this table. That would be your answer." Raysk stuck out his chest. "And your defense against the Lysnapi families."

"Your obsession with this sword perplexes me," Irin growled. "It was hidden in a tomb before and it's hidden somewhere else this day. Whether it's in one hiding place or another makes no difference."

"A great many swords concern me, but the Bleedin' Blade isn't one o' them," Hanngoh whispered. "The thousands o' swords controlled by the crowns are what I mind. Travelers tell me o' the comin' war with the Crimson Crown. The lords with their lands against the Paders have less loyalty to the Emerald Crown than us. Methinks the time's come to throw our lot in with the king and queen to keep the realm green."

"Crowns are for cravens," Raysk cut him off. "We bow to no king. The king bows to us. The Swordfamilies united as one could fetter any crown!" he boomed. "I say we let the red crown and Swordfamilies from Lysnap descend upon our city where they'll be run through by our Greatsword!"

Quivum shook his head violently. "That-that-that's not right," he stuttered. "Not totally right. I know that muh-muh-my family favors a strong crown. A crown at peace with the other kingdoms. It's easier to pay off the kuh-kuh-Kingdom Guard when there's no trouble. They get angry and guh-guh-greedy when there's war. They stop us from peddling goods. They burn our crops and throw our patrons in duh-duh-dungeons. Ashfall wants a strong crown turning a blind eye to our easy coin." Though the room was cool, beads of sweat dripped from his forehead.

Kardas put his hands on the table and pulled himself up. Every eye on him measured how little strength remained in those once powerful arms. "If the crowns clash, we must support our king and queen. A short war that ends with the Emerald Crown's decisive victory will put this all behind us." The years weighed heavily on Kardas's shoulders. "Thundering gods forbid, if the Crimson Crown were to win the war and take Fulccrum, they would sack the city and the Lysnapi would follow close behind. Those barbarians make no vows and honor no code. They know nothing of Sacred Kin. Our Sword-families may survive, but our blood families would not." Kardas frowned deeply. "Honor Thy Debt? They honor nothing. And Screaming Silence...no doubt they would work with the reds to hunt us. They would scream and it wouldn't be silence; they'd scream our names to any knight in their crown's army." Kardas shook his head. "If the Emerald Crown is weak, we must make it strong. If we don't, our families bound by sword and blood will fall."

The Fire Keepers' Swordfather sank back into his chair.

"Under the reds, our Shrines of Solace would fall into ruin. Our family would be enslaved as comfort men and women." Sinsasi betrayed no emotion as she spoke. "If the war were to drag on, even if the borders held, our people may be sent to the front to comfort the Kingdom Guard."

She glared at her fellow Swordfathers. "We are not friends, but we must be allies for peace."

Hanngoh had nodded in agreement with much of what had been said. "The entire realm knows that the Emerald Crown's navy is weak. The Crimson Crown knows it, too. I won't have me ship commandeered and me warriors pressed into their service. If it came to that, we would weigh anchor and take our chances on the open sea. I'd take me pet whirlpool. Pirate for years at a time the way our family used to before we made Fulccrum our home port."

Irin's gaze passed over the dark shadow of Mages' Mist near the city wall. "The crown despises us, but respects us. War makes leaders paranoid even when they're winning. After all, they lose a loyal subject with every death on the battlefield. That paranoia breeds hate that the mind blurs into justice. I'm certain that in a lengthy war with the Crimson Crown, our king would see magic-wielding outcasts as a vulnerability he would gladly do without." She rubbed her thumb across her other four fingers. "And he would act accordingly."

Kardas summoned more strength than anyone in the room thought he could muster. "Then it is agreed!" he bellowed. "We must support the Emerald Crown to protect our realm and our city from the Lysnapi and their handlers." His presence grew as each word thundered. "A weak throne makes weak Swordfamilies. We have thrived together in this long peace. Each Swordfather has gathered wealth that kings envy. To shatter the foundation of this prosperous peace would be a folly that we would all regret to the end of our days!"

Every Swordfather cheered Kardas's words, except Raysk. Irin clapped her hands high in the air, as did Quivum, though he missed a few times as the pills began to fog his mind. Sinsasi clapped her gloved hands as well. She also gave Kardas an admiring look, the highest praise a man could receive from a Syren. Hanngoh beat his fist against his chest. Raysk remained standing with his arms crossed.

Kardas held up a hand and the Swordfathers quieted. He covered his mouth as he coughed with a deep, raspy sound that came from the depths of his chest. "I have one last good battle left in me. I intend to fight it for the Emerald Throne and the good peace among the families." He looked Raysk square in the eye. "In my last battle, the only blood dripping from my blade will be that of my enemies."

Raysk took his seat. His mind moved faster than his war hammer in battle. "Answer me this, Kardas Fire Keeper. If the Emerald Crown can't protect itself, how can it protect us? If our crown needs us to survive, how can it preserve our peace? Steel is strong and gold is weak."

Kardas swallowed hard. "With our support, the king and queen can stop the Crimson Crown from sacking Fulcrum and the Lysnapi from breaking our families." He leaned over the table and spoke only at Raysk. "If we aid them, mayhaps the Emerald Crown will protect you from the ghastly family that stole the leaky sword."

"The colors of the banners in the throne hall matter naught." Raysk shrugged. "If the banners that hang so high today lie crumpled on the floor tomorrow, the families will remain the strength in this city. Debts from commoners and royalty who require our favors will flow to us like the River of Plenty."

As Sinsasi stroked her hair, it flashed between red and blonde. "You say that you're a reasonable man. Beneath the Emerald Crown, we've known nothing but plenty. Why throw the dice and hope the Crimson Crown is friendly to us and keeps their Lysnapi families at bay?"

"Those Syren tricks don't work on me anymore," Raysk growled. The mask of scars that covered his face twitched. The Colosseum where his family's warriors and captains took their vows stood tall in the distance. "The Heavies will withstand anything. Peace. War. The Lava Sea spilling over the Pader Mountains. We could crush the Kingdom Guard and the Crimson Crown at the same time. But I don't see the coin in it, so why bother?" Raysk scratched at his throat. "You want the Emerald Crown in the castle so Minacia remains queen. You want one of your own on the throne with her thrall seated next to her."

Sinsasi smiled with her mouth but not her eyes. She began to protest but Quivum regained his senses and spoke over her words.

"Enough!" the Ashfall Swordfather barked. "You've said your puh-puh-piece. If it's war, each family will lend the crown their strength or not." The effort of speaking made him slump against the back of his chair.

"Very well," Raysk said as he yawned. "The king is but a fool in the court of the six great families."

Icy silence fell over the council. A strong wind gusted through the windows, whipping the Scabbards' heavy cloaks. The guards' steel plate armor made nary a sound as they remained motionless. Throughout the Swordfathers' rancor, the Scabbards had remained still.

Hanngoh held up his hands with his palms out. "Raysk, yer voice sounds to me like two gulls fightin' over a rotten fish head."

The table shook as Raysk pounded his fist on it. "The Swordfathers disappoint me. The thief who stole the Bleeding Blade is at this table. Theirs is a cowardly silence."

The scars on his face reddened. "You talk to me of bending the knee to the Emerald Crown." He spat. "Anyone tells me to bend a knee, I'll bend it all right! After I bring my war hammer down on your knee, it'll bend whichever way ye like!"

Pametan frowned.

"That's enough," Kardas whispered.

"Then it is agreed. Each Swordfamily will forge their own path." Raysk straightened his soft clothes and spoke with a soft voice. "But all paths ultimately lead to me, just as all rivers flow to the sea."

With those words, every Swordfather in the room understood that war had been declared.

"Violent families will meet violent ends," Andra said.

Raysk stood and turned in a fury. He stormed from the table without another word. Pametan hastened to follow.

Around the table, the Swordfathers and their advisors slowly began to leave. Andra moved toward the door quickly, leaving Kardas in his seat. Sinsasi was no more than three steps from departing when Andra deftly stepped in front of the Syrens' Swordfather.

"I thank you, my Blade," Andra began. "For standing up to that brute. To him the world is a giant rock to be smashed. You made a noble effort to reason with him."

"The effort seems to have been in vain," Sinsasi said plaintively.

Andra looked up and down Sinsasi's body, forcing her eyes open wide to try and appear suitably impressed. "You aren't wearing much, but what you have on I find fascinating. You're the only people in Fulccrum who look their best wearing clothes so thin that you may as well be wearing water." She smiled. "What I find most interesting are your gloves. Pure white and made of fine silk.

They are truly fit for a queen. Are they a gift from Minacia?"

"No," Sinsasi replied in a tone devoid of warmth.

Andra reached out to slide her hand along a glove.

Sinsasi recoiled at her approach. "Do not presume to touch me," she growled, clenching her hands tight. She stormed past Andra.

The only other person remaining in the room was Kardas; even the Scabbards had retired. The Fire Keeper hobbled over to Andra and put his hand on her shoulder for support. Together, they began the long descent from the top of the Gods' Blade. Kardas winced as he took each step.

"Many steps and much pain for the privilege of listening to Raysk spew threats," Kardas groaned. "He's never more confident than when he's utterly wrong."

"His obsession with the Bleeding Blade has clouded his judgment," Andra replied. "I suspect that blade will be the death of him."

As the pair descended through the monument, they passed by cavernous rooms.

"My Blade, we have been rewarded for our suffering."

"Rewarded? The Heavies refused to back the Emerald Crown and declared the first war in dragon's years. Raysk's war hammer would agree to peace before the man himself would consider it."

A tug on Andra's shoulder let her know that Kardas needed to stop for a moment to gather his strength. They both looked up and down the curved stairs and listened for footsteps. They saw and heard no one, but spoke in whispers in case the stones around them were listening.

"The Heavies will work against the crown to strip away our cloak of protection," Kardas said between breaths. "They'll do this at the same time they slash at our dragons.

They'll attack us from both sides, like a piece of metal being pounded between a hammer and anvil. It's impossible to defend. I've failed."

"The council wasn't a failure. You're always telling us that eyes without a mind see only as much as a mind without eyes. That's what I did during the council. I studied the Swordfathers and I discovered something important."

"What did you learn, my captain?"

"I know who holds what Raysk covets."

CHAPTER ELEVEN
DARK WATER

Three moons hung low in the night sky. The middle moon shone just above the two other moons that nearly kissed the horizon. If a line traveled between all three, it would form a wide triangle. They each shined a jagged streak of light over the calm water in Fulccrum's port.

The largest moon was made of many dark shades of gray. Sometimes a plume of bright red fire would shoot from its surface and a spot on the moon would glow red. Some fires traveled so far from it that people in Fulccrum would stop and point at the fiery moon. Nobody in Fulccrum could predict where or when the red bursts would appear. The townsfolk called this fire-breathing moon Dragon Without Wings.

Light from the second largest moon shone a bright white. It looked as smooth as a giant pearl. About as often as fire shot from Dragon Without Wings, this moon would spit out wisps of dense white fog. The moon was so bright that the wisps were hard to see unless they puffed out from its edge, against the black night sky. The people of Fulcrum who had traveled to the east side of the Pader Mountains thought the wisps looked like the boiling hot water that shot from the ground at the Land of Dancing Water. This moon was named Rain Above Rain.

The third moon was much different than Dragon Without Wings and Rain Above Rain. Those two moons were disks in the sky. The third moon changed shape. Sometimes it looked like a circle, the same as the other moons. Then it would turn so that it was a wide and lumpy line. It seemed to spin end over end like a coin flipped from a giant's thumb. This moon was more colorful than the others, a dull yellow hue. Because of its color, and the way it moved, it reminded the townsfolk of a gold scythe tumbling through the air. They named it Night Scythe.

Other than a few eccentric old men and women who stared at the night sky through long tubes with glass at both ends, nobody paid attention to the fourth moon. Most commoners didn't know it existed. It was small and dark and rarely noticed unless it passed in front of bright stars, blocking their light. Even then, people would think that a bat had flown overhead. The fourth moon didn't move at the snail's pace of the other three moons. This moon flew fast as an arrow and wobbled as it glided across the night sky. The path it took crossed the other three moons' paths at sharp angles. Tonight, the fourth moon rushed through the sky above Fulccrum and, as usual, it traveled unnoticed. The few people who took interest in this strange moon called it the Wanderer.

After rowing away from *Shark Queen*, two Dark Water captains took a roundabout course through the port, staying close to ships tied to the dock. They did this to avoid unwelcome eyes spying them in the light of the three moons. They lashed their rowboat between two large ships, under the bowsprit of one and behind the other ship's stern. After heaving a sack onto the dock, they began their long trek.

The two men moving along the dock were grateful for the fast approaching clouds. They tried to step lightly, but one man was nearly twice the size of the other and he had precious little luck in muffling his footfalls. For now, they were not concerned about the noise from the creaking wood planks under their soft leather boots.

The ships in the port didn't move, as if the water were solid ice. They were cogs and carracks and other sailing ships of many sizes and flags. With their sails stowed, the ships' masts stabbed at the sky. Voices that spoke with strange accents and even stranger words could be heard below the weather decks. Many ships had a guard stationed by the gangway. Those guards took little interest in the two men on the dock.

"Did you hear about the place Sinsasi lives in?" Bajak asked. When he received no reply, he punched his intended audience on the arm and said, "Faomen, I asked you a question."

"Ow, stop that. My arms are sore from rowing us here," Faomen replied. "My mind was somewhere else."

"I'd wager it was somewhere underneath Jyfa's cloak. Probably underneath whatever's underneath her cloak," Bajak said. He punched Faomen on the arm again. "You sure this arm is sore from pulling an oar? Maybe it's sore from pulling something else?" he laughed.

"Quiet. We still have a ways before we get to her shop and you know how voices carry over water," Faomen said in a whisper. "Anyway, yes, I heard about Sinsasi's palace. You know how the Swordfathers live. They're kings without crowns."

"Aye, all of them 'cept Kardas. I heard he's a simple man in a simple house in Forsbeme." Bajak tugged on his long black beard. He granted Faomen's wish and kept his voice low. "The other Swordfathers don't seem to keep their coin. The coin flows through them; they earn it with their right hand and spend it with their left."

"I'd wager they have a few gold scythes tucked under their beds," Faomen said.

"Anyway, Sinsasi's palace is one big room. No walls. She has some thin silk that hangs from the ceiling. There're cushions and beds everywhere, soft as your Jyfa's sweet bosom," Bajak said.

Faomen expressed his opinion on the jibe by driving an elbow deep into Bajak's enormous gut.

"The Syrens use some potions that smell nice in their shrines. Sinsasi's palace is filled with it. She built the place over hot pools. They put stones around the water so it's like one of them wooden tubs the royals use to bathe, only made of stones. They say the hot water angries up the loins. Every man and woman whose gone in there gets swallowed by their own desire. They'll do anything for her. She takes their minds."

"Maybe some people want their mind to be taken," Faomen mumbled.

"Not some, *many*," Bajak replied. He combed through his beard with his hands. "With the Syrens so easy on the eyes, it's a wonder why Hanngoh chose who he chose."

"How do you mean?"

"Don't get me wrong, the lass is comely. She'd be welcome to stow away on *Shark Queen* during a long voyage." Bajak screwed up his face. "The two are so different, though. He's a Swordfather; she's a warrior."

"Captain, now."

"Captain, what have you. She's no Swordfather, but he is. Our ships are made of wood and ply the waters of open seas. Her lot worships fire."

"He's had his eye on her for eclipses now," Faomen said as he pondered his fellow captain's words. "Mayhaps they're not so unlike. Dragons have scales, same as fish."

"They can breathe *fire*, but I wonder if they can breathe *water*? Should've found out when we had the chance."

Faomen glared at Bajak, then held up his hand, ordering silence.

The Dark Water captains neared their destination. They were careful to step on the nails in the dock's wooden boards. The planks made less noise when the men stepped where the boards were hammered into the supports below. Now their footsteps were nearly silent.

Wordlessly, the two put more distance between themselves and the place where they tied up their boat.

"There it is," Bajak whispered. His voice was so soft that Faomen could barely hear him. "Up ahead."

Faomen nodded and Bajak shifted the heavy sack he carried from one shoulder to the other. A puff of thin, gray smoke escaped from it as he cinched it tight.

They took dozens of careful steps, but no matter how lightly Faomen treaded the sound of sloshing liquid came from beneath his cloak. The dark leather they wore helped the Dark Water captains disappear into the shadow of a large ship near their destination. Safely concealed, the men squatted down and studied the shop on the shoreside of the dock.

Above the door to the windowless shop were carved the words "Emerald Ezzy's Curios and Oddments."

"You ever been in there?" Bajak whispered.

Faomen shook his head. "I hear that if you go in, you have to buy something. If you walk out empty-handed, you're just as like to walk out without your hand."

"Weird the shop is over the water. Look at it, must be held up by tree trunks," Bajak said under his breath. "The dirt barely touches that back wall."

The two men checked their surroundings to find the dock was as empty now as it had been when they'd tied up their boat. They crept across the dock and crouched near the door to the shop.

Faomen blew on his fingers and pulled slivers of metal out of his pocket. He stuck the pieces into the keyhole. The metal scratched inside the lock, but didn't produce the click that he expected. His brow furrowed as he stuffed the metal back into his pocket.

Bajak reached over Faomen and grasped the handle. When he pulled on it, the door opened a finger's width. He pulled the door only far enough that the men could squeeze through—after Bajak sucked in his gut. The two Dark Waters entered to find a darkness so black it seemed their eyes were filled with ink. Bajak lowered the heavy sack from his shoulder.

Searching a pocket, Faomen pulled out a candle. Then he uncorked a bottle tied inside his cloak and dipped the candlewick into it. The candle dripped as he pulled it from the bottle. Bajak felt the wick to aim his dagger as he struck it against some flint. A few sparks landed on the wick and an orange flame instantly sprang to life. A moment later the flame stretched so high and burned so bright that Faomen shut his eyes.

Some heartbeats later, the flame shrank down to the size of an arrowhead. Faomen held his hand steady as Bajak used the flame to light his own candle. Each man held their burning candle in one hand and used their other hand to grip the hilt of their sword.

"Wasn't locked," Faomen whispered. "Someone else is in here or Ezzy forgot to lock the door before she set sail."

"Hanngoh said she boarded the *Green Flash* this morning," Bajak replied. "It weighed anchor and sailed out of port before midday."

The two Dark Waters shared an uneasy look.

With candles held high and their swords gripped tight, the two men went separate ways to search each side of the shop.

Along the walls, shelves made of pine stood from the floor to the ceiling. They were lined with exotic objects gathered from every point on the compass in the Emerald Kingdom and beyond.

The skull of a troll startled Faomen as his candlelight flickered over it. The low, sloped forehead joined a massive maw filled with teeth bigger than a man's fingers. Lines of sharp horns were on its crown and jaw. Faomen's heart sank when he realized that the grotesque skull seemed to smile at him.

Farther down the wall, a sheathed longsword lay on a low shelf. Bajak knelt to inspect it. The candlelight shining on the sword's grip showed a figure made of gold. When he moved the flame closer, it revealed the gilded hilt's detail. It was a goblin head made narrow enough to fit in a hand. The goblin's wide ears formed the sword's cross guard. Between the top of the goblin head and the scabbard was a short length of blade that glowed green.

Setting the candle next to a shark's tooth bigger than

his head, Bajak picked up the sheathed sword. Dim, green light shone in the room when he pulled the blade from its scabbard.

Faomen spun around to find the source of the strange, pulsing light. The liquid in the bottles under his cloak sloshed as he turned.

With both hands, Bajak thrust the longsword's point deep into a trestle table near the middle of the room. It stood up straight. Green light from the goblin blade barely reached the shelves against the walls.

A giant battle axe stood next to the glowing sword. It was braced by wooden beams that bowed from supporting its great weight. Faomen approached the weapon. His mouth was agape as he studied the impossibly huge axe. Its double-bladed head was wider than Faomen was tall. He saw deep notches and scrapes in the blades. His eyes grew wide as he realized they were battle damage. The haft was made of a single piece of wood, thick as the trunk of an ancient oak. The wood in the haft's midsection was darker than the rest, where huge hands seemingly had gripped it.

Faomen resumed his search. A snakeskin lay in a pile on the lowest shelf. Dark purple scales covered the skin, except where white stripes wrapped around the width of it. The skin was wide enough that had Faomen stretched his arms apart, he couldn't have touched both sides. He reached to feel the scales, but snapped his hand back as his mind suddenly imagined the gargantuan snake that must have shed this skin.

His eyes drifted upward to a shelf where an iron pot sat on a flat stone. On its front was a crude depiction of a dragon and a shape like a raindrop. When Faomen neared it, he could feel the heat radiating from the pot as it glowed red.

Faomen quickly finished his search and returned to the door where Bajak waited for him.

"Anything?" Faomen whispered.

"Nothing," Bajak replied. "This place is crazier than the rumors. I saw an iron shield with something black and shiny over its face." He paused. "What's that battle axe? The man that swung it must've been big enough to wear those great sabatons by the port."

"You ever seen a glowing sword before?"

"Aye, I've seen swords glow," Bajak replied. "When they're pulled from the forge."

"Where does she find these things?" Faomen asked, his voice full of awe. "Some of it we've plundered for her, but there are things in here that simply shouldn't be."

"Past the Paders?" Bajak offered.

"No, there's a reason she's here by the docks. The Ring Islands or Dallu Isles, maybe? Or the Isle of Doubt, that's the strangest place I've seen and we didn't even go ashore. Could be some kingdom across the Angered Sea." Faomen pointed to a row of wood boxes near the back of the shop stacked waist-high. "Wouldn't be surprised if she sold a few things right there that came from the stars above."

"Those are strange marks on some of them boxes," Bajak said. The boxes were bare wood except for one that had two black handprints on it. "Only the thundering horde knows where all this came from. Well, them and Ezzy. I heard rumors of islands in the Lava Sea. If anyone could steal from a place like that, it'd be her."

Faomen caught a strange scent. "Something's not right. It's not just these things that I'm like to see after too much of Jyfa's drugs. It smells strange in here."

Bajak wrinkled his nose. "I smell it, too. Smells real nice in here. Like one of them plants with all the colors."

"Could be some of those," Faomen said, pointing at some dried flowers tied together and hanging from the ceiling.

"I wish Hanngoh would've sent some warriors," Bajak whispered.

"Aye, I'd much rather Yamsi and Wilde were here instead of us."

Shrugging, Bajak opened the sack that the Dark Waters had carried into the shop. It was filled with fine, powdery ash. A puff of gray rose as he scooped out a handful. The flame on the candle in his other hand flickered as he moved.

"Let's find this thing and get back to the ship," Faomen said. "Watch the ash as it falls. When it lands on the Shard of the Specter, you'll see the shape. Ezzy said it was shorter than a Kingdom Guard's blade. It's real sharp, so try to grab the hilt." He buried his hand in the ash and pulled out a mound. "Keep your candle high so you can see where it lands."

The captains moved through the shop, shaking their hands to scatter the ash. They began spreading it on the highest shelf before methodically coating the lower shelves. The tiny cinders wafted down onto Ezzy's goods, the shelves, and the floor. The pair worked to sprinkle it evenly and inspect where it fell.

Faomen spread ash over the dark purple snakeskin streaked with white stripes. He watched closely as the ash became a film over the skin that revealed no sign of the invisible blade.

Bajak repeated Faomen's efforts on his side of the shop. When he ran out of ash, he reached into places where he couldn't see and slowly felt for the sword. Finding nothing, he retrieved another handful and began anew.

The shop was mostly covered in a thin gray film when

someone sneezed. The sound hadn't come from either of the Dark Waters. Faomen and Bajak dropped the ash in their hands and drew their swords.

A cloud of ash rose from a corner.

"You fellows made quite a mess," Hallita said as she threw off the purple snakeskin and drew a dagger with each hand. "Most fellows make a mess when they're with me." She pointed a dagger at the floor. "When Ezzy sees this, she's going to make you swab the floor with your own blood."

"Hallita?" Faomen's eyes widened. "I didn't know that Syrens were allowed to wear real clothes."

"We dress for the occasion," Hallita replied. She was clad in a brown cotte and trousers. "Tonight, I don't benefit from drawing the attention of admirers."

"I should've known that smell," Bajak growled. "Syren's perfume."

"Washing off that scent is an arcane art," Hallita sighed. "I must've missed some."

"Browsing Ezzy's wares for something to dicker over?" Faomen asked.

"Searching for that glass blade, same as you." Hallita shrugged. "Ezzy blamed us for stealing the Shard of the Specter so we may as well take it. I could use an invisible sword to match my invisible dress."

"Did the king believe she spoke the truth?" Faomen asked.

"The king swallowed her lie, but the queen saw the truth of it. Ezzy is almost as good at beguiling men as a Syren. She convinced the king to offer fifty gold scythes to throw her innocent husband into the dungeons," Hallita replied. "That requires skill."

"Where's the Shard of the Specter?" Bajak pressed.

Hallita held up the daggers. "Do you think I would be holding two daggers if I had a sword that you couldn't see?" She marched past the stack of boxes. "You pirates should leave. This ship is getting too crowded."

Bajak and Faomen put more distance between themselves. Their naked blades reflected the glow from the goblin sword.

"We came here for a sword that can't be seen, not a sword that glows," Faomen said. "I'm no good with figures, but even I can count that there's two Dark Waters here and only one Syren. We have swords and you have daggers. If you leave now, we'll go about our business and you can go about yours."

Wood boards creaked beneath Bajak's boots as he advanced on the Syren. "You should walk straight out of that door."

Hallita kept facing the Dark Waters as she moved toward the door. "If I scream for the Kingdom Guard, you'll have to swim back to your boat faster than a fish or rot in the dungeons."

"If the Kingdom Guard comes here, you'll be rotting in the dungeons with us," Bajak shot back. The two Dark Waters and Syren circled.

Lowering her daggers, Hallita smirked. "Why do you think I'm here?" she asked. She edged past the pair as she spoke. The faces of her audience became crimson as they slowly understood her words. "If I scream for the Kingdom Guard, they'll hear me through this door." She dragged the point of her dagger in curves against the door. Metal clinked as she tapped the blade against the door handle. "My dear friend happens to be a prince. Any Kingdom Guard foolish enough to touch me would be more like to spend time in the dungeons than myself."

Bajak and Faomen stopped circling. Bajak lowered his sword as his brother-in-arms kept his high.

"I'd rather die by your hand than go back to my Sword-father without the Shard of the Specter," Faomen said.

"I'd rather kill all three of you than listen to more of your bickering," a voice called.

The intruders turned to face the back of the shop.

Emerald Ezzy stood on the stacked boxes with a crossbow at each of her hips. A long whip coiled in tight loops hung from her cockeyed leather belt. The whip was made from the skeleton of a snake. The green light from the goblin blade made her shadow a towering phantom looming on the wall behind her.

"You folks come into my shop to browse or buy? Anyone takes from me, I take their life."

She was dripping wet. Her hair was slicked back and her cotton clothes clung to her body.

Bajak pointed his sword at Ezzy. "You should be leagues into the Angered Sea. You were on board the *Green Flash*," he said, incredulous.

"Pirates' heads are filled with seaweed," Ezzy scoffed. "You think the king was the only marionette that danced while I was pulling strings at court?" Her eyes narrowed. "Why play one fool when you can play the whole lot of 'em?" Ezzy turned her eyes to Hallita. "I'm disappointed in your families. I can tell where you're from by the way you look. I expected Dark Water to show up tonight. Maybe Ashfall, too, if their minds weren't dribbling out of their ears. But the Syrens should have known better. Your trade is turning people into puppets. Of course, what you pull to make the men do your bidding isn't a string, it's their manhood."

With fire in her eyes, Hallita hissed at Ezzy.

"Enough!" Bajak roared. "You have two bolts and there are three of us. You can't reload fast enough to kill us all."

"Better men than the likes of you have tried to kill me. I sent them all to be trampled by the thundering horde," Ezzy said. "And if you kill me, how will you ever find that pretty sword you're trying to steal?"

"Is it real?" Hallita growled. "Or were you lying about that, too?"

"It's real. Lies grow best from a kernel of truth. They taste sweeter that way, too. Makes the bitterness of the lie easier for the witless to swallow." Ezzy held the crossbows wide, pointing one at Hallita and the other at the Dark Waters. "I can sell a real sword for real gold. When it's found later, that clumsy husband of mine is to blame. Nobody would think that poor little Ezzy, who shed *so many tears* before the king, could be responsible." Ezzy sighed. "Truth be told, my husband's wits are as dim as yours. He better hope the king and queen find him before me. And if the crown wants me to offer them my rare goods first, well, they need to pay fair coin for a fair chance."

As Ezzy spoke, the Dark Waters surveyed the room for strong barriers.

"We're not leaving here without the Shard of the Specter," Faomen said in a cold voice. "You can either give it to us or we can burn down your shop. With you inside."

He spread a side of his cloak wide to reveal glass bottles filled with light brown liquid. They were tucked in pockets sewn on the inside. The liquid sloshed as the bottles swayed.

"What's that?" Ezzy asked. She raised the crossbow aimed at Faomen.

"Magic water that we take from whales," Faomen replied. "This water burns like dragon blood. If you put one of those bolts in me, when my body hits the floor the candle goes with me. The bottles will break and when the flame hits that brown water, everything in here will be turned into the same fine ash that covers your shelves." He raised his eyebrows and tilted his head. "Now, where is this sword that can't be seen? If you tell me, that will be the only thing you lose tonight."

Ezzy hooked a crossbow onto her belt and grabbed her whip. She stood with her legs spread wide, a crossbow resting against her shoulder, and the whip twitching at her feet.

"Nobody tells me what to do in my shop. Not the crown, not the Kingdom Guard, and not the Swordfamilies. I don't care if a Swordfather walks in here, this is my castle and my keep. The four walls around you are the borders of mine own realm. I own everything and everyone in here." She pointed the whip's handle at the Dark Waters. "Get out of my sight and I'll consider not putting a bolt in your back as you leave."

Faomen kept the side of his cloak pulled open. With his other hand, he moved the candle near the bottles of brown water. "I'd rather die than fail my Swordfather." He brought the flame closer to a bottle, where it licked at the glass.

"I wonder," Ezzy laughed. "When they throw you down that whirlpool does it suck out your brains?"

Faomen heard the thrum of her crossbow and the crack of the bolt piercing Bajak's skull. The Dark Water crumpled to the floor with the bolt's fletching pressed against his forehead.

In the same instant, Ezzy brought around her whip. Its snake bones clacked as it lashed Faomen's candle, snuffing out the flame. Faomen's hand sprouted a bright red streak where the tip snapped, but the bottles in his cloak didn't move.

The candle fell to the ground as Hallita ducked for cover.

Bajak's enormous body fell back against the shelves behind him. They rocked under the force of his weight. The iron pot on the flat stone rested on a shelf above him. It swayed from the impact and the pot tipped from its stone base. Dragon's blood glowing like lava splashed over Bajak's quivering body.

Smoke filled the shop as Ezzy gripped her loaded crossbow and fired a bolt at Faomen. His reflexes were quicker than his wits and he dodged it. Instead, the bolt sank so far into Bajak's gut that the head, shaft, and fletching disappeared to become the dead captain's last supper.

Ezzy screamed about the torture she would inflict on them. She produced another bolt and reloaded a crossbow.

On all fours, Faomen crawled to Bajak and the thick smoke pouring from his body. He pulled a bottle of brown water from his cloak and dragged the top of it through a puddle of smoldering dragon blood.

With the acrid smoke and putrid smell of burning flesh driving tears from his eyes, he lobbed the bottle at Ezzy as she finished reloading the crossbow. She dropped flat against the boxes and the bottle flew over her. It shattered where it landed. Ezzy roared as the dragon blood set the brown water ablaze at the back of the shop. Pulling herself up, she scrambled away from the fire that grew with a voracious appetite.

"I'll drown every one of you Dark Water scum!" she yelled so loud that the Swordfamily on *Shark Queen* may have heard her.

On her knees and searching through the thickening smoke, Ezzy loosed another bolt. The bolt pass through the purple and white snakeskin. Almost as fast as the bolt had sped away, a dagger from Hallita streaked toward Ezzy. In its wake, it left a deep cut through Ezzy's cheek.

Hallita clutched her remaining dagger and sprinted past Faomen. She lowered her shoulder and crashed against the door. It clattered open and she disappeared into the night. A man on the dock shrieked in pain and the sound of her footfalls receded in the distance.

Faomen uncinched his cloak and rolled it into a ball. The bottles of brown water inside it clinked as he worked behind a veil of smoke. He gave Bajak one last look. Then he heaved the cloak into the flames behind the stacked boxes. A ball of fire blew out the back of the shop.

Ezzy's enraged howl eclipsed the flames' roar. Then came the sound of splashing water.

The heat from the fireball pushed Faomen to the doomed shop's front. In a daze, he sat with his legs splayed. The gaping hole where the back wall had been now pulled the smoke and fire out toward the city.

As the smoke rushed away from Faomen, he saw the shape of a sword pierce through the gray. The point was lodged in a rafter that supported the swaying roof. The sword hilt hung above the giant battle axe.

Faomen became detached from his surroundings, as if he were falling deeper into himself. Time slowed. A stack of shelves collapsed to one side. Flames burned on his other side, consuming the remains of Bajak's body. Cold wind gusted in from the back of the shop. It fanned the flames around him and hit Faomen's face like a volley of ice-cold daggers.

Thick cinders swirled as the thundering gods taunted

him for the ash that he had thrown earlier that night. His arms screamed as he pushed himself from the floor. He drew one last deep breath and held it tight as a jealous lover. Stomping clouds of ash into the air, he ran to the battle axe and grabbed tight to its haft. Faomen's muscles throbbed as he awkwardly climbed the axe. His eyes felt as if they were the bright coals at the bottom of a raging fire.

The axe wobbled as Faomen put his knees on either side of its head. He saw nothing more than waves of heat and black smoke. Thrashing his arms above his head he felt only air, nearly hot as flame. Then he swung around and skin from his forearm was shaved off. It fell like a dry leaf in late autumn.

Blood poured from the wound. Denying the pain he knew would come back to collect its debt a hundredfold, he groped at the air. Something cold and unseen knocked against his hand. Reaching his fingers with a feather touch, Faomen felt the hilt of the invisible sword. He grasped it with both hands. With his failing strength he tried to wrench it free from the rafter.

It did not budge.

The giant battle axe shuddered. Its blade fell through the wood plank floor to smash open a gaping hole. Faomen's legs flailed as he clutched the invisible grip tight. His heartbeats launched spurts of blood from his wounded arm. He moved one hand, then the other, to the cross guard above the grip.

His body spasmed as he pulled hard with both hands. Kicking his feet, he struggled to bring down the sword with all of his body's weight. Sweat rained from him as the flames greedily devoured every piece of wood above the water.

He accepted death, but he would not accept defeat.

Another blast of frigid air swept into the doomed shop. With blood trickling from where his hands gripped the cross guard, Faomen curled his legs up to the ceiling. He placed his feet on the rafter above as his eyes fixed on the water below.

Faomen thanked Hanngoh for the honor of serving as a Dark Water captain. Then he pushed against the rafter, only to find that his strength had fled. The force was little more than a man twice his age could muster.

But it was enough.

He freed the Shard of the Specter from the wood. Faomen fell headfirst into the gaping hole the battle axe had smashed open. The splash as he plunged beneath the water sent a bolt of fear through him.

Salt stung his eyes and his wounded arm. He thrashed in the water, searching for an escape from the collapsing shop. Flaming chunks of wood hissed as they rained down around him. He stabbed the sword at them in a frenzy.

Faomen clawed at the water. He desperately tried to get away from the shop before it collapsed. The burning in his lungs was now hotter than the flames above him. Yet he held the Shard of the Specter tighter than the precious air in his chest.

His vision darkened as he struggled. The bright flames shining above became dim.

The sea beneath him began to swirl. The first white wisps were small. They spun in wide circles. When the current touched Faomen, he felt the same warmth he'd enjoyed in his youthful days playing on the sun-soaked shores south of Fulccrum. The water caressed his body, soft as a Syren. The white water spun all around him as its circles flowed ever closer.

Water, warm as blood, gripped Faomen tight.

The whirlpool spirited him away from the shop, fast as a courser in an open field.

Faomen had one thought before everything went black. He trusted that Hanngoh's loyal servant would carry him home.

CHAPTER TWELVE
EMERALD CROWN

A crimson fire blazed. The stones of the fireplace mantel were hot, as though they had washed up on the Lava Sea's shore. Fed with dry wood that burned like kindling, the flames rose high into the flue.

Voden and her king stood before the fire. They both stared into the same flames, but their minds were in far different places. The beads of sweat that sprang from the king's face were only partly due to the roaring fire.

"Pity the king who struggles to rule the dais in his own throne hall," Fallov whispered. His eyes did not leave the beckoning flames inside the fireplace. "It's said that across the Pader Mountains there's an hourglass so huge that instead of sand, it's filled with the skulls of men." He ground his palms into his eyes. "I don't believe it myself, but I've often lain awake at night between my silk sheets thinking about those skulls dropping through the neck of that hourglass. Do they shatter into sand when they fall to the bottom? Mayhaps they break apart slowly, after many trips from one end to the other. I ponder how many are stubborn and refuse to split, damning themselves to an eternity of futility."

As the fire crackled, a flaming cinder jumped onto the hearth.

Voden cleared her throat. "Your grace, I'm afraid that I must be the bearer of painful tidings."

"You have something painful to tell me?" he chuckled. "Good. It'll prepare me for when my wife arrives."

"It's your nephew."

"Oh? Did the Kingdom Guard find him? Or did Lord Wrand stumble upon him skipping stones on the Lava Sea?"

"How I wish that were the case. Sadly, he met a cruel end." Voden wet her lips. "His bones were discovered in the dragon refuge."

"Bones?"

"Yes, my king. His charred remains were found in a field. The earth around them was scorched. The dragons burned him."

The king closed his eyes tight. "Are you certain? If the bones were badly burned, it could have been anybody. Foolhardy townsfolk wander out there all the time."

Voden placed her hand on the king's shoulder. "The bones were about the same size as Romlad." She cleared her throat. "And the skull in the remains had three gold teeth."

"Three?"

Voden squeezed the king's shoulder. "No more. No less."

Fallov closed his eyes and bowed his head. He sighed, pulling the hot air deep into his chest. "You're telling me that Kardas's dragons killed Romlad?"

"I am," Voden whispered.

Empty suits of armor stood rigid around the war room.

Each one of them had been worn by the fighter who bested every other man and woman in the Melee of the Risen Knight. The tournament was a grand battle among scores of the strongest fighters in the realm. Unlike most tournaments, the Melee of the Risen Knight was a battle to the death. Only the victor left the Colosseum in Stonebann alive.

The victor basked in magnificent glory and was feted by the entire realm. If they weren't a knight before, they were knighted on the arena floor. The crown offered each one a momentous prize and the townsfolk made certain that no champion ever paid for a tankard of ale in Fulccrum again. Only one man had declined the crown's prize.

Gouges, dents, and punctures marred every suit. Some of them were missing entire pieces, such as breastplates and gauntlets. Half of a great helm was missing from one. Each suit of armor stood on a pedestal made of marble. In the stone, the knight's name was carved along with the year they had won the melee. An inscription told the tale of how the knight had battled. Words etched in marble did not tell the story of harrowing violence as deftly as the mangled armor standing above it.

One suit of steel armor was adorned with spikes and blades. The knight who wore this armor had won his melee after falling into a pit in the arena floor. The pits were narrow and deep so that the knights who dropped into them only had one way out—kill the others and climb their bodies. The pits were lined with copper so the opening above was the only escape, even for spilled blood. The copper lining made them watertight. To keep out rainwater, the pits were covered when the Colosseum was dormant. The townsfolk called these pits the Copper Crucibles. Flecks of copper had been wedged in the gaps on this suit of armor, where the knight had slammed against the pit wall.

Trembling with rage, Fallov walked to this suit of armor. Its steel rattled as he grabbed the morning star clutched in its gauntlet. The king tugged at the handle, but the empty armor refused to yield its weapon. He put his leather boot on its cuisse and pulled hard. The morning star broke free with the gauntlet still attached.

Fallov stormed back to the fireplace. Clutching the weapon's haft, he brought the spiked steel ball down onto the roaring flames. Red hot embers leapt as the king smashed the burning wood again and again. His sweat fell to the hearth, where it sizzled away. Voden took two steps back, distancing herself from the rain of cinders.

"*Damn! Damn! Damn!*" King Fallov raged.

The middle of the burning logs collapsed into a heaping pile of red coals. Fallov's strength fled. He left the morning star lodged in the pile where the flames licked at its iron-wood haft. The gauntlet still held the weapon tight, hanging just above the hearth.

Fallov put his hand over his eyes and permitted himself a sob. Struggling to remain kingly, he swallowed hard and cleared his throat.

"The boy was always wandering out to that treacherous refuge. He was so cross with me when I sent him to Lord Wrand's care. Kept yelling nonsense about how the dragons were part of his spirit." The king punched a fist in his palm. "Who found him?"

"A group of Kingdom Guard assigned to search the refuge discovered his remains late in the morning several days ago. It took the guards time to confirm they were Romlad's bones."

"Why did he keep sneaking out there?" Fallov used his

heel to crush some embers on the hearth into black smudges. "That's how he got those gold teeth in the first place. He knew they were dangerous. Why would he travel all the leagues back from Wrand's holdings to make the same mistake twice?"

"Dragons have an allure that some simply cannot resist."

"Indeed. I must speak with Kardas." Fallov ran his fingers through his dark brown hair. "Has there been any word from Lord Wrand?"

"No."

"He failed to protect my nephew and now he fails to tell me of it," Fallov said. "Is there anything more?"

Voden shook her head.

Fallov sighed and his shoulders sagged.

The oak door to the room was adorned with carvings of predators found in the land, sea, and air. Pounding on the door made those adornments tremble.

"Her majesty Queen Minacia has arrived," Melyq shouted through the door.

Voden strode across the room. She laid her hand on the pull and paused, looking back at the king for his assent. Fallov's royal blue mantle rose as he shrugged. Cold air rushed in from the hall as Voden opened the door.

Melyq passed by Voden without a word. Chill air followed him into the war room.

The queen, prince Opvolk, and the oldest princess, Silny, marched toward the king in single file.

"King Fallov, we meet again here in our bedchamber," Minacia said. She smiled with her mouth and frowned with her eyes. "Pardon my mistake, this isn't our bedchamber. It's our war room. Ofttimes I confuse the two because we tend to discuss hostilities in both places."

"We also tend to shout at each other in both places," Fallov replied in a disinterested tone. "Of course, the same could be said for every chamber in our castle. Wherever we meet has all the warmth of an ice house. But I didn't call you here to trade insults. We need speak of an urgent matter. Before we do, I might ask why you've brought Opvolk and Silny here. This isn't a game to entertain ourselves. We're discussing the defense of our realm."

"One day our children will be charged with protecting our family's crown. Best they learn the paramount importance of strategy now, lest they sit on the throne and believe these figures on the table are playthings."

The king stood at one end of the war table. Minacia put her hands on her hips after she moved to the opposite end. The counselors positioned themselves near their respective sovereigns. Prince Opvolk and Princess Silny stood midway between their parents.

"What happened there?" Silny asked, pointing at the fireplace.

The gauntlet finally released its grip on the morning star's haft. It fell to clatter against the hearth.

"I was tending the fire," Fallov replied.

On the table before them was a map depicting the territory held by the Emerald and Crimson Crowns. The table held far more than a flat painting that showed the realms. It was covered in miniatures of the land's features. The Pader Mountains stood tall between the two realms, their peaks colored white to show the snowcaps. Mount Densmore, the tallest of them all, loomed over the range. Servants had cleared away the gems that Fallov's scepter had littered on the map when the king had attacked a Pader Mountain with it.

Near an edge painted blue with the Angered Sea, Fulccrum had been carefully crafted by artisans that labored day and night for many eclipses. The Gods' Blade stood high over everything else in the city, except the nearby castle towers. Even the bases for the planned grand statue of a knight were included in the map's details. A brown line that began at the capital city's East Gate represented the Shamrock Road meandering through the Emerald Realm. On its route were most of the realm's largest cities, such as Alermond, Caviskillen, Salamar, and Forfur.

"I admire the artisans for including those little white flags over the Shrines of Solace," Minacia said as she studied the Satinwind district.

"We're inside there, right?" Opvolk asked. He pointed at a high tower in the castle.

"That's right," Voden replied.

"Making those little shoes out by the port must've been quite a chore," Silny said.

"They're not shoes," Melyq corrected. "They're sabatons. Knights in armor wear them on their feet."

"Isn't there supposed to be a knight straddling the entrance to the port?" Silny pressed. "When will the rest of the statue be finished?"

The queen roared with laughter. The king felt very tired.

Melyq waited until Minacia had quieted before he spoke. "The Whenyards, who preceded your parents on the throne, began building the Grandest Champion of Fulccrum. Progress on the statue has been...slow."

"I expect that our great-great-great-grandchildren will sit upon the throne when the last stone is laid," Minacia said dismissively.

Servants cleared the gauntlet from the hearth. They dropped more logs into the fireplace, where the flames immediately set upon the wood.

"This is a war council?" Silny asked as she slid her hand along the table edge.

"Of late, every discussion in this castle is a war council," Fallov sighed. "Breakfasts, lunches, and suppers all devolve into war councils. The only difference is which war is discussed. Here and now, we're not talking about the war within the castle walls." He put both hands on the table and leaned on them heavily. "We're discussing the threat from beyond the Pader Mountains."

"The Crimson Crown?" Opvolk asked.

"Yes," Voden replied. "They have all but declared war against us. The fools believe that we're weak. They mistake the quarreling that sometimes exists between the king and queen as a lack of resolve. They couldn't be more wrong."

Fallov labored for a few breaths before he managed a smile. "When your mother and I engage in spirited discussion, we're sharpening each other's minds the same way knights hone their skills when they're sparring."

Minacia threw her head back and laughed until she snorted and covered her mouth.

Fallov wiped the sweat from his brow. He unclasped his royal mantle and threw it on a plush chair. The light shirt that he wore underneath was soaked through.

"Do you see those?" Fallov asked. He pointed at figurines in the Emerald Crown's realm. They were made of emeralds larger than a bird's egg mounted to wooden bases shaped like crowns. Next, he gestured at the pieces on the other side of the Paders, in the Crimson Crown's territory. The pieces for their rivals were similar, except that the gemstone on each base was a ruby. "The gems are our armies and those of our enemies. The emeralds are ours; the rubies are theirs."

Minacia strolled over to stand next to the Emerald

Crown's castle. She raised her hand to show the king the diamond bracelet wrapped around her wrist. The rouge flames in the fireplace made the stones flicker like candle flame.

She used her teeth to rip a stone from the bracelet and spit it into the Emerald Crown's castle.

"I gave that to you at our coronation ceremony!" King Fallov protested.

The queen smirked. She pulled another diamond from the bracelet. It landed in the castle and rattled against the walls. She wrenched free six more diamonds and dropped them into the same spot in the castle's bailey.

"Why would you do that? You've ruined a thing of beauty," the king said in exasperation.

"The emeralds are the Emerald Crown's forces and the Crimson Crown has its armies." Minacia plucked a ruby token from the map. With her other hand, she picked up the diamonds. "These are the children, my counselor, and myself. They are *my* forces. We aren't armies, but what we lack in numbers..." She winked at her husband and returned the six diamonds to the bailey. "We make up for with our cunning."

The king sighed. His eyes wandered through the Emerald Kingdom to settle on a piece of land some leagues from the capital city. The verdant ground was marked with streaks of dark black soot. Boulders were strewn about its rolling hills. Near the Pader Mountains, the king latched onto a familiar sight, the Castle of Towers. He squinted at the towers where he saw tiny eggs in the dragon nests.

Opvolk followed his father's eyes. "Does the Castle of Towers have no moat? I don't see any water around it."

The shadow of a grin fluttered over the king's mouth. "Oh, yes, it certainly has a moat," he replied. "But it's not in the ground. It's in the air and it's made of fire." His brow furrowed as he stared at the dragon eggs. "Mayhaps my old friend Kardas could be of some aid here. The dragons aren't the terrors they once were, but they're still potent. No doubt they could be used to cut off the mountain passes that the Crimson Crown would favor. It wouldn't take many dragons to seal them off. A little fire could burn a long way."

The queen's mustard yellow dress swished against the stone floor as she stomped to the fireplace. Grabbing the fireplace tongs, she reached deep underneath the blazing flame. She snapped the tongs together and grasped a large coal that glowed a brilliant red.

A curl of thin smoke followed the coal as the queen returned to the map. She swung the tongs around and held the coal above a field in the dragon refuge. Part of the refuge was circled by boulders. With movement that was both careful and slow, the queen set the coal down in the center of the circle. Puffs of black smoke rose as the coal smoldered on the wood map.

"Why are you destroying the war table?" King Fallov asked warily. "What's that supposed to be?"

"Romlad," the queen said. She whipped the iron tongs to the floor, where they left a black streak on the stone. "Your favorite nephew. Or what's left of him. You do remember him, don't you? That bright-eyed youth that used to make you laugh so hard that your crown would fall off?" The queen folded her arms and glared at her husband. "You propose to ask the Fire Keepers for aid? A jest! You should bring them all into court and make them answer for the murder of Romlad."

The king sensed the air around him become heavier.

"The boy was ofttimes found in the dragon refuge, it's

true," Melyq said as he stood next to his queen. "But that does not excuse the Fire Keepers from making the lands outside of Fulccrum dangerous for the Emerald Crown's leal subjects, particularly a blood relation of our king. Their group has an ability to influence the dragons in a way that others cannot. They should have used that power to tame those dangerous beasts." Melyq's head trembled. "Romlad's blood is on their hands. No, that's not right. Romlad's ash is at their feet."

Thin gray smoke spread over the dragon refuge and wafted toward Fulccrum. Moments later, the smoke tickled at the old city wall within the capital.

Voden glared at Melyq.

Fallov remained silent.

"Why are there only green and red pieces on the map?" Opvolk asked. "What of the other kingdoms? What of their colors? I don't see a single amethyst here."

Melyq picked up an emerald token and held it close to his eye. "The Amethyst Crown's two kings are one of many powers near and far. There are others, such as the Garnet Kingdom. Some kingdoms bow to no king; the realms rule themselves." He peered into the emerald and returned it to the map. "That host has an imperfection."

Voden shook her head. "They won't interfere. The distance between us and the amethysts is too great. Even if they desired a conquest, the reward of our kingdom would be too difficult to hold. Our friendly ears near the Crimson Crown are the only ones who have told us of interest in our lands. The two red queens believe the time to strike is ripe. Depending on how the king and *queen* handle this situation, they may be correct."

The fire kept crackling as it burned.

"What was the name of that lord?" Silny asked. She

always wore blue feathers in her black hair to highlight the pale shade of blue in her eyes. "The man who asked you about the gold when we were in court?"

Melyq pointed to a castle nestled tight against the west side of the Paders. Its walls were smooth as pond water because the castle had been carved from the mountain. "That was Lord Kellington. His castle and keep are there."

"Yes, Kellington, that's right," Silny said. "He spoke of loyalty and moving mountains for the crown. He mentioned gold and Father acted like some beggar down by the docks with his hand out." She leaned over the table and pressed a finger on Kellington's castle. "You have a problem and I've put my finger on it." She withdrew from the castle, dragging her finger across the map. "Look at all the mines on his land. I suspect your mapmakers understand how much wealth that lord surely harbors. That gold could supply an army or two, no? I imagine your words put most of it in fat pouches hidden under Kingdom Guard armor."

A suit of armor standing in the room had belonged to a woman, judging by the breastplate. Silny left the map and neared it. She briefly inspected the large hole through the plackart that was punched through both its front and back. Silny wrested the sword from the armor's gauntlet. As she walked back to the war map, she dragged the sword point on the floor.

"Look at this pass right here," she said in a controlled tone as she brought the blade around in a great sweeping arc. It came down hard near the Pader Mountains and cut so deep into the wooden foothills that when Silny took her hands off its grip, the sword remained lodged in the map.

"We have wooden rods that you can use to point at places on the map," Voden said through teeth clenched. She gestured at several long, straight pointers leaning on a rack.

Silny shrugged. "You see where that blade is wedged, Father? In the pass next to that pretty castle with all that gold flowing out from the mountains. That's just one pass on his lands. There are others. If those passes are wide enough, the Crimson Crown could bring many, many knights through the mountains."

"Kellington will remain loyal," the king growled.

His daughter shook her head.

"Kellington will remain loyal *enough*," King Fallov said, his voice tempered by some long-forgotten bit of patience. "He's been a leal vassal so long as your mother and I have sat upon our thrones. I offered him a fair compromise. You desire the gold, you pay the tax. That's life."

Silny spread her olive hands wide as she leaned over the map, toward her father. Voden winced as the princess's right hand crushed a small village. "What if you're wrong? What if Kellington isn't as loyal as you think he is?"

The king stood well away from the fire; nonetheless he kept dripping sweat. "He's not the only lord who's loyal to us near the Paders. We also have the Bynningtyn, Faremother, and Wickundun Houses. Also, that other one, the lady who runs the castle perched high on the mountains."

"Slaeton," the queen said as she yawned.

"Yes! That's the one. Must have taken her family almost as long to carve the castle from the mountains as it took the thundering horde to lift the mountains from the soil." Fallov clawed at his neck under his collar. "And Lord Wrand on the east side of the Paders remains loyal as ever. He may be our only friend under the Crimson Crown, but he is a good one."

"The same Lord Wrand that lost Romlad and fed his well-cooked flesh to a dragon?" the queen asked.

Melyq cleared his throat loudly. "We've heard nothing

from Wrand since his men brought that strange chest to Fulccrum. Need I remind you that it was filled with lava rock! The lord may be loyal, but are his men?"

The king ignored them both. "Each one of those houses would send messenger pigeons at the first sign of the Crimson Crown. I've given them all very explicit commands to do so." Fallov nodded, as if trying to convince himself more than his audience.

"I don't see many emeralds near the mountains," the king's daughter sneered. "Will they be enough?"

"Why don't you ask your mother?" Fallov sputtered. "She would know whatever the Crimson Crown is planning better than me. Between our dueling spies, for some strange reason, hers seem to know more about the reds than mine."

The queen had her retort nocked like an arrow and ready to loose, but Melyq cut her off. "Your grace, the crown is unified from top to bottom. From this high tower all the way to the bottom of the port. All of our listening ears and seeing eyes toil as one. They provide the same secrets to our rulers who sit on the throne, no matter the color of their mantle."

Voden scoffed at him.

"Enough," the king barked. "This squabbling is a distraction from the greatest threat that our family has faced. The reds see the Unbloodied Throne and think us weak. We can join together to defend our crown, or we can watch green bleed into red. Make no mistake, that red won't be mere banners hanging in the stead of our own. There will be fires sweeping through our lands like a plague, laying waste to everything that we hold dear. Our family's blood will be spilled in the throne hall, mayhaps on the throne itself."

The queen plucked an emerald token from their realm and sauntered to the reds' territory.

The castle from which the Crimson Crown reigned over its lands stood in their capital city of Lysnap. The towers seemed to grow from the ground as if they were crystals of rock thrust up from beneath the land. Not one stood up straight and all of them had tips with sharp points. The outside walls were ringed with a moat made of lava. The drawbridge was made of iron. When it was lowered, it lay high above the moat so that the iron wouldn't melt and the riders wouldn't linger.

Ruby tokens ringed the castle and lay thick as dragon scales across the Crimson Crown's lands. One patch of land was littered with tiny arcs of blue that represented Dancing Water. It had four ruby tokens on it placed so close together that they touched each other.

In the castle's bailey stood two ruby tokens. "The gems are supposed to be guards, but let's call these two in the bailey queens," Minacia said as she caressed the two rubies. "The two queens that rule the Crimson Queendom have always struck me as capable leaders. Their people are content. They wave their banners high at every festival. Sometimes I wonder…" She set the emerald token atop the two ruby tokens. "If their people and court might be eager to add a third throne. It is said, by me, that the only thing better than *two* queens is *three* queens."

The king slammed his fist on the table. "Thu'gods! I should have just thrown the emerald tokens in the fire!" He paused, trembling with his jaw clenched tight. "This is why the reds are massing their forces. It's why there're twice as many rubies over there as emeralds over here." He brought his fist down again. This time, he made the Gods' Blade shake.

Voden placed some tokens in the Emerald Kingdom, halfway between Fulccrum and the Paders. They were spaced apart by leagues. "The numbers heavily favor the Crimson Crown. Many times, war is little more than figures. That's why I counsel moving the majority of our Kingdom Guard to the middle of the realm, with some leagues between them." She adjusted the spacing between two tokens. "We can't defend every pass between here and our enemy. But if we have our forces positioned at these intervals, we can lie in wait until they begin dribbling through the narrow passes. That's when we attack, when much of their strength is trapped in the mountains. The Kingdom Guard assembled out in the field will be coiled like snakes, waiting to strike."

The flames in the fireplace had shrunk to half their earlier size. King Fallov's skin was dusted with salt where his sweat had dried.

"That's a sensible approach," Fallov said to himself. He eyed the tokens arrayed near the Paders. "We can plug the gaps by quickly deploying our hosts where they're needed." He pushed one token to the east, near a pass. Then he slid a token close to where the defending token had stood. "That scheme won't provoke the Crimson Crown, but it will give them pause. Then we can maneuver diplomatically to stave off war. And the Kingdom Guard can be recalled to Fulc-crum should the need arise." He gave his counselor an approving look. "The gambit carries risk with it, to be sure, but it strikes a good balance between aggression and patience."

"Men lay plans that the thundering horde tramples," Silny whispered.

Servants mounded more wood on the fire and stoked its

flames to new heights. Opvolk helped himself to a goblet of wine.

Queen Minacia made her way around the edge of the war map. She picked up as many emerald tokens as she could carry. She returned to stand behind the reds' castle.

The king was filled with dread.

She placed the green tokens by the moat surrounding the Crimson Crown's castle.

Opvolk took a deep pull from his gilded goblet.

"War," Minacia said, her voice tempting as a ready lover. "We march every Kingdom Guard outside Fulccrum through the passes and lay waste to the reds." One at a time, she picked up an emerald token and used it to knock down a ruby.

"Kill them all. Let the thundering horde trample the bodies," Opvolk said. He sipped from the goblet.

"This is the first time that you've been tested," the queen continued. "Your father before you never had need of armies and bloodshed. His mind was far sharper than his blade." She gave her husband a patronizing smile. Fallov recognized it as the same smile that she showed their children the first time they walked. "Upon the Unbloodied Throne sits an untested king."

The fire crackled as the suits of armor maintained their silent vigil.

"There's that Syren charm of yours," the king grumbled at the queen.

"You know what charms I have. Or, you used to know," the queen said. She glared at Voden. "I'm not ridiculing you. I'm offering sage advice."

Silny pressed on the longest blue feather in her hair. Opvolk drank more wine.

"You would sacrifice our kingdom, our castle, and our

family to spite me. You would smash our thrones into kindling and feed it into the reds' castle hearths," King Fallov sputtered, reaching his open hand toward the queen. "Please tell me that I am mistaken."

"I will tell you this. When I choke the life from you, I will use a rope because I would not deign to place my hands on the throat that has spewed so many lies." The queen spoke to the king as she again glared at Voden.

The eldest daughter and son of the royal couple continued to play with feathers and drink wine. The two counselors locked eyes.

The king's hands shook on the war map as he struggled to compose himself.

"With or without your aid, I will defend our kingdom," he said in a tremulous voice. "If the reds dare to worm through the passes, the Kingdom Guard will build new mountains within the Paders from piles of their dead knights!"

Snarling in disgust, the queen marched over to a candelabrum that held a score of candles. Wax hugged the sides of each candle, as if the flame's tears were frozen against it. She yanked two from their holders. As she stomped back toward the map, the flames grew taller.

"This is your proposal?"

She leaned over the map and stretched her slender arms to hold the thick candles over the Paders. The candles were directly above narrow passes. As she tipped them, the wax poured down and splattered into the troughs between the tall mountains.

Her family and the counselors watched as the rain of wax became a mound in the valleys between the Paders' peaks.

"We defend ourselves by using the dead as rock?"

Minacia asked Fallov. "This wax would be a greater obstacle for the reds."

Her husband ground his teeth louder than the crackling from the fire. "I will array the very best knights of our Kingdom Guard near the Paders. Sir Rausthall, Medam Nepvand, Sir Yttrub, and Sir Thenkjen will be at the fore. They'll be joined by Sir Lindenfyre and Medam Irristax." He paused for a moment. "There must be others outside the Kingdom Guard that I could summon. There's the one with that peculiar armor called the Medam Murderer...the Dread Dawn...if she can be found."

"What about the Swordfamilies?" Princess Silny asked. She put her hand over the heart of Fulccrum. "The ones here, inside the city? They can force their will on others. The townsfolk certainly fear them. Maybe the Crimson Crown would, too." Silny closed her eyes tight. She snapped a blue feather in two. "The crown raises hosts from the realm. Inside the city walls, the families are their own hosts. Some commoners say even the Kingdom Guard fears the Swordfamilies. One family has a boat in the port that's bigger than anything in our navy."

King Fallov gave his daughter a genuine smile, surprised at her welcome change in tone. "I favor my approach, but yours is certainly a proposal worth pondering." The king crossed his arms. "Your strategy could make better mine own. If a family lent its strength to the Kingdom Guard, the fields in our realm would be more torturous to cross than the highest peaks in the Paders."

The king's eyes fell on the dragon refuge.

"You won't choose the path of strength, you won't attack?" Queen Minacia said in an even voice. "If I told you I was surprised, it would be a bigger lie than your wedding vows."

"My dear wife, I am bringing our approaches together. We will not attack, but we also won't hide the Kingdom Guard in Fulccrum. Instead, we'll station the Kingdom Guard as I suggested, and strengthen that force with the wisdom of our eldest daughter." The king offered the queen a timid smile. "Not too strong, not too weak. The right balance is struck. On the morrow, Voden will relay the plan to Sir Dadinaz, High Commander of the Kingdom Guard."

The queen smiled in an odd way. She tossed the burning candles onto the Lava Sea and strode toward the door.

Fallov quickened his steps to catch her. He grabbed her by the elbow and spun her around. "My queen," he began.

Before he could utter another word, she wrenched herself free and stormed away. The folds of her yellow dress snapped behind her like whips lashing at a rotten servant.

Fallov retreated to hunch over the Emerald Crown's castle.

The queen paused a few steps from the door. She stared at a suit of armor festooned with streaks of crimson. It had suffered merely a few nicks and scratches, a remarkable lack of damage for a Melee of the Risen Knight champion.

"Mother," Opvolk said in a whisper as he arrived at her side. "You must calm yourself." He took her hand in his own dark hand, squeezing it tight. "I would counsel you as you've done for me since I was a boy. Emotions are your enemy. Throw them in the deepest dungeon of your mind."

A flaming log rolled onto the hearth. Servants rushed to herd it back into its place.

Silny passed by them as they spoke, uninterested in their words. "If we don't master our emotions, our emotions will master us." The queen gently placed her palm on his dark cheek. "That's why you must guard your feelings as if they were more dear than your own life. Especially against family that is not your blood."

The cheek on the side of Opvolk's face that was white as bone turned a bright shade of red.

"You've taught me well, Mother," Opvolk whispered.

The queen pulled her hand away from his face.

"I'm not Hallita's thrall."

"To be a Syren is to have a power that few understand," the queen said. "If you truly believe that you are above her charms, you may well be under her spell." She sniffed at him. "You reek of her perfume."

"I know when to wear the mask to make her believe," Opvolk replied as he looked at his feet. "You know that I don't fancy her, or any of them. The dragon spike powder helps with that. She doesn't suspect."

"All the same, beware of her. Where there is love, there is vulnerability." Minacia put her hand under her son's chin and brought his face up to hers. "You are there for information, not satisfaction."

"Your teachings haven't fallen upon deaf ears," Opvolk assured her.

Queen Minacia kissed her son on his dark cheek.

The queen disappeared from the room. Opvolk drained the last of his wine. A suit of armor missing a cuisse was positioned with its gauntlet thrust out. Opvolk put his empty goblet in the steel glove's palm. Without another word or a glance toward his father, he slid through the doorway.

Voden shooed away the servants who had tended the fire. One of them took Opvolk's goblet from the gauntlet before they left. Voden slowly closed the door behind the last servant. Metal ground against metal as she spun the iron lock.

The king tapped his finger against the tiny tower that represented the place where he had just suffered his most recent defeat at the hands of his queen wife. His attention wandered to the port.

"Emerald Ezzy may be of some—" Voden began.

The king interrupted her. "Sometimes I dream of boarding a ship at dawn and ordering the captain to sail into the Angered Sea. I could throw the captain overboard and let fate have her way with me."

Closing his fist tight, Fallov punched the Gods' Blade. He yelped in pain as it stood firm. Then he grabbed the obelisk and pulled with all of his might. With a groan and a crack, the monument broke at its base and tumbled to the floor. The king kicked it under the war table.

Voden undid the clasps on her armor. Her practiced fingers worked methodically. Piece by piece she removed the steel and set it down by the fire. The gold ornamentation lost much of its majesty on the floor.

"My armor is getting tight in places," she said, scratching her flanks.

She wore only the linen privy clothes and woolen hose that had kept the steel from chafing against her skin. She joined king Fallov on the Emerald Crown's side of the war table, bringing a goblet of wine with her.

"She spat on your plan," the king said.

"*Our* plan," Voden corrected. She handed him the goblet.

Fallov looked into the wine and watched as his reflection rippled in the tiny waves. Then he drank it all in a single motion and refilled it.

"Don't let her Syren's charms cloud your judgment. Dispel any lingering memories of the woman you once knew," Voden said. "Your mind has deceived itself into believing the myth of a king and queen who were once madly in love. There's no more truth to it than a story a minstrel would tell by a fire on a summer's eve."

The king drank too much wine. It was not nearly enough.

"My father could control people without uttering a command. He had a gift of thought and influence so great that he convinced a realm to give him the throne without unsheathing a single sword," Fallov said. He snickered as he found his own reflection in the wine again. "I could slay every dragon in the refuge and it wouldn't win Minacia's respect, only Kardas's ire." After a few more sips, the king set the goblet down on the war table. "I must see him soon. It's been too long."

Voden put her hand on the king's shoulder. "I'm sorry that I've done this to you," she said.

"You haven't done anything to me," the king said. "We did this." He put his hand on her belly. "It's the only thing that keeps me from drowning in either the Angered Sea or the bottom of a flagon." He raised the goblet to his lips, but he didn't drink from it. "What will you do when your armor won't fit anymore?"

The low flames in the fireplace flickered.

Voden shrugged.

The king pulled off his clothes and threw them on top of his royal mantle on the plush chair. He pulled off his counselor's woolen hose and linen privy clothes, dropping them into a crumpled pile on the floor.

King Fallov stood so close to her that he could feel her breath on his bare chest. He caressed her arms, moving to her breasts and then to her belly.

"It won't be long before I'm well swollen," she said,

returning the king's affection. "Soon, if I lay on this map, I'll be more of a mountain than the Paders."

The king didn't respond with words. He pressed his lips hard against hers. As the two closed together, his hands reached at the war table behind her. He carefully moved aside emerald tokens.

When Voden dug her nails into his back so deep that she drew blood, she backed herself farther into the Emerald Realm. Fallov put his knee on the edge of the map and threw himself on top of her.

They gripped each other hard as he entered. From a slow and methodical beginning, they worked into a quivering frenzy. Their arms and legs thrashed over the map.

Emerald armies, holds, and castles all went tumbling off the war table. Voden's foot kicked away a green token that shattered against the stone floor. Fallov's hand swept away half of Fulccrum, smashing it from the realm. The Emerald Crown's castle crashed against the stone floor, where it fractured into shards beyond counting. The more their passion consumed them, the more they flailed around the war table. Armies fell and allies disappeared.

When Fallov and Voden finished together, the end of their passion was the beginning of their regret. After spending their last full measure of ecstasy, the Emerald Kingdom lay in ruins beneath them.

CHAPTER THIRTEEN

HEAVIES

The frigid stream was clear as the air that Droena breathed. Like many mountain streams in the Emerald Kingdom, its bed was coated with smooth, flat stones. Their shades of brown, red, and gray shone brightly beneath the surface.

Large stones and boulders stood in the middle of the stream. Some were so tall that their tops were dry. Others had been split in two and both halves lay beneath the rushing water. These large stones under the surface were smooth all over, except for the jagged surface where they had cracked down the middle. The water coming down from the Paders that flowed over them had many years of work ahead before the newly exposed surface would be as smooth as the other rocks.

Upstream from where Droena stood, the water widened before narrowing again. The stream slowed at this point and became very still. Hidden beneath some low-hanging branches was a deep pool.

Near where the Heavy captain stood, sunlight sparkled like diamonds on the flowing water's rough surface. Birds sang as they darted low over the water between the trees near the stream. Schools of tiny minnows swam near the banks, flitting from the shelter of one shadow to another. In a copse on the far side of the stream, two fawns followed their doe. The deer idly nibbled at leaves and buds. In the deep pool upstream, a few ducks plunged their heads underwater.

Amid the idyllic grandeur of this natural beauty was a scene of ugly humanity.

A tall stone was particularly wide. Kneeling by this rock, on the upstream side of it, was a Heavy warrior. He wore nothing but the length of strong rope that bound his hands behind his back.

The kneeling warrior was Zrobik. Droena recognized the drawing of a horse inked into his back. What she didn't remember seeing on the warrior was a stab wound in his side that had not yet fully healed. It was raw and tender. Yellow pus oozed from it. He shivered from the cold mountain water rushing over his bare calves. It splashed up against his arse and back.

On the other side of the wide rock stood Raysk. The Swordfather loomed over the warrior. He was also stark naked, although much of his skin was hidden. He was covered in thick, woolly hair that grew like weeds all over his body. The only part of him that wasn't hidden behind a black coat was his scarred head that could sprout neither a beard nor hair on his crown.

As she drank in the scene before her, Droena was thankful that she didn't have to endure the sight of whatever remained of Raysk's manhood. *Even when that man is naked he looks as if he's wearing winter furs.* She stood farther back from the stream's bank than the other Heavies. In front of her stood Vasarox. His arms were stained dark red all the way to his elbows, a memento from his failed attempt to capture the Bleeding Blade. To her left was Kraaft, his arm still bandaged from the dragon fire he and his shield had endured in the refuge.

"You failed me, Zrobik," Raysk growled. "It was such an easy task that I gave you." The shaft of his war hammer lay on his shoulder. Sun reflected off its steel head as Raysk paced.

Tears fell from Zrobik's eyes, surviving for only a moment before they disappeared into the rushing water that swept them downstream.

"Please, my Blade. I beg you. Please. Have mercy," Zrobik said in between sobs. "Send me to debtor's prison. Please. Anything but this."

Raysk smiled at the warrior. "This *is* mercy." He laughed. "The last man that failed me, I hanged him from a tree and used his own entrails as the rope!"

Consulary Pametan frowned.

"The weaker the throne, the stronger the Heavies!" Raysk boomed. Water licked at his knees as he paced in the stream. "To weaken the throne, I must needs weaken their allies. The Shard of the Specter would've hastened a decisive blow." The scars on his brow became a darker shade of red as he clenched his eyes shut. "That sword could be more useful than the Bleeding Blade." Dipping a cupped hand into the stream, he splashed the water on his face and the back of his neck. "A blade that cannot be seen gifts its swordsman the advantage of surprise. A child could kill with an invisible sword. Even *you* might've been able to do it."

Teska looked up at the sun and sneezed loud enough that a fawn across the way raised its head in alarm.

"To me, swords are little more than daggers," Raysk

said. "But if I had the Bleeding Blade in one hand and the Shard of the Specter in the other, the Swordfathers would be the ones begging on their knees before me. Not you."

Vasarox tensed at the mention of the Bleeding Blade. He clasped his hands behind his back to hide the red stain on his arms that was even darker than his skin.

Raysk sat on the tall stone. He faced the bank where Vasarox, Pametan, Droena, and Teska stood. Behind them was a group of warriors, one of which was named Nasabrun. Sitting with his shoulders hunched over and the war hammer resting on the stony streambed, the Swordfather drew a deep sigh.

"When I told you that taking the sword was important, did you understand its purpose?" Raysk glanced over his shoulder. Zrobik shook his head. "I could have used it to kill Kardas. With a single stroke I could've weakened the throne and beheaded the Fire Keepers." Raysk ground the war hammer's steel head into the small stones of the streambed. "And with thorough planning, it could have been used to deceive the other families. They would have blamed each other for Kardas's death." Raysk rubbed the scars on his temples. The palms of his hands were almost as scarred as his face. "In one swift stroke I would have undermined the throne, killed the Swordfather whose power is second only to my own, and put the blame on another Swordfamily."

Zrobik bowed his head. "I am sorry, my Blade," he muttered. The water was so cold that his calves had turned bright red.

Raysk laughed. "Feelings are folly."

"Please have mercy."

"Begging for mercy is also folly."

The doe and her fawns enjoyed their midday meal,

unperturbed by the theater taking place in the middle of the stream.

"So long as the Fire Keepers have their Swordfather and their dragons, the crown will be too strong for my liking. The royal row has weakened the throne, but the time is not yet ripe to strike. And I only throw loaded dice." Raysk stood and began circling his prey. "If you had done your duty, I would've made you a captain. You had only to take the sword."

A thick tree branch drifted by the wide stone. Raysk snatched it from the water before it sped past. The smaller growth had been stripped away from the limb.

"Do you see this piece of wood?" Raysk asked.

Zrobik shivered in response.

"It's probably been traveling for weeks now, carried by the stream's current. Do you know what this is?" He gripped the thick branch near each end. It was gray and rotted.

"Deadwood."

"That's right. Do you know what you are?" Raysk asked.

Zrobik didn't answer.

Raysk pulled the ends of the wood toward each other. The branch broke in the middle with a terrific crack. Splinters shot through the air as it shattered. Raysk dropped the two halves. They bobbed in the ripples on the surface. The pieces resumed their journey down the stream. In time, they would enter the Wandering Waters before finally being swept into Fulccrum's port and the Angered Sea.

The two fawns huddled close to their mother. The birds sang less now.

"The stream dragged that wood to us. It is nothing but a burden to everything around it. The water bore its weight." Raysk rubbed his hands under the surface, washing off the filth from the branch. "Just as you are a burden to my Swordfamily."

"My Blade, please," Zrobik said through gasping sobs. His bare legs trembled in the water that was nearly cold as ice. "I've done much for your family, *our* family. I have served loyally as a warrior for years." Zrobik's arms wiggled as he made a pathetic attempt to wipe the tears streaming down his face. The rope thwarted his efforts and kept his hands tight behind his back. "I've killed so many dragons to weaken the Fire Keepers. I risked being roasted like a pig on a spit when I obeyed your orders."

Where the stream was wide and still, a pair of mounted Kingdom Guard guided their horses to the water's edge. The ducks paddled away from the large animals. As their horses drank, the guards looked toward Raysk. He tossed his war hammer in the air and caught it, as if it was a small tree branch. Zrobik was naked and kneeling in the stream with his hands bound. The Swordfather motioned for the guards to continue their rounds. Obediently, they pulled on their reins and rode away from the Heavies.

"Killing dragons can be easy," Raysk continued. "Look at Kraaft's arm." The bandages wrapped around Kraaft's forearm were stained with dark red blood and bright yellow pus. "That was hard. He wasn't sneaking up to kill a sleeping dragon. He met one on a field of battle! Better still, the queen's man paid handsomely for it. Men like Kraaft are who I want by my side in the coming war."

Raysk set the head of his war hammer in the middle of the tall stone between himself and the warrior. He squatted across from Zrobik so their eyes were at the same height. The war hammer's shaft was centered exactly between them.

"I told you our family's code when you joined," Raysk whispered. "If you fail to execute my orders, I execute you."

Zrobik clenched his jaw. "Vasarox didn't get the Bleeding Blade. He didn't follow your commands and yet he stands over there on the bank." He spat on the wide stone, away from the head of the war hammer.

"It's true that Darker Hands came back from Auzken's tomb empty-handed."

"Blood red empty hands," Zrobik muttered.

"His failure and yours are not the same," Raysk said. Vasarox crossed his blood-stained arms across his wide chest. "That blade was gone when he arrived. He could not succeed. With no chance for success, there is no failure." Raysk contorted his face into a grotesque likeness of a smile. "Besides, Vasarox is a great captain and you are merely a warrior...who let the Shard of the Specter slip through his fingers."

Raysk stood and grabbed the war hammer's haft. He pressed the hammer's head under Zrobik's chin. As the bound warrior's head rose, he squinted from the brilliant sun behind Raysk's head.

"Yes, yes," Zrobik stammered. "But I have *earned* your mercy. Don't forget that me and Vasarox killed those Kingdom Guard."

Vasarox laughed hard. "Standing lookout is not the same as breaking the bones."

The doe and her fawns resumed grazing on a low bush.

"You failed to make the Heavies strong. If you are not strong, you are weak." Raysk rested the hammer's head on the streambed, leaning on it like a cane. "A Syren was closer to seizing the Shard of the Specter than you. Is that not true?"

Zrobik did not answer.

"I see that wound in your side. It's barely healed. That's how I know you're not a real Heavy. My family heals fast," Raysk said.

Zrobik trembled harder. "I know who has the sword," he gasped.

"I don't believe you."

"I heard Ezzy scream that she would drown every one of them. Right before the girl stabbed me and the shop fell into the water." He gasped for air. "It was Dark Water."

"Who was it? Which Dark Water took the sword?"

"I don't know. I didn't see."

"If you didn't see it with your own eyes, might be Ezzy still has it. Whoever Hanngoh sent could've failed him, just like you failed me."

"The Syren fled empty-handed."

"One of her hands wasn't empty if she stabbed you with a dagger."

"She didn't have the sword, I know it. If she did, the Dark Waters would've chased her. They wouldn't have stayed in the shop while it burned." Zrobik's head bobbed. "I fell when she cut me. That's when I saw swirling white water below the dock. It was strange. The port was so smooth. It went under the dock and when it came back out, I saw the shape of a man inside of it. The rushing water carried him."

"How do you know he had the Shard of the Specter?"

"The blade can't be seen." Zrobik shook his head. "But I know Dark Water has it. Ezzy wouldn't have yelled that way if they didn't."

"So you don't know."

Raysk walked toward the warrior and stood behind him. Using the war hammer, he pressed Zrobik's head against the wide stone.

"Please, my Blade. Let me put my head over the water. Use a sword, not the hammer. For all I've done for the family, you owe me that much," Zrobik begged between sobs. His tears pooled on the smooth stone.

The doe flicked its tail many times.

"You know our way. Only those who are too weak to wield a war hammer use a sword." He laughed. "You enjoyed sparring with anvils. Think of your head as hot steel and that stone as your old plaything."

Raysk moved to where Zrobik could see him. He gripped the end of the war hammer's haft with both hands. Its steel head lay in the water. The skin over his knuckles turned white.

Droena folded her arms across her chest and looked down at the green grass sprouting by her feet.

"I will not permit you the honor of spilling your blood on my armor."

"He says that every time," Droena murmured. "I think he does this naked just so he can feel the bone hit his skin."

Nasabrun nodded.

"If you have prayers for the gods, now is the time."

"Hear me, thundering horde! The fields of copper will yield me a bountiful crop! I shall bathe in the lakes of silver to cleanse myself of this world! I shall scale the mountains of gold that you protect! I will stand above all, casting golden boulders down upon my enemies!"

The puddle of tears on the stone grew bigger. Slaver oozed from his lips.

Raysk yawned. "Any last words?"

"You live by the blade, you die by the blade."

"I wield a war hammer."

A crescent of ice-cold water trailed the war hammer's head as Raysk swung it in a terrible arc. The weapon moved so fast that it sounded like the thrum of a bowstring. As the hammer came down, Zrobik's head burst into a pink mist of blood, brain, and chunks of skull. Some of what had been the warrior's head an instant earlier splattered on Raysk's body. The rest splashed into the stream.

The wide stone coated in the ruins of Zrobik's head split down the middle. The two pieces were smooth all over, except where it cracked. They toppled into the stream with the jagged, newly exposed rock facing the sky. The new fragments looked just like the many other halves lying on the streambed.

Birds ceased their songs.

Ducks splashed the water in the deep pool as they flew away.

Minnows darted to the refuge of dark shadows.

The doe and her fawns sprinted through trees.

"The only headsman in the realm that uses a war hammer." Vasarox grinned.

"The man with no stones who likes to split them," Pametan whispered into Droena's ear.

Raysk tossed his war hammer onto the bank where the Heavies stood. He stepped to put a foot on each of the two jagged halves of the freshly split rock. His legs were spread wide. He arched his back and made water into the stream.

The current grabbed the Heavy's corpse. Its legs swung and pulled the torso around. Limp arms dragged against the bed as the body began its journey downstream. The ripples in the stream made the horse inked into his back look as though it was galloping.

His chore finished, Raysk walked against the current to the deep pool of still water. He pushed aside the low-hanging branches and slowly dipped into the blue. He clutched at rocks and branches, always keeping his head above the surface and his feet planted firmly on the streambed.

When he had finished rinsing off the blood and bone, he joined the other Heavies on the streambank, shaking himself as if he were a dog. Droena and Pametan each took a large step back from the mist of water.

"Zrobik's skull must have been thin. It was easier to crush than a dragon egg." Raysk sighed. "The problem with using a war hammer to behead failures is all the filth," he mused, admiring the head of his war hammer. "The stream's cold. If any of you fail me, do it in the middle of summer when the heat makes waves in the air. That way I can wash off in a cool stream." He dragged the hammer's head across some new leaves to wipe the last few drops of watery blood from it.

Sitting on a stump, Raysk began to pull on his linen, wool, and armor.

Vasarox handed a breastplate to his Swordfather. "This stream joins the Wandering Waters about a league from here. Won't be long before he's in the port."

"Maybe he'll float by *Shark Queen* and steal that sword back from Dark Water." Raysk laughed at his own jest. He put a dented pauldron on his shoulder.

"Now that Zrobik's failure has been addressed..." Droena began. She became more comfortable with each piece of armor that Raysk put on his body. "What is our course? How do we find the Shard of the Specter, my Blade?"

Raysk frowned. "We will do what we always do...take what we want." He pounded a steel-clad fist against his breastplate. "To my mind, it's either with Dark Water or Ezmerelda, not the Syrens." Raysk scratched at a particularly deep scar on his face. "I'd bet my last gold scythe that

Dark Water stole it. Ezzy's shop burned down to the water. If she couldn't stop them from putting her shop to the torch, she couldn't stop them from stealing that sword. It's either lost in the port or with those pirates."

Vasarox raised his eyebrow. "You want to raid *Shark Queen*?" His voice was dripping with anticipation.

"I'd prefer we didn't have to, but if we raid Dark Water I either get the sword or send a message to the other Sword-families."

"Who's going to fetch the sword this time?" Droena asked.

"I am. And I'm bringing captains and warriors with me."

"They drowned the last Swordfather that tried to destroy Dark Water," Vasarox said.

"That isn't my intent. I'm simply retrieving what is rightfully mine."

"It's said the water around *Shark Queen* is cursed," Droena added.

"That's because it is," Raysk responded. "But I know how to get through it. We'll have to kill, oh, I don't know, half a hundred men. That shouldn't take long."

"Who?" Vasarox asked.

"Could be anybody. They need to be big, though. No runts. Then we wait for three or four days. After that, I raid *Shark Queen* and take the Shard of the Specter."

Vasarox gave Droena a confused look, which she returned in kind.

The Heavies strode away from the stream, leaving the water to begin smoothing the jagged faces of Zrobik's split stone over untold ages.

"What about the Fire Keepers?" Droena asked. "If Dark Water didn't pry the invisible sword from Ezzy's hands, we would have to find another way to get at the dragon family. Even with Zrobik and the others thinning their herd some, a battle with the Fire Keepers right now would mean a fiery death."

Raysk put his war hammer on his shoulder. "That it would, but not long ago a little dragon told us that the Fire Keepers have the Bleeding Blade. We'll have to find a way to break them. And you're going to tell me how."

"My Blade..." Droena began as she shook her head.

Raysk cut her off. "When we're back in the cavern, you and Kraaft will tell me again about your escape from that dragon when you dropped the bones." He turned his mask of scars to Droena. Years of practice kept her from grimacing at the sight of his face so near to hers. "I must know every detail of your escape. It's very important."

Droena nodded.

"We'll need every advantage to defeat the Fire Keepers, including surprise. We must make haste to take them unawares." Raysk scratched at his face and neck as he thought. "Teska, bring me the three fastest, strongest horses in Fulccrum. If they're not for sale, steal them from whoever owns them. I expect they'll pull wains, so make certain they're suited to that task. They can't be skittish. If they spook easy, they're no good to us. Understand?"

Teska gave her Swordfather a shallow bow.

Vasarox rubbed his soft cheeks with his dark red hands. "Once we attack, we've crossed the Paders. There is no going back."

"You're right, my loyal captain. That's why we're treading lightly. First, we raid a weak family—Dark Water—and take the Shard of the Specter. We can use that invisible sword to kill Kardas without a single Heavy getting burned." Raysk narrowed his eyes. "If Dark Water doesn't have it, we hit the Fire Keepers. Their dragons are nasty, but it'll take too long to thin their herd enough to make the fight painless. We'll lose Heavies, but the war will be won in a single battle."

"First the Shard of the Specter, then the Bleeding Blade?" Vasarox asked. He flexed his arms. "Then you'll be the third sword...the Greatsword."

"Indeed," Raysk replied. "And the last fire to burn after our battle with the Fire Keepers will be Kardas's funeral pyre."

CHAPTER FOURTEEN

FIRE KEEPERS

Andra trembled so violently in her saddle that the palfrey she rode became confused. Her legs knocked and squeezed against its side. The horse mistook the movements for commands. As her left leg pounded against its ribs, the horse turned to the left. Andra jerked the reins, commanding it to the right. As it returned to the middle of the well-trod path, Andra's right leg rattled against its rib on that side. The horse whinnied in protest.

The source of her trembling rage was the man riding the rouncey behind her. He kept his head bowed and the hood of his cloak pulled up.

"I don't know what's making me angrier right now, you or my horse," Andra yelled at him as she turned in her saddle. "How many times have I told you no?"

"I'm sorry," he mumbled. "You know how much I want this."

"You can't have it, Mistahn," Andra shot back. "I don't know how many more times I have to yell this at you, but it must be at least one more time. You can't join my Swordfamily. The Fire Keepers won't take two people from the same family. You are my brother, I am a Fire Keeper, and that is where this ends!"

Andra reached into a pouch tied to her belt and clutched the small carving of their home that Mistahn had given her. She remembered the pathetic look on his face when he handed over the carving. The memory tempered her rage for a few heartbeats.

In the saddlebag on the back of her horse, Furwing meowed in protest.

Mistahn responded to his sister's fury with repentant silence.

"You have another sister. Why don't you ask her?" Andra seethed.

"Because I don't want to live at home with Lecata any longer. That life is over for me. That's why I'm here."

"Not that sister, the oldest one."

"No. Never."

"If you try to throw your dice with me, you're doomed. You've got a better chance to join her."

"I'd rather rot in the woods," Mistahn said.

"This will be the last time that you trouble me with this childishness. It ends tonight. You won't listen to me when I say no, but you *will* listen to Kardas. He is the Swordfather and you will hear from his very mouth why you can never be a Fire Keeper."

Hooves clopping on the hard earth were the only sounds as the pair rode single file through the dragon refuge.

"You will have a brief audience with my Swordfather and then you will return to our mother. This evening, Kardas has far more important supplicants to receive than your like. Now keep up. We're late," Andra barked. She leaned into her palfrey. The horse responded by galloping forward. Mistahn drove his heels into the ribs of his mount to give chase.

The two thundered over the path. The dark red sun was low in the sky, casting shadows like long, dark blades.

Over a rise and down, Andra's horse pulled up quick. A mother and father dragon stood over their children. The young dragons were gorging on a large carcass. The kill had happened not long ago; tendrils of smoke rose from the body. What the young dragons fed on, Andra couldn't say. She and her brother stopped close enough to the feeding dragons that they could hear the unmistakable sounds of snapping bones and tearing flesh.

"Stay close to me," she whispered. "The dragons know the Fire Keepers and our friends. They don't know you. If you fall too far behind, you could end up like that supper over there."

Andra again pressed her heels against her palfrey's ribs. The horse and rider kicked up a tail of dust as they thundered on a course that gave the feeding dragons a wide berth. When the sun was so low in the sky that it touched the horizon, Andra and her brother neared the Castle of Towers. Mistahn pulled up next to his sister as the two slowed.

"Is this the place?" he asked in a hushed voice.

"This is the Castle of Towers. The Fire Keepers' home."

Dragons hopped along the tops of the towers. Small dragons enjoyed the meals that their parents dropped. Some larger dragons, sated from taking an early supper, lay on their backs.

When Mistahn and Andra entered the bailey, the Fire Keepers' towers cast a shadow dark as the scorch marks on the ground. Away from the light, chill air nipped at bare skin. The dragons outside the castle had frolicked and played, but inside the bailey was a haunting stillness.

Andra looked at the large tower in the back of the castle, to the east. She permitted her thoughts to briefly wander back to the ceremony that raised her from warrior to captain in that eastern tower. She smiled, remembering Kardas's kind words.

At the middle of the bailey, Andra turned her horse sharply to the left. Mistahn followed obediently. When they tied up their mounts, Andra noticed that only one other horse stood nearby.

The door to the northern tower swung open with surprising ease. Torches mounted in sconces lined the walls. All of them were lit and burning brightly, revealing a room that was smaller than the one where Andra had become a captain.

Inside the circular room was a dragon sculpted from red marble. Squatting on its hind legs, the dragon held its wings high. Spikes surrounded its head like a lion's mane. Many scales graced its skin. Its teeth were carved sharper than daggers. The tail resting on the ground behind it had a cluster of spikes on the end, a terrible mace poised and ready.

Claws on its forelegs served as its hands. They raised an hourglass above the dragon's head. The hourglass top was filled with specks of gold as fine as soft sand. It fell into the bottom, where a human skull rested. Little gold had fallen to cover only a few teeth.

More sculptures of dragons stood near the walls. The room was a refuge for lifeless dragons made of stone. Furwing pranced to the base of a dragon carved from basalt. She lay there, licking her paws zealously.

In the center of the room, Kardas sat on a simple

wooden chair. He was not far from the menacing red sculpture. His arms were crossed and his ruined sword leaned against the chair. Glass shards were piled so close that if he stretched out his legs, Kardas almost could have kicked them.

The Swordfather was fast asleep and snoring loudly. To wake him from his evening nap, Andra slammed the door behind her. He sounded like an angry bear arising from its winter's respite. Kardas blinked his eyes and smacked his lips.

"Andra!" Kardas bellowed with glee, his wits quick to attention. "I was beginning to think that you'd never come. Or was that a dream? No matter. It's good that you're here."

"My Blade," Andra replied, bowing her head. "I'm grateful beyond words that you would invite me here. There are other captains my senior who are worthier of this honor."

"It's not an honor, it's business," the Swordfather replied flatly. "You have an aptitude for diplomacy. Your blade is friendship and you wield it well. That's true within your own family, and the other Swordfamilies, too. I see this in you, even if some others do not. I need someone who can help me navigate the treacherous waters that lie ahead."

Andra's visage didn't betray the pride that swelled inside of her.

"I want you here to observe and hone those gifts of yours. We need allies and you can help win them." Kardas stopped and turned his attention to Andra's brother. "Who's this young man you've brought with you?"

"I'm Mistahn. Andra's brother."

"My *younger* brother."

"Of course! I can see the resemblance." Kardas tipped

his head back and inspected the youngster. The Swordfather was equally adept at understanding dragons and men. He betrayed no discomfort at the sight of the crimson red birthmark that streaked across Mistahn's face. "Welcome to my family's home."

"Thank you, Swordfather," Mistahn said as he bowed deeply. "I've wanted to meet you my whole life. You look much as I had imagined. Though I must ask, why do you have a dragon fang hanging from your neck?"

The Swordfather pursed his lips. "When a man reaches a certain age, it's wise for him to distract people from his face. The dragon fang helps me with that, like it did just now." He smiled and patted the fang. "And the Fire Keepers' Swordfather always wears this dragon fang. It's one of our most sacred traditions. On the back of it, I've carved the name of the Fire Keeper who I've chosen to succeed me as Swordfather, after my blade is sheathed in darkness." His cheeks puffed like bellows as he chuckled. "Sometimes I think this fang must surely hang from a noose!"

Words rushed from Mistahn's mouth like fire from a dragon. "I'd be honored to serve you or whoever's name is on that fang. Ever since the day I learned about the six great families and all of the—"

"Yes, yes," Kardas interrupted. He offered a sad smile as recompense for the rudeness. "Andra has told me all about you. Sounds as though you have an aptitude for the hunt. Good instincts and you're loyal." Kardas wrapped his fingers around the hilt of his blade and leaned on it heavily as he stood. "What she hasn't told me, but I can easily guess because you're standing here, is that you are persistent. Andra would probably say stubborn. You won't take no for an answer. Is that true?"

Mistahn smiled broadly and nodded at the Swordfather.

"Kardas, my brother's visit was unexpected. He ambushed me on my ride here. I've brought him because he simply will not listen to me. I've explained again and again that he can't join the Fire Keepers. I traveled to my childhood home not long ago and told him the very same. He listens worse than the stone dragons in this room. This must end, hopefully before your guest arrives. Mistahn refuses to listen to me, but he *will* obey you."

"Sir, uh, Blade...Swordfather," Mistahn began but was quickly silenced when Kardas raised his hand.

The blunted point of Kardas's cane tapped against the stone floor. "I've been Swordfather for a long time now. Maybe too long." He sighed deeply, admiring the bright flames in the orderly sconces around the room. "The Fire Keepers had fallen upon hard times before I took the reins. Many things went wrong. Some were inevitable, but some were unfortunate mistakes." Flecks of stone spit from where he ground the point of his sword on the floor. "Tell me, youngster, why do you badger your sister so? Why do you want to become a Fire Keeper?"

"I know of your reputation and that of your family," Mistahn replied, speaking as many words as possible before being ordered into silence again. "The city adores you and the Fire Keepers. You have power beyond..."

Kardas guffawed. The brown robes around his belly shook like tournament banners in violent winds. "Your kind words are not unappreciated. But I sense there's something more. A yearning that's deeper than this not-unwelcome flattery." He again tapped his sword on the floor. "Tell me of it."

Mistahn took a deep breath. Now he spoke slowly and

deliberately. "I am a ghost trapped inside the body of a man. I am nobody. If I don't become somebody soon, I will die as nobody. All I ask is a chance, because without that I will die without even the dignity of failure." He swallowed hard. "Any stone may serve as my headstone, because there will be nothing to write. But if I join your Swordfamily, I can be somebody. I can master a dragon and maybe live a life that's worthy of a few words etched into a stone." His black-tipped fingernails dug into his palms. "Even if I fail as a Fire Keeper, I will die as somebody." He shuddered as he drew a deep breath. "Minstrels will sing of you. Only the wind will sing of me."

"You are haunted by deeds undone."

"I see my fate." Mistahn nodded. "I will die an old man mourning a life unlived."

The Swordfather put his hand on Mistahn's shoulder. "I sense you have a good heart, Mistahn. That is a tremendous liability in our work."

Mistahn tried to speak but Kardas silenced him with a look.

"When I became Swordfather, we were a Swordfamily in name only. Most warriors and captains died in a battle known as the Clouds of Flame. Some of those who lived went on to desert our family in its time of need. The rift that nearly destroyed the Fire Keepers forever was caused by two brothers who were captains. They both yearned to become Swordfather, and if they couldn't, each one would rather see the family burned to the ground by its own dragon fire than cede control to the other. They warred, and in so doing they betrayed their Swordfamily."

The air in the room was still, but the torches flickered.

"The threat that came closest to destroying the Fire Keepers wasn't another family. It came from within. That's why I've made it our way to never blend *blood* family with *chosen* family." Kardas said this in a tone that would brook no argument.

Andra moved to stand by her Swordfather's side. "As I told you, Mistahn. I wish you would have listened to me. Now you will heed my Swordfather."

Grains of gold sand slipped through the hourglass neck and rolled down the skull.

"A man with conflicting loyalties has no loyalty at all." Kardas rested both hands on the pommel of his sword. "Passions within families can burn with love or hate so powerful that it consumes them like dragon fire." Kardas sighed. "Those two brothers didn't want to be Swordfather. Each merely sought what the other coveted. What they truly desired was to destroy each other." His eyes were glassy as he spoke. "Instead, they nearly burned the Fire Keepers to ash.

"We have captains who married after they became Fire Keepers. Yutago and Xutsuh are very happy together, but they do not share the same blood. They do have a daughter. She's young, but even when she's older, she won't be permitted to join us. Her blood is already here."

Mistahn sighed.

"Do you see now?" Andra asked softly. She pressed her hand against the pouch that held the carved house. "Kardas is our Swordfather and his word is our law."

After swallowing hard, Mistahn nodded his head. "I understand. I'll obey."

"Good, now it's done. You must leave here." Andra moved to grab her brother's arm and lead him from the tower.

She had only taken a few steps when a knock at the door stopped her with a jolt.

"What do we do?" she whispered to her Swordfather. "They're early."

"We'll be fine," Kardas replied in an even lower whisper. "But he shouldn't see your brother." Turning to Mistahn, he said, "Boy, go hide behind a dragon."

More knocking came from the door. This time the rapping was louder and sharper, as if made by metal. Mistahn secreted himself behind the basalt dragon favored by Furwing.

"I'll speak for the family," Kardas said as the two Fire Keepers stood side-by-side. "But I want you to listen hard and think harder. Understood?"

Andra nodded.

"Enter," Kardas called.

The door swung open and two guards in full plate armor entered the room. They stationed themselves on either side of the open door. In unison they announced that his majesty King Fallov had arrived.

Andra's eyes grew wide with anticipation. She had only seen the king seated on his throne in the great hall. She always wondered why he looked more miserable than the commoners on the back benches.

The king stepped into the room wearing a mantle of royal blue with silver trim. He was sullen, quiet, and slouching so low that the trim on the bottom of his mantle dragged on the stone floor. He dismissed the knights with nothing more than a look. They turned and he paused for a moment before the door slammed behind him.

The mantle trim rose from the floor as he pulled himself up. His windblown cheeks were flushed red and his eyes shone bright in the torchlight. His royal mantle commanded an aura of power. The gold and silver crown he wore was rife with blue sapphires, as was his gold scepter.

The Emerald Kingdom's ruler marched across the room. He stepped high and beamed a genuine smile at Kardas.

Gold poured through the hourglass and Furwing twitched her tail.

The king stood before the Fire Keepers. In a swift movement, Fallov bowed. The king's knee drove into the pile of shards by the Swordfather's feet, shattering pieces of glass. His scepter lay flat on the stone floor as he bowed so deeply that his crown nearly fell from his head.

The king bent the knee.

Andra stared with her mouth agape. For her, time slowed and the gold specks falling in the hourglass froze in the air.

Then Kardas laughed, so hard that he nearly lost his grip on the sword that held him upright.

"Fallov Lutish, what are you doing?" Kardas exclaimed. He took a deep breath. "Ah, begging your forgiveness, where is my proper obeisance to the ruler of our fair realm? Or should I say, *your* fair realm. What I mean to say is, King Fallov Lutish, why are you bowing before me? And in that blasted glass I put there to keep my guests from kneeling, *you* most of all!" the Swordfather admonished.

The king remained in his genuflect long enough to make clear that his gesture was sincere. When he rose, shards of glass fell from his knee while others stubbornly clung to the cloth of his riding breeches.

"My Blade, it's been too long," King Fallov said. "Worry not about the glass. I have the poleyn from my armor on underneath my breeches. My knee is perfectly fine, other than the aches that I always feel after a ride. But this will be the last time that I wear these breeches."

"I wish that you wouldn't insist on bowing. Friends do not kneel before friends."

"There are few men in this realm who are worthy of my respect," the king replied. "You are one of them. Mayhaps the only one." The king looked down and seemed to lose some of his vigor, as if it escaped with his breath. "You also have power, my dear friend. And it happens that I am in grave need of it." The king crossed his arms. "How I wish the purpose of my visit was to share meat and mead, but I find the thundering gods seldom offer me such mercies."

Sinking into his chair, Kardas held up a hand to cut off the king's speech.

"Be that as it may, before we continue I believe it wise for us to observe social graces." Kardas gestured to the Fire Keeper standing beside him. "This is a newly made captain of mine. Her name is Andra. She's equally adept at wrangling dragons and men." At this, King Fallov raised an eyebrow. "Some Swordfathers afford her more respect than they do each other. I fret that they may steal her away! One day she'll perfect the art of outfoxing sharp dragons and herding dull men. Hahr!"

Fallov doffed his crown to Andra. She bowed her head in response.

"Kardas flatters me with his kind words. Any victories that I have won, or will win, are because his wisdom has been a whetstone that has sharpened my mind."

The Swordfather asked the king if he would like a chair. The king responded that after the ride, he would prefer to stand.

"Who rode with you?"

"Voden and my personal guard await me in the bailey."

"They wore the dragon wing cloaks?"

"They did. Had they not, we may have arrived as a cloud of foul smoke. My mantle would burn like paper, no doubt. I wore no cloak, but they remembered me. Thank the thundering gods, the dragons have those long memories that you've told me of."

"They never forget a friend, and the dragons know that anyone who wears a dragon cloak is a friend of ours," Kardas said.

"And *your* friend wears a royal mantle." The king drew in a deep sigh. "These days I fear that I'm aging faster than a dragon in ice."

Kardas coughed hard. His chest sounded like it held half-full wineskins. "We have that much in common!"

A torch devoured the last of its cloth. Its flame vanished into thin smoke.

"You have provided me generous aid in the past, my Swordfather." Fallov puffed out his chest. "Without the threat of your dragons, torrents of blood might have rained down on the throne as my family took it. Many of the dead would have been my kith and kin. For your aid to my parents and myself, I thank you. Though sometimes I wonder if spilling some enemies' blood on the throne may have served as a useful threat today."

His mantle billowed as the king turned and inspected the red dragon sculpture. His eyes fell on the skull trapped in the hourglass.

"Your loyalty to the Emerald Crown has been repaid by my loyalty to your Swordfamily. My Kingdom Guard have turned blind eyes to many Fire Keeper...indulgences. Commoners who petitioned my court complaining of missing gold went missing themselves." Fallov tapped his scepter on the hourglass. "My men ensured they were never found." The gold sand continued to fall apace. He looked the red stone dragon in its eye. "When bones covered in soot lay on scorched earth, more oft than not it was my men who covered them with dirt."

"I sense that you are going to ask something of me, my king."

Fallov turned to Kardas. "I say all this so we both understand that the debt I owed has been repaid. You helped my family win the crown. In return, I gave you free rein over the city." Fallov put his hands on his hips. "Now my family and the Swordfamilies are in grave danger. Our border with the Crimson Crown has been quiet for a great many eclipses. Of late, I have learned that the Crimson Crown intends to move against us. They will invade the Emerald Kingdom by crossing over the Pader Mountains."

Kardas tugged at his beard and frowned.

The king scratched at his neck. "I cannot protect the realm alone. As it happens, alone is precisely where I find myself. It's been so many years that the queen and I..." The bitter words caught in his throat. "That's why the Crimson Crown moves to strike. My crown is divided and weak. I no longer have a single lord on the red side of the Paders who I can truthfully call a friend. Lord Wrand was the last one. After my nephew Romlad had that trouble in your refuge, I sent him to Wrand to keep the boy safe and strengthen our bond with a critical ally. That gesture was not rewarded. Romlad escaped and, for reasons that I still don't understand, Wrand sent me a chest full of lava rock. Was it a threat? Did his men steal whatever was supposed to be in the chest?"

Kardas wore an emotionless mask. Andra clasped her hands behind her back so the king would not see them shake. She suddenly felt as though the gold sand in the hourglass were pouring down her throat.

"Whatever the answer, I must assume that Lord Wrand is no longer an ally," the king continued. "If I've sent one messenger pigeon to him, I've sent a hundred. There's been nothing in response."

"That is vexing indeed, my liege," Kardas offered.

"It seems I can't even trust birds anymore. I've created a relay of coursers with loyal riders to send my most vital messages." Glass broke as the king absently pressed the tip of his riding boot into the pile of shards. "I have nary an ally across the Paders, and there are few leal houses on the west side. I hope against hope that Kellington remains loyal. There are others, like Slaeton and the Wickunduns, but they are precious few." The royal mantle that had concealed the king's lack of bulk now shrank against his body.

The king pulled off his crown. He held his scepter in one hand and his crown in the other. He held them wide.

"I'm begging you. Pledge your dragons to me. I only need them in the mountain passes for a time. They can return here before the next triple eclipse. My Kingdom Guard are stationed near the foot of the mountains. They'll do the killing, but they'll need time to get there. Your dragons will slow the Crimson Crown and my men will stop them. That is all I ask of you."

Kardas rose from his chair, leaning heavily on his sword. "My king, I would do nearly anything for you. But I cannot risk my dragons. Without them, we have only empty land and a strange castle."

The Swordfather rested his hand on Fallov's shoulder. "I have a war of my own in the offing. Raysk intends to seize the Bleeding Blade and declare himself the Greatsword who rules the families. Doubtless his first strike will be against the only family that can stand against him by itself. Mine."

Kardas dropped his hand. Torchlight flashed on the glass at their feet.

"Without your aid the Emerald Crown will surely fall.

My family partnered with the Fire Keepers to win the throne. I'm asking you, as your friend, to help me keep it. Lend me your fire."

Kardas hesitated. The king glared at his subject.

"My king, our dragons are not well. Many have perished on the refuge at the hands of men. Some eggs and young have disappeared. We've had poachers in the past, but this is different. The mother dragons are ill at ease. They won't abandon their nests, let alone the refuge. I want to strengthen your house, but I can't weaken my family as we ready ourselves for our own war."

The king frowned. "Did you hear what Melyq reported at court?" he growled.

"Yes, he spoke of Romlad."

"Do you know where the boy was found?"

Kardas glanced at Andra, who shook her head.

Fallov returned the crown to his head. He pointed a knobby, trembling finger at the door that led to the bailey.

"Romlad was found out *there*, in *your* dragon refuge! Where your fire-breathing pack mules harvest their crop of souls!" He curled his hand into a fist and shook it in front of Kardas's face. "Romlad was found by my own Kingdom Guard as a pile of charred bones!"

Fallov kicked the glass pile on which he had knelt when he first arrived. Nearly every glass shard scattered around the room. Some pieces bounced off the red dragon's feet.

The king turned on Kardas in a fury. He pressed his scepter hard against the dragon fang that rested on Kardas's chest.

"Romlad was of my blood! You owe me a *blood debt!* I am your *king* and I *order* you to pay that debt in the same coin you used to borrow it. *Fire!*"

Torches around Kardas burned bright as he locked eyes

with the king.

"This, I will do for you, King Fallov Lutish," Kardas said. The wrinkles around his eyes deepened. "By the thundering gods, I will send as many dragons as I can spare." Kardas tugged at his white beard.

King Fallov nodded.

"I do ask something in return. At court you sentenced a man to the dungeons. Called himself Skail. In the bowels of your dungeons he'll die before the next eclipse. Give him to me."

Fallov approached the Swordfather. "The man the queen wanted to free? He's yours. Do with him as you will."

The two men embraced over the spot where the glass had lain. The gold in the hourglass flowed more quickly as they pulled each other close.

Without another word, the king turned and walked out the door.

Kardas's sword wobbled as he sank back into his humble wooden chair. He sat for a time and stared at the glass shards lying all around the room. Andra stood as still as the dragon statues.

When Mistahn cleared his throat, the Swordfather and his captain jerked out of their trances.

"I...apologize, Swordfather," Mistahn said. His eyes were wide. "For, uh, intruding on your...audience. I didn't realize...please forgive me." He knelt on the floor.

"There is nothing to forgive," Kardas replied in a warm tone. "Please, rise. Go to your home. Enjoy your quiet life. Surely you see that the perils of a Swordfamily are a burden that you would not want to bear, even if you could."

Mistahn stood before Kardas. "Never in my life have I seen a king bow. My Blade, if there's ever anything that I can do for your family, you have but to ask." His usually mischievous eyes adopted a deep sincerity. "I would do anything for you."

He turned to his sister.

"You should leave now," Andra said. She saw the panic flash over his eyes. "The dragons will remember you. We were together on the ride here," she reassured him. "Besides, nearly all will be in their nests with their young. Stay on the paths and you'll be safe. Ride fast. If you see a dragon, ride faster." With that, she dismissed her brother.

When he pulled the door behind him, Mistahn left it open the width of a rapier's blade.

Andra moved around the room, dropping the torches in a bucket filled with water before returning them to their sconces. Instead of light, the smothered torches produced a hint of gray smoke. When she had extinguished all but a few torches, she returned to her Swordfather.

He groaned as he reached deep into a pouch that hung from his waist. Andra realized she had never seen the pouch before. It was made of heavy cloth and cinched together with a length of flax string.

"I've pledged our strength to the wrong war," Kardas moaned. Opening the pouch, he drew a long, narrow stone from within. "The Fire Keepers should have every dragon prowling the refuge right now. From every tower around the bailey we should have fire hotter than the sun poised to strike." Kardas held his sword with the point resting on the stone floor. "I wouldn't have done it, but we owe the king for Romlad. Blood debts are the priciest of all debts. They cannot be repaid with gold. They demand blood for blood."

The grating sound of stone against steel filled the room as Kardas slid the whetstone down the length of his cane. The captain watched in confusion as her Swordfather nimbly moved the stone along the edge of the sword.

"What are you doing?"

"I'm sharpening my sword," Kardas replied in a casual tone that, contrary to the condition of his blade, suggested he used a whetstone every day.

"Don't you mean your cane?"

"After speaking with the king, methinks it'll be much more useful as a sword than a cane. Hopefully my old whetstone is up to the task."

Light from the torches that still burned cast sharp shadows across the two Fire Keepers. The darkness danced through the smoke lingering in the air.

"Andra, what do you remember about the bones?" Kardas's eyes never left where the stone caressed the steel. "Inside that chest we stole from Lord Wrand's men."

"Besides what I already told you, I remember they were burned so dark that it was hard to see them inside the chest."

"Was there anything more?"

She furrowed her brow as she struggled to recall. "There were some gold teeth in its mouth. Not many, less than it would take to cast a gold scythe. Tyv said something about how the only gold in the chest were the teeth in the skull."

"Do you know how many teeth were made of gold?"

Andra blew out air like a great gust of wind. "No. I think Tyv said there were a couple. Not sure if he meant two or a few. It was difficult to see and we were short of time. Why?"

Resting the whetstone and sword on his thighs, Kardas turned his attention to Andra. "One of our dragons hurt Romlad, the king's nephew. The boy snuck onto the refuge. With its tail, the dragon knocked three teeth from the boy's mouth. They were replaced with gold."

"If only I could go back. I can't be certain."

Furwing padded to Andra and wrapped her body around the captain's boots.

Kardas snorted. "It matters not. The bones we stole might have been what was left of Romlad after some cruel turn of fate. The boy wasn't leery enough to avoid dragons when he was here in Fulccrum and the Lava Sea isn't far from Wrand's land. Romlad may have sought that fire instead." Kardas scratched his chin and narrowed his eyes. "Even if the bones found on the refuge were from that chest, I damn well couldn't tell Fallov the truth. I sense that sword and burned lamb we found before your ceremony had something to do with this." He grimaced. "I could neither confess to the king nor refuse him. Our bond is too strong. Our fates have been woven tight since he first grasped his scepter." The Swordfather pursed his lips. "Melyq and I must needs discuss the depths of his debt."

Kardas scratched Furwing behind the ear. Many flecks of gold fell before he spoke again.

"The whole realm is half-truths that bloat into lies before they rot into myth," Kardas groaned. "Like as not, our mothers lied to us about our given names! Hahr!"

"I fear we'll drown in our own lies. But perhaps one more won't matter." Andra rubbed the bridge of Furwing's nose. "You don't have to send the dragons. So long as the herd stays here in the refuge, Raysk would never dare to attack. He doesn't fear much, but he would cower at the sight of our dragons breathing a wall of flame."

Furwing hissed.

"Aye, I could break my word. But I won't. There is honor among the Swordfamilies, all of them. When I'm faced with an opportunity to choose honor or treachery, I ask myself one question."

"What question is that?"

"Will doing the honorable thing get me killed? If the answer is no, I do the honorable thing. If the answer is yes, I do the treacherous thing." Kardas tapped his whetstone against his blade.

"How do you know if you're safe choosing honor?"

"Honor is always the riskier throw of the dice."

Andra did not doubt that her Swordfather spoke the truth.

Kardas smacked his lips. "Fallov has blessed us with many years of favor. His generosity helped make us the most powerful Swordfamily. There is much risk in this honorable act, but half the herd is stronger than any force in the realm. And we will harvest a great debt."

Andra could not suppress her doubt. "If we split ourselves, we may well be conquered."

"I summoned you here for a few reasons. You needed to meet the king. It's important for our family and the crown that you two respect each other. Today is the first stone in the foundation of that respect." Dark shadows streaked across Kardas's face as he spoke. "I also suspected that he would plead for our strength." Kardas regarded Andra with pride. "You're going to lead our dragons into the mountains. You will slow the reds for the Emerald Crown. This is vitally important to the future of our family."

Andra searched for the words that would convey her thanks, but found only doubt. Though her lips moved, she remained silent.

"We must be thoughtful about how thin we spread our dragons. I intend to send you with the stronger dragons. Take most of the largest ones with you. Not all of them, but you will need many to harry the reds in the mountain passes. You must leave the mothers and their hatchlings here in the refuge. The young couldn't defend a pass wider than the blade of my sword. Their mothers won't leave the refuge anyway, not while their hatchlings are in danger. If Raysk dares attack, our mother dragons alone will fight like flame to protect the refuge. They are a fury the thundering hells couldn't hold."

"I thank you, my Blade. This is an honor that I will never forget," Andra said solemnly.

"Hahr! We all forget everything eventually," Kardas shot back. "The good and the bad. The things that made us shed tears of joy and the others that make us sob tears of sorrow. Eventually, it's all lost as our minds fade."

Andra felt much older.

"What's important isn't the memories that you struggle to never forget or your hopes for the future. What will make your life a success or failure is how you respond in the moments that you're truly tested. When others are foolish, will you be wise? When others are weak, will you be strong? When others are less, will you be more?" Kardas smiled at her. "I'm gifting you one of your moments."

Andra didn't bother to search for words this time. She knew they didn't exist.

"You're here tonight because I believe the answer to each of those questions is yes."

She tensed herself, as if a great weight had been placed upon her shoulders.

"We're going to the rushes. I'll call the Fire Keepers here to the Castle of Towers. I should've done it earlier. That business with the bones is troubling. There is much that I do not know, but I can feel the war nearing." Kardas's face paled. "I fear that I may have made a misstep. I've led the Heavies to believe that we have the Bleeding Blade. I didn't expect that the king would ask so much of us." He sighed. "One of our dragons is worth more than a hundred Heavies.

Still, the timing of all this makes our throw of the dice a far greater risk than I'd prefer." He squeezed Andra's hand. "Don't worry about the Castle of Towers while you're away. If the Heavies want our fire, we will give them fire. Concern yourself with those passes. We will speak more of your journey to the Paders on the morrow."

Andra patted Kardas's hand. She turned to leave. Her eyes lingered on the hourglass clutched between the dragon's wings. She noticed that the skull was still sitting above the fine specks of gold. After all the time that she had been in the room, and all the gold that had cascaded through the neck of the hourglass, the same amount of glittering metal still rested in the bottom. The skull with its grotesque grin had not been buried.

Cool night air rushed in as Andra pushed the door open. She turned in the doorway and watched her Swordfather for a long time.

Kardas remained seated in his wooden chair, sliding the whetstone over the length of his blade. He worked with natural precision that was a generous gift from the thundering gods. He handled his sword the same way a loving mother tends to her newborn child.

Andra turned and walked away, leaving the door open. Although she didn't watch Kardas all through the night, she knew what would happen. When the last torch burned out and the room was black as pitch, Kardas would keep sharpening the blade. The Swordfather would slide the whetstone and an oil-cloth along the blade more times than there are scales on a dragon. After a final stroke, soft as a lover's lips, the sun would rise over the Paders and lighten the bailey.

By the new day's light, the Swordfather's feeble cane would vanish and his fearsome sword would be born anew.

CHAPTER FIFTEEN
HEAVIES

Raysk stood on a raft buoyed by the corpses of dead men.

Three days earlier, his warriors slew dozens of townsfolk. They chose men who were tall and wide and plump. The warriors were forbidden from using war hammers or even their fists to kill the men. All of them were strangled by hand so their skin remained whole and strong. If the warriors found a fresh wound on the victim, they dumped the body deep in the forest where foxes, ravens, and the like enjoyed a feast.

The bodies with whole skin were laid in a field for days in the direct sun. Warriors poured pitch in their mouths, on their eyes, and over the places where their legs met their trunk. With the naked bodies laid flat on their backs, the warriors placed heavy stones on their hands and feet to keep their limbs straight. The corpses were guarded day and night to keep away scavengers that might gnaw a hole in the watertight skin.

By the grace of the thundering gods the skies were cloudless and the spring sun warmed the bodies. They swelled like sausages cooked over a hot fire. The big, plump men grew bigger and plumper. They smelled worse than rotting eggs. The longer the bodies lay in the sun, the farther away the warriors on watch stood from the corpses.

Heavies placed the bloated men in the backs of wagons. Each wagon had layers of shelves made of flat wooden planks. Lying on the shelves, many corpses could be hauled without pressing against each other. This arrangement protected the body's skin and ensured that it would float like a piece of cork.

At the darkest place on Fulccrum's docks, the only townsfolk who lingered were so full of ale they couldn't see what was happening even with their eyes wide open. That's where Raysk set his plan in motion. Warriors pulled bodies from the wagons and floated them into the port. The bodies were laid so that one man's head was near the next man's ankles. Then the warriors bound them together.

After the ropes were pulled taut with the bodies side-by-side and shoulder-to-ankle, wide wooden planks were laid across them and cinched fast. The planks made a firm surface over the buoyant corpses to ensure that the Heavies didn't lose their footing.

The macabre fleet's maiden voyage began when the rafts departed the docks carrying dozens of Heavies. They were bound for the *Shark Queen* anchored in port. The night air was still as rock. The water was mirror-smooth and the reflection of the three moons above looked exactly like the sky.

War hammers served as the Heavies' oars. They dipped the hammers into the water sideways so that the heads' width served as the oar blade. The Heavies pulled the hammers back in rhythmic and synchronized strokes. They pulled their weapons through the water with the same effort as a rower on a galley, and no more. A war hammer's weight was a trifling burden for a Heavy.

"Did we need to kill so many men?" Droena whispered as she tapped a foot on the raft. "Their stench makes my nose burn. The thundering gods have favored us with a westerly breeze. If it came out of the east instead, the Dark Waters would smell us coming."

Raysk grunted. "There's some ill sorcery in that family. Mayhaps they've been friendly with Iron Wand. Many eclipses ago we tried to raid them and lost warriors before we even made it to their boat. Seemed impossible to get there from dry land. Our men would get sucked down in a whirlpool. Or those sharks with fins like sails on their back would tear holes in the bottom of our boats. As we struggled across the port I noticed their thralls avoided our dead.

"When you're on the water, you're at their mercy." Raysk tapped the point of his sword on the plank beneath him. In his other hand, he held a sack speckled with dark red stains. He kept his voice low. "It took many dead to find out which bodies floated best. I don't know if it's the thundering horde of gods or the hellish smell that keeps Hanngoh's playthings away. Don't care, either. Whatever magic protects their boat won't come near the corpses of dead men."

"You're carrying a sword tonight?" Droena asked.

"The war hammer is my true weapon. I choose to wield something weaker tonight, but I have my reasons. Mayhaps I'll trade a sword that can be seen for the sword that is unseen."

Sounds traveled over the water almost to the horizon. Droena was grateful that the taverns near the docks were open late and entertaining many loud, drunk sailors. The raucous din veiled the Heavies' sounds of rowed water and whispered words.

When the rafts were far enough into the port that they passed a ship resting at anchor, the first shark fin pierced through the surface. A rippling wave in a V shape trailed behind the fin. The V spread wide as the shark sped toward the raft that held Droena and Raysk.

"This is when they come for us. When we're far enough from the dock that trying to get back would just make us tired before we filled the sharks' bellies," Raysk said. "I should cut those fins off their back with my sword, but I don't want to risk the noise."

As the fin cut through the water so close to the raft that Droena could have reached out and touched it, the shark turned and sped off. The fin sank lower in the water before it disappeared. The wide V of its wake spreading across the surface was the only sign that something below the water had hunted the Heavies.

More fins cut through the water, but none came close to the rafts.

"I hope Zrobik was right," Droena said. "Elsewise, this voyage is for nothing."

"Even if Dark Water doesn't have the Shard of the Specter, our presence will cow Hanngoh," Raysk replied. "He will understand that I now rule the Swordfamilies."

"This will be the first of two blades," Teska added.

"One for each hand," Raysk replied. "You're certain that this Fire Keeper warrior of yours has told you true?"

"About the Bleeding Blade? He's always been truthful in the past. He won't play me false."

"You had best be right. I don't want to march into the dragon refuge in force for naught. *Shark Queen* is one thing, the Castle of Towers is something else entirely."

"Glas told me that the Fire Keepers have the Bleeding Blade."

"If you're wrong and you fail me, you know the price."

"The Fire Keepers possess the Bleeding Blade," Teska repeated with confidence.

"Why did he tell you this?"

Teska faced her Swordfather. The Night Scythe was a full disk in the sky, its dull yellow shining like a bastard sun. The moonlight fondled her light hair and the fair complexion of her homely face. Her dark eyes were drops of mystery.

"The Syrens aren't the only ones with charms."

Raysk grunted. "Did you get the horses?"

"Yes," Teska replied, smirking.

"Good."

Shark Queen was anchored on the south side of Fulcrum's port. Not a single light shone from her deck or the portholes that lined her hull. Her sails were raised, which Droena thought was strange for a ship lying at anchor. Ropes dangled from the corners of the sails to rest on the weather deck. The black sails were adorned with a swirling white pattern in the center.

The noise of drunken sailors shouting and fighting in taverns became muffled. Those sounds were overpowered by a dull roar. This new noise began as a whisper before growing loud enough that it sounded like winds, strong as gales, roaring by the rafts.

Smooth reflections in the water began to dance and shimmer. The moons' reflections on the water looked as if they had been dropped from a great distance and shattered into countless tiny pieces. Droena planted her war hammer on the planks and braced herself. The dirty water hit the raft, which rolled and pitched, sending the Heavies to their knees.

Fins that had harassed the rafts scattered as the water became rough. The whirlpool, a twisting funnel of angry water, slid toward Raysk. The raft heaved with so much violence that Droena feared the bodies hadn't been tied together with strong enough rope. She crouched down to steady herself.

Raysk reached into the sack and pulled out a severed head. "This is from a body that was too small for our rafts," he informed Droena in a casual tone.

Holding the head by its long hair, Raysk eyed the distance from where he stood to the whirlpool's white water. As it dangled from Raysk's hand, the head swayed like a pendulum while the raft rocked.

In a fluid movement, Raysk hurled the head at the whirlpool. Tumbling end over end, it sailed through the air with speed and power greater than some arrows. It landed in the whirlpool and disappeared without a sound or splash.

The swirling waters tightened around the spot where the bloody head landed. They collapsed to spin in a narrow circle of raging water. After long moments, the rough water that harried the rafts began to calm. The moment Droena let loose her sigh of relief, the head shot from the whirlpool. With its long hair flinging streaks of water, the head flew in a high arc to land on the deck of a nearby galley. A watchman yelped when the head landed at his feet with a sickening thud.

The whirlpool disappeared and the port waters returned to their placid state. Heavies now returned to their feet.

Teska had fallen to her knees as the raft heaved beneath

her. Before she stood, her eyes lingered on the water. A piece of something drifted to the surface. It looked like a cloak that someone had thrown into the port. Its cloth had strange coloring, dark purple with white stripes wrapped around the width of it. By the time she stood, it had vanished into the dark fathoms below.

"Learned that trick on one of our earlier voyages through the port," Raysk said, chuckling at the startled watchman. "Damnable whirlpool made the waters so rough that it nearly ripped apart the bodies. The ropes that bound those corpses started to saw off arms and legs. A couple bodies floated free into the port. A warrior had brought a sword. We cut off a head from a body and threw it into the whirlpool. Hanngoh's pet must not like the taste. That whirlpool doesn't fear bodies, even headless bodies, but it hates severed heads." He admired the blade that he carried this night. "That's why I brought a sword. If Hanngoh sends his pet whirlpool again, I can cut off plenty of heads."

Droena's face was a sickly shade of green as she leaned heavily on her war hammer's haft. "Dark Water is more like Dark Magic," she whispered.

"Might beats magic," Raysk replied. "Every time."

Shark Queen tugged at its anchor chain. To Droena, the sides of its hull looked gray and rough. The other ships in the port had sides made of smooth, dark brown wood. She didn't spend much time in the port, but she found the strangeness of Dark Water's ship to be unnerving. She noticed that the other boats inside the port were anchored far from the Swordfamily's ship.

Sea creatures that slithered like snakes passed through the water in front of Raysk's raft. The surface churned as the slender animals wriggled close before turning away.

Closer to the hull, the details of *Shark Queen*'s appearance were revealed. The sides of the ship were covered with large teeth shaped like wedges. The teeth were almost as big as Droena's hands. The edges of them were ridged like the blade of a saw. They stuck out from the side without any pattern and pointed in all directions.

Droena stared at *Shark Queen* with her mouth agape.

"Hanngoh added the big shark teeth after the last time I boarded his boat," Raysk said. "That's why I had the warriors get us boots with steel soles."

The ghoulish fleet of rafts pulled against the starboard side of *Shark Queen*. After a wordless signal from Raysk, dozens of men and women lit torches. Grappling hooks were swung in tight circles before being heaved onto the deck above. After pulling on the ropes to make certain the hold was true, the Heavies put their torches between their teeth and scaled the hull. The shark teeth on the ship crackled as the steel soles of the Heavies' boots crushed them.

Raysk was the first Heavy to reach the deck. He vaulted over the railing, sword in hand. The entire Dark Water Swordfamily was on the ship's far side. Their weapons leaned against the railing or hung from their belts.

Instead of steel armor, they wore the garb suited for the sea: loose clothes that, during the day, invited the breeze to carry away heat from the unrelenting sun. On their heads were scarves or hats with wide brims that shielded their eyes. To a man and woman, their skin was thick and leathery, a gift from their long days on the water.

The other Heavies joined Raysk on the starboard side of the ship. They held burning torches in one hand with their weapons in the other. Neither Heavy nor Dark Water moved or spoke.

A light breeze gently filled the sails and made their lines squirm on the deck.

On the quarterdeck of *Shark Queen*, at its stern, Hanngoh leaned heavily on the wheel. The light from the moons made the earrings dangling from every part of his ears sparkle. The gems of all sizes and colors on his necklaces did the same. He held a long bottle.

"Want a drink?" Hanngoh asked. He raised the bottle and wiggled it at Raysk. "The best rum comes from west o' the Rin' Islands." He turned the bottle upside down and swallowed a few gulps. After the last swallow, he wiped his mouth with the back of his hand.

"I'm here to take what is mine," Raysk growled at him. Droena stood behind her Swordfather, along with her fellow captains Kraaft and Vasarox. "Give me the Shard of the Specter and I won't send your boat to the bottom."

"This is a ship, not a boat," Hanngoh sighed. "And apologies me whole family isn't here to greet ya. Sadly, we lost a few overboard in a fierce storm not long ago." Hanngoh took a swig. "For someone who likes war hammers, ya spend much o' yer time huntin' for swords. Ya dragged all the Swordfathers to the Gods' Blade to cry about Auzken's tomb. I'd wager the Night Scythe above that ya sent a warrior to try and rob Ezzy. Then I'd go double or naught that ya sent him the night she boarded the *Green Flash*, and he came back with excuses instead o' a glass blade." Hanngoh took another long drink. This time, he didn't bother to wipe the trickle of rum dripping down his chin. "That reminds me, we found that flotsam in the port. It belong to you?"

Hanngoh pointed his bottle to the whalebone plank that stuck out over *Shark Queen*'s port side. A naked body with bound hands lay facedown on the plank. Droena couldn't see if the body still had a head, but she didn't need to. The ink stain on his back in the shape of a horse told her the body had been Zrobik.

"You can have him," Raysk spat. "We're here because he was weak. If he'd been strong enough to get the Shard of the Specter, he'd still be sparring with anvils."

"Raysky, Raysky, Raysky," Hanngoh slurred. "Always with the swords. What's that in ya hand there? *Another sword?* Ya can't seem to get enough of them. Does that one have a pretty name, too?"

"You aren't worthy of my war hammer," Raysk growled. The mask of scars over his face turned a darker red.

"As ya can see, I'm unarmed. Except for me bottle o' rum, o' course. Let's settle this like sailors."

"You're a pirate, not a sailor."

"Every sailor's a pirate after he's drank enough rum." Hanngoh grinned. "I say we drink until the loser crumples like a struck sail." The dark brown rum sloshed as he shook the bottle. "I would drink ya under the table. Then I would drink what was left in yer bottle."

"I'd rather strangle you with that rope," Raysk said, pointing his sword where a frayed line dangled from the corner of a sail.

"That's not a rope, it's a line," Hanngoh yawned.

"You sailors have more words than brains. What do you call that wheel you're leaning on?"

"It's a wheel, ya fool." Hanngoh took another pull of his rum. "I'm surprised ya made a return voyage. I thought the only time ya got in the water is when ya slaughter yer own. Like the fella who's a head shorter over there. I'm sure ya stand real tall in that safe, shallow stream. But yer in deep water now. *Dark Water.*"

Hanngoh's crew was still as their Swordfather spoke.

They remained along the railing. Some stayed attentive, with their eyes darting between the families. Others looked as though they might fall asleep. A few of them enjoyed their own bottles of rum, taking even more drinks than their Blade.

"Give us the sword and we'll consider leaving without turning your boat into a floating funeral pyre," Droena said. Some Heavies held their torches high.

"Ahr, if I were you I'd be thinkin' real hard about what ya do to me ship. Leaving her on this side o' the water be in your interest and mine. True that me warriors and captains can't outfight ya, but we can out-swim ya. Our friends in the sea won't touch those filthy rafts ya crafted. But we will. If *Shark Queen* burns, and some o' me crew were to reach out o' the portholes and cut loose those ugly rafts, this port will become a red sea o' your Swordfamily's blood." Hanngoh spun the wheel around and gestured at the water. "You should be beggin' us not to scuttle *Shark Queen*. Ya don't look like ya swim much, Raysk."

"Water is for those who are too weak to fight on land," Raysk said with confidence. "I'd sooner breathe water than learn to swim like a fish."

"Look into the port, Raysk, and tell me what ya see." Hanngoh smiled, adding a few more wrinkles to his young, but weathered, face. "*Tell me what ya see.*"

Raysk glanced over his shoulder. Then he turned to face the port. A forest of large fins circled the hull of *Shark Queen*. They all swam in the same direction, so close that the sharks must have rubbed together. Droena sensed that the Heavies now stood on a ship in the center of a giant whirlpool made of teeth.

Hanngoh turned his bottle bottom up to drink down the last few drops. Then he whipped it overboard. Where it landed, the sea became a white foam and the crowd of shark fins moved like the teeth on a saw.

"Where do ya think all the shark teeth on me boat came from? We didn't kill the shark to get our hands on them. That would be like a Fire Keeper killin' a dragon for its win's. No, we summoned our friends and pulled them out real gentle-like. Then we sent them on their way. Sharks have lots o' teeth, rows and rows of them. They don't miss the ones we use. They grow new teeth and we grow stronger. In the sea, strength begets strength."

"That's what those were?" Raysk feigned ignorance. "I thought I was crushing barnacles when I stomped on the side of your boat."

"Ship."

"You have something that I want. Either give it to me or I'll take it from you."

"Oh, I'll give you somethin'. I'll add a fresh scar to that ugly collection on ya face." Hanngoh spun the wheel next to him. "O' course, your deepest scar isn't on ya face; it's between ya legs."

Raysk growled.

The Heavies began to advance from the starboard side of the ship. The Dark Waters remained loose near the port-side railing. Their weapons remained pointed at the deck.

"Raysk, I'm a reasonable Swordfather," Hanngoh called. Faomen shot him a worried look. "If our families fight, my warriors will be swabbin' the decks for an eclipse to wash away all ya Heavy blood. Tell yer thugs to wait. We'll settle this Blade to Blade."

The scars on Raysk's face crackled as he frowned.

"Ya sent one o' yer glorified cupbearers to fight Emerald Ezzy for the Shard o' the Specter. Seems to me that fightin' an unarmed sailor would be the manliest thin' you've done since ya declared yer silly little war for that bloody Bleedin' Blade."

Hanngoh held his arms wide with his palms open and facing up.

Gripping his sword so tight that his knuckles turned white, Raysk growled. "Hanngoh, if you promise to shut your fish mouth, I'll grant you the honor of dying by my hand."

Hanngoh smiled and beckoned his opponent. The Heavies retreated back to the starboard side of *Shark Queen*.

Raysk raised his sword. "One dead Dark Water or a hundred dead Dark Waters. Makes no difference to me." He spun the blade that he pointed at Hanngoh. "Now what weapon will you use? Foul language?"

"Words are weapons," Hanngoh slurred. "And I wield them well." He staggered down the steps from the quarter-deck and approached Raysk.

"Have it your way." Raysk shrugged as he raised his sword. "It'll be easy to bury you at sea. I'll just drop a torch and throw you over the back of the boat."

"Transom." Hanngoh clucked his tongue. "If ya burn *Shark Queen*, ya will envy the dead men that carried ya here."

"Looks like someone already tried," Raysk said. He pointed at a narrow burn mark that stretched across the deck, all the way from the portside to starboard. A few more streaks of blackened wood scarred the deck.

"Not all o' our passengers are as friendly as ya."

Hanngoh approached to stand within easy striking distance of the Heavies' Swordfather.

Raysk brought his sword around in a sweeping arc. Hanngoh raised a hand above his shoulder as the blade sliced down toward his head. The sound of steel striking hard rang out.

The two froze for an instant. Hanngoh's arm quivered as he pushed hard against his opponent's strength. Then he relented and spun around to sprint back toward the quarterdeck. He stood on the steps near the wheel, holding out the same hand he had raised to parry Raysk's attack.

"That's a wise place to hide an invisible sword," Raysk said. "Because now you can hand it over to me. Then we'll leave you and your Swordfamily to cleaning barnacles off your ship or whatever it is you do out here."

"The only way I'm cleanin' barnacles off me hull is keelhaulin' ya when we're headed downwind at full sail."

"Is that a threat or your next voyage?"

"Both," Hanngoh replied. He leapt toward Raysk with his arm whipping around. Raysk blocked with hesitant cuts, trying to anticipate where the unseen blade sliced through the air.

The Heavies grew nervous. Most of them now clutched their weapons tight. Droena had never seen Raysk spooked in a fight.

Grasping the Shard of the Specter with both hands, Hanngoh hacked away at Raysk's blade. Raysk parried the blows once and again, but the Dark Water swept his blade across the Heavy's gut. A line of crimson drops fell from the shallow wound.

Droena gasped.

Raysk pressed his fingertips against the cut. When he pulled them away, they were caked in blood. "Congratulations are in order," Raysk said in a droll tone. "Few Swordfathers have drawn my blood. When I give your eulogy before I dump your corpse into the Angered Sea, I'll be sure to mention your greatest feat."

He charged at Hanngoh, who quickly rolled to the port side of *Shark Queen*. Raysk gave chase. He brought his steel blade down twice, which Hanngoh dodged. The blade left deep gouges in the deck. Hanngoh fled to the edge of the ship, next to a line dangling from a sail.

Raysk charged like a bull.

Hanngoh clasped his hands together. When he pulled them apart, he feinted with the empty hand and Raysk slashed the air where he thought the invisible sword lunged. With his other hand, Hanngoh swung the Shard of the Specter by Raysk's face, drawing more blood from the Heavy. The fresh cut on Raysk's cheek was deep enough that it would leave a scar.

Raysk responded before the first drop of blood fell from his face. Faster than Hanngoh could move, he brought the sword down. It sliced across Hanngoh's chest and he howled in pain. The Dark Water grabbed the line hanging from a sail and swung from it. His grip slipped and he let go an instant too soon, slamming into the deck where it met the plank.

Grimacing, Hanngoh rose to his feet and staggered down the plank. He kicked Zrobik's corpse and it splashed into the water below. Then he scampered to the end of the whalebone and turned to face Raysk.

"Ya fightin' or tryin' to make me chest look like yer face?" Hanngoh growled.

"I don't care where my enemies bleed from," Raysk said. He stood where the plank met the deck. The Dark Waters near him edged away. "So long as they bleed."

"Dark Water...it's time to abandon ship," Hanngoh said.

His Swordfamily followed the order. Every warrior and captain that served Hanngoh had been sitting or leaning on the portside railing. At their Swordfather's words, each one gathered their weapon and leaned back to tumble into the waters below. The sounds of splashes filled the night as they dropped from the ship.

"Take another look out there, Raysk," Hanngoh called from the plank. He pressed hard against his fresh wound. "Put me ship to the torch and me sharks will make sure that if ya ever set foot on shore again, it will be yer foot alone and nothin' else. The rest o' you will fill their bellies." Hanngoh clenched his teeth. "Even if they must die jumpin' onto those nasty rafts ya built."

"Surrender the Shard of the Specter and you have my word as a Blade that I won't burn your ship."

"The only thin' ya can hope to get from me is safe passage back to the docks. I'll only surrender that much if ya leave without harm to *Shark Queen*." The forest of fins continued to swirl around the ship. "This is our castle and keep. If ya sink her, ya will learn a reason why we're called Dark Water. It's not because we ply deep seas. It's for what happens under the water if ya wrong us. Ya will meet pain so terrible that ya will blow the air out o' yer lungs to hasten the sweet release o' death. Ya will find no mercy from our horrors below."

"Give me the sword now or I'll keep returning until you do."

Hanngoh laughed hard before pain and a wave of spasms gripped his body. "I'll tell you true, Raysk. You won't see me with the Shard o' the Specter again. Seein' you in anger as I hid it has given me more joy than a bottle o' rum the size o' me ship. I swear on me honor as a Swordfather, this is the last night that Dark Water will hold this blade."

"What will you do with it?"

"Might be I drop it to the bottom o' the Angered Sea.

Could give it to someone who gives it to ya by plungin' it into yer neck. Wherever it goes, it won't be here," Hanngoh said through gritted teeth. "Now I'll take me leave. Yer welcome to join me."

The whirlpool swirled in a foamy white circle directly below Hanngoh.

"Come with me and ya will swim with the fishes forever."

The plank bounced as Hanngoh sprang backward. He arced his back and his body turned down. He sped toward the whirlpool headfirst. There, he disappeared without a sound.

Raysk walked to the end of the plank. He held his sword like a dagger. Then he threw it down with the blade pointed at the whirlpool. The white water spun away and the steel barely made a splash where it landed in calm water. Raysk turned to his Swordfamily.

"What is thy bidding, my Blade?" Vasarox asked. "Shall we torch the ship?"

"No," Raysk said as he scratched his jaw. "I want Dark Water gone. If we destroy their boat, they have no choice but to stay and fight. If the seaweed in Hanngoh's head dries out, he'll understand that if they stay, we'll keep coming back until the Shard of the Specter is ours. If we leave their ship, they'll leave Fulccrum. That'll be one less Swordfamily."

"What is our plan of attack?" Vasarox asked.

"The Shard could have made the path to victory shorter and less bloody. But it's not necessary for me to rise as the Greatsword." Raysk smeared the fresh blood on his trunk and face. "Now I march the path soaked with the blood of Swordfamilies who dare oppose me."

CHAPTER SIXTEEN
FIRE KEEPERS

The Scabbard patted down Andra the moment she entered the DragInn. When he had finished, she handed the man two silver crowns out of habit. He took both coins from the Fire Keeper, then handed one of them back to her. She shrugged before tucking it into a pocket.

Empty tables and chairs filled the tavern before Andra. The few patrons in the room were hidden in corners. They faced away from the door with their heads hanging low. They didn't come to the DragInn for companionship. They came for the drink, and the drink alone.

The sign above Andra read, "No swords, war hammers, daggers, dirks, dragons, wands, or anything else that would make the Scabbards angry." Before Raysk declared his war, the sign was a friendly jest. When she saw it tonight, Andra felt a pang of sorrow.

On the far side of the tavern, behind the bar made of dark wood, the innkeeper stood by himself. He leaned on the bar, staring at some place halfway between himself and

Andra. Only a single cask of ale on the stack behind him had been tapped.

She walked to the bar and rested her elbow on it. "No minstrel tonight, eh, Reddy?" she asked.

The innkeeper didn't budge.

"Reddy, you here?"

"Huh?" Reddy shook his head, shooing away unseen cobwebs. "Oh. Hello there, Andra. Thanks for comin' by. Don't see many Fire Keepers these days. Don't see the other families either, for that matter." He sighed.

The bar was immaculate. There were no rings of dried ale where tankards had been set. Scraps of food brought from the kitchen were nowhere to be seen. If every morsel on the floor was swept into a pile, it wouldn't have been enough to feed a mouse.

"The Scabbard only took one silver crown."

"Aye, I asked 'em to take less. Tryin' to get more patrons in here. Soon I won't need a Scabbard at all. There's not much to guard." He absently rubbed a rag inside a spotless tankard. "I've spent days just standin' here. There's nothin' to clean. Almost no one to serve. Real quiet here. I feel like a statue most o' the time." He clutched at his beard. Andra noticed many more rows of worry lines than the last time she had seen him. "I hope this gets sorted out soon. Don't know how long I can last without servin' anyone anythin'. Enough of my woes. Innkeeper is supposed to listen to problems, not burden others with his own."

A patron in a corner took a drink and set down his tankard. He sobbed loudly.

"Have you seen Glas in here with that Heavy?"

"Not since the talk of war got loud. Like well-nigh everyone else."

Andra tapped her fist on the bar.

"What'll it be?"

"Sorry, Reddy," Andra said, patting his hand. "Nothing for me tonight."

"Oh, right! I'm sorry, I forgot about him. He's upstairs in the usual room."

Andra put three gold scythes on the bar and winked at the innkeeper. "We may need the room tomorrow morning." She thought for a moment. "And tomorrow night, too."

He picked up the gold coins and saluted her with them. "It's yours as long as you want it."

"Don't tempt me!"

The rickety wooden stairs to the inn above the tavern squeaked as Andra stepped on them. The boards beneath her feet rubbed hard against the nails that were losing their struggle to hold the wood tight.

As she mounted each step, a charge shot through her. Some of it came from eager anticipation of the night to come. The rest was her fear of delivering bad news. The two sensations alternated with each step, one after the other, dread and desire.

Walking swiftly down a hallway with more loose boards, she arrived at a familiar door. She knocked three times and waited a moment. Hearing nothing, she slowly opened it and entered.

Some candles burned inside the room. Their flames danced from the change in the air as Andra closed the door behind her. A hot fire crackled in a small fireplace.

Andra's heart beat faster than the wings on a panicked dragon. She locked the door and hung her cloak. Her eyes lingered on a small looking glass.

She had a friendly smile that flew like a welcome banner in soft wind. Her large eyes were hazel and warm;

they made her many quick friends even before she spoke a word. The natural beauty of her young face was tempered by the burden of decisions that meant life or death for her —or someone else. Streaks of auburn curled playfully through her tawny hair. She had dark eyebrows, plump lips, and smooth cheeks.

When she turned to face the room, her smooth cheeks quickly turned bright red.

"Are ya a Syren? Because I have The Need," Hanngoh said. He sat on a chair across the room. A candle sitting on a table next to him bathed a side of his body in warm, yellow light.

"Why are you naked already?" Andra asked as she put her hands on her hips.

"Because it gets us halfway to the time when we're both naked," Hanngoh replied. He took a drink and wiped the dribble of rum from his lips with the same hand that held the bottle.

"What happened to your chest? That cut looks deep."

"That little scratch? 'Tis a gift from Raysk," Hanngoh replied, looking at the deep cut with contempt. "He and his family were unwelcome stowaways on *Shark Queen*. Told him I didn't much appreciate him tryin' to make me chest look like his face. Didn't like the cut at first but I think it makes me look tough as boiled leather. Like I been nursin' a hungry baby shark with me blood!"

"Can I dress the wound?" Andra asked.

Hanngoh took another swig from his bottle. Then he poured some of its liquid on his cut.

"Old medicine woman lived on some tiny speck o' an island. The horde o' gods had forsaken that place long ago, but she taught me the only thin' I know about healin'. She said that rum kills whatever makes a cut turn yer blood bad." He took another pull from the bottle. "I pour the strong drink *on* me and *in* me. I figure that way both sides o' the wound will heal."

Hanngoh stood. The two walked toward each other until they stood close at the foot of the feather bed. Hanngoh handed the bottle of rum to Andra, who drank it greedily.

"Ya don't usually drink like that. Not the rum," Hanngoh said. "Let me take yer mind off whatever troubles ya."

He moved his hand slightly and, although he didn't touch her, the top button on Andra's jerkin sprang off. She looked down to find that the top had fallen open.

After Hanngoh flicked his hand, and more buttons jumped in the air, the front of her jerkin opened wide.

"I paid good gold for this!" Andra protested.

"There's always more gold in the world," Hanngoh said dismissively.

The jerkin's lowest and final button fell to the floor. Then the jerkin itself hastened to follow.

"I sense that you're not telling me something," Andra said as her eyes narrowed in suspicion. "This isn't how you normally undress me."

Another quick snap of Hanngoh's hand and the privy clothes that had been under Andra's jerkin fell away. Her chest was now bare. Gooseflesh erupted over her exposed skin.

"Ow!" she said. "You scratched me."

Three tiny drops of blood sprouted from a thin pink line on Andra's stomach. He poured some rum on the scratch.

"I taught ya somethin'!" Hanngoh laughed. "Now every time ya pour rum on a wound ya'll think o' me."

Hanngoh moved his hand up and down. The drawstring

that held up Andra's trousers was sliced into two pieces. The trousers fell to the floor.

"You better not cut my privy clothes," Andra said without looking down. "I wore them for you. They're your favorite."

"Aye, they are. But that's where me treasure lies!"

Andra pushed him on the shoulder.

"Ah, careful. Don't move. I'm still not sure how long this is," Hanngoh warned.

Her last bit of modesty floated to the floor. Andra made no effort to conceal herself.

Their naked bodies told the tale of two very different lives. Hanngoh was younger but the sea, its hard weather, and years as a Swordfather gave him wrinkles that belied his youth. Hanngoh had seen the same number of eclipses as any other man his age, but he had lived harder years.

Andra's body was made of gentle curves that she thought curved a little too much. Her skin was smooth as a carefully polished gem, except where a few long scars served as unwanted reminders of her own slow decisions in the presence of her enemies' fast blades.

A black flame was tattooed over her heart. Fyur had inked it for her the day she became a warrior.

"How am I supposed to leave the DragInn now that you turned my clothes into rags?" Andra waved her hands at the pile of cloth lying on the floor at her feet.

"Who said yer goin' to leave?" Hanngoh asked earnestly.

"How in the realm did you get the Shard—?" Andra started.

Hanngoh waved his hand, silencing her. He moved his arm toward the chair and opened his hand. Something made a thud and a hole sprang open in the cloth seat. The two wrapped their arms around each other and kissed hard. Feathers sprang into the air as they collapsed onto the bed together. Their skin pressed tight as the two fought to become one. When they pulled back, Andra brushed her hand against the fresh pink wound on Hanngoh's chest.

"Don't worry yerself about that," Hanngoh said softly, pushing her hand away. "I'll be fine. Maybe the scar will cover up some o' these wrinkles the sun insists that I wear."

They wrapped themselves together tightly and nestled between inviting pillows. Hanngoh put his head on Andra's shoulder. He caressed her with hands calloused from pulling thick lines and turning a rebellious wheel. His fingers scratched the Fire Keeper's skin, but she didn't mind.

"I have ill tidings," Andra said. Her voice felt and sounded empty.

"Then *we* have some ill tidin's," Hanngoh sighed. He squeezed his love tight.

Running her fingers through Hanngoh's curly black hair, Andra drew a deep breath. "I have to leave the city for a time," she said, all at once. "Kardas is sending me to the Paders to aid the Emerald Crown."

Hanngoh raised his head and furrowed his brow. "Help the *crown*? Why?"

"The Heavies will come for us first. Fallov is our ally. Kardas says that a strong crown makes our family strong, and the other way around. Since the reds are like to come through the Paders, we're going to send some dragons into the passes to slow them down."

"He's sending ya with them," Hanngoh groaned as he nuzzled at her neck. "Why go? Quit the Fire Keepers. Join me Dark Water. A war between crowns is no war for us.

This kingdom is just the sea where the Swordfamilies set their sails. A green sea, a red sea, it matters not."

"I'm not just *going* with them, I'm *leading* them," Andra corrected him. "Me, who wasn't even a captain the last triple eclipse. I'll be the one giving orders instead of taking them. Kardas has put his faith in me."

"Ah, what's a triple eclipse but a time when the sea's tides and the townsfolk's passions are high?" Hanngoh asked.

They both closed their eyes and enjoyed each other's welcoming skin. Even after a length of silence, surrounded by a soft feather bed and warm bodies, neither one was near sleep.

Andra's heart beat even faster than when she'd arrived.

"I want ya to have it," Hanngoh said in a whisper.

He ran a finger along the shallow scratch on Andra's belly that he had made.

"Have what?"

"Is yer head full of ash? What do ya think?" Hanngoh said, pinching her side. Andra slapped his hand away. "I'm talkin' about that sword ya can't see. The one Ezzy called the Shard o' the Specter." Andra parried his attack when he poked at her navel. "The one I used to slice off all o' yer fine clothes bought with yer precious gold. Take it. Make use of it in yer battles, however ya can." Hanngoh pressed against the fresh wound on his chest. "If I was quicker with a blade, or hadn't drank so much rum, I could've thrust before Raysk made the first strike. I wish chance was a mermaid, then she might've favored me. With Raysk gone, maybe Kardas wouldn't care so much about the greens and reds. If I weren't so damn slow, maybe ya wouldn't be headed into so much danger."

"How'd you get it?"

Hanngoh sighed. "Drownin' in all the lies that Ezzy spewed before the king and queen, there was precious little truth. But there was *some*." He clenched his hand into a fist. "Me captains took it from her shop while other families tried."

Andra wound one of Hanngoh's dark curls around her little finger.

"You knew she had it."

"I didn't. But there was lots o' talk about that sword down on the docks. Where there's smoke, there's dragons. I knew that if she had it, she'd never let it go without someone payin' a handsome price. And I don't mean coin. Cost me a great captain." He closed his eyes. "She'd never let that oaf husband steal it from her." He laughed. "He used to be a great hunter of relics, himself. Now he can't even find where his wife keeps their treasures! He probably ran his hands over the whole shop searching for it."

"Like this?"

Andra slid her hands up and down her love, pinching in spots and fending off an elbow being driven into her side. Their pinches and laughter went on so long that a candle burned out before they calmed themselves.

"I don't know what that sword is made o', but it must be tough. Raysk's strokes didn't break it. Might be there's a nick in the edge now."

"Why not leave it with Ezmerelda?"

"Same reason the families are startin' to fight," Hanngoh sighed. "If we didn't take it, one o' the other families would've. They'd have the sword and the advantage o' surprise against anyone who didn't know they wielded it."

Andra pulled him close. She swatted his hand away as he pinched her nipple.

"What happened to Ezzy?"

"Last my captain saw, she disappeared inside o' her shop as it burned down into the water," Hanngoh said. "Me whirlpool saved Faomen. Mayhaps I could ask the swirling white water. If Ezmerelda's still alive, I expect she'll surface when and where it suits her. She harbors more than a little hate for me, no doubt."

Hanngoh petted Andra's belly for a time, careful to avoid the scratch.

"I've never trusted Raysk. Never trust a man who can't swim, that's what I say. Raysk can't swim any better than he can show mercy." Hanngoh's eyes narrowed and he shook his head. "I took that sword, but I cannot hold it. If we tried, the Heavies would keep boardin' us until they found it or sent *Shark Queen* to the bottom o' the Angered Sea. If any family can guard that blade and use it, it's yers. Just promise me somethin'."

The hairs on the back of Andra's neck stood up. "Sword-fathers don't give gifts; they trap the unwary in debts. What do you ask of me in return?"

Hanngoh raised his head from Andra's shoulder. "If ya get the chance to kill Raysk with that sword, do it. The Shard o' the Specter should make him a ghost."

"I will," Andra replied, kissing him on the forehead. "I promise."

Hanngoh pulled himself up. They sat next to each other with their backs against the wall.

"So yer goin' to the Paders?"

"I am." Andra patted him on the thigh. "I'll be back soon. Then we'll be together again." She smiled at him, but he was looking away. "Why are you so sad? It won't be long. I'll be back in the city after we slow the Crimson Crown."

Hanngoh reached out and wove their fingers together.

"I, too, must go," Hanngoh said. He spoke the words

softly, but they hit Andra like a lance to her chest. "For the good o' me family."

Andra started to ask why. Then she closed her mouth without making a sound.

"Even if the Heavies stay out o' the port, we're not strong enough to shape this war. I must do what's best for me family. If I stay while we're weak, the best I could hope for are the right friends in the right families." Hanngoh stared at the ceiling. "I drift in a sea o' doubt. I would much rather be sailin' the Angered Sea."

Andra squeezed his hand. "Where will you go?"

"We'll weigh anchor and sail past that statue they'll never finish. From there, I do not know. Maybe the Ring Islands or farther west to the Land o' the Setting Sun. Could go t'other way, head to the east and the Rising Gold. Strange ships say there's good ports there. Could go north to the lands that wear the Night Crown. Don't think I could abide the Realm o' Rime, though. Even me rum couldn't keep me warm there. Mayhaps to the south, see if we can get through the Timeless Tempest. They say so many ships have wrecked in that storm there's a pile o' treasure taller than Mount Densmore."

Andra put her arm around Hanngoh's shoulders and pulled him tight.

"I love you, but that's a terrible plan. You're just sailing away from problems on that boat you won't let me board."

"She's not a pretty ship. And yer not wrong," Hanngoh said, caressing the arm that Andra had put around him. "The important thin' isn't *where* we're sailin' to, it's *what* we're sailin' to. Dark Water is leavin' because we're weak where it matters most. The Fire Keepers rule the air and land because they have dragons. They're strong because of dragons. Me family is weak because we're strong in the wrong place. Every ship for a thousand leagues, and another thousand leagues, knows that Dark Water's sails are victory flags. The Heavies and the rest o' the families know that our sails are flags o' surrender soon as we disembark and put our drippin' wet feet on dry land."

"If only there was some way to know the future before it becomes the past," Andra mumbled.

"Ahr, some o' me family is friendly with Ashfall. It's said they have some drug that gives ya visions. Whether it's the future or past or somethin' else, I don't know. Ashfall probably doesn't either."

Andra grunted.

As the two sat together in silence, another candle guttered out.

"I must find somethin' that gives us strength where the dirt is above the water. We'll never be the Heavies or the Fire Keepers, but we have to be somethin' more than a piece o' driftwood for Raysk to break over his knee."

"I could speak with Kardas. Our families could band together."

"A kind offer, but our only allies lie beneath the waves." Hanngoh hesitated for a moment. "Kardas has been cold to me since the misfortune with Fyur."

Andra wiped a tear from her cheek.

"I'll try to send word by messenger pigeon. I swear the ones we have are part seagull. The whole sea is their nest. I wish we could get pigeons sent to me ship, but when yer castle moves through waves like mine, there's no way for the birds to find me."

He bit the bottom of his lip.

"I'll leave some o' me family in Fulccrum. Faomen will stay behind. He's a good captain. The wound from stealin' the Shard hasn't healed yet. His arm's in bad shape. He shouldn't be at sea. Some others will be here, too. Might leave Hazord. He's a captain. Me best warrior is Rooker. He'll remain." He pressed the fresh wound gifted by Raysk. "If ya need anythin', ya know where to find them. Me people never wander from the water for long. They'll keep an eye on ya and yer families. Both families."

"The Fire Keepers honor Sacred Kin, but I fear that nothing is sacred to some families." Andra sighed. "You remember what Lecata and Mistahn look like, right?"

Hanngoh nodded.

"Good. Make certain whoever you leave behind knows, too."

The Swordfather nodded again.

Hanngoh pulled Andra's hand to his lips. Then he kissed it, soft as sin.

Andra's chin trembled.

"When should I watch for you?" she asked.

"Can't say. When I've made me Swordfamily strong."

The wood in the fire popped, throwing an ember onto the hearth. The last candle's flame withered into smoke. The only light that graced the room came from the small fire.

"Let's make love until the feathers in this bed are all in the air," Hanngoh whispered.

"For now, let's enjoy each other this way," Andra said as she wrapped herself around Hanngoh. "I may need this memory for a long time. I want it to stay in my mind like it's carved in stone." She bit her lip. "And I need some time to distance my thoughts from...him."

Hanngoh unleashed a frustrated sigh. Andra released him.

"I'm sorry. I know it's been months, but Fyur was very dear to me."

"Well I'm here, and yer dear to *me*." Hanngoh curled his hands into fists. "I told ya I did all I could to bring him back."

Andra crossed her arms, covering her breasts. "This pain feels so familiar. I've lost Fyur forever and soon you'll be gone."

"I'll return. I can't stay away. I'd do anything for ya."

Andra smiled at him.

He cupped her breast in his hand and squeezed it tight. She grabbed his wrist and pushed it against his wounded chest.

"Let's stay like this. Give me tonight to quiet my memories."

He groaned and covered his face with both hands. Then he rolled over.

"Don't be cross," she said, smacking Hanngoh on his arse. "I gave Reddy enough gold for another night...or nights."

"I'll think of ya while I'm at sea. The memories will be worn thin by the time I return."

With a final crackle, the flames succumbed to the cold. But the lovers' bed remained warm.

CHAPTER SEVENTEEN

IRON WAND

Sunlight drenched the gently winding streets of Fulccrum's Satinwind district. Draught horses pulled wains with fresh vegetables piled high. Some were loaded with casks of ale that sloshed with each step. Others carried salted meats covered in tight cloth to ward off bugs, scavengers, and desperately hungry men. Each wain smelled like a banquet of sumptuous plates gracing the table at a royal feast.

The bright spring day reminded children that summer was nigh. Packs of them chased each other across the wide cobblestone streets as they squealed in delight. Merchants hawked their goods from wide stalls hoping that country-folk, pleasure-seekers who entered the city through the southernmost gate, would surrender their copper, silver, and gold.

Patrons circulated through taverns and shops where the crowds milled about. Many who wandered from a tavern to a shop to an inn marveled at how each stop in their journey was more expensive than the last, but not as costly as the next.

Three figures walked together. Despite the sun and heat, each wore heavy robes with the hood pulled up. They looked down and kept their hands hidden inside their sleeves. Instinctively, those who traveled this street kept their distance from the trio.

"Are you certain this is wise, my Blade?" Guiden asked.

"It is a risk, but one that I have measured with great care," Irin replied quietly. "If the Syrens truly desire something from us, mayhaps we can sow a favor and reap a debt."

"The Syrens are beautiful things full of rot," Guiden grumbled.

A child with his head down sprinted toward the Iron Wands. When his eyes rose to find the mages, he skidded to a stop and ran back in the direction from which he came.

"I reason that most families will not yet attack each other," Irin said. "This is Raysk's war, and his alone, until it spills over to the rest of us. It would be folly for the other Swordfamilies to fight so long as the Heavies and Fire Keepers maintain their strength. I don't think this invitation was a ruse. Of course, even if they're not trying to kill us presently, we must remain cautious."

A driver called to his draught horse and steered his wain away from the three Iron Wands.

"For now, any enemy of the Heavies is our friend, it would seem," Guiden added.

"Indeed," Irin agreed. Her bright white robes flashed in the sunlight. "Many eclipses ago, the Syrens and Heavies were, how shall we say, friendly. That is, for some time while Minacia was the Syrens' Swordfather, she and Raysk were romantic. It is said that when he spurned her and she left the family, it drove him to disfigure himself."

"Do you believe that?" Lisha asked. "What they say about his worst scar?"

"I do," Irin answered. "The Syrens have a perverse ability to command the minds of those who fall under their spell." She looked up, squinting in the sunlight. "Their control is more than a primal desire for flesh. Syren power transcends lust and what most refer to as love. It's something more, an ability to make their prey desire them more than the air we breathe. The victim's mind is changed to believe that their Syren master is the font from which their own meaning and happiness flow."

"We must shield ourselves from their charms," Lisha observed.

"Did you drink the potion?" Irin asked. Her captain and warrior nodded in response. "Good. If Hiamoe is right, it's as good a protection as one can find against the Syrens' powers."

Turning a corner, Lisha sensed a palpable change in the atmosphere. The sun shone just as brightly here, but the townsfolk's mood changed dramatically. Some of them stood in the street looking directly into the sun. Others sat on the ground with their backs against the buildings as they sobbed into their hands. One man yelling gibberish sprinted toward the Iron Wands. Guiden pulled a dagger from his robes and plunged it into the crazed man's chest. He crumpled to the ground.

"Freedom," the man moaned as a red puddle spread beneath him. "Sweet freedom."

The blade disappeared beneath Guiden's robes as quickly as it had appeared.

"I have The Need!" a woman who was nearly naked screamed. She tore at the tattered remains of her clothing.

Next to her, an old man sat on the ground with his legs

splayed wide. He brought a large stone down on his manhood again and again, grunting each time it landed.

A young woman whose skin was tight against her bones hobbled toward the Iron Wands. She begged for a gold scythe. Her eyes were dark. The trio passed by her without a word. She leaned against a stone wall, exhausted from the effort of begging. Each breath she drew was a struggle for survival.

Before the Iron Wands could see the entrance to the Shrine of Solace, they could smell the bodies. Strewn about the street were many corpses. Some of them had been dead for days, and some were so fresh that their eyes had not yet sunken. Among them, many were naked.

Long white banners swayed in the light breeze above the Shrine of Solace.

"Look at them," Lisha whispered, gesturing at the dead. "Their mouths look strange. As if they're smiling."

"It must be the way their skin shrank after death," Guiden said.

"No. They all have much the same look. The fresh and the rotten," Irin replied.

Near the shrine's entrance, a woman sat on the ground. She drew deep breaths. Her grin was so wide that each corner of her mouth seemed to touch her ears. Her eyes were vacant. Blood streamed from somewhere under her clothes to pool around her threadbare trousers.

No door hung in the entrance to the Shrine of Solace. Instead, strings of gems dangled in the doorway. The gems were red and purple, pink and white. The pattern they formed gave the impression of a naked body's inviting curves.

"Please! Please! I'm begging you!" a voice screamed from inside the shrine. "I'll do anything! I'll clean the worst floors! I'll haul out the bodies! Anything! Don't make me go! I have The Need! *The Need*!"

The Iron Wands backed away from the entrance.

Strings of gems clattered as two men burst through them. Between them a much smaller man tried to dig his heels into the ground. He succeeded only in clearing lines in the dust outside the shrine. After advancing a few steps outside, the large men threw the smaller man to the ground. As he lay in the street, he drew himself into a tight ball and sobbed almost as loud as he had screamed in protest.

The two large men returned to the Shrine of Solace.

Before the Iron Wands could follow them, a young woman raced inside. A pouch full of coins jingled merrily on her hip. She was a pale waif clad in a simple dress. Her brown, feathery hair was so long that it reached the small of her back.

The gemstones hanging in the doorway were light and surprisingly soft. Lisha felt as though her robes had fallen to the floor and the gems had become soft hands caressing her body.

The Shrine of Solace was decorated much like the attire worn by Syrens. The walls were made of silk so thin it was transparent. It hung from the ceiling to offer patrons only a whisper of privacy as they indulged. The songs in the shrine were not sung by minstrels. They were the moans of satisfaction, cries of delight, and screams of pleasure the patrons sang to the accompaniment of a harp.

Candles burned with flames barely bright enough to reflect off of quivering flesh. Lisha felt herself being pulled deeper into the shrine by some unseen force. The perfumed air permeated her body, luring her with the promise of an ecstasy that went far deeper than skin.

Saliva dripped from Guiden's bottom lip.

Lisha crossed her legs absently.

"Welcome to our principal Shrine of Solace, my Iron Wand friends," Sinsasi said elegantly. "You will not find a more epicurean collection of men and women to satisfy your appetites. Join us and relax for a time. *Indulge yourselves.*"

"We're here to speak with you. We will not succumb to your enticements," Irin said in an icy voice.

"Of course," Sinsasi said. She smiled with her mouth, but not with her eyes. "Please allow me to introduce you to some of my family. This is Hallita. She's our most promising warrior." Sinsasi gestured with one of her gloved hands at the warrior, who gave their guests a shallow bow. "And this is one of my captains, Ederron."

The Syren captain took Lisha's hand in his and gave it a gentle kiss. Gooseflesh raced from her hand to spread over every part of her body. She looked down to ensure that her robes still concealed her nipples that felt as though they might've jumped from her breasts. Ederron bowed deeply. His skin was bronze and his eyes were light gray. His wavy black hair bounced like a flat stone skipped across a still pond. In the dimness, Lisha wondered that he might be some beautiful apparition, a shadow of a winsome ghost.

"We are honored that you've accepted our invitation," Ederron said.

The three Syrens were clothed in sheer satin. It clung tight to their bodies, but still concealed that which made their guests' loins ache with hunger. The younger Iron Wands stared at the flesh rarely seen, but found only inviting forms and shadows that inflamed their imagination.

Beads of sweat clung to Guiden's forehead despite the coolness inside the shrine.

A young woman screaming words the Iron Wands couldn't understand was carried out by two much larger women. They carried her by the wrists and ankles. Guiden ducked behind his Swordfather to avoid the chaos.

"What's happening in this place?" Lisha asked. Her eyes lingered on the woman writhing in anger. "There's something wrong with these people."

"We must politely ask some of our patrons to leave," Ederron said. He had a light sweat over his torso and legs. The thin satin that he wore soaked in the sweat to cling tightly against his well-defined muscles.

"There are a number of bodies lying in the street," Guiden added.

"A somewhat regrettable consequence of our work here," Sinsasi replied coolly. "They'll be cleared away soon."

"The patrons seem quite desperate for your affection," Guiden said.

"That's our secret," Ederron replied. "Or should I say, one of our secrets. Yearning is better than having. Desire is the master of control. We are quite skilled at prolonging the moment of...anticipation. Sometimes we stretch our patrons' desire so far that we rip apart their minds."

"That explains the people screaming as you drag them out of here," Lisha said. "But what about the dead fouling the air in the street?"

"Those are our former patrons," Hallita replied. "They no longer possessed the coin to enjoy our charms. That circumstance was very upsetting to them and they made their choice."

Lisha and Guiden shared a look.

"Your Swordfamily's home is quite a spectacle," Irin

said in a dry voice. "We do enjoy spending time drinking in the sumptuous beauty of your family. That said, we are here on business and I insist that we now attend to it."

"Of course. Please, follow me through the main floor," Sinsasi responded.

When the Syren Swordfather turned to lead the party deeper into her shrine, Guiden's eyes rampaged up and down her backside. He clenched his teeth. Lisha drove her elbow into his chest. Irin hastened to walk between the Syrens and her Iron Wands, but even she found her eyes lingering on Ederron's toned flesh.

The group meandered through a maze with walls of thin silk. The Iron Wands couldn't ignore the decadent orgy surrounding them. This shrine was a battlefield of desire clashing with satisfaction. The battles were fought on a field of feather pillows. The views were more than the Iron Wands' imagination could muster. They were enraptured.

In a silk-clad chamber, a naked Syren sat on a throne carved from stone. Fires with tall flames burned in small braziers on either side of the woman. Above her was a statue of a cherub spilling a small cauldron. Liquid silver fell from the cauldron onto the woman's neck. From there, it cascaded over the woman's breasts and into her lap before it flowed into a pool at her feet.

"We use quicksilver, but never like that," Guiden said. "It's driven more than one of our mages to madness."

"There are different kinds of quicksilver," Sinsasi said as she pointed a gloved finger at the woman clothed in the shimmering metal. "She's wearing the kind that lets you keep your wits. It's what we use in all of our Shrines of Solace, not just this one."

"Liquid privy clothes. Interesting," Guiden mused, his

eyes lingering on the woman dressed in flowing silver. "We must experiment with this metal."

Lisha scoffed at him.

"To expand our knowledge of its attributes, of course."

In another chamber, the stone cherub poured its cauldron of quicksilver onto the seat of an empty throne. The Syren and his patron thrashed about in the silver pool at the foot of the throne. Where the waves of silver spilled over the pool's edge, on the side farthest from the braziers, the liquid silver froze into hard dollops.

Guiden reached down and picked up a piece of frozen quicksilver. As they walked deeper into the Shrine of Solace, the rock-hard silver melted into a drop of liquid in his palm. He dropped it to the floor, where it splattered.

"Do you think Hiamoe's potion is working?" Lisha whispered to Guiden.

He shrugged in response.

The noises in the shrine became stranger as the group delved deeper. An animal brayed in the distance. Lisha swore that she could hear a buzzing sound.

"Where are you taking us?" Lisha asked. She looked over her Swordfather's shoulder, hoping for a glimpse of their destination...and hosts.

"We're going to a place in the shrine where we can speak in private. There are precious few," Sinsasi replied. "We're going to the privy."

Lisha and Guiden shared another look.

"She dragged us here to show us a glorified chamber pot?" Guiden grumbled to Lisha.

The hosts and their guests meandered past more see-through silk. In one room, a Syren played a lute as another Syren played a patron. After a few more paces they saw a woman drink wine served from a naked man's navel. A third room held a pool filled with warm water. In that pool, eels slithered between a half dozen women and men who sat with only their heads above the water.

All around them was the sight of bare flesh tensing and relaxing. Fingers grasped at skin as if it covered the only source of joy in the world. Mouths licked and pulled with the ferocity of feral animals. Legs shook as if the ground beneath the shrine were quaking. The naked bodies shone in the candlelight, as if warm mist fell on them.

Each room was a theater of beauty and beast. There was no modesty here where the patrons satisfied their most carnal desires.

The group arrived at a door made of dark wood. It looked almost exactly like the wooden walls that stood around the silken maze. Sinsasi unlocked it and the Sword-families filed into the large privy. Ederron pulled the door shut behind them. Then he locked and barred it.

Hanging directly above the hole in the privy was the Bleeding Blade. It was long as a greatsword, but narrow for its length. The hilt was pure black, like a moonless night made solid. The blade's steel was dark red.

It was held by a length of rope tied to its grip. The sword pointed straight down. A steady trickle of blood fell from the blade and through the opening. A rushing stream below swept away the blade's leavings.

"You stole it," Lisha whispered.

"We didn't *steal* anything," Hallita said dryly. "Auzken had no more use for it. We merely retrieved it for safe-keeping."

"A privy is a curious place to hide a sword," Guiden said.

"The stream below flows to the River of Plenty. It's the only place we could keep the sword without its blood washing over us like a cursed flood," Ederron replied.

"From here, the blood will make its way to the port and the Angered Sea. The stream and river flow fast enough from the spring snowmelt that not even the fish will notice it."

The privy hole was wide enough that none of the blood falling from the sword splashed against its edges. The hole was so wide it alarmed Lisha; a small person could fall down the hole and no one would ever know.

"My congratulations, vexing Raysk is a noble feat," Irin said. "But I fail to see what this leaky sword has to do with the Iron Wand."

"I want you to take it," Sinsasi replied flatly.

Irin raised an eyebrow. "You want to give us the Bleeding Blade? Forgive my skepticism, but in Fulccrum gifts are usually drenched in poison. Why would you want us to have this?"

Without a word, Sinsasi peeled off her long white gloves. One after the other, she pulled them off to reveal that her hands and forearms were covered in dark red stains.

"I made a careless mistake and touched the damnable thing. Now my arms have this heinous crimson on them," Sinsasi sighed, crossing her befouled arms over her chest. "You wield wands as we wield our charms. Our bodies are powerful weapons and the Bleeding Blade has desecrated my sacred skin. A Syren without her beauty is a mage without a wand."

Irin eyed the Syren Swordfather's arms. "I fail to see what this has to do with me or mine. Give it to some other family if you don't want it."

"Because I want something in return that I suspect only the Iron Wand can provide." Uncertainty flickered across Sinsasi's face. "I propose an exchange. I will give you the

Bleeding Blade. In turn, you will restore my arms to the same beauty that the thundering horde of gods intended."

Taking a few steps closer to the Bleeding Blade, Irin eyed the sword made of maroon steel. Blood seeped from the blade the way sweat beads on skin.

"My family wields wands, not swords. Why would I want this?" Irin asked.

Hallita took a few steps forward to stand next to her Swordfather. "This blade is a useless ceremonial sword to most families, but the Iron Wand is different. You have the power to make wands, do you not?" she asked.

Lisha nodded.

"A short, narrow piece of wood can serve as a wand. Sharp steel, like a dagger, can serve as well?"

Guiden muttered his agreement at this.

"Then I would think a wand made of a sword, not just any sword, but the legendary Bleeding Blade, would be of great interest to your family."

"Mayhaps." Guiden shrugged.

"The nature of this sword would call for study, wouldn't you agree?" Sinsasi asked, directing her question to Irin. "I understand that your family has a laboratory where you conduct experiments."

Irin drew a deep breath and frowned. "Why did you take this? Why not leave it sealed in the tomb, resting on Auzken's chest?"

A smile crept across Sinsasi's lips the same way a cat creeps up behind its prey. "Because if I have the Bleeding Blade, Raysk does not."

"You took it because Raysk wanted it?" Lisha asked. "That strikes me as half an answer. Maybe less."

"Before Raysk donned his mask of scars, he and Minacia found something in each other," Sinsasi said. "In Fulccrum, loyalties slip through fingers faster than quicksilver. Enemies are more predictable than allies. Whoever our friends might be, I know that Raysk is not among them. His disdain for his old lover tarnishes her old Swordfamily. I don't want the Heavies to garner more strength. I trust that, on this, we are of like mind."

Irin again leaned in close to inspect the Bleeding Blade. The blood that dripped from the steel maintained a slow but steady flow. "Raysk isn't the sharpest war hammer in the armory," she said. "This blade has been a curiosity and a symbol for a great while. The only thing that seems to make Swordfathers desire it is pride. We may be able to enhance this sword to make it a weapon once again. Or there could be another use for it."

"What of my price?" Sinsasi asked. Her hands and arms were stained almost up to her elbows. She held them out from her sides. Lisha noticed how the imperfection dramatically lessened the aura of beauty that the Swordfather projected.

With a glance, unspoken words traveled between Irin and Guiden.

"I believe we can devise a way to rid your arms of those dark stains." Irin studied the disfigured skin. "To remove them, you may need to dip your arms into a scalding hot cauldron."

Sinsasi didn't hesitate. "I will do whatever must be done. Just make certain that you can restore my body to its rightful beauty."

Irin clucked her tongue. "Before we agree on anything, we must be clear as the air we breathe. Your gift of this blade is no gift at all. It is a burden upon my Swordfamily and myself." Irin and Sinsasi neared each other. "The Iron Wand is relieving the Syrens of the Bleeding Blade *and* performing a favor for you that no other family can. This blade doesn't lessen your debt. It doubles what you owe me."

Sinsasi clenched her jaw tight. "You have my thanks."

"Your thanks is not my price. The Syrens have not always honored their debts. This is known," Irin said, her face hard and her eyes narrow.

Sinsasi tensed. She opened her mouth, but did not speak.

"Do you understand the nature of this agreement?"

"I'll beg if you'd like."

"I would."

"I'm begging you to take that blade and make me whole again." Sinsasi looked at her feet. "I agree to your price. The debt is mine."

Blood continued to fall from the blade and splash into the stream. Irin's eyes were wary as she looked it over.

"I will do this for you," the Iron Wand Swordfather said. She frowned deeply. "Do not forget that I have given you a gift on this day. You will Honor Thy Debt."

"On my honor as a Swordfather, I will."

"You Syrens," Irin said as she shook her head. "Your vanity will be the death of you."

CHAPTER EIGHTEEN
FIRE KEEPERS

Dragons frolicked on the west face of the Pader Mountains. Their long claws grasped outcroppings of rock. Wings flapped even when the dragon had no intention of taking flight. They breathed fire into the sky, and onto each other. When a mountain goat wandered too close, they gave chase.

A hard morning rain had passed and the Paders shined in the full sun. Midday was upon the Fire Keepers and with it came warm and comforting air. Weeks of spring showers made the flora near the mountains lush and verdant. As the mountain snowpack endured the same fate it suffered every spring, waterfalls cascaded from cracks high in the mountains. The dragons deftly avoided the cold water by making short flights around where it fell.

Plodding along the foot of the mountains were the older dragons that preferred the company of a rider against the merriment above. They bore a saddle and Fire Keeper with a set of reins in their hands. When drops from the waterfalls strayed out to where these dragons marched, they lifted their heads and used their fiery breath to boil away the cold water before it splashed down onto their scales.

"The thundering gods might be smarter than we think," Andra said. She held her arms out wide. "How could a wild pack of gods create beauty such as this?" She stroked the dragon she rode on its neck. Its scales were red as the sun-facing side of a ripe apple. "And only gods with an eye for true beauty could create you, Uther."

Andra's dragon raised its head and shot fire above them as they approached a waterfall. The water hissed into a cloud of steam as they passed underneath it, without a single drop falling on them.

The pale orange dragon next to Uther nipped at Andra's toes. Berg yanked on its reins. Gray smoke poured from the dragon's nostrils in protest.

Berg scoffed. "The thundering gods stampede around gold mountains and silver lakes. I doubt they give much thought to anything other than the riches they guard." He slapped a spike on his dragon's back. "Or they were so busy making your dragon pretty that they forgot to give mine some manners."

"When the male dragons get together, they listen for prey instead of listening to their riders." Andra shrugged. "But Kardas told me to leave the mothers and young behind."

"How much farther until we arrive at Lord Kellington's castle? I can't stomach any more burned meat and the dragons keep charring everything they hunt," Yutago said. "Including you," she admonished her dragon that was adorned with scales of mint green and auburn.

Glas rode behind them on a small dragon whose color was the same dark yellow as the tumbling moon called Night Scythe.

The dragons that Andra and Berg rode scrambled over some jagged rocks. They came to the edge of a wide stream. Its water flowed fast and rough. The ripples in its surface became deeper as the dragons flapped their wings to jump far enough that their feet wouldn't land in the chill water.

"Kardas should've heeded my words," Andra said. She turned her eyes to some billowing white clouds lumbering across the sky. "After the Council of Sheathed Swords, I told him who'd stolen the Bleeding Blade. It had to be Sinsasi." She opened and closed her fist. "The Syrens are nothing if not vain. Doubtless their favorite thing to do is gaze upon themselves in a looking glass. They want everyone else to stare at their bodies and envy their beauty," Andra spat. "Sinsasi wore a pair of gloves that covered most of her arms. That's the only time I've seen a Syren conceal their body behind cloth."

Berg was quiet. He stared out into the distance.

"What if the gloves were a feint?" Yutago asked. "Maybe she wanted the Swordfathers to believe she was trying to hide something. She could have been playing a game with the families."

"They don't play games with their bodies. That would be like a Heavy wielding a blacksmith's hammer instead of a war hammer," Berg said, shaking his head.

"At the council, Raysk said that Vasarox came back from Auzken's tomb with dark arms and dark tidings. The blood from the blade must've stained his arms red. Sinsasi would only cover her body if she was ashamed of something. Those gloves are a telltale that she took the Bleeding Blade."

"She wore gloves to cover bloodstains?" Berg asked.

"I'm sure of it," Andra replied.

"Did you see the stain?" Yutago pressed.

"No," Andra admitted. "But I don't need to. Syrens don't cover their bodies around other families like that. For their Swordfather to do it at the council shows weakness. She'd only do that if the other Swordfathers seeing her would be worse than looking weak. The only thing worse than being weak would be revealing that she had the blade."

Yutago and Berg rode in silence.

"Kardas thought I had the right of it, but he didn't want to take the blade from the Syrens." Andra ran her fingers through her hair and pulled at the ends. "He said we didn't need the Bleeding Blade. Called it a relic of a bygone time. If we tried to seize it from them, and they didn't possess it, we would reveal to the Syrens that we lacked the blade, too. Said we might make a family into an enemy when the Heavies are the true threat."

"He's right, of course," Berg said firmly. "Our own swords are sharp and strong. We don't need useless steel that makes a mess."

Andra clenched her teeth. "Kardas thought the same as you. Said that he was more like to slip in a puddle of the sword's blood and crack his skull open than slay another Swordfather with it." She wiped away some sweat. "I think he's moving too slow. The Heavies aren't the sharpest family, but they're decisive. I told Kardas that we should plunge the Bleeding Blade into the bailey of the Castle of Towers. Its blood spilling inside our stronghold would be an insult to Raysk. He wouldn't tolerate that disrespect. He would've attacked. Our dragons would have turned the bailey into flames thicker than the Lava Sea."

"Maybe, maybe not," Yutago said in a grave tone. "Show more respect for Raysk's wits. Just because he's strong doesn't mean he's stupid." She sighed. "I don't think he'd rise to that bait. If he didn't, then he'd know for certain that we had the Bleeding Blade and he could chip away at our strength one dragon at a time. I'm of a mind that Kardas has us on the best course. This way, the blade stays hidden at all events."

"Unless he puzzles out what I discovered."

"Beliefs aren't truths. You're peddling a guess as lore," Berg admonished. "And there's risk in every throw of the dice."

The dark yellow dragon that Glas rode snapped at the wagging tail of Andra's mount.

"With the trouble on the refuge, might be we could use some of those," Yutago said as she pointed at a ledge high on a mountain face. Large feral dragons were perched on either side of their nest. Gray smoke wafted from it.

"Those wild dragons are a handful. Bigger and meaner than ours. Unbroken dragons are a menace, like a spell that won't obey a mage," Berg said.

Glas eyed the wild dragons.

"Nobody on watch has answers for dead dragons and missing young, only unsettling tales," Yutago growled. "When Mwizi returns from watch, she yells about making captain. When Grouss returns, his shoulders are slumped and his head is bowed."

Andra laughed. "Mwizi is that eager to make captain, eh? Thu'gods, why not Swordfather? Could be that her name is carved on the back of that fang hanging from Kardas's neck!"

Berg's eyes narrowed. "Mwizi is ambitious, I'll give her that." He straightened up, sitting tall in his saddle. "If it's her name on the back of that fang, I'm like to join Ashfall."

"You don't know whose name's on it?" Yutago asked in disbelief. "I thought you snuck up on Kardas while he slept and read it a long time ago."

Berg snorted.

Hissing above made the trio of Fire Keepers turn toward the mountain. Halfway up a low peak, two dragons hung from a rock with their mouths wide open. Smoke poured from their nostrils. One was colored black with crimson spots. Its neck moved like a wary snake as it snapped at the other dragon with scales the color of dried mud. The spotted dragon brought its tail around and slammed it against the rock below its adversary.

Large chunks of rock fell from the place where the tail struck. Then the entire outcropping the brown dragon clung to plummeted. Falling through the air backward, it twisted around and spread its wings. It shrieked in anger as it glided, landing at the rear of the long column of dragons behind Andra.

From its perch high on the mountain rock, the spotted dragon threw its head back and breathed a column of flame into the sky.

"Those wild dragons," Berg said, pointing at the dragon with red spots. "Ours are strong but those untamed dragons have the strength and rage of the wild."

Glas rode up close to the three captains. "Shouldn't we be guarding our refuge instead of the Emerald Kingdom? The refuge is the only truly safe place in the realm for our dragons and we've left it unguarded."

Andra flashed the warrior a friendly smile. "Glas, my Swordbrother, your question is a good one. This is not the path that I would have chosen. But our refuge isn't bereft of strength. The mothers remain with Kardas. Their fire is just as hot as any other dragon's."

"That's some comfort." Glas nodded. "I haven't slept much these past nights, since Kardas had me tell Teska about the Bleeding Blade. I hope he's right and the war will be nipped in the bud."

"We won't be long," Andra said. "The Crimson Crown began its march sooner than expected, but it's of no matter. We need only slow them and the Kingdom Guard will stop them. We'll soon see our dragons home."

"Who's going to send word to the Emerald Crown?" Yutago asked.

"Kellington or whichever lord is closest to the Crimson Crown's approach," Andra replied. "And us, too. We have our own messenger birds to send back to Fulccrum."

"Crimson Crown? More like Crimson Crones," Berg spat.

The pale orange dragon that Berg rode nuzzled with the dragon that carried Yutago. Berg pulled on his dragon's reins.

"If he saw this, my brother would kill to be here. Or he would kill me for not letting him be here." Andra turned in her saddle and looked back over the long column of dragons that followed her. "He keeps torturing himself trying to join us. I finally had Kardas himself tell him no. My brother can question me all he likes, but there is no questioning our Swordfather."

She reached into a leather pouch on her hip. She found the small wooden model of her old home that Mistahn had carved. She squeezed the carving twice before tucking it away.

"When will we get there? I'm starting to get saddle sores," Glas complained.

"Think of them as dragon kisses on your soft arse," Berg replied.

Andra pointed ahead. "The Paders turn to the east past that mountain. Lord Kellington's castle is a ways from there. We should arrive before nightfall. We'll take our places at the passes on the morrow, before first light."

"Or we could turn around and make for the refuge on the morrow," Glas offered.

"I'd rather be home on the refuge, too, Glas. But you know how Kardas is about the king," Andra replied.

"I can feel our dragons are uneasy," Berg said. "So am I. It's best if we start early tomorrow. Out here, if the sunrise doesn't wake you, a knife in your throat will."

"We must step light and sleep lighter," Yutago agreed.

Deer, rabbits, and wild birds all sprinted away when they saw the line of dragons marching along the foot of the mountains. The male dragons scrapped and played. They breathed fire on each other's tails. When one dragon wandered too close to another, their wings were nipped at the edges.

The sun blazed above the western horizon. The Paders' gray and white rock glowed in the bottomless orange of late day.

"The mountains look like dragon fire," Yutago mused.

Fire Keepers leading the dragon column reached the place where the mountains bent to the east. Glas rubbed his rear and grimaced as he stood in the stirrups of his saddle.

As they turned the corner and Lord Kellington's castle came into view, Yutago gasped.

This lord's castle was not pieced together with stone and mortar. Instead, its smooth walls and towers were carved from the mountain itself. The tapered towers looked like sword blades pointed to the sky. The walls around the bailey curved back and forth with an elegance that made them equal parts protection and sculpture. The battlements atop the walls rose and fell with the grace and weight of rolling waves in the Angered Sea.

Waterfalls spilled from the mountains on either side of the castle. They poured into the moat that surrounded the outer walls. Their water didn't simply spring from the cracks that were chiseled open by time. Instead, where the water fell from the mountain had been carved into two scenes.

The massive carving on one side showed a fight between two knights. One knight plunged his sword into the armored chest of his opponent. The waterfall cascaded from the spot where the fatal sword pierced the wounded knight's chest.

On the other side, Kellington's men had carved a jester in motley that wore a cap 'n' bells. He juggled three moons —Dragon Without Wings, Rain Above Rain, and the Night Scythe. The mountain had been carved so the waterfall fell onto the top of Rain Above Rain. From there, it splattered over and around the moon before continuing down the mountain and into the moat.

The keep stood far from the drawbridge and close to the mountains at the back of the bailey. Its shape seemed impossible to the Fire Keepers who noticed that the tower's base was narrower than its top.

"This place makes the Castle of Towers look like an outhouse," Glas said, his voice full of awe.

"That may be true. But I'll take dragons and an ugly castle over a pretty castle with no dragons," Berg growled.

"You say that now, Berg, but I don't think they're done building it yet. Look," Yutago said.

The men hanging in baskets and hammering the rock were difficult to see across the distance that still lay between the Fire Keepers and Lord Kellington's castle. But their work was plain to see. Puffs of gray rock sprang from the mountain where hammers and chisels struck. The mountain shed rock the way a man without coin sheds tears as he begs a Syren for one last taste of her charms. The workers carved the mountain above the castle's keep.

"Must've cost a Greatsword's ransom to build that place," Glas said.

A messenger pigeon appeared from a tall tower. It sprinted to the north and disappeared.

After the Fire Keepers made camp, the three captains rode their dragons to the castle. What they saw on their path suggested that Lord Kellington's town around the castle offered much the same grandeur as the finest districts of Fulccrum.

Taverns and inns lined the streets. Fine wine and hearty ale flowed in the taverns. Men and women wearing little more than privy clothes beckoned from the doorways of pleasure houses. The mouthwatering smell of rich meat cooked over an open fire saturated the air.

Outside a tavern where a minstrel belted out a lively song, a group of Kingdom Guard crowded around a table. Flagons full of red wine sat on the table while more flagons lay empty all around their feet. They pushed and yelled, then one of them threw a pair of dice. When the dice rolled to a stop, the pushing was harder and the yelling was louder.

"Look at that pile of gold," Yutago mumbled. Near the center of the table, gold scythes stood high enough that when a Kingdom Guard slammed his hand down, it sounded like bells ringing. "Could be the Emerald Crown pays their Kingdom Guard more coin the farther they serve from Fulccrum."

"Could be," Andra replied.

Outside of a pleasure house, a Kingdom Guard had a bag of gold tied to her belt. The coins were so heavy that they pulled the belt down to bare nearly all of her hip. She had a lad on each arm as she strutted inside.

A line of Kingdom Guard stretched outside of an armory. Their brethren leaving the shop carried armfuls of armor resplendent with polished metals and inlaid with precious gems.

"Are they here to protect the realm or parade about the next Festival of the Eclipse?" Berg growled. "From what I've heard about the Crimson Crown's knights, they'd be better off buying the heaviest steel instead of that jewelry. The fancy armor will make their corpses look nice, though!" He laughed at his own jest.

As the three neared the carved castle, the buildings around them grew taller and more ornate. Perfumes filled the air, overpowering the smell of exotic foods. The dragons' claws scraped on the neat cobblestone streets. Townsfolk walked on paths that were carefully decorated with plants unfamiliar to the Fire Keepers.

The workers hanging on the mountains that the Fire Keepers struggled to spot before were now plain to see. Rock shards plummeted below each man like sand falling through an hourglass. The pieces caromed off the rock face and the dust drifted down in plumes.

"What do you think they're carving up there?" Berg asked.

"Giant statues of themselves," Andra replied. "They'll probably look like that."

She gestured at two gold statues standing at the edge of the castle moat. One depicted a towering man, tall and wide with a barrel chest. He had a large nose and glaring eyes. His head sat atop shoulders that spread like mountain ridges. His hair and beard came together in a brilliant leonine mane.

Next to the man stood a golden statue of a woman. She was tall and lean with a pronounced hourglass shape that Andra doubted could be achieved, even by pulling the strings on a corset tighter than those on a minstrel's lute. With long flowing hair and a beckoning smile, she looked more radiant than the shining gold from which she was sculpted.

Braziers burned with high flames around both statues. They were also made of gold.

"The way they've decorated this place, you'd think that copper townies were rarer than gold scythes," Yutago muttered.

Andra, Berg, and Yutago arrived at the moat's edge and dismounted. Schools of floppy fish meandered through the water below them.

"The drawbridge is raised. They must fear attack by the Crimson Crown," Berg said. He crossed his arms.

Andra put her hands on her hips. "Or he may not be the Emerald Crown's most loyal subject. Hopefully he's loyal enough to send a pigeon when the reds try to cross the Paders. Even if he doesn't, that's why we brought our own birds."

"That was a wise decision." Yutago nodded.

"The only thing I trust is the certainty that I'll be betrayed," Andra yawned.

The sigil of Lord Kellington's family was engraved on the underside of the raised drawbridge. The etched lines had been charred black. They formed the simple outline of a mountain, jagged as virgin rock on one side and smooth as a gentle arc on the other. Inside these lines, pieces of gold were embedded in the wood, filling the entire mountain from its base to its summit.

Above the sigil, written with inlaid gold, were the words "Gold Springs Eternal."

"Fire Keeper captains seek an audience with Lord Kellington," Andra called to the guards above the castle wall.

Three guards spoke to each other in hushed tones.

"Those dragons, have they been broken?" one shouted down.

"Better than tame, they are our friends and servants. They pose no threat to you or your lord. We're here at King Fallov's request for the good of your lord's lands," Andra replied. "I swear it upon the honor of my Swordfamily."

The guards disappeared. They stayed out of sight for so long that Andra was about to wonder aloud whether the Fire Keepers would be admitted.

With a loud thud and a lurch, the drawbridge began to lower. The chains on either side jerked alive and grew longer. As it lowered, the glimmering yellow portcullis hiding behind the bridge was revealed.

"Of course their gate is made of soft, useless gold," Berg growled. "Is anything in this city made of hard metal? Have they no steel?"

"Either that gate is a strong metal that's been gilded, or they're very sure that no one will lay siege this city anytime soon," Yutago replied under her breath.

The drawbridge settled at the Fire Keepers' feet. More metal chain clanged as the portcullis was raised to reveal the bailey. Two dozen guards in gilded armor marched in formation to line each side of the drawbridge. The armor worn by the guards closest to the Fire Keepers' dragons shook at the poleyns.

A man and woman holding hands shuffled out from the castle's shadow. They both looked like mountains, short as they were solid. They each had snow-white hair, which, for Lord Kellington, included a long beard.

Yutago gasped when the couple neared and she saw Lady Kellington's eyes.

"Lord Kellington, we are in awe of your lovely city. No doubt your castle is as sturdy as it is stunning." Andra gave the lord a shallow, but courteous, bow. "We're here on behalf of the Emerald Crown and King Fallov."

The lord dropped his lady's hand.

Berg pointed at the gilded statues. "Who are they? Relatives of yours?"

Creases appeared around Lord Kellington's lips as his frown bowed sharply. "Those statues are my dear wife and myself, of course."

The statues' proportions and beauty could not have been more different than the man and woman standing on the drawbridge.

"Of course," Berg said unapologetically. "It's all that gold, makes it hard to see the features."

"Ah, yes," Andra said breathlessly, her tact smothering her mirth. "There's a striking resemblance. But why are there braziers burning below the statues?"

"So my people can see who they depend upon for their safety whether it's morning, noon, or night," Kellington replied coldly.

Lady Kellington's face was dour and wrinkled, similar to many the Fire Keepers had passed on their way to the castle. Except in one way, and that was the lady's eyes. Other than two black points in their centers, they were dark red. Her eyes looked like two boils so full of blood that they could burst at any moment.

"Might we enjoy a bit of your renowned hospitality?" Andra asked. "We've had a long ride. Our mounts and men are weary. If we could summon some of them to enjoy your hearths and halls, we would be most grateful."

The beard flowing from Kellington's chin quivered. "We're dutiful allies of our beloved crown. Our loyalty is lodged with the queen and king, even whilst they're not loyal to each other."

Stone and white dust fell from the cracks where the men on the mountain swung their hammers.

Kellington tugged at his beard. "Regretfully, you cannot join us behind the castle walls. As you can see, we're carving more castle from the mountain. If misfortune strikes, the falling rock can kill. We've lost more than one servant that way." He waved at the workers hammering at the rock. "What's more, my wife, although she has thankfully recovered from her illness, is not able to host guests. Fatigue and other…infirmities…are lingering effects from the potions that spared her life."

The work on the mountain continued at a frenzied pace. The lines, details, and proportions of where the men hung resembled the figures of two people rather than towers or battlements. The carvings didn't extend the castle outward; instead they stretched high above the keep. Most workers dangling from the craggy mountainside were above the castle, not beside it.

"If you stacked up all the gold scythes to pay for that kind of work, it would be taller than the mountain they're carving up," Berg said, his head tilted back.

Lord Kellington cleared his throat. "We are a humble folk, scratching out an honest living here by the Paders. What you see before you is a grudging indulgence. A rare opportunity for us to enjoy the fruits of our very difficult labors."

Lady Kellington remained nearly as still as the statue that depicted her so falsely. Her red eyes were vacant and unmoving. Without the subtle movement of her chest to show her breathing, Andra would have judged her a particularly fresh corpse.

"Those fruits of your labor must be very ripe," Berg said. "At your visit to court you mentioned a mere vein of gold. What I see here makes me think these mountains are more gold than rock."

Uther perched himself on the edge of the moat. Craning his long neck down to the water, he drank deeply. The guard on the drawbridge nearest to the dragon broke formation and shuffled closer to another knight, away from Andra's dragon.

"The king and queen told me what they expected of my house, and we have obeyed," Lord Kellington said to the Fire Keepers while his head was turned toward the dragon. "I've sent enough gold to Fulccrum that if they wanted courts for each of their children, they could make the colors in the Throne Hall look a flower garden and stuff the place with servants." He grabbed his lady's hand.

Water splashed below the drawbridge. Andra's dragon whipped its head up from the moat, sending a stream of droplets arcing through the air. A writhing fish disappeared to become a lump sliding down the dragon's long gullet.

"You needn't worry about us squealing to the king and queen," Andra said patiently. She yanked on Uther, pulling him back to the other dragons. "It's true that we're here at the Emerald Crown's behest, but we're not here because of anything that you've done."

Yutago smiled at Lady Kellington, whose face remained

an expressionless mask. "We're so glad to see that you've recovered from that grave illness."

"Yes, yes, indeed!" Lord Kellington bellowed. His wife remained still. "We're all jubilant that she has escaped the clutches of death to grace me and my kingdom with many more eclipses."

"How was she restored to such...vigorous health?" Andra asked. "A healer or some other who's skilled in those arts?"

A red flush washed over Lord Kellington's face. "We tried everything on this side of the Paders. There wasn't enough time to seek aid from across the Angered Sea, or a far kingdom." The lord bowed his head and took a shuddering breath. "We sought aid from across the Paders."

"The Crimson Crown?" Berg asked. "I didn't know they had such powerful skill to heal."

"No," Kellington replied. "The red crown doesn't have that kind of skill. But Winged Mind does."

As he spoke the name Winged Mind, all three Fire Keepers went rigid.

"You put your house in the debt of a *Lysnapi* Swordfamily," Yutago said. Her accusatory tone hammered harder than the men working above. "The family that pushed out Ashfall, no less. You dared to turn your back on the Swordfamilies of *Fulccrum*."

Lord Kellington took a step backward. Then he pulled his lady a step back as well.

"I had nowhere else to turn!" His pleading was so loud and guttural that Yutago's mount reared in alarm. "Ashfall had *nothing* for me. Their herbs break minds the way my stonecutters break rock. They were powerless to cure my wife's affliction. I did what I had to do to *save my lady*."

With those words, a powerful righteousness seemed to strengthen him. "And I would do it again."

Before she spoke, Andra waited in silence long enough to show her control. "If you turn to the Lysnapi families again, you will feel a blade in your back. You would do well to remember that gold is soft and steel is strong."

Berg moved closer to Kellington, towering over the squat man. The guard nearest to the Fire Keeper curled his fingers around the grip of his sword. Some gauntleted hands moved to rest on hilts.

"Never forget where your loyalties lie," Berg said as his shadow swept over the lord and lady. "You *should* remain loyal to the Emerald Crown. You *must* remain loyal to the Swordfamilies of Fulccrum." All three dragons reared and spread their wings wide. "Winged Mind is a Lysnap family. Their business stays where it's from and where it belongs, in the Crimson Crown's capital." Berg took a step forward. All of Kellington's guards put their hands on the hilts of their swords. A few pulled their swords far enough from the scabbards to reveal a threatening length of blade. "Look me in the eye and tell me that you will never again do business with a Swordfamily that's not one of ours."

The tip of Berg's finger was so close to Kellington's face that when the lord tried to look at it, his eyes crossed.

"I had no choice," Lord Kellington began as he clutched his wife's hand tight. "She was going to die."

Berg curled his other hand into a fist. Each knight drew his sword. Their blades pointed at Berg, but their eyes didn't leave the three dragons.

"You're lucky we're here for our king. If we weren't, I'd give the order to burn down this city with flames so hot the moat below us would boil. If I have to ask this again, you'll join the fish inside the belly of our dragon." Berg waved at

Andra's mount. "Swear to me that you will never again betray the Swordfamilies of Fulccrum."

"I swear it," Kellington replied quickly. Tears fell into his great white beard. "On all the gold in my chests and mountains."

Berg withdrew.

The knights released their hilts. One of the knights, whose poleyns had been shaking, now stood in a small puddle.

Planks of wood shuddered as a young page dressed in a floppy hat and an odd collection of silk, leather, and fur, thundered toward his lord.

"Lord Kellington! My lord!" the page yelled between gasps for air. "You told me to inform you the moment we heard." The page put his hands on his knees. A long, thick strand of his slaver dripped onto the drawbridge.

"What is it?" Kellington asked coolly.

"Begging your forgiveness, you told me to inform you about this straightaway," the page replied. His cheeks were smooth and ruddy. Several varieties of fruit had more hair on them than this lad's chin.

"Mayhaps we should speak of this inside the keep," Kellington said, the words escaping between his clenched teeth.

"Let's hear what the boy has to say," Andra said before the lord and page could turn away. "What tidings do you bring to Lord Kellington, child?"

The boy pursed his lips. Kellington glared at him before relenting with a shallow nod of assent.

"Our sentinels at the passes have sent word. The Crimson Crown's march west has been swift," the boy said breathlessly. "They are moving with much quickness."

Lord Kellington darkened at the news.

"Prithee tell, how many days' ride are they from the Emerald Kingdom?" Yutago asked.

"The Crimsons are moving with haste but they have mustered a considerable host. Thousands at the main pass alone. I don't partake in games of chance, but if I did, I'd wager no sooner than three days from the morrow," the page replied.

Kellington glared at him.

Andra turned to Lord Kellington. "You will send messenger pigeons to the Emerald Crown forthwith." Though she was barely taller than Lord Kellington, her words loomed large over him.

"At once, Fire Keeper," Kellington said in a whisper. "The birds shall be sent straightaway."

"Excellent," Andra replied. "Our Swordfather will hear of your faithful service to the Fire Keepers and the crown."

Lord Kellington bowed deeply while his lady maintained her vacant vigil. "Begging your forgiveness, I must attend to urgent matters and my wife requires her tonics."

He turned toward the castle without looking at the Fire Keepers. His wife followed, after her husband tugged at her hand. The page gave a bow so deep that his floppy hat landed on the drawbridge. After he retrieved it, he scampered after his lord and lady.

Lord Kellington approached the keep in the bailey with his knights in tow. The golden portcullis dropped as the last knight stepped off the drawbridge. Chains clattered against wood as the drawbridge rose haltingly.

The Fire Keepers again stood before the sigil of a mountain filled with gold.

"Do you trust that he'll send the birds?" Yutago asked.

"No more than I trust he'll stop crawling to Winged Mind for more elixirs to keep his wife alive," Andra said.

"You call that life? Fyur was more alive than Lady Kellington after his funeral pyre burned out," Berg said, shaking his head. "Let's get back to camp. I'm hungry enough I could eat my mount."

Andra said nothing.

"We should scout the pass that boy spoke of. The more we know about the Crimson Crown's approach, the better we'll be able to defend it," Yutago replied.

Berg moaned as he climbed onto his dragon.

"Fyur should still be alive today," Yutago growled.

Andra tensed.

"A job that needs two families is one family too many," Berg spat. "Having Dark Water carry Fyur across the Badwaters to the Mountain of Blue Ice was folly."

"Agreed, but there was no other way. You can't sail any old cog into those waters. It's said there's tornados under the waves. Sailors speak of tentacles thicker than the trunks of the tallest crimsonwoods. The sharks are the size of ships!" Yutago spoke with an awed tone.

"Braving all that just to dump Fyur and his dragon on the Mountain of Blue Ice to find a book seems needless," Berg shot back. "Why not have Hanngoh send Dark Water into the caves to find it?"

"Because the only thing that can melt that blue ice is dragon fire," Yutago answered. "Fyur was only there to loose Hoqqes's dragon fire."

"Bah, to the thundering hells with it then!" Berg yelled. "Let Ashfall melt the blue ice with their burning cigars. They should've gotten the damnable book themselves if they wanted it. No treasure in the realm is worth Fyur's life."

Andra remained still and controlled as they spoke. She

fettered her thoughts, keeping them far from the memories of her lost love.

Berg shook his head. "It was all a jest before he left. Said he was taking his skin ink with him because he heard some islanders on the way had the best needles. He said they could make the best lines."

"Why Kardas agreed to that madness is beyond me." Yutago shook her head.

Andra wiped something from the corner of her eye. "Let us make haste." She pressed her mount hard and shot ahead of her companions.

The three made their way along the mountains to the north, away from their camp. A quiet fell over them. When countryfolk saw the three dragons approaching, they quickly scattered.

Away from the outskirts of Kellington's town, the buildings became shorter before they were reduced to hovels. Then the Fire Keepers rode past farms and fields. Finally, the well-tended fields became wilder and yielded to trees that were untouched by a woodcutter's axe. The raw wilderness was filled with the primal sounds of animals as they went about their evening struggle for survival.

Sounds of hammering, much like the noise made by the stonecutters above Kellington's castle, overpowered the sounds of nature. The Fire Keepers neared the entrance to a mine. Great animals with thick gray skin and shaggy hair pulled large carts from the mine burdened with boxes full of rock. The lumbering animals, four times the size of a dragon, had tusks that were long and straight.

"Mammophants," Berg muttered as he nodded at the beasts. "Their tusks make 'em look like they're ready to joust two knights at once."

Next to the entrance to the mine, a half dozen hefty

Kingdom Guards lazed on large wooden boxes. Every guard had at least two skins of wine hanging from their leather belts. Their armor was piled on the ground. The sacks sitting next to their armor were strained almost to the point of bursting. The cotton threads were pulled so wide in spots that they didn't conceal their contents of gray rock streaked with glittering yellow.

"Travelers from Fulccrum!" a guard called, slurring merrily. "A sight for sore eyes. Miss me station back near the refuge!" He tipped his head back and squeezed wine from a skin down his throat.

The dragons slowed, but didn't stop. The opening to the mine was so large that Kellington's drawbridge wouldn't have covered it all. Men struggled to move heavy wooden boxes placed near the guards. The boxes were stacked like towers.

"What kind of wine is that?" Yutago asked the guard who called to them.

He finished his drink and replied that it was a Kabern.

"No doubt," she muttered under her breath.

Great columns of smoke billowed from the top of a large building made of tree trunks. Dozens of guards armed with bows and swords were positioned all around the structure. Stout men carrying boxes that jingled emerged from the building. They loaded the boxes onto wains before returning to the building from whence they came.

Three wains pulled by hardy draught horses lumbered down a dirt path that, leagues away, joined the road to Fulccrum. Each one of these wains carried six wooden boxes and a single guard wearing boiled leather armor.

Four more wains carrying the same kind of boxes departed down a path that stretched to the north, away from Lord Kellington's castle. A pair of men clad in steel armor traveled on these wains. Their armor matched the knights' who earlier had stood on the drawbridge.

As the wains traveled the path headed north, the dragons fell in behind them. The Fire Keepers kept enough distance between themselves and the draught horses so the animals wouldn't be spooked by the fire-breathing mounts.

"If this is what Kellington's able to pull from his grant, how much gold are the other lords at the foot of the Paders mining?" Yutago wondered.

Andra fixed her eyes on the wains they followed. "The lords that tend the lands against the Paders will be richer than the Emerald Crown." Her mount nipped at the neck of Berg's dragon. "Methinks Kellington didn't go to court for himself alone."

"You think the other lords sent him?" Berg asked.

"Where the road forks, most men choose the Gilded Granite Street. If they know the crown's price, the lords can weigh that against how much coin it'll take to hide their gold," Andra replied. "If the king was reasonable, the lords could've mined their gold and paid some coin to Fulccrum. From the look of it, Kellington's chosen to pay for the Kingdom Guard's silence. The king wasn't generous to his lords and I'd wager Kellington isn't generous to his king."

"We had a warrior at every court after Kellington petitioned the crown," Berg said, scratching his beard. "I don't recall hearing of any other lord make the same appeal after him. Didn't see Faremother, Lady Slaeton, Wickunduns, Zellmast, or the others. Might be they agreed to make up for any lost gold."

"Could be they didn't find as much gold as Kellington," Yutago offered.

"Mayhaps." Andra shrugged.

Berg whistled. "That was a bit o' gold for the Kingdom

Guard." He furrowed his brow. "I should leave the Sword-family and join up with the Kingdom Guard lazing about for an angry lord! Hah!"

The sun's last sliver disappeared below the horizon, but the sky remained bright. The wains ahead of the Fire Keepers bounced so violently that the knights splayed their arms to stay balanced. Dust from the wheels rose in the breeze and lingered long enough that the dragon riders coughed. Yutago's mount sneezed, sending more dust from the bare trail into the air, along with a puff of smoke.

Where the Fire Keepers had departed from Kellington's town, the road was made of smooth dirt with wain ruts notched deep in the earth. Here, loose rocks were littered all along the path. Some were small as pebbles while others were the size of ripe gourds. A few were even bigger than dragon eggs. All were jagged and sharp.

"The dust their horses are kicking up is strange," Berg said. "It's not dark like dirt. It's too light."

"It's pale," Yutago added. "White. Dust from smashing rock apart."

Andra nodded in agreement. Then the two wains ahead of them vanished.

"Did we lose them?" Yutago asked.

"No, they turned," Andra replied.

Dragon claws scraped against the fragments of rock that covered the path. Where rocks were gathered into deep piles, the Fire Keepers found that the two wains had turned east.

Before them was a mountain pass that had been carved wide. The sides of the pass weren't smooth like Kellington's castle, but they had an unnaturally steep slope. Chisel marks marred both sides. The path was wide enough that two wains could travel beside each other. It stretched to the east.

"Before they took their hammers to it, this pass was probably no more than half this wide," Yutago whispered. "I wonder how many they've widened."

Sounds of rock crackling under rolling wheels echoed off the pass walls.

Berg dismounted and reached down between a few large rocks. He pulled a chisel from where it had been buried.

"There's barely any rust on this steel," he said in a grave tone.

Andra nodded. "Some of this work wasn't done long ago."

"Looks wide enough for the thundering horde of gods to stampede all the way from here to the Crimson Crown," Berg said. "Or t'other way around."

Yutago looked far down the mountain pass. "I've never seen this pass before, but I don't like it," she said absently. "We should turn back."

"We carried enough pigeons for each pass," Berg said. His eyes didn't leave the east. "When we know which passes the reds have chosen for their march, we should send more than one."

"Agreed. If the Kingdom Guard doesn't come we could get caught out here, trapped in the mountains," Yutago added. "And this battle is not ours to fight."

Andra nodded in agreement.

A clump of rocks spilled from the side of a tall cliff. They clattered into the pass, sending a mountain goat leaping away. Where they landed, a cloud of dust rose.

The newest captain shook her head. "Kardas sent us here with our strongest dragons. We have their flame.

Inside their bellies is a fire like the sun." Andra petted Uther's neck. "The fire of our suns can't be defeated, even by eclipses."

"Grouss has been a captain longer than Kardas has been our Swordfather," Yutago said. Her gaze was cast to the shadows darkening in the east. "When our warriors are fearful, Grouss laughs. After his belly stops shaking, what does he tell them?"

"If it burns, we can kill it," Berg said with an edge in his voice.

"That's right. Now come, we've lingered too long," Andra said. "Torches and dragon flame must show the way back to camp."

In the last faint whisper of light, the Fire Keepers saw a pigeon flap its wings above them. It turned to fly east over the carved pass.

"What if the thundering gods have forsaken us?" Yutago asked.

Andra pulled the head of her dragon close and rubbed his scaly cheek. Then she answered Yutago's question.

"We must be our own gods."

CHAPTER NINETEEN

SYRENS

"To thrive in this war, we must not fight the Swordfamilies," Sinsasi hissed. "That's how we emerge from Raysk's folly stronger than before." She tugged at her long gloves. "The Bleeding Blade is an illusion of power. A clumsy trick coveted by an even clumsier Swordfather. While the Heavies chase a brazen symbol, we will gather veiled power."

She sat at a table in the Shrine of Solace's back room. Unlike much of the shrine, the walls and door to this back room were made of heavy wood. Adjacent to the room was the shrine's main floor where patrons satisfied their cravings for a hefty price. Two Syrens guarded the door.

The back room held a collection of artifacts as valuable as it was diverse. Coins from realms near and far spilled from wide jars. Animal pelts with fur that shone like polished metal hung from the walls. Golden braziers burned with many different colors of flame, none of which were red or yellow or orange.

Long strings near the ceiling stretched from one wall to

another. Hanging from them were hundreds of rings, bracelets, and necklaces. These festoons of jewelry glimmered like decorations for an impossibly decadent festival. The inside of a dragon skull was filled with gold teeth pulled from patrons' mouths. Keys to some of the most heavily guarded places in Fulccrum were thrown in a wooden box sitting on the floor.

All of these treasures had been offered as payment by patrons after they ran out of coin, but before they died an unnatural death.

Served on the table before Sinsasi were serving platters piled high with delicacies. Among them were roast eel coiled on a bed of rice and smothered in sweet plum sauce. Shark teeth ringed the platter as cutlery to slice the eel. Roast messenger pigeon nested in honey and orange slices. Stuffed in the bird's beak was the message it carried on its last flight. Had the message been delivered, it would have done harm to the Syrens.

An ornate silver platter, that a patron handed over a day before he mysteriously fell from the top of the Gods' Blade, held a poached dragon egg. Dark green yolk spilled from the cut in its side.

A naked man lay face up on a trestle table. His only movement was his chest rising and falling as he breathed. His eyes were shut. Eyelashes were the only hair on his body that hadn't been shaved off. On each of his six pronounced abdomen muscles was a morsel. The food had been wrapped in strips of sour bread, peppered, and rolled in pine nuts.

Flagons of water, Kabern, and fire wine were held by servants eager to pour.

The men and women in the back room who weren't Syrens could neither hear nor speak. They had pledged their service and silence for the remainder of their lives in exchange for one last indulgence with a Syren.

Dining at the table were Sinsasi, Hallita, and Ederron. All of them wore thick robes made of wool and lined with soft velvet. The thick cloth hid nearly all of their bodies below their neck. Under their heavy robes were the sheer silk garments that revealed nearly everything. Here in the back room the Syrens sheathed their most potent weapon.

A rapturous squeal sounded from the floor of the Shrine of Solace. The noise from the woman was so loud that it penetrated the heavy door and sent a foreign coin, which had been teetering on the rim of a jar, tumbling to the floor.

"It's bad enough they're all so ugly. Why do they have to be so noisy, too?" Hallita sneered in disgust. "They even *sound* ugly! And thundering gods the smell! When they don't lie with us are they in the stables rolling around in horse droppings?"

"It's difficult to choke back the bile that their hideousness pulls like water from a well. But you must not forget, my warrior, their weakness is our strength," Sinsasi admonished. "If everyone in the realm was blessed with our beauty, subjugating them would be more difficult." She grimaced as she wrung her hands. "It's painful waiting for the Iron Wand to devise the cure for my arms. The stain makes me feel like a commoner, like one of them." She pointed at the door to the shrine's main floor. "As if my beauty is mortally wounded. The Shard of the Specter wouldn't have done this to me." She glared at Hallita.

"I've apologized, my Blade. Time and again. There were four others that I had to contend with." She frowned and made a tight fist. "Ezzy will not soon forget my visit, nor will that Heavy." Hallita shook her head. "I know that you speak the truth about our strength." She cut a length of eel with a shark tooth. "I only ask that we require any commoner who dares ask us for an audience to cleanse their filthy bodies. They must do what precious little they can to make themselves less repugnant."

"A modest request," Ederron said impassively. He scooped dark green yolk from the dragon egg and poured it into a jewel-encrusted bowl. "Only a Syren can truly please a Syren." He winked at Hallita as he slurped the yolk from a gilded spoon.

"That's another problem. Even if they had handsome bodies, they utterly fail to grasp the art of pleasure," Hallita fumed. "Our patrons must learn the subtleties of love-making by watching farm animals in heat."

The door creaked open. Into the room walked a tall, lean, and beautiful woman who moved like a whisper. Her hair was a mosaic of yellow, orange, and red that resembled a cloak of flame as it fell down to the small of her back. She wore the Syrens' transparent dress.

"Sinsasi, there's trouble in the shrine. A patron has no more coin and refuses to leave," the newcomer said. She walked over to the dragon skull and dropped five gold teeth into its mouth.

"Fann, why are you troubling me with this? Simply have them removed and make it painful enough that they won't soon forget," Sinsasi replied with her mouth full of messenger pigeon. "I'm not to be disturbed when I'm taking a meal. You were made a captain days ago. You know better than to bother me with such trivialities."

Her fiery hair was a shimmering cloak as Fann moved to the naked man with the six morsels on his abdomen. She pointed at the food. "Are those what I think they are?"

"Yes, they are," Hallita replied.

Fann snatched her finger away from the man and moved to stand by the Syrens.

"The stubborn woman, girl really, claims to be one of the queen's servants. I didn't have her thrown out because I thought that she may be of use to us."

Sinsasi stopped chewing.

"The queen and I can never have too many mutual friends. This one may be of interest. Bring her to me," Sinsasi ordered.

The rings and bracelets hanging overhead clinked together as Fann stomped from the back room without another word. Sinsasi tore off a piece of bread and soaked up some dragon yolk before chewing it with relish.

"Messages relayed by our man in the castle dovecote have been quite revealing. The gods have favored us with the great distance between the queen and the Crimson Crown. The glimpses of the queen's scheming he's passed along may give us an advantage in our dealings with the Emeralds." The Swordfather pointed at her captain and warrior. "Don't forget that our perfume must always be cleansed from our thralls in the castle to ensure they remain hidden from the queen."

"The powerful always rely on the powerless," Ederron said through the well-seasoned food in his mouth. "That reliance can make a person who is without power nonetheless quite useful."

Sinsasi picked up the knife by her plate. The blade made a scraping noise as she pulled it between her teeth. "I see you've been studying our patrons, Ederron. That's perceptive of you. I hope you make a habit of it." She returned her knife to the table. "Hallita, be mindful of this understanding. It separates captains from warriors, and Swordfathers from captains."

A pale waif followed Fann into the back room. The young patron had long brown hair so feathery and curled that some of its tips almost pointed up. She shook hard enough that her simple dress trembled against her skin.

"Thank you for hearing me," she squeaked in a small voice that matched her small body. She curtsied with far more elegance than her appearance suggested.

"What is your name, my little friend?" Sinsasi asked with a smile that radiated a well-practiced warmth.

The girl replied that her name was Belna.

"I understand that you're a servant in the castle. Tell me, Belna, what are your duties? What do you do for the queen?"

"I do quite a lot for the queen," the girl replied in a voice that trembled as much as her body. "Why, I clean her bedchamber, beating the rushes and dusting the top of her four-poster bed. I make sure the sheets are soft and her pillows full of down. I fill her glasses with wine. She always has lots of glasses of different kinds of wine. It's real hard to put the right wine in the right glass." She paused and thought for a moment. "Oh, and I check the candles so they're always as tall as my hand."

"She's wasting our time. Throw her out," Hallita scoffed.

Ederron pressed his index finger against his lips.

"Do you prepare the queen's food or serve it to her?" Sinsasi continued, ignoring her warrior.

"I don't make anything for the queen," Belna replied softly. "The only time I serve food is if the platter is too big for one girl to carry."

Hallita yawned.

"You said that you cleaned the queen's rushes. What else do you clean?" the Swordfather pressed.

"I don't clean her majesty's dresses or special clothes. But I make all of them so there aren't any wrinkles. The queen gets real mad if her dress has a wrinkle in it. I set out the dresses she could wear. Then she chooses which ones she likes best. We do that in the morning and sometimes before she takes her supper, too."

"Those sound like very important tasks."

"Oh, they are! The queen put me in charge of them because I do things so good," Belna said, swelling with pride.

"Which clothes do you mean by 'special clothes'?"

Belna looked at her feet. "Well, uh, they're…" she began. Sinsasi squeezed her hand and nodded, encouraging her to continue. "They're the queen's privy clothes. You know, what's under her dresses and the like. The type you all don't wear."

"No need to be embarrassed. We know all about privy clothes. Now, what kind of privy clothes do you mean? The top *and* the bottom?"

Belna blushed as she nodded wordlessly.

"Do you give her different privy clothes to choose from? The way you do with her dresses?"

"No, ma'am. She doesn't care what the special clothes look like, so she doesn't pick them the way she does the dresses. I just pull them from her wardrobes and she wears the special clothes that I put on the table. They're all much the same."

"Do you help her dress?"

"Yes, me and the other girls, too."

"Do you do the same things with the dresses and privy —*special*—clothes whether you're dressing the queen in the morning or for supper?"

Belna nodded. "Mostly so. Only difference for the

suppers is that I always put good-smelling things on the special clothes. The perfumes." She cleared her throat. "I put lots of them on because the queen likes them lots."

"Do you put the perfumes on the top and the bottom?"

"Yes, both."

Sinsasi leaned back in her chair and crossed her arms. Lines pulsed on her neck as she tensed.

"When she puts on these clothes for supper, who does she dine with?"

"Always with the king and they always drink *a lot*. He doesn't talk much. She yells at him, mostly. No matter how loud she yells, when they leave together they hold hands. I help clear the table when they're done."

As Ederron stood, his thick robe made of wool swayed. He undid the rope tied loosely below his navel. He pulled at the right shoulder of his robe as he angled his chest toward Belna. Half the thick robe fell away. Pausing for a deliberate moment, he locked eyes with the waif. As he slowly pulled off the robe's left shoulder, Ederron flexed every muscle in his body at once. His gentle curves were suddenly forged into hard lines.

The sheer robe that Ederron still wore concealed nothing except that which Belna most desperately wanted to see. Belna blushed again and this time her cheeks were an even deeper red. Her eyes were wide and her mouth fell open.

Taking his plate from the table, Ederron walked to the naked man and eyed the morsels on his midsection.

He leaned over and paused.

Belna chewed on her tongue with her mouth open.

"Are these what I think they are?" Ederron asked. He straightened his body.

"They're Pader Mountain Stones. Brought in yesterday," Sinsasi replied. "Very fresh."

Belna furrowed her brow.

"Those are the little round bits between the legs of mountain goats," Fann explained to Belna. "They taste like lamb."

Hallita frowned.

"Good thing you're deaf. Because I find it sad that the best use of your unsightly body is a serving platter for my food," Ederron whispered. "But at least we didn't make you serve your own tongue."

After plucking three Pader Stones from the man's abdomen and depositing them on his plate, Ederron strolled back to the table. He locked eyes with Belna. Before he took his seat, he pressed a hand against his chest, bringing the thin robe flush against his skin. Then he slid that hand all the way down to his thigh, providing his audience a fleeting glimpse of his manhood.

The waif gasped.

"Now, Belna, my friend here tells me that you've no more coin. But you also wish to stay and enjoy our company here in the Shrine of Solace," Sinsasi whispered. "That's a very big problem."

Belna nodded her head very slowly. "Please don't make me leave. *Please*. I'll do *anything*," she offered. Her chin shook like a late autumn leaf in strong wind. A thick tear trickled down her soft cheek.

"I'm so very glad you mentioned that," Sinsasi said, her voice as genuine as the gold hanging above.

Sinsasi rose and took Belna's limp hand. The Swordfather used a soft cloth that had been under her knife to gently wipe away the girl's tear. "What if I told you that there was a way that you could stay with us?" Sinsasi smiled the way she had seen mothers smile at their children.

"I don't have any gold teeth. Like what's in that skull," Belna said plaintively.

"No, of course you don't. Not a young, healthy, beautiful woman such as yourself. What I propose is this. I want you to do something for me. In return, I will let you enjoy as much time as you would like here in our Shrine of Solace."

The girl's face lit up, as if the thundering gods had just gifted her a mountain of gold. "*Really*?" she asked, her mouth agape.

Hallita stabbed her knife into a pheasant drizzled in acorn sauce. She withdrew her hand to leave it there, sticking up.

Sinsasi knelt before her prey, pulling her thick robes tight so they wouldn't brush against the puddle that had formed beneath the girl. "Yes, *really*! In return, I will ask you to do something for me. Not today and probably not tomorrow, but I *will* ask. When I do, what I tell you to do will be our secret. Only you and I may know of it. Do you understand? Can you do that for me?"

Belna's head bobbed up and down like a cork in rough water.

"That's good. Very good. Now you go and pick out your favorite Syren or two. Tell them that Sinsasi said they should make you *extra happy*. Even if they're with someone else, you can have them."

"*I can*? Are you sure?"

"I'm certain. But remember, if you want to enjoy the Syrens, you must do what I say and keep our secret."

"Oh, I will. *I will!*"

"Wonderful. Enough talk, my dear. Now go and enjoy

our pleasures. Splash around with a Syren in our quicksilver. Indulge yourself."

Fann took Belna's hand and led her from the room. Hallita followed them through the door. After they'd left, Ederron wrapped his wool robe around himself. He plucked a Pader Stone from his plate and nibbled at it.

Sinsasi looked down at the slippery puddle where Belna had stood. "Disgusting," she said. "They get so aroused before we even touch them. I'd wager the skin on the inside of that girl's thighs is pruned."

Grimacing at the puddle, Ederron shook his head. "Mayhaps I shouldn't have pulled my sheer robe so tight." He shrugged. "I could hear you purring as you finessed her."

Snapping her fingers, Sinsasi commanded a deaf and mute servant to clean the floor.

Throwing the Pader Stone in his mouth, Ederron crossed his arms. "You have something in mind," he said as he chewed on the morsel thoughtfully. "What is it?"

Sinsasi finished the roast hen in her mouth before responding. "You see all these shiny things around us? For a handful of these riches, a pirate would sink a ship and slaughter its crew." She laughed. "The crown would steal it all and call it a tax." She reached down and picked a gold coin from the floor. The coin was wide enough to cover her entire palm. It had been lying on the floor for so long that dust covered most of it. She tossed it carelessly into a jar nearly filled with smaller gold coins. "And what we keep here in the back room is nothing compared to the treasures in our vault."

Ceremonial gold swords that leaned against a wall shifted, clanging as they toppled to the floor. Each one of them had been a cherished family heirloom for generations.

That is, until the last descendant inherited the sword and traded it for the Syrens' charms.

"Everything in our back room and our vault, it's all a pittance compared to knowledge and influence. In here, we can't see the control that we have over Belna. It doesn't glitter like gold. But power over a miserable waif may one day become as valuable as controlling the Emerald Crown."

After picking up another Pader Stone, Ederron put it back on his plate. "She's close to the queen, that's true. But it's not the queen we want dead, it's Fallov. I could see gifting Syrens' pleasures to someone in the king's court. But one of the queen's servants? Whatever the queen's feelings toward us from her time as a Syren, she doesn't seem to harbor much enmity. Our time would be better spent on patrons who offer valuable secrets that concern the king."

"We're not fighters, but we do have weapons." Sinsasi clasped her hands. "You were such a promising captain once, Ederron. You yearn for power but first you must learn the art of scheming. There are other captains passing you by each and every day."

Stabbing a Pader Stone with a knife, Ederron ripped it from the blade with his front teeth.

A deep bucket sat on a three-legged stool. From a distance, the bucket looked as though it was filled to the brim with shimmering water. What the bucket actually held was hundreds of polished diamonds.

A deaf servant poured fire wine into Sinsasi's jewel-encrusted chalice as she held it up. She drank half the wine before returning the chalice to the table.

Noise that sounded like a drunken audience at a bawdy play flooded into the back room as the door opened a crack.

A Syren with a stubbly beard and green eyes poked his

head into the room. "There's a man out here who says he's willing to give us his body for one last night with a Syren."

"Is he able of body?" Sinsasi asked.

"Yes, strong back and has many eclipses ahead of him. If he wants them."

"Did you offer him the chance to become one of our silent servants?"

"I did. He's not agreeable to it. Said he'd rather die. He said we could take whatever we wanted from his body. He'll die for this, but he won't live if he isn't whole. He won't submit to being a slave."

"Our servants aren't slaves. They're free to leave whenever they'd like," Ederron protested.

Sinsasi closed her eyes and her breathing slowed.

"You hunt for worth even in the most common of commoners. What are you thinking about now?" Ederron asked after he finished the last Pader Stone on his plate.

"Whether someone I know might have use for something inside the commoner's body." She shook her head. "I don't think he does. Not now, anyway."

"So this commoner will be another raving lunatic outside our shrine," Ederron said.

"Yes. Despite his refusal, he will become our servant by showing the city how desirable we are," Sinsasi said. Then she raised her voice and said, "Remove him." She fidgeted with her knife. "Some are able to forget our charms eventually. Vanishingly few though, the poor fools."

The head with the green eyes disappeared and the door closed.

"Even if they do, I suspect they're never the same," Ederron added.

Sinsasi took a few sips of her drink. Ederron played with his food. The two sat for a time and enjoyed the quietude.

Hallita stormed through the door. "It's so much easier to vomit in the privy without that wretched sword dripping blood over it," she announced. Then she returned to the table and wiped her mouth with the small cloth that sat next to her plate. "Now I can enjoy the second course of my meal."

Drinking deeply from her chalice, Hallita swished the wine in her mouth before she swallowed. Then she ripped a leg from a chicken drenched in lemon juice and dusted with pepper. A servant refilled her chalice.

Returning to the back room, Fann sprinted over to the dragon skull filled with gold teeth. She set down a handful of rings next to the skull.

"I'm too busy to string these up right now," she said, pointing at the rings festooned above. "And I'm not touching these rings again. Some of them came from the patron's nose. You should've seen the blood pour when they ripped them out."

Hallita coughed as she choked down a mouthful of lemon chicken. "If there wasn't a hook or clasp or something, how did they get in there?"

Fann shrugged. "Why do we let them pay with these disgusting things?"

"Gold is gold," Ederron replied.

Grabbing an unused small cloth from the table, Fann dipped it in a flagon filled with water. "There's something else." She wiped her hands on the wet cloth vigorously. "A man on the main floor claims that he's Emerald Ezzy's husband. He seeks an audience."

"What does he look like?" Sinsasi asked.

"A bit like a toad. He's short, wide, and his chin bulges." Fann handed the wet, sullied cloth to a silent servant. "He's out of things to barter."

"Then he's run out of the treasures that he stole from Ezzy," Ederron corrected.

"Are you certain it's him? He's lain with some Syrens since Ezzy told the king that he disappeared, but he's kept to the shadows to avoid the Kingdom Guard and his wife. Odd that he would now be so heedless, even with The Need." Sinsasi rubbed her temples. "Ezzy's husband has never paid us in coin. Tell this man to remember the last time he was in the Shrine of Solace. Ask him, what was the last treasure he used to pay us, and which Syren did he see?"

"What are the answers?" Fann asked.

Sinsasi lowered her voice. "He called the artifact Steel Ice. He saw Glatt and Lunyu. But make sure you ask him which *Syren*, not which *Syrens*. Doubtless he'll remember both of their names if he is who he says he is."

Without another word, Fann left the room.

The candles burned low. With a movement of her hands, Sinsasi commanded the servants to light more of them. Pulling her heavy robe tight, she rose and paced around the dining table. Hallita continued the second course of her meal. Ederron took a drink of sweet wine.

"What's Steel Ice?" Ederron asked his Swordfather.

"He said it's a shield that can stop dragon fire. It's supposedly made from the hide of some kind of salamander that can run through fire the same way a fish swims through water," Sinsasi replied. When Ederron searched the back room with his eyes, she told him: "It's not here, it's in the vault."

"Can it truly stop dragon flame?" he asked. "Mayhaps it can't even protect us from Fann's blazing hair."

Sinsasi shrugged. "Depending on how this war goes, we

may find out. I sincerely hope not. Our strength lies in dark bedchambers, not a fiery battlefield."

After a rapping at the door, Sinsasi summoned her audience.

The man that Fann had described walked into the back room. His eyes grew wide as they darted around its treasures. They lingered longest on the jars filled with coins. He folded his arms and drummed his fingers against his flabby biceps. Fann remained outside and pulled the door tight.

"Nuryam, welcome back to the Shrine of Solace," Sinsasi said in a pleasant tone. "To what do we owe this great honor?"

"I, uh, I..." the man stammered.

"Oh, come now. Compose yourself. I'm wearing a wool robe. Let's talk about how we can help one another before we discuss pleasure."

"It's, uh, it's not you, that's got me wound up. Begging your pardon. It's the-the-the gold. The treasures you hold here." His eyes wandered all around the back room, except for the bodies of the Syrens.

When Nuryam's eyes raced past Hallita without hesitation, she glared at him and pulled her wool robe tight.

"I'm told that you've run out of valuables to exchange for our company," Sinsasi said with a smirk.

His skin dimpled as Nuryam scratched at the side of his neck. "Yes, that, um. Well, the whole Emerald Kingdom knows that my wife and I are having a bit of a tiff right now." The Syrens had the grace to suppress their laughter. "Sometimes I think the Kingdom Guard are reading my mind, they're so close." He chewed on his tongue as he spoke.

"That's just awful," Sinsasi said deliberately.

Now that his attention was on the Syrens, Nuryam held his hands over his crotch.

"I had armloads of treasure. Some of it was so old that Ezzy and I stole it together. But, ah, it's all gone now. That shield I gave you the last time I was here, I found it in the port beneath where our shop used to be."

Sinsasi tilted her head.

"I was there to look for my dear wife, of course! Hoping she hadn't met her end in the fire. While I was there, I checked around to see if anything else survived. Steel Ice was all right since fire can't burn it." For the first time since he entered the room, the servants caught his attention. "Are they…?" he began.

"Don't concern yourself with our silent servants. They could not betray us even if they so desired," Ederron said.

"I understand that you are unable to pay our price. Therefore, we have little to discuss." When Sinsasi spoke these words, Nuryam's eyes became glassy. She raised her gloved hands, as if presenting the treasures inside the room for consideration. "Do you have anything like what you see here? An invisible sword, perhaps?"

"I didn't steal that sword!" Nuryam roared. "I took a few worthless trinkets, that is true enough. But I did *not* take that sword! I don't even know where she kept it!"

Hallita regarded him carefully.

"Is there anything other than your own bounties that you can offer?" Sinsasi asked.

Nuryam began to tremble. His lips moved but he made no sound.

Sinsasi clucked her tongue. "If there's nothing you can offer us, there's nothing we can offer you. That's how we throw our dice."

A gloved finger pointed at a servant, then Nuryam, then the door. The servant advanced on Nuryam.

Ezzy's husband put his hands up with the palms out.

"Please, please wait," Nuryam begged. "Me and my wife were partners for many years. There must be something you want to know. Please, please, ask me something!" His bulbous neck jiggled as he spoke.

A quick gesture from the Swordfather returned her servant to his station. "There is one question that has been vexing us of late."

"Where is she?" Hallita growled. She sliced some eel into small pieces with a shark tooth.

"Ah, yes. I understand that the whereabouts of my wife are of keen interest to some," Ezzy's husband replied.

"We've heard tales spun by desperate men and women about your wife fleeing to the Ring Islands, or climbing Mount Densmore," Sinsasi said dismissively.

The dragon skull caught Nuryam's attention. Hesitantly, he walked on the balls of his feet to peer inside of it. He put his hand deep into the pile of gold teeth. "Mount Densmore, eh? Ezzy hates snow and the top of that mountain is always white, even in the middle of summer."

"Make sure there's no gold between your fingers when you're done fondling our treasures," Ederron hissed.

After Nuryam reluctantly pulled out his hand, he showed it to the Syrens.

"Is she alive?" Hallita pressed. "Might be that she perished in the flames. Or the smoke put her to sleep and she drowned in the water below. I heard the fire was like dragon breath."

"She's alive, I'm certain of it. I didn't find any sign of her in the ruins of our shop," Nuryam replied as he faced Hallita.

"Ezzy built that shop so she could get out fast. That's why it was over the water, one more direction to leave. Down. She'll turn up, if only to skewer me with that strange sword."

"Where would she go?" Sinsasi asked. Her voice was hard as diamond. "I've heard rumors about her collection. The things that she swore she would never sell at any price."

"Whatever rumors you've heard about her stash, they're all true." Nuryam pinched the saggy flesh under his chin and pulled hard. "Before I go on, what's this worth to you?"

"I can't tell you the value until I've heard all that you have to say," Sinsasi replied coolly.

"Can I trust you?"

"No."

Nuryam loosed the sigh of a man with few options. "Her hidden collection is far more valuable than what she had in our shop." Sweat dribbled down Nuryam's temples. "If she still has that glass sword, it's with her cache of the sweetest plums hidden in the catacombs."

"Iron Wand makes their home down there," Ederron said, scratching his chin. "Is she in league with them?"

"Ezmerelda? Friendly with the mages?" Nuryam scoffed. "I think not. The catacombs I speak of are under the Old Town Market Square."

Sinsasi moved to stand near the man. "If you're telling me that she has buried her treasure in the ground, that is of no value to the Syrens." She put her hand on his shoulder.

"Uh, but, it's not that at all. She doesn't drop the relics in the catacombs and throw some dirt over them." He began chewing on a ragged thumbnail as he spoke. "I can't lead you there because I don't know where it is. Ezzy blindfolded me whenever she took me there. She didn't trust me."

"Of all the things Ezzy possesses, her good sense is undoubtedly the most valuable," Ederron mused.

Nuryam grunted. "There's a chamber deep in the catacombs. She protects it with many traps. When she led me there I coughed on smoke. My head ached after I breathed it in. I heard stone grind on stone, the crackling of flame, and some other sounds I didn't recognize. We turned so many times that I was dizzy by the time Ezzy took the blindfold off me. And there's more than one path to her treasures."

Hallita grabbed a flagon from a servant and poured herself some more drink. "What treasures does Ezzy have stashed in there? Are her mounds of gold taller than ours?" She gestured dramatically at the sparkling yellow metal in the back room.

Shaking his head, Nuryam pulled his fingers from his mouth and spit a piece of thumbnail. "Gold bores Ezzy. She fancies herself a seeker of fantastic relics." Nuryam closed his eyes. "I saw weapons that glowed. Things she said came from the Bottomless Well and the Harbor of Shipwrecks. A wand made of fire and another made of ice. Eldritch things."

Sinsasi beckoned for more fire wine. "The Syrens have an aptitude for acquiring relics as well." She nodded at the pile of ceremonial swords lying on the wood floor. "If we were to seek Ezzy's collection, where would we begin?"

"The answer to that question changes all the time. She has a stall at the market that hides the entrance to her catacombs. Every time she took me there, someone different was standing in it. She was always changing the cloth over it, the wares, everything about it. The shopkeepers have no idea what's hidden behind them. I've been there when the square is empty and not even the cobblestones will betray her secret."

Fire wine burned Sinsasi's throat as she swallowed a mouthful. "Which leads us back to Emerald Ezzy. Where is she?"

"Truthfully, I do not know. She'll want to protect what she has left, and that's in the catacombs. If I were searching for her instead of hiding from her, that's where I'd go hunting for my dear wife Ezmerelda."

The Syrens fell silent, except for the sound of Ederron chewing on a boar's rib soaked in Kabern wine and rolled in mustard seeds.

"She...hasn't been here, has she?" Nuryam scratched the back of his neck.

"If she could, there's no doubt she'd search for you here after what she told the king and queen." Sinsasi grinned. "But she is not permitted within these walls."

"I thank you for letting me use the lesser known passages in and out of here." Nuryam cleared his throat loudly. "Can I...see the Syrens now? The lad and the lass? Glatt and Lunyu."

Sinsasi finished her fire wine. "You've given us a map without a path marked on it. What you've told us is as useful as a gold scythe without the gold. A scythe alone is merely a helpful tool used to harvest with much work."

"Please, I beg you. She's there and she might still have the Shard of the Specter," Nuryam blubbered. "Maybe I'll learn more later! Maybe she'll find me! If she does, I'll bring her to you, I swear it!"

Sinsasi waited until she saw beads of sweat glistening on his brow. "You may enjoy half a night with Glatt alone," Sinsasi said. "If you desire more of our company, and more of Lunyu's company, you must mark the path on that map."

As his jowls shook, Nuryam bowed deeply before Sinsasi. "I thank you, Swordfather. I will do anything for your family. Anything at all!"

Without waiting for a word of dismissal from his hosts, he sprinted out the door and into the Shrine of Solace to search for his prize.

Sinsasi summoned Fann and instructed her to follow Nuryam to make certain he enjoyed only half a night of Glatt's pleasures.

Hallita shook her head. "There's no way that tower of jelly could bring Ezzy to us. That woman was loosing crossbow bolts from her hips."

"Ederron, when we're finished here, you'll order a warrior to shadow Nuryam when he leaves." Sinsasi shrugged. "Doubtless he'll go to the market and search for the stall that conceals Ezzy's treasures. We must know if he finds it."

With a subtle gesture, Sinsasi commanded the silent servants to fill the chalices with each Syren's drink of choice and leave the room. Hallita touched the hand of the naked man lying on the trestle table. Opening his eyes, he took the remaining Pader Stones off his body and put them on a silver platter. He walked out the door to leave the back room and return to the main floor, naked as the day the thundering horde of gods had made him.

Sinsasi, Ederron, and Hallita sat at the table with their chalices full.

"The silent servants' ears hear no better than their feet," Sinsasi said. "But this discussion is for Syrens only."

Ederron stood. He went to the bucket of diamonds and inspected one nearly the size of his hand.

Hallita pushed away her plate. "The Fire Keepers draw strength from the king, and the king draws strength from the Fire Keepers. If we weaken one, we'll weaken the other. Attack wouldn't be difficult. I've seen the way their captain Berg looks at me. I haven't even used my charms on him, but whenever I'm near him he holds his helm over his crotch."

Silence flooded into the back room. Sinsasi slid her palm down her face.

"Your hearing is worse than our servants'. I will tell you once again. The key to winning this war is *not* fighting the Swordfamilies." Sinsasi strolled over to lean against the trestle table where the servant had lain. "Our goal is not a bloody victory." She rubbed her gloved hands on the table top. "We must make our greatest enemies as obedient as the servants who lie still to serve us delicacies.

"The key to our victory is to seize control of the crown and wear the royal mantle as a cloak of protection. In time, Raysk will find the Bleeding Blade. If the Iron Wand has any skill at stealth, they'll keep it from him long enough for us to control the Kingdom Guard." She petted the table behind her. "Raysk may wield the Bleeding Blade after the Syrens wield the throne."

The rings strung above the Syrens jingled as Hallita stomped across the room.

"If that's our aim, then I bear glad tidings." The Syren warrior sneered. "We need only kill the king so that my thrall Opvolk takes his rightful place on the throne. Opvolk's mind is no battlefield. I am his queen and he is my loyal subject." Hallita put her hands on her hips. "He will rescue me from our patrons that reek like chamber pots."

"You must demonstrate the prince's supposed loyalty to you," Sinsasi hissed. "He *must* have The Need. You will be engaged to marry him, and soon. If you cannot seal this union in marriage, then I will finish what you have begun."

"The Prince of the Eclipse is powerless against my charms," Hallita said sternly. She glared at her Swordfather.

"I cannot have this discussion again," Ederron groaned.

Sinsasi ignored him. "The king is only one side of the royal coin. It will do us no good to secure half the royal court if the other half will dominate Opvolk."

Ederron began tossing the huge diamond in the air. "Your concern is that our smitten prince would be no more powerful at court than the herald because Minacia would control her young pup." The diamond sparkled as it went up and down, up and down. "We could solve that riddle by murdering the king and queen at the same time. Fallov is wed to a Syren. When they're gone, Fallov's son weds another Syren. The arrangement would be familiar to the townsfolk." He caught the diamond and held it toward his Swordfather. "The banners in the throne hall will be made of Syren silk."

One more toss of the diamond proved fatal for the supposed gem. Ederron pitched the stone into the air but failed to catch it. Crashing to the floor, it shattered into tiny shards. The Syrens all stared at the ruined gem in disgust.

"One of those bastards paid with a false stone," Hallita said, spitting on the shards. "Our master of treasure must be whipped for this."

"Thu'gods I hope the warriors scrubbing our scent from our castle thralls are more thorough than the treasure master," Ederron added, shaking his head.

"I will punish those who fail me appropriately," Sinsasi seethed. "As for emptying both thrones through regicide, even the dimmest candles in the royal court would know the killings were done by those with the most to gain. Melyq and Voden have many unsavory qualities but stupidity isn't among them."

Hallita picked up a gold nose ring and threw it in a jar of rubbish. "Then we kill Fallov first and divine Minacia's untimely demise later. How hard could it be to poison a king?"

"Using our skills, poisoning most of the royal family wouldn't be difficult. But you can't poison the king. He has servants that taste his food and wine," Ederron said dismissively.

"You speak the truth, my captain. Though if the king were to die, and the court believed the queen was responsible, then for us the war for the Greatsword would be a tourney of no consequence." Sinsasi wrapped her heavy robe close and scowled. "The Shard of the Specter is the perfect weapon to kill one enemy and pin the blame on another. Hide the blade, cut the foe, smear the blood on whoever you like."

"Forgive me, my Blade," Hallita said apologetically. "I failed you."

"You have indeed, but not all victories are won with blades." Sinsasi laid her hand on Hallita's shoulder. "Knowledge can be far deadlier than any weapon made of steel. Tell me, what do you know of the king and queen's intimacy? They quarrel in the throne hall, but is there still some lingering passion in the bedchamber?"

"The flame between the two has gone out, but there are still some warm embers. They will bring no more children into the realm." Hallita's head bobbed. "The king no longer plants his seed in the queen's garden, although she permits him to pleasure her in other ways."

"What ways?" Sinsasi pressed.

"She only permits the king to use his mouth. She says they have their best conversations in the bedchamber because she's the only one who can talk." Hallita smiled. "That usually happens after they're both full of wine."

Ederron raised his eyebrows.

Gold scraped against the floor as Sinsasi grabbed the hilt of a ceremonial sword that had fallen over. "You know all of this from Opvolk?"

"A secret whispered inside the castle is like the court herald blowing his horn and announcing it, and the queen didn't whisper this one," Hallita replied. "She wants the royal courts to know that while the king sits higher on the dais, she sits above him in the bed." Hallita flashed her Syren's smile. "The Prince of the Eclipse does not ask about what his parents do in their bedchambers, but neither can he escape hearing of it."

"She rules in the throne hall and the bedchamber," Ederron said absently.

Hallita nodded. "The queen still has her Syren's appetites. She keeps a smooth rod of gold within arm's reach of her four-poster bed. It's curved in the way that women enjoy. The queen calls it her bedchamber scepter."

Ederron smirked.

"Opvolk suspects that the king satisfies his other desires with other women. If he does, it's a secret that hasn't been whispered to him," Hallita added.

Sinsasi admired the sword's polished gold. "The king is quite safe inside his castle but he's still vulnerable where all men are, in the bedchamber."

Ederron and Hallita shared a quizzical look.

"I find it amusing that our queen wears privy clothes. She's not one of us any longer." Sinsasi ran her finger down the golden blade's dull edge. "We don't have a single thread of privy clothes in any Shrine of Solace. Except for the ones our patrons forget when they stumble home." She felt the sword's point with her finger. "Our best poison is Syren's Silence. It's potent and has neither odor nor color. It's only fatal when swallowed. We shall use it to kill King Fallov and throw Queen Minacia in a dungeon cell."

"How? We just spoke of the king's servants and guards," Hallita said. Her words were laced with anger.

"No servant tastes where we'll place Syren's Silence." Sinsasi dropped the golden blade on the trestle table where the naked man had lain. "That waif who's probably howling in delight right now, Belna, she'll deliver the poison. It will be dribbled onto the queen's privy clothes, along with her perfume. The privy clothes that cover her sex." She petted the sword slowly. "Belna will do this when the queen asks for fresh clothes before taking her supper with the king."

Hallita's eyes grew wide.

Ederron's mouth fell open.

"The next morning, the servants who tasted the king's supper will be alive and well. The king who tasted the queen will be dead. And the queen will be the last person alone with him before he dies."

A long moment of silence passed amongst the Syrens.

"We're going to kill the king using poison between the queen's thighs?" Ederron asked, his voice full of disbelief.

"Do you know what Minacia calls the king's face?" Hallita asked.

Ederron shook his head.

"The queen's second favorite throne."

Ederron burst out laughing.

"That's how we empty both thrones at once. We kill the king and the queen takes the blame to rot in the dungeons. After years of open enmity between the two, no one would think to look into the tragedy any further," Sinsasi replied.

"The queen will protest her innocence, but to the Emerald Realm her guilt will be certain. Both thrones will be ours for the taking. We must move with quickness. The sooner we seize the Emerald Crown, the sooner we escape Raysk's farce of a war."

The three Syrens touched their chalices together high in the air. To the Swordfather, the captain, and the warrior, the sound their chalices made was a celebration bell.

"We'll doom the queen, who was once the Swordfather of our own family," Ederron said with awe. "One day I hope to lead the Syrens with the same brilliance as you."

"You have much to learn and little to learn it with." Sinsasi clasped her gloved hands together.

Ederron glared at his Swordfather.

"Pity that Rumam isn't here to enjoy this moment," Sinsasi said.

"He's still missing?" Hallita asked.

"His whereabouts are unknown." Sinsasi frowned. "When he returned from Auzken's tomb with the Bleeding Blade, covered in red and sobbing, I feared for him."

"Life without beauty isn't worth living," Ederron said morosely, sipping from his chalice.

"Nothing could be done for him?" Hallita asked.

"There's a terrible mess of blood-red stains over his chest and arms and legs. Whatever cure the Iron Wand devises for me may be too late for him," Sinsasi replied. She stared at the drink in her chalice.

Ederron frowned. "The blood from that wretched blade could stain water."

"He will cleanse himself of the stains in the lakes of silver guarded by thu'gods," Hallita said with conviction.

"I, too, fear the worst. But I will not abandon hope so easily," the Swordfather added. "I've doubled the number of warriors searching for him. If the thundering gods are just, he will return to us unharmed. Let us hope it's soon, for our sake and his own. If word of his condition spreads, so will the truth of who took the Bleeding Blade. The Heavies will be wroth."

For a time, the Syrens remained silent.

"My Blade, I must ask," Ederron said, clearing his throat. "We traded the Bleeding Blade for more debt. I can't help but think that we would be a stronger family today had Rumam never opened that accursed tomb."

Sinsasi paused long enough that Ederron recoiled.

"Though we don't need the Bleeding Blade, we must be certain that Raysk never wields it." She folded her arms, suppressing her rage. "We must secretly fear Raysk. I despise the man but admire the deed. He sacrificed much of his manhood to be free of our charms. He is the one man of power in the realm who will never again suffer The Need. Our charms break upon him like water on rock. His shield is that scar between his legs. That is what makes him our greatest threat." She bit her lower lip. "My intent wasn't to possess the blade. We had to secrete it from our most dangerous enemy." She tugged at the gloves that she wore. "I would prefer that we still controlled it, but I have my own needs."

Rapping came from the door. After she was summoned, Fann entered the room.

"I told you to stay with Ezzy's husband," Sinsasi growled. She made no effort to conceal her disgust.

Fann fidgeted with the ends of her long, many-colored hair. "Apologies, my Blade. There is much happening in the shrine today. Word of a possible war with the Crimson Crown has spread amongst the commoners. They are desperate to forget the danger, if only for a time." She glanced at the captain and the warrior, then returned her attention to the Swordfather. "Quivum requests an audience with you."

Sinsasi's rose-red lips curved like a crescent moon.

"Leave me," she said to her Syrens. "Fann, do not permit him to enter until I summon him."

After her Swordfamily departed the back room and the door was closed tight, Sinsasi's wool robe became a crumpled pile on the floor. Next, she pulled off her sheer silk that landed on the wool. She was naked except for the snow-white gloves that concealed her stained arms.

Sinsasi took the golden sword from the trestle table. She walked to the center of the room where she faced the door. There, she placed an arm across her chest. In her other hand, she held the sword with its point resting on the floor between her bare feet. She held it such that the gold blade's broadside hid the place where her thighs came together.

In the Shrine of Solace, her body was the greatest altar upon which men and women would sacrifice all. For a patron under her charms, nothing was sacred except for Sinsasi herself. Her skin was white as a cloud against a blue summer sky. She was a medley of graceful curves, as though her body had been shaped by wind alone. The woman's beauty didn't end with her skin; that's where it began. She seemed to glow not with light, but cherished memories. Those who looked upon her felt the warmth of returning home after a long time away and the same all-consuming desire they felt the instant before they first indulged their most carnal desires.

After pausing for a moment to take a deep breath and summon her most powerful charms, she called for Quivum.

The Ashfall Swordfather stumbled through the door. He trembled so violently that the dark blue cloak over his white jerkin flowed like waves in heavy seas. He needed both of his unsteady hands to close and lock the door behind him.

Sinsasi remained where she stood. As Quivum approached her, he kept his eyes fixed on the floor. When he was within a sword's length of her, he stopped. As his eyes slowly rose to meet hers, he savored her body the way a man lost in a desert drinks water from an oasis. Then he dropped to one knee, bowed his head, and asked her a question.

"What is thy bidding, my Blade?"

CHAPTER TWENTY

FIRE KEEPERS

Andra's heart beat faster than she would admit to any mortal man. She pressed her thighs tight against Uther. The dragon that bore her settled above the mountain pass near Kellington's castle. She was high enough that she could see the Crimson Crown's knights advancing out of the east, but low enough that nearby warriors could hear her.

What she saw made her yearn for the wretched hovel where she spent her youth fighting with her blood family and dreaming of being anywhere else.

A line of knights clad in steel plate marched through the wide pass. The column was unbroken, except for the intervals where destriers pulled carts laden with large wooden boxes. An unarmed man knelt on top of each box. They wore simple clothes and a felt cap. Andra could see they also wore gloves and an apron, both made of leather.

Dragons gripped the mountainsides where Andra had ordered them. Each one was positioned for the greatest advantage against the Crimson Crown's force. Some were concealed by an outcropping of rock or greenery that had taken root inside a crack. Others hung from a spot where they could quickly glide down while raining fire from above. All were concealed against the eastern eyes.

Andra signaled to Glas, beckoning him to near.

"The Kingdom Guard was supposed to be here by now!" she yelled, her breath hot against his cheek. "This is Kellington's Pass. Where in the thundering hells are his birds? When did Kellington send the messenger pigeons?"

"Days ago," Glas said, the words rushing in a shrill tone over his thick tongue.

"Days ago, he told us he sent them days ago!" Andra shot back.

"I saw the pigeons flying to Fulccrum, to the southwest."

"But you didn't see the message."

"No, but I sent our own pigeons myself," Glas protested. "They flew to the Castle of Towers." Glas ran his hand through the sweat-soaked mop of his hair. "Even if they all failed to get there, surely some lord at the foot of the mountains would have told their king. They wouldn't *all* betray him."

"My Swordbrother, the king has been betrayed by either the Pader lords or his own men. Mayhaps Fallov is betraying us," Andra said breathlessly. "To me, it matters not. I'm the one on this mountain facing a river of red banners without any aid from the man who begged for our strength. Gods, I wish Fyur was here with me now."

A war horn sounded from the east. The noise was so low and loud that Andra could feel her dragon shake. Some small rocks came loose from the mountain faces to cascade around them.

"Fletch!" Andra called to the rider of a dragon gripping the mountain face on the other side of the pass. He pulled aside some moss hanging between himself and his captain. "Take your dragons and get as high on that wall as you can. Push around to the rear of their line. Glas and I will strike them here on the west side. When you light up their rear-guard, we'll do the same to their vanguard." She squinted from her perch high on the mountain but couldn't see the far end of the Crimson Crown's line. "Stay high on the mountain and bathe them in flame. Don't go down into the pass. That's their strength. We must preserve our dragons by fighting our kind of battle." She held her hands apart and then clapped them together. "We'll crush them into ash between the jaws of a fiery vise. If it goes bad, get out of there, past the rock hanging over the entrance pass farther to the west. Understand?"

Fletch replied with a shallow nod. "Born to burn!" he cried and pressed his heels hard against his dragon's ribs. A group of his fellow warriors and their mounts followed him eastward. The swarm of dragons was nearly half the Fire Keepers' force in Kellington's Pass. They climbed and flapped along the rock. Almost immediately, Andra lost them in the morning sun that shone low over the Paders.

The small wooden house carved by Mistahn was tucked inside a pouch tied to Andra's belt. She undid the string that held the pouch and clenched the carving of the tiny home tight in her hand.

"My brother made this for me," she said absently. "Every time I've seen him since I joined the Fire Keepers, he's begged for adventure saddled on the back of a dragon. I wonder if he would still beg to join with a column of Crimson knights bearing down on us." She frowned. "Mistahn had great fortune when he hunted. He would always return with as much game as he could carry. I hope his token brings us some luck."

Glas eyed the keepsake. "It's well-crafted. You can tell he put much time into it. Maybe he'd be good with a blade. Just because someone begs you for something doesn't mean they'll fail at it."

With movements as quick as they were deft, Andra returned the carving to its pouch.

Another war horn sounded below. Andra beckoned Glas to follow her.

The two Fire Keepers were the point of a spear made of dragons and warriors. Their mounts crawled along the mountain face. The dragons picked their way along the craggy rock. Their movements were slow and controlled to knock loose as few rocks as possible.

Guiding her force quickly, Andra brought the dragons to a halt on the side of a spur where they could hide from the advancing knights. Small ledges provided the mounts with firm footing.

A patch of gray clouds bunched over the sun. The flat light let Andra study the advancing force in detail, all the way to the column's rear. The knights clad in full armor, with shields painted red as blood, marched in lockstep. An impossibly long snake made of steel slithered to where Andra's force was tight on the mountain face.

"We wait for Fletch to light a fire under their arse," Andra said. "When the fire comes down on them and they break ranks, that's when we hit them in the front."

As she stopped speaking, the sound of dragon fire echoed against the craggy mountains.

Smoke darker than the gray clouds above began to fill the air. A flock of small birds sprang from somewhere in the distance and raced the length of the mountain pass, squawking in a furor as they flew past the Fire Keepers.

After the birds passed, the air became still again. The

smoke became darker. Spots of white on the mountainsides began to move west, bouncing high above the ground. Andra squinted at the strange white splotches. As they neared, she could see they were mountain goats. They jumped from rock to rock with enough agility to make a dragon envious. Andra gave another signal to stay back.

Screaming like men stabbed in the gut, the goats scrambled past the dragons. They bounced and lunged through the dragons so fast that it seemed as though a snow squall was sweeping through the pass.

One goat trailing the rest paused. It bleated a lone scream as it stood on a nub of rock beside a gold dragon. Before Andra could bark a command or move a muscle, the gold dragon's head swung close to the mountain goat. It loosed a flame that enveloped its prey's body. The snow-white fur disappeared under the dragon fire. When the flame stopped, smoldering meat and charred bits of bone caromed off the mountainside as it tumbled to the pass below.

A dragon shrieked.

"Quiet!" Andra hissed.

Expecting the sight of onrushing knights, she turned to face the Crimson Crown's strength.

Each knight stood rigid. None showed any sign that they had noticed the gold dragon's flame. Behind them, the smoke had become darker and thicker, like the clouds of a powerful summer storm rolling in quickly.

"There's smoke to the east, but where's the dragon fire?" Andra asked.

"That's odd. I don't see any archers down there," Glas said.

"I don't like that they've halted. Don't they see the

dragons burning the tail of their column?" Andra asked, taking a deep breath.

A straggler mountain goat, far behind his herd, hopped lazily between the dragons. Neither man nor menace paid it any mind.

War horns sounded for the third time. Dark smoke in the east billowed as the sound of the horn's long call echoed off the mountains. More rock shook loose to fall like rain.

"Fire Slayers! Let slip the slashmanders!" a gruff voice yelled below. The words were so loud that they sounded as if they had been blown through the war horn itself.

"Fire Slayers, loose slashmanders!" a chorus of voices yelled in response.

The unarmed men dressed like blacksmiths grabbed the center of each large wooden box. Wood planks clattered throughout Kellington's Pass as doors on the roofs of the boxes were flung open.

Pitch-black animals with shiny skin sprang from the openings. They had flat heads, wide bodies, and short legs. Their bellies were flush against the ground where they scurried and the mountain rock where they climbed.

"What's a slashmander?" Andra asked.

"Don't know. Maybe some kind of salamander?" Glas replied with a question of his own. "You know, those slippery-looking things. I see them climbing trees sometimes. But those things down there are far too big to be salamanders."

Dragon fire sprouted in the distance like Dancing Water. Commands screamed by warriors that had followed Fletch echoed off the jagged rocks lining the pass.

The Crimson Crown's dark animals moved with much more speed than their low profile would suggest. The blood flowing through Andra's racing heart ran cold when she saw that the animals moved just as fast on the mountains as they did in the pass.

Slashmanders sprinted up the mountain on the side of the pass opposite from Andra.

Smoke to the east turned black.

"That smoke is too dark to be from dragon breath. It's black," Glas said. "Could be dragon blood."

This mountain pass looks like the belly of a soft man after I've gutted him. The foulness is rushing everywhere.

"It's time to close the vise," Andra said to Glas. Then she turned to face the warriors and dragons waiting for her command. "Stay high and rain fire from above. I want every last dragon with us when we return to the Castle of Towers!" She yelled so loud that her voice broke. "Fire Keepers, with me! Rain down thundering hells! We keep the fire and they suffer the flame!"

The warriors roared: "Born to burn!"

Andra charged and her force rushed with her. Dust and rock fell into the pass in a sloping line as her mount drove his claws deep into the steep mountain face. The captain stood tall in her stirrups, bending her uphill leg as she stretched her lower leg to stay upright. She unsheathed her sword and raised it high.

Smoke trailed behind her mount's nostrils.

Andra's dragon Uther, and all the dragons that followed behind her, held a terrible fire in their bellies. The air near to them became so hot that it rose in waves. As the dragons charged, the mountain rock looked as though it flowed like a river. As if the rock itself was pulled by a current.

The knights at the column vanguard unsheathed their swords and held them at the ready.

"Uther, fail me not!" Andra cried.

As she charged, Andra could see how steady the knights held their swords. They were unafraid as they faced a fiery death. Wind rushed through her hair. The cold blood coursing through her veins became even colder as she saw her enemy's posture.

So many knights pointed their blades to the sky that the mountain pass sprouted a forest of sharp steel. Some knights cried their allegiance to the Crimson Crown. Others shouted loyalty to Lord Vlymner. Those knights' shields bore the sigil of a streak of blue that arched across a field of red. Whatever other names the steel skins yelled, Andra could not hear and she did not care.

"Loose flame!" she commanded her mount.

Uther sprayed a column of dragon fire over the Crimson knights. As his breath blasted down, the dragon spread its wings wide to glide through the mountain pass. Knights fell in his wake as the hot steel scorched their flesh. By the time Andra's dragon crossed the pass, the acrid scent of burning flesh hung thick in the air.

Safe above the steel-clad men, Andra watched as her fellow Fire Keepers swept over the pass. The plumes of flame that the dragons launched destroyed the red knights' order and discipline. Long lengths of the column collapsed into ruin as the survivors dropped their swords and ran back east, or into each other. A few sprinted down Kellington's Pass to the west. They didn't look back.

The roar of each blast of her dragon's fire deafened Andra. Between those blasts she was struck by a shrieking that made the hairs over her backbone stand on end. Her eyes grew wide and she forgot to breathe. It was the most awful noise that Andra had ever heard.

Black tendrils reaching for the Fire Keeper captain streaked across the face of the mountain. She and her mount stood ready. A short distance, that was quickly becoming shorter, separated the slashmanders and Andra.

Thundering horde those beasts are darker than pitch and move faster than quicksilver.

When the slashmanders charged so close that Andra could almost feel them, their hellishness became clear. The monsters had gaping maws lined with rows of narrow teeth sharper than knives. Much smaller than a horse, but bigger than a hound, they snapped their jaws tight with each step they took. Their flat tails dragged against the rock as they approached.

"Halt and ready flame!" Andra cried.

Every dragon behind her drew a deep breath and raised its head.

A single dragon disobeyed to charge past Andra. It loosed a cloud of scorching hot fire that burned with a roar like rolling thunder. While the huge plume of fire was still blazing in the air, slashmanders attacked. The first dark beast to reach the dragon launched itself into the billowing flame. It passed through the cone of blue fire burning near the dragon's fangs.

Teeth whiter than bone bleached by the sun clamped down on the dragon's neck. The slashmander wrenched its body, ripping open a wide hole in the dragon's flesh. Flame poured from the terrible wound and onto the attacker's head.

The fire burned over the slashmander's black body. The monster licked at the dragon's flame with ravenous zeal. It bit at the air, trying to pull the flame deep inside its belly.

As the mortally wounded dragon's head swung wildly, the slashmander dug its claws deep under its victim's scales. The small beast ripped at the dragon scales, sending them to the mountain pass below like dead leaves in winter. The slashmander crawled to the fiery creature's soft underbelly. It ripped and tore at the dragon flesh with a whirlwind of razor-like claws and teeth. Before the dragon ceased to blow its hellish inferno, scalding hot blood poured from its belly.

Fire from the dragon vanished and was replaced by wisps of thin gray smoke. Its life ebbing away, the dragon's grip on the mountain face loosened. Before it fell, the slashmander dove into the yawning hole it had ripped open in the dragon's belly. The dark body disappeared inside. The dragon screeched so loud that nearly every knight below turned to find the beast that made such a terrible noise. The dragon's body went limp. It lost its grip on both the mountainside and its life. As it fell, torrents of dragon blood followed. The only part of the slashmander that showed was its black tail poking out from the belly. The tail wagged as if it belonged to a joyful dog welcoming its master home.

When the dragon landed, it exploded into a towering ball of flame. The billowing black smoke rose in the air to form the shape of a mushroom. The knights who had stood where the dragon's body landed were reduced to piles of steel that glowed red hot.

A stiff breeze blew down the mountains and through the pass. Moments later, the smoke cleared enough that the fate of the men beneath the dragon became apparent to many in the red column.

The knights close enough to feel the heat began to smash their way through the column. Discipline and order dissolved as the panic that seized the knights cascaded in waves that spread from where the dragon fell.

"Tear them apart with your fangs!" Andra yelled to her charges. "Claws and fangs! Shred them! Take to the sky!"

Uther stretched his wings and lunged away from the

mountain. He hovered over the pass, laboring mightily with each flap of his wings. The dragon rose and sank as he held his rider in the air, as if jumping and falling to the ground before repeating the effort.

Slashmanders advanced west along the mountain faces. One that scampered high above Uther crouched on its haunches before leaping at Andra. She yanked on the reins of her mount. The monster's snapping teeth were closer than the tip of her dragon's wing as it plummeted past her, into the chaos of the knights panicking below.

From the east came the sound of stampeding dragons. Their bodies were concealed by the dark smoke, but they screamed with fury and their blasts of red flame showed through the smoke.

Rock fell from the pass walls. They shook so much that some slashmanders lost their grip and fell to their deaths.

A line of dragons shot through the dark smoke, sprinting along the mountainside in a frenzied terror. Their eyes were wide. They fired their breath wildly without thought to where it hit. Some had slashmanders latched onto their backs or tails.

The dragons that Fletch led to the east had become a thundering horde retreating to the west.

Andra couldn't feel her lips. "Fall back!" she screamed over the growing anarchy. "Fall back to the Emerald Kingdom!"

Fall back to where an army should be advancing to relieve us. If I don't see a column of Emerald Knights stretching to the horizon, I'll bring the Gods' Blade down on Fallov's castle like a headsman's blade.

"FALL BACK!" she cried, pressing her heels hard against her mount. She yanked on the reins and the dragon wheeled away from the horde of slashmanders. Andra whipped the reins hard and Uther pumped his wings in response.

The pair dipped toward the ground as they lurched backward. Andra spun in her saddle to find a slashmander with its teeth sunk deep into her dragon's tail. "Whip!" she cried to Uther. The dragon's tail flicked in the air. Andra threw her sword at the slashmander. The spinning blade struck true, slicing the black beast's head from its body.

The lifeless body fell away and disappeared inside the writhing mass of knights below. The head with its wretched teeth still held tight to the dragon's tail.

Slashmanders raced on the walls of the pass with the sure feet of mountain goats. When they climbed to a place high above a dragon, they leapt at their prey below like a deathly hail. One of them landed on the head of a dragon struggling to fly near the wall, driving the straggler into the ground, where it crashed with a sickening thud.

Andra felt the rhythm of her dragon's wings slow. The two sank lower to the ground.

Slashmanders crave dragon flame, but men still fear it.

Pounding her fist on the flank of her mount, she dove Uther to the pass. He landed at a gallop, slamming knights aside with his bulging muscles.

"Loose flame!" Andra shouted.

Fire billowed and red knights parted. Andra kept pounding her dragon and he responded, sprinting through the mass of knights faster than he could fly.

Through the smoke, Andra could see the western end of the pass as Uther hurtled through the crumbling column of knights. They reached the column's west end and without the steel-clad bodies before it, the dragon darted through Kellington's Pass.

Mounted Kingdom Guard lingered at the entrance to

the pass, where the mountains finally surrendered to the foothills. As Andra neared them, they vanished. By the time she reached the pass's west end, the only thing that remained of the Kingdom Guard was dust in the air from their hasty retreat.

Andra turned to look back into the pass that she had escaped.

She saw the Crimson knights in disarray. They stumbled around the pass in every direction. Dragons scrambled toward her. Slashmanders harried the Fire Keepers, diving from places on the mountain above the dragons.

Four warriors mounted on swift dragons ran the gauntlet to meet Andra.

"See that rock?" Andra said between gasps. She pointed where high mountain rock leaned over the pass. The granite beneath it was covered in a spiderweb of deep cracks. "All of you burn the rock under those ledges until it falls into the pass." She felt consciousness slipping away until a warrior yelled her name. "Do it! Burn it now before those knights get here!"

Dragons and Fire Keeper warriors bounded from the pass, most collapsing after they escaped. Smoking blood from the dragons streaked the mountain walls.

Some slashmanders, driven wild by their feasting on the dragons, set upon the red knights in the pass. The column's advance was little more than a crawl.

Above the Crimson Crown's knights, the dragons ran along a mountain wall or glided over the pass. The Fire Keepers' strength fled with speed that Andra had never before seen.

Our dragons have never fled in terror.

Near the back of the mass of dragons sprinting away from the Crimson Crown, Fletch gripped the reins of his mount and leaned forward in his stirrups. Andra's eyes locked on him as he wove through the slashmanders hurling themselves at his dragon.

The four dragons Andra had ordered to lay flame to the granite blasted away at the deep cracks below the overhang. With the dragon fire merging together, the rocks began to glow a sunset red.

Fletch's dragon flew low over the red knights, beating its wings unevenly. Its rider was bleeding from his head and leaning to one side.

"Fletch, hurry!" Andra yelled, her voice high and shrill. "They're above you!"

The wounded warrior in the pass did not hear her. Two slashmanders jumped from their places high on the mountain wall. With speed as harrowing as the beasts themselves, one hit the dragon and ripped off its head. The other landed on Fletch and plunged its teeth into his chest.

The dragon and its rider were dead before they slammed into the ground, their blood redder than the knights' shields.

Smoke dark as a shadow rose from Fletch's funeral pyre.

Andra howled in rage so pure that her dragon lowered its head and backed up several paces.

War horns sounded to the east. They blew a long, low call followed by two short blasts.

Slashmanders that had been scrambling along the mountain walls slowed, then stopped. Some obediently turned east. Others lingered and took halting steps forward before grudgingly abandoning their hunt.

The men in leather aprons atop the wooden boxes herded the slashmanders back into their pens.

Sweat poured from Glas's head. His dragon staggered from the pass to join Andra.

"Damn the horde!" Spittle flew as Andra yelled. "This was not our fight! Fletch was not meant to die defending a *lowly king*!"

"Thu'gods! Those monsters hunger for more than dragon flesh!" Glas screeched. "They crave the dragon's very flame!"

Where the four dragons blasted the mountain, granite glowing brilliant red flowed down the mountainside. Thick and slow, the rock slid beneath the four columns of flame.

Shattering rocks cried out as the mountain above the dragon fire yielded to the great weight it now supported without foundation. As the granite was torn asunder, the massive ledges tipped down. After a final blast of dragon fire, the ancient rock surrendered its battle against a dreadful weight. The overhangs tumbled into the mountain pass with a roaring crash, shattering into dozens of huge boulders. The ruins filled the pass with a pile of rock taller than an oak.

The captain and her warriors shielded their eyes from the cloud of dust that swept over them. A small rock loosed by the violent collapse rolled to the foot of Glas's dragon.

Over the boulders, dragons continued to climb and fly. Most trailed blood that smoked in their wake. A smaller dragon limped over the boulders. It reached the top to roll down the west side, its body flopping like a piece of cloth. The dragon wobbled as it rose to its feet and staggered to its masters. Then it collapsed at Andra's feet to die where it lay.

"How many did we lose?" Andra whispered between gasps, her eyes on the dead dragon. She coughed on the terrible smoke from the blood of her dead and dying. "How many did we waste?" Tears birthed by loss streamed from her eyes.

Glas shuddered. "At least half," he replied in a voice even smaller than hers. "I pray to the thundering horde that the other passes aren't this bad."

"More than half of our strongest. What have I done? How do I tell Kardas? I've failed him. No. *I've ruined him,*" she whispered. "*And Fletch.*"

The warriors that survived the slaughter, unlike their mounts, pulled themselves over the boulders. Andra ordered those who could fight to provide cover for those still retreating through the pass.

Glas reached over and put his hand on Andra's shoulder. She paid his gesture no mind.

"Take the warriors with the fastest mounts and get word to the other captains." She swallowed the thick spittle that had pooled in the back of her throat before she barked the orders. "Pull them from the passes. Horde, I hope those monsters haven't set upon them yet. Tell them all to make haste for the Castle of Towers. We must retreat to our stronghold, the refuge. It's the safest place in the realm for our dragons." She grabbed Glas's chin and pulled his face close. "I'm trusting you with our Swordfamily's lives. You've earned that trust, but you must not fail."

Reins snapped and Glas spun his dragon around. He yelled orders and galloped away with mounted warriors following close behind.

Andra and the warriors that remained with her rounded up their wounded. Dark smoke hung in the air like a whisper of night.

Many dragons had gaping tears in their wings. Some bled from gashes where a slashmander had ripped away their flesh. One dragon, soon to join the thundering horde, was missing a leg. Needle-like teeth sprouted from bloody wounds.

It took three strong warriors to pry off the slashmander head still clenched to Uther's tail.

"Tyv, listen closely. Blocking the pass will slow those knights but it won't stop them. I'll take the dragons that can keep a good pace back to the refuge," Andra said wearily. "You gather the wounded and move them somewhere safe. Save the ones you can; show mercy to the ones that you can't." The frown on Tyv's face deepened, but he nodded just the same. "Get them back to the refuge as soon as they're able." Andra closed her eyes tight. "I have to go to Kardas. He must know what's happened here."

Tyv bowed to his captain and immediately began to follow her orders. Andra wove her way through the thin group of dragons. She signaled to most of those who had survived unscathed to follow her. The dragons, those with and without a warrior, slowly obeyed. Andra began to lead them away at the best pace the drained mounts could muster.

Her band passed Kellington's mine that lay south of his pass, where she had seen mammophants hauling gold. There were no boxes and no guards.

Before her defeated group had traveled far enough to see Lord Kellington's castle, a dragon carrying a Fire Keeper charged up to Andra.

"Mwizi, why aren't you with Kardas?" Andra asked before the warrior could speak a word.

"It's the Heavies!" Mwizi blurted out, gasping for air. "They're going to attack! Kardas sent me as soon as we heard they were coming. You have to bring the dragons back to the towers!"

"By the horde, it just keeps getting worse!" Andra growled. "I can't. Many are dead and the survivors can't charge into battle. If we ride them too hard, they'll die before we get to the refuge."

Sorrow burned in Andra's chest like a dagger buried to the hilt. She looked at Uther.

"Get this group back to the refuge as fast as you can. But make certain they get home alive. We have none to spare," Andra ordered Mwizi, waving at the group of ragged dragons and warriors behind her. "I must ride alone."

With a heart far more calloused than it was before she rode into Kellington's Pass that day, Andra accepted the sacrifice that must be made.

CHAPTER TWENTY-ONE

ASHFALL

"Quivum, you're crazy!" Moshen yelled.

"I'm not crazy! At least, that's what the voices inside my head keep telling me," Quivum protested. He shrugged and drew a breath through his vision pipe. "Why would they lie to me? They sound like *very* honest people."

Moshen grabbed his stomach as his laughter became painful.

"I don't know why they keep saying that. I've never asked them if I'm crazy." Quivum threw back his head and blew out smoke like a young dragon. "They're probably just being friendly."

As he convulsed with more laughter, Moshen toppled over backward.

Swordfather Quivum sat on a giant mushroom the size of a tall stool. His greasy brown hair was still matted against his head; he hadn't washed it since the Council of Sheathed Swords. He reached down and pulled a chunk from the mushroom's cap. After inspecting the morsel, he popped it in his mouth and chewed thoroughly. He swallowed and pulled more smoke from the vision pipe. Then he closed his bloodshot eyes.

Blue fire drenched the den with its light. The flames weren't focused and intense. Instead, the blue light came from flickering candles and braziers.

The Ashfall den occupied the top floor of a building. The den's only window framed a giant blue flame atop a column in New Valois. The towering flame served as a beacon to attract all those who desired escape from the inescapable. It burned in the market where Ashfall peddled its drugs.

The expansive den was filled with a haze composed of many-colored smoke. Some smoke was as orange as a tree welcoming autumn, some was gray like the fog that rested on the port waters early in the morn, and some patches would flash and change color as if a rainbow had shattered.

Smells swirling around the Ashfall den were as diverse as the smoke. Near a corner, if one closed their eyes and drew a deep breath, they would swear spring lilacs were blossoming. Above a hookah made of fine pottery, the air smelled as if a skunk had been crushed by a war hammer.

Near the middle of the den sat a man and a woman, both naked and strumming lyres. The notes from the dueling instruments melded into calming sounds that soothed the warriors and captains littered about the room. The Ashfalls lay on feather beds resting on the floor, reclined on benches placed around hookahs, and sat on mushrooms so big they served as stools.

On the floor next to Quivum's mushroom was a large tub. A croaking noise came from inside it.

The sound was so loud that Moshen stopped laughing and pulled himself up. He straightened his dark blue robes and smacked himself on the head twice. He had olive skin, brown eyes, and straight black hair. His arms were pock-marked from his shoulders to the tips of his fingers with dark burn marks.

"The warriors say there's word from our patrons that the Fire Keepers think we stole their youngling dragons," the Ashfall captain said casually. He scratched at a burn mark on the back of his hand.

"I heard that, too, Moshen. I was sellin' some dragon spike, might've been at the DragInn," Jyfa said. Her sunken eyes had dark rings around them. "They always accusin' us of somethin'. First they say we're killin' they dragons 'cause they burn our crops. Then they say we're stealin' them. Why would we want a baby dragon? The spikes don't get good and ripe until they old enough to fly. It'd be like having a little pet whose only trick is burnin' your arse. Might be I'm not thinkin' about this the right way. The good shrooms grow outta cow dung, right?" Jyfa asked.

"If you're lucky," Moshen replied. He puffed from a thick cigar made of silver leaves.

"The good shrooms are good, right?" Jyfa pressed. "I mean really, really good."

"They're kind of small." Moshen shrugged after he blew a plume of silver smoke over his head. "You can't sit on them when you eat them. But they're better than the kind they put in the stew at the DragInn. Those don't do anything but fill your belly."

"We may be all wrong 'bout the dragons," Jyfa mused.

"You want to steal a little dragon? What would we do with it?" Moshen asked. "Can the smoke take you anywhere?"

"No, no, no," Jyfa said, shaking her head. "If good shrooms grow from cow dung, what kind of shrooms grow in dragon dung? That could be the fieriest trip you ever take." She stopped shaking her head an instant before she lost her balance and toppled over.

Moshen puffed his cigar. "Those dragon spores aren't for us to eat, we put them in that potion the Heavies crave. It's worth more than gold to those oafs."

Jyfa leaned over a trestle table. She began to speak, then passed out cold and crumpled to the floor. Two warriors lifted her up and laid her on the table.

"The Swordfamilies don't respect our family, let alone fear us," Threll, an Ashfall captain, said. "They think we're only a threat to ourselves."

Quivum eyed Threll suspiciously, sensing the meaning behind her words. "Don't talk about that filthy Bladeslayer lie again," he said, grabbing a handful of his mushroom cap. "I didn't kill Elemon. She had too much dragon spike powder. Everyone knows this! Elemon couldn't handle her dragon spike powder! I did not kill our Swordfather!"

Threll smiled and tilted her head. "If Elemon was buried under a mountain of dragon spike powder, she could have snorted her way out of it."

She pulled her dark red robes tight around her slender body. She had straight black hair and skin the color of sand when the sun is high. Her orange eyes beamed like two lilies blooming in early summer. She had a small scar on her chin and another one above her eyebrow, mementoes from her youth that she tried to erase with Ashfall's goods.

"Mayhaps someone put something bad in her powder, I know naught!" Quivum yelled, mushroom crumbs flying from his mouth. "If you weren't a captain I'd have Moshen drop you deep in the refuge covered in dragon yolk!"

"I'm just suggesting that a family led by a man accused of killing his own Swordfather has to earn the fear of his enemies." Threll shrugged.

"Wrongly accused," Quivum mumbled.

Moshen took another deep puff from his silver cigar. "The problem isn't how Quivum came to be Swordfather," he said with glittering silver smoke pouring from his mouth. "The problem is that the other families think we shouldn't be here at all. Our family should have stayed in the Crimson Kingdom and fought Winged Mind to the end. Traveling all the way here just to end up crushing Green Star was a waste. If the alliance had worked, we could have tossed the Bleeding Blade to the bottom of the Angered Sea. The Greatsword symbol would be a giant cigar made of silver leaf instead of that leaky blade." He took the cigar from his lips and became mesmerized by the blue light in the den reflecting from the shiny leaves that he smoked.

"Instead of a Bleeding Blade, the Swordfamilies would be lusting after the Silver Cigar," Threll said.

"Long may it smoke," Moshen added.

A tall man with skin brown as the last stubborn leaves of early winter towered over Threll and Moshen. He wore a toga made of wool dyed purple as a plum. The captain's bulbous muscles were covered in veins that looked like bark on a tree. His nose was crooked from a particularly savage beating he took in his youth.

"None will fear us until we beat the fear into them," the giant man said. His voice was deeper than the Angered Sea. "Which is exactly what I'll do at the next Melee of the Risen Knight."

Quivum groaned. "Shujaaq, that's no tourney fight. The battle isn't over after you're beaten down. That's a fight to the *death*." The Swordfather was very serious, which was apparent because he didn't eat a bit of mushroom as he spoke. "It's a fatal trap for men that value glory more than their own lives."

"You're mistaken, my Blade," Shujaaq said. "It's a fight to the death for the others." Every tooth of his smile was made of gold. "For me, it's a fight to glory forged in the crushed hopes of the dead."

Moshen looked up at him. "You've been taking too much of what we sell to the Heavies. It's making you big and angry like them." He shook his head. "You're beginning to talk like them, too."

Shujaaq didn't respond.

Another handful of mushroom filled Quivum's mouth. He chewed for long moments.

"Bring me the only thing that can help me divine our family's future," Quivum said after he swallowed hard. "Bring me the *Toadfather*." He pointed at Threll.

Moshen put his meaty hand over his eyes.

"He's right next to you," Threll replied, waving away plumes of silver smoke.

"Really? Where?"

"In that big tub, on the floor. Right below you. That's where the Toadfather is. That's where he always is. I can hear him croaking."

Reaching into the deep tub next to him, Quivum grinned so hard that his cheeks hurt. He pulled out a toad as wide as a dinner plate and as tall as a tankard of ale. Its brown skin was dry and covered in warts. He set the large toad in his lap.

"Ah, my Toadfather. You've been with me since the beginning. I don't know what I would do without your learned counsel." He petted the toad on its head. "What's that?" Quivum brought his ear close to the toad. "You want me to lick you? As you command, my Blob."

The toad croaked as Quivum lifted him up. With the

Toadfather's back close to his face, Quivum took three long licks over the full length of the animal's back.

After a final croak, the Toadfather was returned to the tub. Quivum tilted his head back and whispered the word "colors" again and again.

"Quivum's a few arrows short of a quiver," Moshen said, pointing his cigar at his Swordfather. Flakes of ash drifted to the floor.

The mushroom below Quivum bent slightly to the side. "The Swordfamilies don't respect us. They think us intruders and call me Bladeslayer. They only talk to us when they want something that makes them feel good, or like lightning, or stronger." He frowned and scratched at his neck. "Ingrates. They treat us as little more than barkeeps. Purveyors of poison and nothing more. As if we're in the employ of Reddy, serving swill that tastes as though it was brewed in a chamber pot." The Swordfather pounded his fist on the mushroom. "There must be a way to seize respect. After all, respect and fear are two sides of the same gold scythe."

Moshen rubbed his eyes hard. "Respect or no respect, the smoke will still feel good. Why fight this war at all? Whichever Swordfather gets that slobbering blade, every family is going to throw their dice, same as always. Heavies will beat everyone down. Syrens will keep pulling the souls of men out through their cocks. Dark Water will do...whatever it is they do in the port. We should stay here in the den where it's safe and let the other families bash each other."

Quivum frowned. "We must fight because if we don't, the others will crush our family and steal our game. If we don't make allies then we're all dead. Same thing we did when we took this game from Green Star. They had no allies, and they had no fight. We ground them down like dragon spikes."

"I'm always just a little dragon spike powder away from a fight." Shujaaq grinned. "Give me some brown powder and point me at whoever you want dead."

Threll rolled a green leaf cigar. "You should try this, Moshen. It's something that I made special."

Moshen eyed his fellow captain's handiwork. "The only reason I would smoke green leaf is to get warm. It's weak. I get a stronger reel when I hold my breath too long."

She shook her head. "This isn't like the green leaf you've had before." She dragged the cigar under her nose, savoring the pungent odor. "One night when the sun was coming up, I was leaving the DragInn. More like escaping, I s'pose. Anyway, some Iron Wand warrior headed out at the same time. I had some green leaf in my hand that I hadn't sold. The Iron Wand slurred something and pointed his wand at the leaves. Now when I smoke 'em, I fly over the Gods' Blade."

Moshen raised an eyebrow. He put out his silver cigar by pressing it tight against his forearm, adding another dark burn mark to the collection on his shoulders, arms, and hands.

Plunged into a brazier, the tip of Threll's green cigar began to glow. Threll brought the cigar to her lips, winked at Moshen, and drew in the smoke. When she blew it out, the white smoke spun like a whirlpool in the air.

Her pupils doubled in size. The small scar on her chin became dark red.

She looked at Moshen and said: "You look so small from up here."

Then the green cigar fell from her limp fingers. Her

fellow captain picked it up and dusted it off. He took three deep puffs, one right after the other.

"Careful, too much of that and your mind will chase the smoke like a hound," Threll told him in an airy voice.

Nodding slowly, Moshen returned the cigar to her. "All three moons are on the ceiling. They're bouncing in the night sky," he whispered. "Dragon Without Wings is trailing flames like they're dragon fire. Rain Above Rain is pouring water into the den. It's going to put out the braziers. Night Scythe is harvesting sparkling stars with a big golden crescent blade."

Threll squeezed Moshen's hand.

"We should get back to the den now," she said in a very serious voice.

Moshen nodded at her solemnly. The two trained their eyes on their Swordfather. After a time, the fantastic yielded to the mundane.

Warriors knelt around a well-worn patch of wood floor. Piles of gold scythes, silver crowns, and copper townies lay around the patch, each a small shrine to the thundering horde of gods. Vranc, a warrior, whispered a small prayer to the five copper townies in front of him, begging the guardians of riches in the afterlife to guide his throw and grow his shrine to their greatness. He tossed a pair of iron dice onto the light patch of wood. The hooves of the thundering horde must have pounded too loudly, for the gods did not hear his prayer. The dice rolled badly and his coins were chosen to join the shrine of another warrior called Bunkun.

Vranc was pious and, despite the loss, his faith was unshaken. He pulled more coins from his wrinkled leather pouch to wager another modest shrine. The prayer before his next throw was louder.

The cap of Quivum's mushroom was now considerably smaller. He pondered how much more he could eat before either being forced to sit on a wood chair or ordering a warrior to harvest another mushroom.

Threll and Moshen rested on pillows before their Swordfather.

"You three are my best captains," Quivum said to Threll, Moshen, and Shujaaq. "I need counsel from someone other than the voices in my head. So tell me, are you here? Is your mind here in our den?"

The three captains nodded slowly, as if their minds might fall out if their heads moved too quickly.

"We must plot a course through this war," Quivum said. "The Fire Keepers think we kill their dragons and steal their young. This must be remedied."

Shujaaq sighed. "It's true they burn our purple leaf on the refuge, but we have so much of it that some goes to rot before we can sell it."

"We plant it there for a reason," Moshen added. "The dragons are going to burn some of it, sure. But they keep away the bastards that would steal our crops. I'd rather see it burned than stolen. We get more gold if thieves can't sell stolen leaf. Us killing a dragon would be like killing our own guards."

Quivum plucked another morsel from his mushroom.

"Kardas and I have seldom clashed. He's got more sense than most Swordfathers, but he doesn't have many eclipses left." Quivum tossed the piece of mushroom in the air and caught it. "There's still some fight in him. He may have seen this war coming before anyone, including Raysk. Some eclipses ago, I gave him lightning in a bottle. The black drink that can exhume youth buried under age. At least for a time." His eyes wandered to the men kneeling around the patch worn on the wood floor. "He's in my debt, though the debt is little more than the coin those warriors are dicing over."

Threll pulled at a loose thread on the pillow below her. "Let's make nice with the dragon wards. Hide behind them while the families bash each other's heads in. There are worse allies in Fulccrum."

"If they knew the truth of it, that we bear them no ill will, I would." Sweat beaded on Quivum's forehead. "But whoever's thinning their herd has done much damage and we've sold too much dragon spike powder to protest our innocence. We didn't kill those dragons, but we did make coin from their deaths. Those dragons are sacred to them." He shook his head. "We should seek a pact with another Swordfamily."

Blue flames flickered around the den. The air was saturated with different colors of smoke that billowed out the only window. In the street directly below that window, an eager crowd of townsfolk had gathered. They looked up to Ashfall's den and reached toward the window from which smoke poured. Most of them had empty pockets, having already handed their last copper townie to an Ashfall warrior who, in return, provided the patron a few flakes of leaf.

These townsfolk looked many eclipses older than their age. Their vigil was equal parts patience and desperation. The street beneath them looked as though a strong rain had swept through, but there was no rain. The dampness on the street had come from the townsfolk's cold sweat.

When a desperate commoner in the crowd fell to the ground and didn't get up, the others paid the fallen no mind. Their eyes remained on the alluring smoke that poured from the open window. They stood as long as their broken bodies would sustain them. As they watched, they prayed to the thundering horde of gods that cold air would cascade from the Paders to thrust the smoke down to the coinless masses for one more reel.

"Melt my mind!" the mass cried to the Ashfall Sword-family above. "Release me!"

They were broken men and women. Their vices had vanquished their virtues.

Jyfa stirred. "Wish we could board up that window," she groaned from her place on the trestle table, covering her ears.

"There wouldn't be enough good air to breathe," Threll reminded her. "If those layabouts down there would make more coin instead of begging for our smoke, we could uncover more windows and get some fresh air in here."

Moshen pushed her shoulder. "Remember how big the crowd was before we closed up the other windows? More smoke means more of those stinking beggars." He shuddered. "And less coin for us."

Quivum ignored them.

"What about Iron Wand?" Moshen asked. "They made Threll's green leaf more powerful than our best silver leaf."

"I've spoken with Irin about joining our strength," Quivum replied. "Much of what she said, I couldn't understand. They may try to create a cult or something of the like. They'd welcome our help to do it." Quivum tossed his mushroom piece but failed to catch it. He picked it up from the floor and threw it in his mouth without so much as blowing on it. "If the mages wanted our help, snaring them on a thread of debt could be helpful."

"They'd be better off using one of our cigars as a wand," laughed Moshen.

"I've heard they have some new blood. Maybe we could

help bring them back," Quivum said absently. "After they help us, of course," he quickly added.

"You seem to have an appetite for Swordfather women," Shujaaq observed.

Moshen nodded.

"Speak of Sinsasi," Threll added. Her lips were tight as she broke into a wry smile. "You spend more time in the Shrine of Solace than you do here in the den."

Moshen frowned.

Another piece of mushroom was liberated from Quivum's chair. "I can use Sinsasi," he said coolly.

"The same way lovestruck fools use the Syrens to empty their pouches of gold," Threll said.

"Tell me one way you can use Sinsasi to help Ashfall," Moshen pressed.

Quivum chewed on the morsel of mushroom deliberately.

"Those who lack the coin to pay for the Syrens' charms will offer that family anything they want. The Syrens have even more control over their patrons than we do," Quivum said.

"You have The Need," Moshen guffawed.

"The only thing I need is for you to shut your mouth," the Swordfather shot back. "You don't understand. They can give us the ultimate reel. Better than that cursed cigar."

The prayers of the crowd beneath the window were heard by the thundering horde. A gust swept down to the street, pulling a great cloud of smoke from the den to the mass below. Cheers of joy and shouts of "Sweet release!" sounded from the street.

"A man with The Need who's out of coin is desperate. They suffer pain that's impossible to describe. It feels as though their loins are pressed against hot coals and the only relief comes from a Syren's comfort. That's why Raysk did what he did. A man will do anything to smother that fire, even the last thing." Quivum watched the smoke fall from the window. "When their life is all they have left, they gladly spend it for one last night with a Syren. They surrender their body and everything inside it."

"You seem to know much about The Need that you don't have," Shujaaq growled.

Moshen furrowed his brow. "You talking about Aduchrome?"

"I am," Quivum said in a deep voice. "It's the most powerful reel I've ever had." His eyes glazed over as he remembered an experience he had tried to forget for many eclipses. "I still don't understand what happened. It makes you see things that happened long ago, or what will happen in the future." Quivum panted as he spoke. "It's either a trick on your mind, or it takes you to those times. Either way, I swear by the thundering horde that *where* melts into *when*."

Threll and Moshen shared a look. Quivum continued.

"Aduchrome must be harvested from the inside of a man, somewhere near his stomach. To get the strongest reel, you must take it from his body at the apex of ecstasy. It has to be cut free at the moment of climax. The Shrine of Solace is the perfect place to find it. If Sinsasi is agreeable, we could harvest much of it from coinless patrons."

The three captains remained silent.

"Sinsasi knows of Aduchrome. I will speak with her about an alliance," Quivum said with finality. "Aduchrome itself could provide us both with an advantage in the war."

"But who owes the debt?" Shujaaq asked.

Quivum didn't answer.

The wind outside shifted to lift the cloud of smoke out

over rooftops, rather than thrusting it down to the street. Moans of discontent and cries of protest sounded below. On this day, the thundering gods were fickle in their treatment of the poor folk.

"Those Emerald Crown kids use our goods. We should get more captains and warriors in the other families using them, too," Threll offered.

"With what, though? Some of them don't care about feeling good. They'd rather be sad or angry," Moshen replied.

Quivum scratched his scraggly beard. "We must satisfy their wants. All the Heavies desire to become stronger, so we sell them things that make them stronger. 'Specially Raysk. He needs us. Turns out much of a man's strength comes from his stones." He laughed. "Not sure he knew that before he gave the order to cut his off."

Threll eyed the green leaf cigar. "Iron Wand captains like to think that they're the cleverest people in the realm. We have plenty of leaf that will make them feel smarter, even if it's only a feeling."

"I think all my best thoughts when I'm smoking leaf," Moshen nodded.

Rising from the mushroom, Quivum stretched his arms high above his head. "Your counsel has been useful. We will wield our goods like the Fire Keepers' dragons or the Heavies' strength. We'll make it so the crown and the families can never stop using what they can only get from us. We will coil a thread of debt around them all and pull it tight."

The Toadfather croaked.

Moshen curled his hand into a tight fist. "We don't have power, but we have paths to it. Syrens, Heavies, mayhaps the crown. Each one of them could lead us to dominate Fulccrum." He gave Quivum a look of admiration.

The naked man and woman continued to play their lyres.

The crowd outside quieted as the wind died down, resigned to their futile struggle against reality.

Quivum crossed his arms.

"Some Swordfathers dream of spinning a web of debt. To the smallest bird, a spider in the middle of its web is like a rich meal served on a platter. We will not cower on delicate threads, hoping to snare our rivals. We will sheathe them in smoke thick as stone and starve them of breath."

CHAPTER TWENTY-TWO
HEAVIES

The dragon refuge in the early evening was filled with lively young animals. Fawns frolicked through the fields. Birds darted between trees, one chasing the other in hopes of winning a nest. Tiny rabbits hid under bushes before darting into the open where their courage vanished and they quickly retreated to cover.

Young birds chirped their meek demands for food. Fox kits slinked behind their elders as they learned the art of the hunt. Fish that had been dormant in the rivers and streams for many months used their renewed vitality to make more fish.

Nests that had once served as the homes for families of dragons sat empty. Some of them were filled with fresh dirt. Others held shards of dragon eggs sharp as shattered steel. The ground around some nests had been blackened by dragon fire. In one, a fox kit joined its mother and father feasting on the sticky green yolk still inside half of a dragon egg.

Many animals busied themselves with their evening routine, but none of them could breathe fire.

The sun began to set in the west. It splashed ruddy light over the Castle of Towers, making the Fire Keepers' home a lighter shade of red than the scars on Raysk's face. The towers in the distance were still small and barely noticeable to the Heavies.

They rode on trotting destriers. A leisurely pace carried them over the rolling hills that were abundant in this part of the refuge.

Riding abreast of his most trusted captains, Raysk always made certain that his horse led the others by a head. The steel bard his destrier wore clinked as he repeatedly squeezed the horse to make certain that it led his captains.

"This will be a great day for me and the Heavies," Raysk said, gazing toward the Pader Mountains. "This night will mark the Fire Keepers' end and the beginning of my absolute rule over the Swordfamilies." Raysk pressed the sides of his horse a little harder, growing its lead over the captains' mounts. "Auzken would be proud. A Heavy Greatsword shall be unsheathed once more."

Despite their power, some destriers struggled under the weight of their riders, armor, and weapons.

Dark clouds gathered in the sky to the east. They raked over the mountains' white peaks that had stubbornly refused to yield their snowpack to the new season. Flashes of yellow rippled through the clouds. Moments passed before the Heavies heard the lightning's accompanying rumble.

A long column, which included nearly every Heavy in the Emerald Kingdom, followed Raysk and his captains. Every captain and warrior on this ride wore their best armor. They carried a heavy pavise for their shield, large enough to conceal even the biggest Heavies against dragon fire.

Half of the Heavies were mounted while the other half marched on foot. They carried weapons almost twice the size of those wielded by the Kingdom Guard. Theirs were greatswords and war hammers too large for all but the strongest men and women to wield in battle. These weapons were suited to the Heavies' size and strength.

Teska had obeyed Raysk's orders. The three coursers that she acquired brought up the column's rear. She had paid a fair price for one of the horses at the Old Town Square Market, using gold scythes she'd liberated from a rich merchant's lockbox. Another she had stolen from a well-guarded stable that was less guarded after she slit a few throats. The third courser's owner had been enjoying a ride through the country when an arrow buried itself deep in his chest. Teska took the reins and finished his ride out of respect for the dead.

These three coursers were the fastest and strongest horses in the Emerald Kingdom. Each one hauled a wain that bounced over sharp rocks concealed within wheel ruts. Wool cloth covered the loads that the wains carried. The sound of iron knocking against iron could be heard each time the wheels hopped over a rock.

The horses had uncommon fortitude so the strange, loud noises coming from the wains they pulled didn't spook them. Nor did the smoke that gathered about them whenever the column came to a halt for a brief rest.

Each courser carried a pack made of crude cloth on its rump. The objects inside the packs were round like the top of a knight's helm and twice as big. They were lashed to the horse with thick leather belts held fast by iron buckles.

Instead of carrying whips to command the handpicked

coursers, the riders for these horses carried long-handled flails. The spikes on the steel heads were nearly the size of dagger blades.

"Yes, Raysk, it will be a great day for the Heavies to be sure," Kraaft said. He rubbed the red scar on his forearm. "But a great day remains a single day. Tomorrow and all the days that follow will judge the victory that we win here today."

"I will concern myself with tomorrow on the morrow," Raysk snapped.

"If we succeed in routing the lizard keepers, I struggle to see how the other families could pose a threat," Vasarox added.

"*When* we succeed," Droena corrected him. "We can't make the dragons do our bidding like the Fire Keepers. But the easiest way to control anything is to make it fearful."

"Fear is the language spoken by all," Pametan agreed. "Fear is what every man understands most deeply; it's what every man responds to most obediently. It is the ether through which control flows."

Raysk pushed his steed a little faster to maintain its narrow lead. "Our decisive victory here will cow the other families. Hanngoh fled as soon as he saw the Heavies' might on the deck of his boat." Raysk dragged a finger along the young scar that Hanngoh had cut that night. "If he ever returns, either his corpse or his boat will sit on the bottom of the port." Raysk flexed every muscle between his waist and his neck. "Mayhaps both."

"So many weak families. The Iron Wand is an empty shadow of what it once was," Pametan mused. "The day that eternal shadow fell upon Raventyn is the day that family became the Broken Wand."

"These days the best use for their wands is kindling," Kraaft said with contempt.

Droena smirked. "Which leaves only the weakest families of all. The Syrens and Ashfall." She glanced at Raysk. "The Syrens no longer pose a threat."

Raysk squirmed in his saddle. "The Need is dark witchcraft. Those naked fools can put a spell on your manhood." His knuckles turned white as he clenched hard on the reins. "The loins yearn for their charms the way a man yearns for air when his enemy's hands are wrapped tight around his throat." Raysk eyed his captains. "Do not toy with their guiles. If I learn that you've been in a Shrine of Solace, you will find no solace from me."

Pametan scratched her chin with her remaining hand.

"I'm surprised the Ashfall Swordfather can find their den. His family could be armed with the best swords and we could crush them with our bare hands." Droena shook her head. "I'll never understand how they were able to undermine Green Star so quickly."

"Maybe Green Star couldn't find *their* den," Kraaft shrugged.

"That's all well and good," Vasarox said, holding reins with his hands stained blood red. "But the other families are for other days."

"Aye," Raysk said. "Tonight is for the Fire Keepers. We will kill them all and let the thundering horde of gods trample their bodies."

"And their dragons," Kraaft snarled.

Teska rode close behind her Swordfather and the captains.

The dark clouds hanging in the sky above the Castle of Towers grew as the Heavies approached the Fire Keepers' home. The light became dimmer, but enough remained to show the clusters of dragons atop the towers. After every few steps that the Heavies' destriers took, dragons on the towers would launch a fusillade of flame that was followed by plumes of gray smoke.

Thunder rolled as streaks of lightning fondled the mountain peaks behind the castle. The Heavies marched in near perfect lockstep. Raysk raised his hand to slow the column's pace. They were now close enough that Raysk could see the details of the towers' stonework and the archers stationed with dragons atop the towers.

The last sliver of sunlight disappeared below the horizon behind the Heavies as their caravan neared the Castle of Towers. Darkness began to fall with unnatural quickness. The dark clouds that had lingered above the mountain and castle hastened to follow the sun and spread to the west.

The castle with no moat loomed before the Heavies. In the twilight, the rolling stone walls looked like the Angered Sea just before a storm. To Raysk, the towers with dragon heads peering down from the battlements looked like rigid, many-headed hydra.

Rain began to fall.

Inside the bailey, the ground was covered with a thick film of ash. Each raindrop that landed on it kicked up a wisp of gray. The piles of bone that were strewn about the bailey began to shine as the drops pattered down. The large tower closest to the mountains became streaked with black as the rain caressed its stone.

Every sconce on every tower that ringed the bailey held a blazing torch. Smoke and light pooled in the space. The torches hissed angrily as they were harried by the falling rain.

The tip of the Heavies' spear now stood under the great

arch that served as the entrance to the Castle of Towers. Raysk sat high on his destrier, flanked by his captains and consulary. They were lined up at the place where every other castle in the Emerald Kingdom had a drawbridge.

Raysk looked over his shoulder. Behind him, outside the castle, the Heavies that had marched as a single column split in two. Half the force moved to the castle's north side while the other half positioned itself to the south. Those on mounts were stationed near the bailey with the Heavies on foot behind them. Teska turned and rode to the south column's rear, behind the foot soldiers.

The three swift coursers pulling their wains rode up close behind Raysk's retinue. The riders turned their horses around so they faced away from the Fire Keepers. They took a position just outside the castle. The wains, laden with their cargo concealed by cloth, continued to make strange noises. Some dragons atop the towers eyed the thin smoke wafting near the horses. The steady rain soaked the cloths, making them cling to the boxes concealed underneath.

After the coursers pointed due west, the riders dismounted to stand between their wain and mount. They each tugged on the cloth that covered the wain, pulling it so that a corner lay in the mud while the boxes remained concealed.

The three Heavy riders stood with their backs straight and chins held high. Each pressed a steel-clad foot firmly on the cloth corner in the mud. They rested the long haft of their flail on their shoulder. Rain dripped from the spikes that bristled from the steel heads.

Scars on Raysk's face crackled as he smiled. *Thundering gods, tonight this is my Colosseum and I'm battling at the Melee of the Risen Knight once again.*

The Fire Keepers' Swordfather was mounted on a

dragon in the middle of the bailey. He unstopped a bottle and quickly drained the black elixir within. He smashed the empty glass against the fang hanging over his chest.

"Welcome to the Heavies' thundering hell," Kardas bellowed with great vigor.

Torchlight glimmered on his rain-slicked armor. His eager sword hung in the leather scabbard on his hip. The dragon that served as Kardas's mount was stocky and gray and had seen many eclipses. Smoke trickled from between her fangs.

Kardas was flanked by the strength of Fire Keeper captains who weren't among the force sent to the Paders on King Fallov's errand. Behind them, mounted on dragons with their swords drawn, was a throng of warriors.

Raysk eyed the massive head of his war hammer. "Lay down your weapons and accept me as your Greatsword." His scars adopted a darker shade of red.

The Fire Keepers did not dignify the order with a response.

"Be reasonable, Kardas. Your weapon is pathetic. I've buttered bread with sharper blades."

Kardas slowly raised his sword high. The torchlight made it glow, as if it had been pulled from the forge instead of a sheath. When a gust of wind blew the rain sideways, the drops that hit the blade's edge were sliced in two. For the first time in dragon's years, this naked blade was an unspoken threat. It was once more a sword for warring, not walking.

"I'm disappointed in you," Kardas called. "You loathed our long peace because you yearn for bloody war. It's what drives your ilk and weakens all the Swordfamilies. Including yours. At peace, we are all strong enough to rule any crown that lays claim to this realm. When the families are at war, a crown could rule us all."

"The Heavies bow to neither sovereign nor sword. You and the other families can hide behind the faded color that pretends to control the realm." Raysk used the head of his war hammer to scratch at the scars on his face. "I have no such intentions for me and mine. We will rule this land no matter who cowers within Fulccrum's castle."

Raysk carried his prized war hammer. Its steel head was crafted in the shape of a large fist clenching a dagger. The blade protruding from the fist's smallest finger served as the claw. The wide handle sticking out past its thumb was the face. The haft was made of ironwood.

Kardas laid his blade across his saddle.

"The last time you set foot in the bailey of our castle, you were a much younger man." The Fire Keepers' Swordfather said. The rain began to pour down on the Swordfamilies as Kardas's dragon carried him forward a few steps. "Back then, you had the excuse of youth. And that was a skirmish; this is a folly."

Raysk pressed his legs against the destrier. It moved forward a length. "The dragons I see here, they look meek." He used the head of his war hammer to point at the tops of the towers. "They're not the same dragons that I remember from my last time. Those lizards were nasty!" He cocked his head to the side. "What kind of dragons are these? With so many in the nests, methinks they're mother dragons brooding on their eggs. Not too many babe dragons on the refuge, though. Pity, that." He surveyed the towers as he spoke. "Where are your father dragons? And where are the rest of your captains? Your warriors?"

A dragon above the bailey stood on its hind legs and spread its wings wide. It hissed at Raysk.

"There are more than enough Fire Keepers and dragons here to turn your bone into ash," Kardas replied serenely.

"They'll look plenty fearful to you when you see them through a cloud of smoke that was your own flesh," Xutsuh added with a crooked smile.

Kardas raised a hand, commanding his captain to remain silent.

"In the old days the Swordfamilies parleyed to avoid bloodshed." Kardas's voice was filled with thinly veiled contempt. "We've had skirmishes, but what you're doing now is different. It's barbaric...*Lysnapi*." He named the city notorious for its codeless Swordfamilies. "Choose the way of peace and strength without burning the blood of your own Swordfamily."

"It's not my Swordfamily's blood that will be spilled tonight." Raysk shrugged. He eyed his war hammer's steel fist.

Kardas frowned hard. "The only thing you'll destroy here tonight are the last shreds of your own honor." He drew a deep breath. "You're the one killing our dragons, Raysk."

The Heavies' Swordfather put his hand over his heart in mock surprise. "Kardas, that is a heinous accusation! If any of your smoke-cursed friends have died of late, I've no doubt that they met their end at the hands of Ashfall. Mayhaps Quivum is angered by the fires in the refuge that burn his precious crops."

All the dragons hissed at Raysk. Smoke poured from their nostrils and rose through the heavy rain.

"The dragons you killed, you could've at least cut off a spike or skinned one. You made no feint."

"But that would've been...dishonest. You should've

yielded when we laid those dragon's wings over its own body."

"The dragons are our blood! You owe a blood debt, and you will Honor Thy Debt!" Xutsuh roared.

"There's less truth to your honesty than your lies. Because of your kind, good men in this realm dig their own graves with honest deeds," Ombran yelled. He spat into the rain.

Raysk glanced back at the three coursers by the archway. "All of Fulccrum saw the better part of your strength ride for the Paders. There's nothing to those mountains except passes and gold." Raysk spoke as if he was bored. "Your dragons weren't carrying pickaxes. I don't require advice from my consulary to know that you sent your best on a fool's errand to slow the Crimson Crown's advance."

Pametan's horse turned and trotted away to the Heavies' rear.

"The Swordfamilies thrived during our long peace," Kardas implored. "When our families are in balance, our blades are sharpest." He rested a hand on his sword. "No blood has been burned yet tonight. Turn back and we can preserve Fulccrum's peace and the families' lordship over it."

Xutsuh's mount hissed and reared. The Fire Keeper captain struggled to bring his dragon under control. He stroked its long neck to comfort it. Ombran scowled at the Heavies.

"The Emerald Kingdom will soon have new blood seated on its throne," Raysk thundered. "Whoever calls themselves ruler here will understand that in Fulccrum *crime rules the crown*! I will be the Greatsword that breaks the realm's royalty! *Kings and queens are my slaves!*"

"The Emerald Crown has friends within the families,"

Kardas said calmly. "I would not presume their defeat until there are red banners hanging in the throne hall."

"You have a soft spot in your heart for our soft king," Raysk said.

"You have a soft spot between your legs," Xutsuh yelled.

Kardas raised his hand again to silence his captain.

"You speak of Fallov as if he's unworthy to empty your chamber pot," Kardas growled. "But you say naught of our formidable Queen Minacia. She, too, sits upon the throne." Kardas smirked. "Her strength is writ large on your ruined face."

Dragons on the towers loosed their fire toward the sky. Some of them dropped their heads low and bared their teeth at the Heavies. Others cocked their heads to the side, hearing faint but familiar noises through the patter of steady rain.

"You will join the ash that blankets the bailey," Xutsuh yelled. "We shall bury you with our boots."

"Your skulls will crush easier than dragon eggs," Vasarox replied.

Droena remained silent. She anxiously searched the faces of the Fire Keepers.

Wind gusted through the bailey. Rain pelted against the large tower at the back of the bailey. The wet stone was black as a moonless night.

Cold rain dripped from the dragon fang hanging from Kardas's neck.

Raysk surveyed the bailey. "I'm a reasonable man. Surrender the Bleeding Blade and there will be no bloodletting," he said coolly.

"Surrounded by dragons in the bailey of our castle is not a place where many men have dared to make threats." Kardas drew a deep breath. "Look around the bailey. Our blades drip rain, not blood. What makes you believe that our family has the Bleeding Blade?"

"A little dragon told me," Raysk said through his bared teeth. He pointed his war hammer at Kardas. "You'd rather beggar the Swordfamilies than see me rise as Greatsword. You're tired and worn, like your sword."

Steady wind thrust the rain against the Castle of Towers and the mountains behind it.

"It's true that I'm no longer the fighter that I once was," Kardas said, eyeing his freshly sharpened blade. The glass shards from the bottle that he had emptied glimmered below him like stars in the rain-soaked ash. "But I will fight with more fury than I ever have before."

"You had your chance for mercy," Raysk yelled.

The Heavies standing next to the three coursers opened the packs on their horses.

Raysk raised his war hammer over his head. He made a fist with his other hand.

Metal struck metal as Raysk's gauntleted fist pounded his steel war hammer. The Heavies by the coursers moved with purpose and precision. Each one kept their boot pressed on the corner of the cloth that covered their wain. The long hafts of their flails came off of their shoulders in a fluid movement.

They whipped their flails down on their horses' rumps. The flail heads crushed the dragon eggs concealed inside the packs. The long spikes drove deep into the coursers' flesh.

The horses screamed and broke into a panicked run. They now had two tails, one made of horsehair and the other made of the wooden haft dangling from the flail stuck in their rump. As the wheels on the wains began to turn, the Heavies shifted their weight onto the steel boot on the cloth.

The wains sped away from the castle as the Heavies pinned down the cloth. The wains' cargo was revealed, dozens of small dragons locked in iron cages. Screams from crazed dragon younglings sounded through the bailey. The crazed young tried to blow fire on the iron cages that held them. Their pitiful efforts succeeded only in belching thin smoke.

From the towers, mother dragons looked down to see their trapped young. The small dragons yelped in terror as the coursers gathered speed and the wains bounced violently. Locks on the cages pounded against iron bars as the imprisoned younglings cried.

Dark green dragon yolk gushed from the packs fastened to the coursers. Wind swept up the smell and carried it through the rain. With their keen noses, the dragons instantly recognized the yolk's telltale odor. Madness spread through them like wildfire.

The dragons on the towers closest to the wains furiously beat their wings as they sprang into the air. The scent defied the rain to reach even the farthest dragons perched near the mountains.

A stampede more powerful than the thundering horde of gods spilled from the towers and bailey. Mounted Fire Keepers shouting powerless commands were thrown from their crazed dragons. They landed on their backs, sending mud and ash spraying into the rain.

Nearly all the Heavies scrambled for cover as the dragons hurtled past them. Except for Kraaft, who swung his sword to lop off wings as he screamed about disrespect.

Archers on the towers who had nocked their arrows were instead knocked from their stations by the dragons.

They joined their brethren in the ashen mud. The Fire Keepers' long falls, especially from the towers close to the mountains, made many of their bodies as broken as the bones littered about the bailey.

As the dragons stampeded from the castle, the columns of Heavies stationed to the north and south collapsed on them.

Flame and fang clashed with steel and muscle. Where the Heavies plunged greatswords into dragons, plumes of pitch black smoke billowed into the air. The immense heat released from the mortal wounds in their bellies easily burned through the rain.

Dragons that evaded the Heavies continued to pursue the wains. They had wings, but the swift coursers had a running start. The horses sprinted over the saturated ground with sure feet. Where the wain wheels struck rocks, some cages would tumble to the rain-softened earth. Pursuing dragons closed around those fallen cages and tore at the iron bars. The Heavies had forged the cage bars as thick as a man's arm. The mother dragons couldn't break them open to free the crying younglings inside, so the cages trapped young and old dragons alike.

Kardas's mount had taken the bait, leaving the Swordfather on his back. Once more, he used his sword as a cane to pull himself up to his full height. As the sword bore his weight, its blade sank into the earth. Mud and ash dripped from his back. By his side, Xutsuh stood ready with a bloodthirsty blade. Behind him, Ombran the warrior stumbled to his feet with a sword in each hand. The other captains and warriors desperately searched for their weapons laying in the mud.

The Fire Keepers had been abandoned by nearly every one of their charges. The dragons that remained were in a wide-eyed, frenzied panic. They sprinted around the bailey, bouncing off the towers' rounded walls. They breathed fire without aim and the rain hissed as it became steam. When they ran too close to the Heavies, blades were plunged into the beast, buried all the way to the hilt.

Dragons fell and black smoke rose as fires broke out that rain could not smother.

The orange and black dragon with the white head that had once carried Fyur as its rider fled into the night, screaming in rage.

Fire Keepers and Heavies charged at each other through the pouring rain. Mud and ash grabbed at their feet like dead men rising from the grave.

The ring of steel on steel echoed off the castle's stones. Light from the guttering torches flashed on the wet metal as the Swordfamilies clashed.

Droena slew many.

Xutsuh dropped to his knees as Vasarox's greatsword sliced the air where the Fire Keeper's neck had been an instant before. Planting a knee and rising faster than the Heavy could bring around the huge blade, Xutsuh jabbed the edge of his sword into the big man's side.

Vasarox grunted as the sword found a gap in his armor and tasted his flesh. Before the Fire Keeper could lunge forward to push the blade deep, Vasarox clenched the blade in his gauntlet.

The Heavy pushed back on the sword to smash its pommel into Xutsuh's gut. The Fire Keeper staggered backward but kept his hand tight on the grip.

For a score of heartbeats, the battling captains pushed and pulled on the blade like two fierce dogs fighting over a meaty bone.

Vasarox had the strength and Xutsuh lacked his mount.

The broadside of the sword faced the sky. Xutsuh wrapped both hands around the grip and yanked back. He pulled a hand's width of blade away from Vasarox.

The Heavy shook his head, flinging the rain from his brow.

With a single hand, Vasarox windmilled his greatsword down onto the broadside of Xutsuh's sword. The smaller blade shattered under the Heavy's massive weapon.

Xutsuh staggered back and gaped at the half blade that remained in his hands.

Vasarox smashed the broadside of his greatsword on the Fire Keeper's helm. Xutsuh dropped what remained of his blade and fell backward, splashing into the mud and ash. He slid into a dark corner where two towers met.

The Heavy was on Xutsuh before the Fire Keeper could get his elbows on the ground. Vasarox pressed his steel boot on the center of Xutsuh's chest. The steel breastplate flexed down as his full weight pinned Xutsuh. The trapped captain pounded his gauntlets against Vasarox's boot, to no effect.

"When we plan our battles, the first thing we decide is the most satisfying way to kill our enemies." In a single movement, Vasarox took his boot off the breastplate and kneeled in the same spot with his poleyn pressed on Xutsuh's chest. His face now loomed over his victim's, a finger's width from the Fire Keeper's flailing gauntlets. "We begin with your death because we know that our victory is inevitable." He paused for a moment. "The game your Swordfamily played with the Bleeding Blade has stained me forever. You took the blade and ruined my hands."

A bottle with a cork stopper hung next to Vasarox's scabbard. The twine that held it snapped as the Heavy yanked the bottle free. He pulled the stopper out with his teeth and spit it away.

"My memento from Auzken's tomb will be his farewell kiss to you."

Vasarox poured the bottle onto Xutsuh's face. The Fire Keeper's head thrashed as he choked on the Bleeding Blade's leavings.

"*My widow shall avenge me,*" Xutsuh yelled, gasping for air.

When he spit in Vasarox's face, the Heavy didn't flinch.

Xutsuh's face was covered in dark red stains.

The Heavy crushed the empty bottle in his gauntlet and tossed aside the shards.

"Your family stole Auzken's blade from me," Vasarox said, rising to his feet and returning his boot to Xutsuh's chest. Now the Fire Keeper's face was red as his lungs became starved for air. "You owe me a debt."

Vasarox placed both hands on the grip of his greatsword. He placed the point next to the toe of his steel boot, directly over Xutsuh's racing heart.

"Now you will repay that debt with a bleeding blade of my own making. A sword dripping blood." The point of Vasarox's sword pressed against Xutsuh's chest harder than his boot. "*Your blood.*"

Awesome strength pierced the greatsword through Xutsuh's breastplate. Metal squealed like a stuck pig as the steel armor turned inward. The point of the sword plunged through metal, then skin, then bone, then the Fire Keeper's beating heart.

The blade plunged through Xutsuh's chest and the armor on his back. Then it sank into rain softened earth. Xutsuh spasmed as Vasarox drove the greatsword all the way down, until its cross guard nearly pressed against the Fire Keeper's ruined breastplate.

Vasarox leaned in close to Xutsuh's face and whispered to him. "I will take the bloodiest blade you can give me."

Xutsuh stopped shaking.

Slow as a spent lover, Vasarox pulled the blade from his victim. He leaned over the sword to shield it from the rain. When the point emerged from the Fire Keeper's ruined chest, he studied the blade's sheath made of blood. Then he lifted the greatsword high above his head.

"This bleeding blade won't make Raysk the Greatsword," Vasarox rumbled. His gaze swept around the bailey where the routed Fire Keepers lost their swordfights or ran for their lives. Xutsuh's blood poured from the sword. "But our victory here tonight *will*."

The last word he yelled echoed around the bailey.

Outside the Castle of Towers, Teska lingered a safe distance from the raging battle. The cries of men and the song of steel beckoned her to join the fray. She had intended to remain away from the fighting, but she was a Heavy at heart. She charged toward the Castle of Towers.

Dragons and their keepers streamed through the archway. The Heavies converging on the castle greeted them with a thicket of blades. Some dragons burned their way through the Heavies, followed by a line of sprinting Fire Keepers. Other dragons were hacked to bits, their blood flowing like lava and belching black smoke. The swordfights ringing through the battleground were short and ferocious. The victor either escaped or began to hunt another Fire Keeper.

Teska made her way to the Castle of Towers' outer wall. She skillfully led her mount around the edge of the fighting and up to a short tower, close to the castle entrance.

With reins held tight in one hand and her sword in the other, her steed trotted so close to the castle wall that her steel-clad leg scraped against the stone. She neared the archway and saw the mud below tremble from the footfalls all around her.

Hard rain fell as Teska slowed her horse and crept closer to the archway. The Fire Keepers who fled the bailey never looked back. When she was closer to the archway than the length of her sword, Teska paused for a break in the melee flowing past her.

A gap opened up and Teska drove her heels into her mount. She pulled the reins over and the horse kept tight against the castle wall as she steered into the bailey.

There she was met by a short burst of dragon fire.

Her steel plate armor deflected much of the terrible heat from her body. But Teska wore an open face helm. As she ducked away, her face roasted inside the intense flame.

Her armor felt as though it had been pulled from the forge that night. Her mount burned like it was thrust into the red coals of a cooking fire. Teska was thrown to the ground as her mount ran screaming from the bailey. The horse was consumed by flames that flew like banners. They grew longer as the mindless beast ran. Its ghastly form looked like a fiery god that had galloped straight from the thundering hells.

Teska sprang to her feet and sprinted, trailing smoke and the stomach-churning odor of burning flesh. The flames greedily fed on her flesh as she ran. Another Heavy warrior saw her. He scooped up a wet, heavy cloth that had covered the wains. After Teska took a few more strides, he leapt at her with the dripping cloth and tackled her to the ground. He wrapped the soaking cloth tight around her body and head. The flames on her face finally went out.

Steam rose from where the cloth pressed against her. The writhing figure underneath the cloth hissed like a snake though her mouth made no sound. After Teska stopped squirming, the Heavy warrior pulled her from the mud. She swayed on her feet like a reed in the wind.

Teska saw Raysk's war hammer. It swung high in the air near the east tower. She wondered why only one of her eyes was open. The warrior that stopped her flames threw her over his shoulder and carried her away from the Castle of Towers.

The battle thinned as Fire Keepers and the dragons that had fought hard accepted that this night belonged to the Heavies. The song of ringing steel slowed and the notes were struck softly. Almost everything ringed by the towers that wasn't made of stone now burned. A pillar of black smoke, nearly as wide as the bailey itself, rose undaunted through the pouring rain.

The battle dwindled but the duel between Kardas and Raysk had lost none of its vigor.

Bolstered by Ashfall's elixir, the old man summoned strength that he hadn't marshalled since his sword was young. He thrust and parried with unmatched skill that was long dormant, but never lost. His armor squealed in delight as he deflected and dodged with moves that knocked bits of rust from its steel. As his reborn blade sliced through the air, it whispered threats more fearsome than any man's words.

"The days ahead for the Fire Keepers' remnants are hale and hearty," Raysk said through gritted teeth. He grabbed the top and bottom of his war hammer's haft and brought it up even with his eyes, parrying another deft stroke from Kardas. "Your family that still draws breath is smart.

They've tucked their dragon tails between their legs and deserted you!"

A sliver of ironwood sprang from the haft where the Fire Keeper Swordfather landed his blade.

"We shall return, and our fire will burn brighter," Kardas grinned, holding his sword straight up. "We're Fire Keepers. If it burns, we can kill it. And the Heavies burn."

Raysk brought his war hammer straight down. Kardas dodged the blow and added a gouge to the side of Raysk's armor. The Heavy sighed as he pulled the head of his war hammer from where it was buried deep in the mud.

"Ashfall must've given you something to make your heart race," Raysk laughed. "It must be beating faster than a dragon's wings...when it can't find its youngling."

Kardas brought his blade around in three quick strikes, each one of them met by the head of Raysk's war hammer.

"Your craving for the Bleeding Blade is madness." Kardas took two more chunks from the war hammer's wooden haft.

Raysk nearly dodged a thrust from Kardas but his armor suffered a streak on the breastplate.

"You're as weak as your steel. Always longing for balance. Suckling at the sweet teat of peace." Chunks of stone the size of a fist launched off the castle wall where Raysk's sweeping blow landed. "Peace only exists among the weak and lasts only as long as the powerful allow it." He took a few steps back and put the haft, badly chewed from the bites of Kardas's sword, on his shoulder.

Kardas was next to the oak door that led to the east tower. As Raysk brought down his war hammer, Ombran struck, driving his sword into the back of Raysk's leg. He fell and the head of his war hammer missed Kardas to shatter the door into a pile of splinters.

Using the haft of his war hammer to pull himself up, Raysk faced Ombran.

"Pitiful Fire Keeper," Raysk said with disdain. "Your attack is cowardly and disrespectful. But the thundering gods have smiled upon you because tonight my war hammer is betrothed to Kardas." He smashed the warrior's face with a gauntlet.

Ombran's head slammed against a stone tower and he went limp.

Kardas and Raysk resumed their deadly dance. As the Fire Keeper slashed his sword quick as lightning, fragments flew from the war hammer's haft.

Raysk advanced and the Fire Keeper backed over the pile of wood pieces that had been the door. His sword was up as the Heavy pursued.

Inside the room was the table made of ash wood in the shape of a dragon's face. Rushes lay on the floor so close together they almost completely covered the stone underneath.

"This is where we almost wiped out your family." Raysk's wide eyes swept over the torchlit room. "Now I'll finish what my forefather began. The Fire Keepers have been a dragon spike in my side for too long."

The notch in the haft became deeper as Kardas landed two quick blows in the same place he had attacked all night. Raysk responded by bringing his hammer down at a sharp angle, but only managed to hit a rush lying on the floor.

Kardas raised his sword and brought it straight down. Raysk defended with the wooden haft. The Fire Keeper's blade struck true. The blade sliced through the ironwood and traveled down to meet the pauldron protecting Raysk's left shoulder. The haft was cut in two.

Raysk whipped the bottom part of the haft at Kardas's face. Then he swung the part of the haft that held the steel head. The war hammer's flat end slammed into Kardas's gut. The Fire Keeper staggered and landed with his back against the ash wood table. His sword slipped from his hand to clatter against the floor.

Raysk pounced and grabbed him by the throat. Kardas struggled against the Heavy's weight, but he was pinned tight against the table.

"Are you wielding a sword or a woodcutter's axe, old man?" Raysk hissed.

"The Heavies have the *strength*. But my family will always wield the *fire*."

Kardas's legs flailed as he struggled in vain. He clawed at Raysk's gauntlet to no avail.

"I've thought about how I would kill you for a long time."

The dragon fang that hung from Kardas's neck shook on his breastplate as he fought to free himself. Raysk grasped the fang and ripped it away, breaking the flax string that held it.

"Give me the Bleeding Blade."

"The only blood that you'll get from me is my own. We do not hold that blade."

Kardas bared his teeth. They were red. He spit blood in Raysk's face.

Raysk found the gap between the gorget around Kardas's neck and his breastplate. The Heavy slowly pressed the sharp point of the fang against the Fire Keeper's chest.

It burned hotter than dragon fire.

CHAPTER TWENTY-THREE
FIRE KEEPERS

Andra's dragon splashed into a cold stream. When they reached the middle of it, the water flowed over Uther's back. As the dragon slowed, clouds of steam rose from the surface around them. Andra felt her face begin to sweat as she squinted through the mist. The gurgling stream was loudest in the deepest water.

Her mount's steps quickened as they reached the shallows on the far side. Looking over her shoulder as Uther raced through verdant grass, she saw that her dragon was already dry and trailing dark smoke.

"I know you're lathered, boy, but this ride may be the difference between life and death." She whipped the dragon's rump with the broadside of her sword. "Forgive me, Uther."

Most of the clouds that had unleashed torrents of rain on the dragon refuge during the night had retreated behind the Paders. The thin laggards that remained made the sky above Andra steel blue. Her dragon's claws sank into the soft ground, throwing chunks of earth as he galloped.

The Fire Keeper's eyes trailed tears from the rushing

wind. Her legs ached from the unrelenting pressure on the dragon as her heart beat faster than her mount's footfalls. Andra focused on every landmark she knew to navigate the shortest, fastest path to the Castle of Towers. Though it made her heart ache, she ignored the smoldering heaps of dead dragons that caught in the corners of her eyes.

The pain coursing through her body surged when she saw the new tower that Raysk had added to the castle. This tower wasn't made of stone; it was thick black smoke rising from the bailey.

Andra smacked her sword against Uther. The ride from where she streaked through the refuge to the Castle of Towers usually would take a turn of an hourglass, even on a fresh courser. She whipped her dragon with the steel once more. She could feel the dragon's heart pounding between her legs, like many hammers falling on an anvil. It shook her as though the horde of gods thundered under her saddle.

Thick strands of dark blood dripped from the dragon's nostrils and mouth. A trail of smoldering grass marked Uther's path.

At a pace faster than any Fire Keeper had ever seen, Andra neared the archway to the castle. She rode through the motionless dragons and Fire Keepers strewn about the ground. When her dragon slowed, its legs began to tremble.

Reaching the archway, at the edge of the black smoke tower, Uther shuddered to a halt.

Andra slid from her saddle and staggered a few steps. *Thundering gods, the battle here must've been worse than our rout at Kellington's Pass.* She rested against a tower that supported the archway to the castle. Now that her mount wasn't careering through the refuge, smoke darker than slate billowed from beneath his scales. *He's lathering so bad the smoke is like wet wood in a fire.*

Uther's head whipped around, his blood and slaver adding fuel to the fires around the bailey. As quick as it started, the dragon went limp and fell to his side. Blue flames peeked out from underneath his scales. Andra blinked twice and her mount was engulfed in flame from the tip of his snout to the spikes on his tail.

Damn the thundering gods, he's become his own funeral pyre.

Andra put her hands on her knees and drew in breath like a bellows. She stared at the ground, pushing back against the black fog that narrowed her vision. Her mount was little more than a smoking skeleton as she found her strength.

She leaned on her sword as she wobbled through the smoke-filled bailey.

"Kardas?" She grimaced. Pain shot through her body as she called. "Xutsuh?" Inside her mind, her voice was screaming. Inside the bailey, it was a whisper scarcely louder than the crackling fires around her. "Ombran?"

The Fire Keepers and dragons in the bailey were still as stones in a graveyard.

The scorching air burned her throat with each breath that she drew. It felt like sharp blades pressed against her eyes. Her lower lip cracked and dribbled blood.

"Fire Keepers?" she croaked. "Dragons?" She stood hunched over her sword near the middle of the bailey. The blade she used as a cane bore more weight than her legs. "Dragons, to me!" Each word felt like the air in her throat was made of hot sand.

The crackling fires were her only reply.

She pressed her hand against the tiny carved house Mistahn had given her. "Just a little luck. Begging..."

Mayhaps I died in that pass and this is my thundering hell.

A small dragon lay on the ground beside her. Its body was azure with black stripes wrapped around its belly, tail, and neck. Its head was the same blue as its body and the spikes on its face were black. Its gut had been shredded and its wings were missing.

She recalled her brief encounter with this young dragon and turned away.

"Here," a faint voice called.

Turning to face the sound, Andra took three halting steps. The same voice called to her again. She and her blade hobbled toward it until she could see Ombran through the smoke. He sat on the ground with his legs splayed out and his back against the castle wall.

Violent coughing racked his body and blood poured from a deep cut on his forehead. He covered one of his eyes. Andra offered him aid, but he waved her off. "No." The single word left him breathless. His eye was dull and glassy and focused on nothing. "There." His arm shook as he dragged his hand from the soft dirt. He pointed to the tower that had no door. "Go."

With three shaking legs, one made of steel, Andra forced herself to the tower that was farthest from the archway. Her body screamed as she willed it over the pile of splinters that had been a heavy oak door.

The dark smoke pooling in the bailey thinned inside the room. Though every sconce held a torch, only a few still burned. A low moan cut through the quiet.

Andra dragged her sword. Its point caught on the rushes to pull them into a useless pile. She hobbled across the room to the dragon face table. Above her, the dark cobwebs hung from the ceiling like banners in a mournful throne hall. When she reached the source of the sound, she dropped her sword and put both hands on the table.

Kardas lay with his back against the ash wood.

The dragon fang that had hung from his neck since the day he became Swordfather was buried deep in his chest.

"My Blade." Tears that would not be denied streamed from her eyes. "I've failed you. Completely." She spied the chalice that she'd drunk from during her captaincy ceremony. "Fletch, so many others...I..."

Kardas raised his hand. "No time for ill tidings," he rasped. "My web will soon lack its spider."

His blood dribbled from the table and splattered on the floor. Andra realized that she was standing in a puddle of it.

"You've lost a lot of blood."

"I haven't lost it. It's right down there on the floor. Hahr."

His laugh, so hearty for so long, was as broken as his body.

Kardas tried to raise himself on his elbow. Andra put her hand on his shoulder and gently pressed him down. It required little force; a soft breeze could have pinned down her Swordfather.

"Save your strength," she whispered.

"There's none left to save," Kardas replied in an airy voice. "I would be dead already were it not for Ashfall's drink. We had to fight this battle. The Castle of Towers was the right place for it." He gasped for breath between his words. "Outwitted by a Heavy...I'll regret it to my dying day. Hahr." Blood dribbled from the corner of Kardas's mouth and into his short beard. "A terrible blunder. I made a feint when I should have parried. It's more painful than this dragon fang."

Andra wiped the blood from her Swordfather's face. "I should have been here, with the family. This is my fault."

"The fault is mine alone. I've paid a dear price for it. I felt my web of debt trembling as the gods trampled my plans like so much gossamer." Kardas grimaced, each breath coming short and shallow. "The trap was right, but the time was wrong. I didn't realize Raysk would move so fast."

"I should have left the strongest dragons here."

"It would've made no difference." Kardas's voice gathered strength born of anger. "Raysk knew the dragons would chase their young. And he drove them mad with their yolk." He made a feeble movement, trying to slam his fist down on the table. It landed noiselessly and he shuddered from the pain.

Andra placed her hand on Kardas's fist. Her tears fell into the pool of his blood beneath her feet.

"I tried to play Raysk to the end. He thought we had the Bleeding Blade. I lured him here to scare the fight out of him. Now he'll fight to the death." Kardas gasped. "Glas told that Heavy warrior we had the blade. Just like I asked him to. He's a good lad and a loyal one at that. Take care of him." He coughed up dark blood. "I told Raysk the truth. We don't have it. Hope that spares the Fire Keepers a battle or two."

His breaths were very weak.

"I hope the Shard of the Specter cut down some Heavies."

Kardas shook his head. "We didn't use it. Wouldn't have done any good in this fight." He wheezed as he spoke. "It's not meant for the battlefield. It's an assassin's weapon."

The fist that Andra cradled felt very cold. She swallowed hard.

"You've taught me so much."

"I should've taught you so much more. Thought I had more time." Kardas looked into Andra's eyes. She saw real fear in them for the first time. "Pull the fang."

"I won't kill you."

"It's not killing, it's kindness." Kardas coughed up thick blood. "Be wary of Berg. His heart will be full of jealousy."

"Kardas. Please don't go," she said in a very small voice, squeezing his hand. Her tears splashed on his breastplate.

"You must keep weaving the Fire Keepers' web, lest it turn to gossamer and vanish in the wind."

Andra covered her face with an unsteady hand, but only for a moment.

"My blood father was murdered. You're not just my Swordfather, you're my *only* father. Stay with me."

She choked back a sob.

"*Do not avenge me,*" Kardas begged.

He took his last breath.

Andra bowed her head. She clenched her eyes tight as tears rained. Biting her lip hard, she broke the skin. Her whole body shook.

Inside her, hope fought bravely against despair. The struggle was fierce.

Andra heard a torch gutter out. She released Kardas's hand.

Her trembling fingers hesitantly clasped the fang. She closed her eyes as it slid from Kardas's chest.

Blood rose from where the fang had been lodged. It flowed onto the ash wood table. There it pooled inside the etched lines that depicted the dragon's face before it dripped onto the rushes below.

Andra held the fang tight. She fought the desire to read the name on the back of it, but she lost that battle.

After a long look at Kardas, she wiped some blood from the fang.

There she saw her own name.

"My Blade, I am eternally in your debt," she whispered. Her tears came so fast that now she couldn't read the letters.

Thus ended the ceremony that raised Andra to Swordfather of the Fire Keepers.

The air in the room was still. The last torches flickered out. Light surrendered to darkness. Andra felt an unnatural chill sweep over her.

She laid her head on Kardas's breastplate and wept.

The moment was morrowless.

Her hands were covered in blood. In one, she clutched the dragon fang that bore her name. In the other, she held the carving of her childhood home.

CHAPTER TWENTY-FOUR
IRON WAND

"I've seen paint on canvas and wood before, though I've never seen it on a woman's fingernails," Guiden said with a quizzical look. "Where'd you get it?"

Lisha sat at a trestle table streaked with so many burn marks that she wondered if it was made of used firewood. On the table lay a ruined book from the athenaeum. She spread her fingers wide over the cover of that book. A small vial filled with liquid, clear as air, was next to her hand. She dipped a tiny brush into the liquid and spread it over a fingernail.

"One of Hiamoe's acolytes gave it to me," Lisha replied casually. "Whatever they were trying to make in the laboratory, this concoction didn't satisfy them."

She stretched out her arm and spread her fingers wide to admire her handiwork. Then she drew her hand back and blew on her shiny nails.

"My sister taught me how to do it. She used to paint her nails a red that was more intense than the sun just before it slips away. Her paint was brought from the Dallu Isles. It's said they have many beautiful flowers on those islands."

"What you've put on is clear, though." Guiden cocked his head to the side.

Lisha gently placed a cork stopper in the vial. "My nails aren't painted with colors; they're painted with memories." She took another breath and continued drying her nails.

Guiden stepped forward. He put his hands on the table and leaned toward Lisha. She finished her breath and reached out with her nails facing him.

Her fingernails became tiny windows to her past. A mound of dry dirt was shown on each of her thumbnails. Streams of water shot out from the dirt and arced against the sky shown on her middle three fingers. The streams of water landed on patches of dark, wet dirt on her little fingers. Each nail showed a different part of the same memory.

Guiden leaned closer, squinting at the exquisite details.

"Somehow it knows where my fingernails are," Lisha mused.

"A stream of water jumps from one spot in the ground to another. Is that the Land of Dancing Water?"

"It is. That's where I'm from. It's where I grew up."

In an instant, the scene changed. Each one of Lisha's fingernails now showed the same image, a slender fist wearing rings. The knuckles were white. Black cloth was bunched in the palm of the hand and it was pulled taut.

Guiden recoiled. Then he gently gripped one of Lisha's wrists and pulled her hand closer. She quickly curled her fingers into her palm, hiding her nails from his prying eyes.

"I don't know what you saw, but I can't control the memories. They're like plays that switch from one act to another without warning."

Guiden released her hand. She plunged her fists into the pockets of her robe.

"What did you see?"

"It looked like a hand pulling on a jerkin. It wore rings."

Lisha shook her head. She wiped the corner of an eye with the back of her hand. Her fist remained tight.

"Open your hand. Let me see."

She shook her head and thrust her fist back into her pocket. Her eyes became glassy and she swallowed hard.

Placing both of his hands flat on the table, Guiden leaned forward. He raised his eyebrows and made his face welcoming. "Please. Tell me of that memory."

She bit hard on her tongue. Then she began to say something but stopped before the first word escaped her lips.

The door to the room flew open and clattered against the wall. "Irin wishes to see both of you," Werevu said in a voice that sounded like a snake whispering closely guarded secrets.

Guiden reluctantly pulled away from Lisha. Together, the three marched through the catacomb tunnels.

Werevu took them to a place in the catacombs that Lisha hadn't seen before. The walls here were made of smooth, brown stone. The stones' shapes and sizes were more consistent than other chambers in the Iron Wands' home. Gaps between the stones she saw were all very narrow.

When Werevu arrived at a door, he opened it for Guiden and Lisha. After they entered, he closed it behind them softly. The circular room was well lit. In the center of the room, the Bleeding Blade was suspended from the ceiling by its grip. The blade hung with the point straight down.

The Bleeding Blade's steel was dark as the blood that dripped from it. The color wasn't from paint on the metal; the steel itself was midnight red.

The blade hung above a naked body that lay on a table. The blade's point was close to the man, almost touching his skin. Rivulets of blood flowed from the blade onto the man's chest. The steady stream ran off the body, onto the table, and finally down to the floor. The stone was sloped such that the blood disappeared into a hole below the corpse.

Next to the corpse stood Irin.

"What is thy bidding, my Blade?" Guiden asked, bowing. Lisha mirrored his genuflection.

Irin stood with her arms crossed and one leg in front of the other. "I grow weary of staring at this body." Her eyes remained fixed on the spot where the stream of blood splashed onto the man's chest.

Guiden cleared his throat. "Mayhaps we should've refused the blade if we didn't desire it?"

The blood from the sword flowed more quickly.

"I didn't want the Bleeding Blade then, and I don't want it now." She inspected the sword. Her face exuded boredom. "But I certainly do want the Syrens in our debt. I could have simply agreed to restore her arms. By also unburdening Sinsasi of the blade, Iron Wand's position against the Syrens is strengthened." Irin sighed. "You see, Sinsasi's vanity will not suffer the indignity of befouled beauty. Our service of curing her arms is vital to her, and Iron Wand is the only family that can perform the service. Because of this vulnerability, she had to relinquish the Bleeding Blade. As soon as she showed us her arms, we would've known which family held it. We could have used that knowledge however best served our aims. The Syrens would have been both indebted *and* vulnerable. By hoisting this useless metal on us, they're less vulnerable but deeper in our debt." She reached down to the still body and pulled an eyelid up to reveal a rotted, sunken eye. "I paid a heavy price to secure that debt. Feels as though it's getting heavier every single day."

"Sinsasi traded one form of weakness for another," Lisha added.

"I'm pleased to see that you're still using that mind of yours after I made you a warrior," Irin said.

Guiden clasped his hands behind his back, as if to protect them from the unnatural blood. "What is the purpose of this...experiment?"

"I had hoped to find some use for the Bleeding Blade. If we can make it do something other than stain things red, that would make me more comfortable about risking the Heavies' ire." Irin sighed. "Our experiments on the blood did help devise a solution for Sinsasi's arms, but I've learned nothing more. It barely shed blood this morning, but for some reason the flow has been building all through the day."

Without warning, the blood suddenly fell in torrents. For long moments, the entire length of the sword was covered in dark red liquid that gushed like red wine from a flagon held upside down. The deluge splattered over the body. All three Iron Wands jumped backward, distancing themselves from the sudden waterfall.

Lisha blinked and the blade shed its red sheath. The blood slowed just as fast as it had rushed. It was now little more than a trickle.

Guiden took a few steps forward and leaned close to the blade, though his hands remained behind him. "Most interesting."

Waiting long enough that she could no longer suppress her curiosity, Lisha asked, "What happened?"

"Swordfamily deaths, bloodletting, and the like cause

the blade to weep more blood. It must have sensed acts of violence that it no longer foresees, at least for a time." Irin shrugged.

Lisha approached the blade but stayed a step farther from the table than Guiden. She cleared her throat. "Wouldn't one use for the Bleeding Blade be to lay claim to becoming the Greatsword?"

"The Blade of Blades," Guiden chuckled.

Irin offered her new warrior a smile that was more condescending than kind. "You're clever, but you're also ignorant. The families that prefer metal over minds have a phrase for that. What is it again?" She stared at the ceiling and tapped her foot. "You have a strong blade with a dull edge."

"My Swordfather, if I may explain to our newcomer," Guiden spoke quickly. She nodded and he continued. "To lay claim to the Greatsword at this time would be fatally unwise." A few tiny drops of blood sprouted from the blade as he spoke. "Our Swordfamily does not have the strength to defend this blade against the other families."

"At present," Irin hastened to add. "But we strengthen every day."

Guiden spoke to Lisha even more quickly than before. "The Swordfather that holds the blade must impose their will upon all the families. If that Swordfamily has anything less than absolute power over the other families, the possibility of bloodshed remains. The sword will bleed so long as that possibility exists." He gestured at the few beads sprouting from the steel blade. "When the blade is utterly devoid of blood and dry, the families will know the true Greatsword holds the Bleeding Blade. A Greatsword with absolute power puts an end to the bloodshed between the families. That, in turn, ends the bloodletting from the blade." Guiden sighed. "Or so our histories say."

Three drops of blood fell on the dead man.

"Listen closely to what Guiden tells you," Irin said with a thin smile. "That's why the Swordfamilies sealed the blade in Auzken's tomb. In the vain hope that balance and the absence of the blade would staunch the bleeding forever."

"As you can see," Guiden waved at the Bleeding Blade, "at present, our dominance is not absolute."

After a lengthy silence, the erratic sound of blood drops on the floor became unbearably loud to Lisha.

"You said that you were trying to discover a use for the blade," she said to Irin. "What exactly are you trying to learn by dripping blood onto this body?"

Irin circled the corpse lying motionless on the table. "I'm trying to bring him back to life." She frowned and made a dismissive gesture at the motionless body. "But he's not cooperating."

"Who was he?" Lisha asked.

A casual shrug served as Irin's reply. "He wasn't with a Swordfamily, so it's of no import."

The blood that dripped from the blade was darker than the petals of a withered red rose.

Guiden grabbed the corpse's big toe. He gave it a slight tug and the toe came off with a cracking sound. "The subject of your experiment is rotten." He tossed the toe down the hole beneath the body.

"Yes, I'll need to acquire a fresh corpse soon." Irin crossed her arms over her chest. "If this blade has any use beyond staining floors, I'm no closer to learning it than I was the day we took it from the Syrens."

The blood drying on the floor seemed to absorb the light from the candles burning around the room.

"You've learned nothing from the blade?" Lisha asked.

"The only secret it has betrayed is that ice can halt the bleeding. We pulled some from an ice house, enough to sheathe the entire blade. The drops froze against the blade while the ice was tight against the metal. When the ice melted, the blood flowed again."

Guiden snorted. "I'd like to throw it in the coldest ice house in the realm and close the door and be done with the damn thing."

The smell in the room began to burn Lisha's nostrils. She pressed her sleeve over her nose.

"What of the grimoire?" Guiden whispered. "Has that tome revealed its secrets?"

"I suspect the author was mad," Irin yawned. "The title loosely translates to *Dungeons for Souls*. The strokes for many letters are elegant and obviously written with a fine quill. The writing where the spells are darkest is jagged and imprecise. As if they were scrawled with a dagger dipped in ink."

"There may be something in the book. If not a spell, a potion? Something less...conventional?" Guiden pressed.

"I have only begun to probe its mysteries." The candles closest to Irin guttered as she spoke. "It is tedious work. Much of its subject matter is ponderous. Given enough time, I am confident that I can unlock its secrets."

Lisha's sleeve slipped away from her hand and she asked, "You mentioned a solution for Sinsasi's bloodstained arms. Have we returned the queen of vanity to her throne?"

"Yes, although she didn't relish being led through the catacombs with a hood over her head." Irin smirked. "Or plunging her arms into a steaming hot cauldron for long hours. Her shrill screams broke glass in Hiamoe's laboratory. Her fingernails remain blood red, but otherwise she's been restored. The Syrens are now firmly in our debt." Irin's smirk spread into a wide smile of brilliant white teeth that contrasted with her flawless dark skin. "Their beauty is both their greatest power and folly."

Lisha put her hands on her hips. "Sinsasi's cured wrists are now bound by our unseen shackles."

"I summoned you here to answer a question," Irin said, her attention turning to Guiden. "Have you made progress on establishing the cult that we discussed?"

A long sigh preceded his response. "The townsfolk of Fulccrum have too little regard for their gods." He spoke to the corpse, as if admonishing the dead man for his lack of piety. "In their defense, the gods are dull. They're an abstract idea, a nameless and shapeless mottle stampeding through the townsfolk's thoughts. The horde's sole purpose is to defend the riches that await the devout in the afterlife. I aim to create a god that dominates the horde and demands obeisance from the living."

"And who will this god be?" Irin asked.

"*Me*," Guiden said with his fist on his chest. "Without a true god, the townsfolk simply worship gold in their Hall of Thunder. I will give them a god worthy of their dreams. To make their minds my throne, I'll need many of Ashfall's goods."

"I spoke with Quivum about our potential needs. Your idea has merit. You are commended for your ingenuity," Irin said.

"Yes," Lisha mumbled. "An ingenious idea." *And it was mine own.*

"You have my leave to use Ashfall for this purpose," Irin said.

"I aspire to finish this work before the anticipated celestial event. A prophecy fulfilled before their eyes would be most beneficial to achieving my goal."

Irin's attention returned to the motionless corpse. "You may go."

"Yes, my Blade," the two responded in unison.

First Guiden, then Lisha, gave their Swordfather a shallow bow and left the room. They meandered through the catacombs for a short time before Lisha pulled on Guiden's flowing robes.

"Celestial. I know many words, but that is not among them. What did you mean?" Lisha asked.

"It means everything in the sky above us at night. The stars and four moons in the ether far above us."

"You mean three moons," Lisha corrected him. "And you spoke of an event?"

Guiden stopped next to a torch and thought for a moment. The uneven light cast shadows across his face that grew and shrank with the flame. "Follow me."

Another short trek through the catacombs followed. The pair arrived at his bedchamber. Lisha was not impressed. The four walls were bare stone, some streaked with black marks above where a candle burned. A wardrobe made of dark, rough-hewn wood sat in a corner. Lisha wondered if Guiden's robes caught on the splinters on the doors.

In another corner a table stood on four legs made of branches with the bark still on them. Papers with worn edges were strewn about the tabletop, beneath a single candle. A crude chair was pushed against it. Most of the papers that Lisha could see had numbers scrawled on them. The others bore drawings made of circles and long lines.

Guiden's featherbed was barely thicker than the papers

on his desk and only as wide as his shoulders. It lay on the floor that was covered in a thick coat of dust and grime.

A large chest sat next to the featherbed. In contrast to the other pieces of furniture in the room, the chest was opulent. Its wood was dark, smooth, and polished so thoroughly that it shined in the faint candlelight. The lid was arched and two ornamental bronze bands wrapped around its width. The handle was tarnished from use and the wood around it was worn where it had been rubbed by many hands.

Opening the lid, Guiden rummaged through the belongings it held. Lisha stood behind him. She leaned to the side for a glimpse of whatever treasures Guiden had secreted inside the chest. The dim candlelight thwarted her effort and the chest's insides remained cloaked in darkness.

"So that's where you're hiding."

He reached deep into the chest. When he stood and turned, he held a copper tube as long as his arm and the same width as a sword's blade.

"What's that, a wand for a giant?" Lisha scoffed.

"Knowledge is the equal of magic. That's why I always strive to acquire both." He tucked the slender tube into a fold of his robes. "Come, I'll show you something that you've never seen before."

He beckoned her to follow and they returned to the tunnels that spread through the Iron Wands' home like veins. A short time and an even shorter distance later, Lisha found herself following Guiden through passages that she didn't recognize. When they reached the bottom of a stairway festooned with moss, he pulled a torch from its sconce. He beckoned her to follow and they climbed the stairs far higher than Lisha had expected. She could feel the dampness surrender to the dry air aboveground well before they reached a landing with a locked door.

Iron clinked against iron as Guiden pulled a key ring from his robes. The fourth key he tried in the lock was the one that fit. After they passed through, he locked the door behind them. Through the doorway was a short flight of stairs and an opening that framed the night sky.

They climbed the stairs to stand atop the city wall, halfway between Wandering Waters and Gilded Granite Street.

Battlements flanked them, the defenses on the inner side of the wall a remnant from the city's violent past. Lisha looked at the city to the west and gasped. In New Valois, the bright moonlight truly made the Gods' Blade a sword raised high. A giant knight wielding that mammoth sword could have sprung from the earth below and charged into battle against the stars and moons. The buildings on the north side of New Valois were bathed in the blue glow of Ashfall's great flame.

To the south, in Stonebann, the banners above the Colosseum hung limp. The circular structure stood taller than the buildings around it, although it did not tower over its surroundings like the monument to the thundering horde of gods. Arches and columns adorned the outside of the Colosseum. During the Melee of the Risen Knight, the roar inside could be so loud that when a land breeze carried the sound out to the Angered Sea, ships nearly a league away could hear it. Tonight, the Colosseum was as quiet as all the knights felled in its melees.

Although much of Satinwind was hidden from her view, she could make out a few white banners above the Syrens' Shrines of Solace.

Closer to the Iron Wands, in Raventyn, Mages' Mist

shimmered in the moonlight. Although the poor folk called it a mist, to Lisha's eyes it looked like silver. A graveyard that was older than Fulccrum straddled the city wall. Some of its bodies had been exhumed for the wall's foundation. Others were buried so deep that they now rested under earth and a wall of stone.

Outside the city wall, buildings and camps huddled near the roads that led into Fulccrum. Past them, a patchwork of sprawling farms and clusters of woods covered the Emerald Kingdom. A few weary travelers plodded toward the city on the Shamrock Road.

The Wandering Waters and Middle River ran fast and rough. Their surface shimmered as if made of flowing diamonds. Through them, the Pader Mountain snowmelt was eager to reach Fulccrum's port and the Angered Sea.

In the distance to the east, storm clouds had retreated behind the Paders.

"What's over there?" Lisha asked as she pointed to the mountains. "It's like a storm cloud, but clouds don't hang so low to the ground. It's so dark I can't see the mountain behind it." She searched the mountain range north and south. "Could it be fog?"

Guiden produced the copper tube from his robes. He brought it to his eye and pointed the other end at the dark smudge that vexed Lisha. "Hard to see. It's black, too dark to be fog." He closed the eye that wasn't looking into the tube. "And it's moving up. Fog doesn't do that. Mayhaps it's smoke."

"That would be quite a lot of smoke. I wonder what it's from."

"Who can say? It's in the dragon refuge. Things burn there all the time. The dragons could be cooking supper for their masters."

"What're you holding?" Lisha pointed at the copper instrument.

Before Guiden could answer, three Kingdom Guards approached.

"You there! What are you doing here on the city wall? State your business or you'll both be so deep in the dungeons your cellmates will be the worms."

The three Kingdom Guards wore heavy armor and swords on both hips. All of them stood at least a full head taller than Guiden. The group fanned out so they stood shoulder to shoulder as they stopped before the Iron Wands. The one in the center crossed his arms over his breastplate.

"An eclipse from now, those cellmates will be eating your rotting flesh."

Lisha took a small step back. She tensed her body and plotted her path for when the time came to run.

"Evening, brave guards," Guiden said in a cool and condescending tone. "On behalf of Fulccrum's townsfolk, I thank you for your diligence in protecting the city from the many horrors that lurk in the night's shadows."

The Kingdom Guard with crossed arms took a step forward. "Jest with us and you won't even make it to the dungeons. We could toss your body into the old cemetery over there."

"That would be a pity. The dungeon worms would go hungry." Guiden cocked his head to the side. His eyes were dull and uninterested. "But we won't be going to the dungeons or suffering your presence any longer. Because, you see, we're with...*the family*."

Guiden pulled down the neck of his robe to expose one side of his chest. From where Lisha stood behind him, she couldn't see what he showed the knight. But she could see strong red light reflected off the Kingdom Guard's armor.

The knight froze.

Guiden released his robe. It again covered his chest.

The Kingdom Guard moved his lips, but the words he summoned were not spoken.

The knights bowed in turn and their patrol suddenly, and unexpectedly, took them back in the direction from whence they came.

"What did you show them?" Lisha asked.

Guiden smiled. "You're adept at chess, are you not?"

"I dispatched my father's learned counselors so easily that I started playing with fewer pieces. Before the first move I'd take a pawn or two off the board. Later, a rook or knight."

"I showed the guards what they needed to see to understand that I'm with a Swordfamily." Guiden patted the side of his chest that he had shown the guards. "The Swordfamilies rule Fulccrum and the Emerald Kingdom. Here, the king and queen aren't the paramount chess pieces. They're more akin to pawns or even the board itself. They merely tend to the squares upon which we play our Swordfamily game."

Lisha's eyes fell on the guards' backs.

"You were asking me about this." Guiden raised the copper tube. "It's a telescope. There aren't many of them in the realm. They're used to look at the stars in the sky and the four moons."

The sky above the Iron Wands was blanketed with points of light beyond counting. They were thick as a crop of wheat before it's put to the scythe. Nearly all of them flickered like a guttering candle. A wide band of sky to the south was lighter than the rest.

"What do they look like? The stars?"

"Not much, to be honest. Most of them look like candles near the bottom of their wick." Guiden blew on the copper tube as if he were blowing out a candle. "Some stars are odd. Their light is stronger than the others; they don't flicker. In the telescope, they look very strange. They move around, too, following nearly the same path every night." He pointed the tube at a particularly bright star. Lisha leaned her head close to his to find the spot where he pointed. She could feel the heat from his skin on her cheek. "I'm not sure why they move that way. Some of the bright stars have little stars that follow them around, too. You can see the little ones with a telescope. Here, I'll hold it steady. Take a look."

Lisha peered through the instrument and gasped as she saw a bright blue dot with a white ring around it. Some smaller white dots shone near this ringed star, all in a line.

"How does this star have a ring around it? It just looks like a white dot to my eye alone," she asked, breathless. "You're very—" Lisha began, speaking loudly into his ear. She stopped and pulled away from him. "You're very curious. You think about things that most people don't, even in our own family."

"A keen mind can be a more potent weapon than the Wailing Wand." He held the telescope as if he were casting a spell. "Do you know why Fulccrum is here?" He nodded toward the city. Lisha shook her head. "Like I told you when you arrived, this is the place where triple eclipses happen twice a year. Every two seasons the three moons pass over the sun, one after another. The founders could mark time knowing that eclipses would divide spring and summer from autumn and winter. The moons separate the warm half of the year for growing crops from the shedding of leaves and cold quiet of winter." He scratched his chin with the telescope. "Preternatural things can happen in the shadow of a Fulccrum eclipse."

Lisha frowned. "You keep saying 'four moons.' But it's called a triple eclipse because all three moons block out the sun. How can you know so much about the sky but not what everyone else sees? There are three moons."

Guiden searched the sky in all directions. "There is a fourth moon that few know about and even fewer care about. It's called the Wanderer. It's small and dark and moves fast as an arrow." He smiled at her with a warmth that Lisha hadn't noticed before. "I wouldn't lie to you. Please trust me when I tell you there are four moons. Not three." He paused and thought for a moment. "Although one day soon you might be right."

He held the copper tube out, offering it to her. She took it from him and was surprised at how little it weighed.

"The best views are of the moons. The three are gorgeous when you *truly* see them for the first time. Dragon Without Wings, Rain Above Rain, and Night Scythe are all out tonight. You won't have any trouble finding them." He put his hand on her cheek. "The night sky is yours."

Lisha raised the telescope to her eye and pointed it to the sky.

"I can't see anything."

"You're looking through the wrong end."

He flipped the tube around and Lisha pointed it at Dragon Without Wings. Her mouth fell open. "There's so much red. It's like a red rose in bloom." She swung over to Rain Above Rain. "Reminds me of windblown snow atop the Paders. It's a little like my old home, too." She turned to face the Night Scythe. "The same god that wields that blade towering over the Emerald Castle put a gold scythe on its thumb and flipped it into the sky. It's a great, worn coin turning end over end. I can see it move." She pulled the instrument away from her eye and inspected its length. "Is this magic? Some kind of wand?"

"It's simple metal and glass. There's no more magic in it than there is in the stones beneath our feet."

"The next time I paint my nails, I hope to see the sky the way I just did."

Lisha looked at Dragon Without Wings with her naked eye. Then she looked at it through the copper tube and sighed. "I could look at the moons all night." She clutched the instrument tight against her chest. "Show me this phantom moon of yours that haunts the sky like an unseen spirit."

Shaking his head Guiden said, "Finding the Wanderer would take more time than we have darkness. And it's almost impossible to follow with the telescope."

She handed it to him. "That's an amazing instrument."

Guiden tucked the telescope into his robes. "Uldritch the Unwise has made observations with it. He believes the Wanderer is black because it's made of pitch. I maintain that it's made of iron. I've been using figures to divine the paths of all the moons. I believe the Wanderer will hit Dragon Without Wings. When those two moons meet, I will convince my cult followers that I am a god."

"You don't have any cult followers," Lisha observed. "Nor did you have the *idea* of creating a cult. Though you made Swordfather Irin believe you were responsible for it."

Guiden paused and gave the young warrior a stern look. "She was more receptive to the idea because a captain, such as myself, made the proposal. Particularly because we haven't any followers...yet." He pulled the key ring from his robes and jingled it in front of Lisha's face. "But once I unlock minds with Ashfall's keys, I will use the power of Iron Wand to teach my believers the joy of obedience. When they see me predict moons colliding, they will believe that I can control the sky above."

"What would happen if the Wanderer strikes Dragon Without Wings?"

"What *will* happen *when* it strikes Dragon Without Wings," Guiden admonished. "I have dedicated considerable thought to this." He breathed out like a bellows. "The fire in the sky will burn twice as bright."

Lisha shrugged.

The sounds of the city drifted up to the Iron Wands. Laughing, crying, screaming, and raucous songs from taverns and inns filled the cool night air.

"Pity that the stars are still in the firmament tonight." Guiden surveyed the sky. "Sometimes there are hundreds upon hundreds that streak across the sky. It always happens around the same times each year. They race away from some unseen point, like loosed arrows of light. Mayhaps they're fleeing from something."

"You jest. To hold a place so high in the sky, the stars must have great strength."

"If I am to be a cult's god, I must be strong." He put his hand on her shoulder. "And if you desire a high station in Iron Wand, so must you. We shall spar."

They retraced their steps down the stairs and through the catacombs. From there, Guiden returned his telescope to the chest and carelessly threw his ring of keys on the table in his chamber. She followed him through another unfamiliar passage that ended at an iron door that was more red rust than black metal.

"This is the armory," he said.

Lisha smiled with her mouth open in anticipation.

Guiden looked down and opened the door with his shoulder. Flakes of rust fell from the door like snow. A hinge broke away from the wall. Guiden lit some candles and placed them around the room.

"If you're going to be a proper mage, you'll require a proper wand. The broken arrows and other detritus you've used to cast won't be adequate to fight the battles that Raysk's war will surely bring." Guiden shook his head. "But only the banal horde knows if you'll find that wand here."

The small room was lined with tables made of wood that had mostly gone to rot. On the tables and rushes lay piles of wands. Dozens of individual wands were scattered around as well, as if a mage had pulled the wand from a pile only to cast it away in disgust.

"This is our...armory?" Lisha asked, incredulous.

"It is," Guiden replied as he scratched the back of his neck.

"Why aren't the wands in neat rows?" Lisha walked into the room, her steps snapping some wands in two. "The stories I heard east of the Paders told of mages in Lysnap wielding gorgeous wands made by skilled artisans." She put her hands on her hips and spat on a wand pile. "To them, this armory would look like kindling bunched together to start a fire."

"The mages of Lysnap have enjoyed a prosperous history, whereas our family has suffered violence and ruin."

After a deep sigh, Lisha sifted through a large pile of wands massed on a trestle table. A plume of dust rose as she disturbed the wands. She pulled apart the tangled mess with her slender fingers.

Fragile, beautiful, and ruined wands were hidden deep in the pile. Lisha blew dust off a golden wand only to find the tip was melted and blackened from a spell more powerful than its caster. Some wands were crude, nothing more than a small branch cut from a tree. Others were carved hardwood with ornate designs. One was cut in the shape of an uncoiled snake, but the mouth and fangs were little more than ash. A piece of steel with the look of lightning caught Lisha's eye, but she cut herself on a jag in the bolt.

"Are there any iron wands?" she turned to ask Guiden.

Guiden shook his head. "Iron is a primitive and inelegant metal."

"Then why is our family called Iron Wand?"

"I suspect the lackwit who chose the name thought that it sounded menacing."

Lisha sighed and shook her head in disgust.

"I suggest you make your choice. We've had a few more warriors join recently. They are promising and they'll choose their weapons soon." The annoyance in Guiden's voice was not veiled. "These wands may not look like much, but many are battle tested. They're capable of channeling powerful magic."

Brushing aside the wands atop a small pile, Lisha spied something unusual. She pulled it from the bottom of the pile and used her robe to wipe away the dust. The wand was long, slender, and mostly clear. It looked like a crystal that had grown tall and narrow. The angular surface was too dull to reflect the candlelight.

"What is this made of? A gem? Diamond perhaps?"

Guiden scoffed. "Salt. It's not the most exotic wand but it will serve." He turned to leave. "You mustn't get it wet, of course."

"Of course."

Traversing long stretches of tunnel, the couple arrived in the arena. The cavernous room spread in all directions beneath a high ceiling. Four torches burned in the sconces that lined the walls. Lisha pressed her finger in a wide divot on a wall made by a poorly aimed spell. The floor beneath her crackled as she stepped on a stone that miscast magic had crushed into gravel.

Black cobwebs dangled in the corners and singed tapestries hung limp. Several suits of armor with an X painted over their breastplates stood against a wall. Archery targets peppered with burn marks were placed near the armor suits. Dry water troughs were placed near the door.

Lisha turned to face Guiden. "I remember this place. You said it was the arena."

"Yes, I brought you here when you first arrived. It is our arena, although of late the only fighting in here has been between the spiders and their prey."

Though the torches were few, they burned bright to cast shadows that grew and shrank in their bronze light.

"Have you used the Wailing Wand in here?"

Guiden paused for a moment as he drew a deep breath. "After the Swordfather of Iron Wand dies or abdicates, their successor is chosen by a single act. The mage must wield the Wailing Wand and live to cast another day."

"The wand chooses the Swordfather? Not the family?"

"Yes. Each family has its own manner of choosing their Swordfather."

"You told me that some people have perished trying to use it."

"Mages with more confidence than ability. They paid for their lack of awareness with their lives. When Irin cast the spell that made her the Swordfather, she was not the first to try to tame the wand. She had to pry it from the charred hand of another mage who sought to lead the family."

"The mages who fail to wield the wand, do they all die?"

"Nearly all."

Lisha gripped the salt wand tight in her hand. "Tell me now, what does it look like?"

"A bouquet of flowers carved from ironwood. Instead of a flower at the end of each stem there's a screaming face. Each mouth on the Wailing Wand breathes a spell the same way the Fire Keepers' dragons breathe fire. When the wand strikes down its caster, it adds a new face to its collection." Guiden pulled his wand from his robe. It was long and thin and white. "The story of my wand is similarly macabre. An Iron Wand captain mocked me. He said that he had more magic in his right arm than I had in my entire body. When he met his end by my hand, I trusted his honesty. My wand is made from his right arm." Guiden tossed the bone in the air and caught it with the same hand. "Though it pains me to admit it, he may indeed have spoken the truth. His arm has served me well."

Guiden began to circle the room. Lisha stayed in the center, turning so that she kept facing him.

"Our magic has a will of its own. Sometimes it does our bidding, other times not. Its nature is mercurial. Becoming a great mage requires far more than simply summoning magic. You must master it. And you must always be mindful of its power, because certain spells can age you faster than a loosed arrow." Guiden kept flipping his wand in the air as he spoke. His robes dragged a path through the dust on the stone floor. "That's what makes the Wailing Wand so dangerous. It's a powerful instrument capable of summoning deep magic that defies the will of all mages, save only for the most cunning.

"Kaato!" Guiden yelled as he whipped his wand at Lisha.

A pale blue fireball streaked across the room. Lisha sprang like a cat to dodge the fire. The errant spell knocked a suit of armor to pieces.

"What's that word you're using?" she asked, rising from the floor. Her words were cool and even. Her voice betrayed no concern at having a fireball cast at her.

"The name of the Iron Wand captain who spake unkind words about my abilities. There are few truly magical words, so when you want to deal some damage it's best to harness your emotions, which in turn summon your magic. If you want fiery anger, think of something that makes you angry.

"Kaato!" he yelled again.

Lisha dodged another small blue fireball, but the robes flowing behind her did not. The cloth smoked and blackened. As she beat on the smoldering threads with her hand, a small hole appeared in her robes.

"This Kaato person must not have made you very angry. Your fire barely burned my robes." She waved her hand at the arena wall. "And that tapestry."

Holding his wand up to his mouth, Guiden blew smoke away from the tip. "I'm being merciful. If I killed a warrior in the arena, Irin might bludgeon me to death with the Wailing Wand so I would suffer more than if she used it to cast a fatal spell."

Torches flickered as Lisha abandoned the center of the room to circle opposite Guiden. Cobwebs above trembled as fires from both torch and wand heated the air.

"Atec!" Lisha yelled.

A pink fireball shot from the salt crystal's tip. It streaked across the room and grazed against Guiden's robe before slamming into an archery target, singeing its cloth.

Repeating the same words, they cast blue and pink fireballs at each other until both of them were dripping in sweat. Their robes clung to their bodies as they danced and dodged around the sweltering arena. The trembling cobwebs above broke from the ceiling and cascaded to the dust on the stone floor.

Gasping for air, Guiden held up a hand. "What is that word you keep shouting? Ay-ket? Some lover who jilted you?"

Her hands on her hips, Lisha's chest heaved as she choked down air. "Ay-tek. It's my mother's name. Atec Vlymner. When I think of her, I get angry."

"Why your mother?"

"My reasons are my own."

Lisha's fingernails each displayed a different episode of violence and hurt.

"Atec!" A pink fireball shot at Guiden and slammed into his shin.

Small flames flickered on his robes. He patted them a few times, reducing them to thin puffs of smoke.

"Good. What you discovered within yourself in the Land of Dancing Water, you may now harvest. Power is not a matter of pronunciation. It is a matter of self. Most mages believe it's in your soul." Guiden ran his fingers through his dripping wet hair. "You can even say something as simple as 'fury,' so long as you feel it." He inspected the hole in his robes. "Your fireball is hot enough to burn cloth, but not through cloth. We'll enhance that."

His shin was light red.

"I prefer spells of ice, but I'll respond in kind. Feel my

wrath!" Guiden yelled, firing off another pale blue ball of flame.

It hit Lisha on her knee. She pulled the sleeve of her robe over her hand and used it to smother the flame.

Lisha smirked. "Your wrath kind of tickles."

Guiden cocked his head to the side. He pondered the best target for his next fireball spell. He pointed his wand squarely at Lisha's chest and yelled, "Kaato!"

She ducked and turned to the side so her shoulder bore the brunt of the spell. She muttered a curse she had learned from hanging near the stablemen at her lord father's castle. Then she glared at Guiden.

Lisha began to raise her wand at him, but stopped when her arm was still angled down slightly. She pointed her salt crystal where Guiden's legs came together. Then she screamed, "Atec!" and a pink fireball, the largest she had cast, raced toward the captain.

Guiden spun around so his back faced Lisha. The pink fireball smacked into his arse, burning away a cheek's worth of cloth. His back arched and he echoed a curse that the former owner of his wand used to hurl at him. As the pain retreated, his modesty advanced. He spun around with his wand ready.

They both broke into grins so broad that the corners of their mouths almost touched their ears.

Pink and blue fireballs flew like a flock of spooked birds. They crossed and collided, their glow blending together to douse the room in purple light. Tapestries burned bright and robes burned brighter. All but one torch went out when it was knocked to the stone below.

When the smoke cleared, both of them realized that the other wasn't wearing any clothes. Only a few stubborn patches of cloth clung to their shoulders. From the neck down, their skin shone light pink from the heat that had disrobed them.

They stood across from each other completely naked.

Lisha's body was smooth as water poured slowly. Her skin was soft as a reverent lover's touch. Her breasts entranced Guiden and summoned him closer every time she drew a breath. The paltry light from the single torch denied Guiden a glimpse of what lay between her plentiful thighs, so his imagination eagerly described that mystery in excruciating detail. She had many dark spots on her pale skin, numerous as the stars in the sky.

Guiden was tall and bristling with muscle. His round shoulders were broad like a yoke. His features were mostly angular, except his stomach that was softer than the robes the two had turned to ash. Either he grew scarce hair on his body, or Lisha's pink fireballs had burned it all away. Lisha had little of the experience that would tell her if his manhood was small or large. As she judged his loins she saw that, unless her eyes were deceiving her, it was getting longer and straighter each time his heart beat.

Thu'gods, he has even less mastery over the wand between his legs than he does the one in his hand!

On the left side of Guiden's chest was a drawing in red ink that glowed bright as dragon fire. It showed a wand casting a fireball spell. The fireball streaked to his heart where it stopped for a single heartbeat. Then it continued on to the right side of his chest where it disappeared. After his heart beat three more times the drawing repeated itself and another fireball sped across his chest, again stopping in the middle for a heartbeat.

Both of them panted from the effort of casting their spells.

"What's that on your chest?" Lisha asked.

"On...*my*...chest?" he asked, struggling to remember that chests other than Lisha's existed. "Oh, yes. Yes, that. It's ink inside my skin. It's called a tattoo."

"How does it move?"

"Uh, Hiamoe put the ink on me. A mage's own magic gives it life. You'll get the ink after you're a warrior. Then you'll make it move. I have to warn you, it can be...mischievous."

"The tattoo?"

"Yes. Magic is wild until it's tamed by your control. Even after you fetter your magic, the tattoos only obey their own whims."

"We don't have *anything* under control! We're naked in the arena!" Lisha sputtered, throwing her hands up.

She noticed that Guiden's face was redder than the rest of his fire-singed body, although she didn't recall any of her fireballs hitting him in the head.

"My bedchamber isn't far and I know these catacombs like the back of my hand. I can quench the torches in the tunnels and we can get there in the dark."

"Then what?"

"I have some...robes there...that...you could wear," Guiden said slowly, as if his mind was entering a dense fog. He felt his loins burn hotter than any spell that had been cast in the arena.

"Excellent, we must go quickly."

She's not making much of an effort to cover herself.

"Snuff out the torch and then we run."

Thu'gods, her nude body should be immortalized on tapestries.

"Be quick about it, we have little time."

Hung on every wall in my bedchamber.

"What're you going to do with that thing, cast a spell?"

She could make the Syrens weep with jealousy.

"Guiden, are you listening to me?"

Mayhaps I could convince her to wear the same transparent robes they do.

"GUIDEN!"

He jumped, as if hearing her voice for the first time in ages.

Then he put out the torch.

Grudgingly.

CHAPTER TWENTY-FIVE

FIRE KEEPERS

"Kardas told you *not* to avenge him!" Mwizi yelled, her voice somewhere between stern and angry. It was a tone that warriors seldom used when they addressed their captains, let alone their Swordfather. "You, yourself, said so. He told you there should be no vengeance."

"Vengeance is merely seeking justice with enthusiasm."

"Andra, he would not be pleased with what you're doing."

"Raysk owes the Fire Keepers a debt that he cannot possibly repay. He will die by the code of Honor Thy Debt," Andra shot back. The dragon fang caked in Kardas's dried blood hung from her neck. The back of it still bore her name. "Kardas told *me* not to avenge him. He said nothing about my brother."

Mwizi folded her arms across her chest and cocked her head to the side.

Mistahn nodded in agreement as his gaze lingered on the red dragon sculpture near the middle of the room. The claws on its forelegs still held the hourglass high. Flecks of gold fell through the glass onto the skull below. The powdery gold only covered a few teeth.

Fire Keepers and Mistahn ringed a table. A candelabrum weeping wax like a mourning mother's tears stood in its center. The gray haze that permeated the room served as a reminder that funeral pyres burned outside to bury the family's fallen warriors, captains, and dragons.

Although no code or tradition forbade it, nobody sat in Kardas's empty chair.

Furwing lay on the table. She hissed at Andra as her tail twitched.

Sitting before each captain and warrior was a cup, tankard, or glass that held their preferred poison. All had been filled recently, but now almost all were nearly empty.

"Why isn't Berg here?" Ombran asked. Cloudy fluid seeped from the cut on his forehead. The swelled skin around it was bright pink. He wore an eye patch.

Andra slid her finger around the brim of her glass filled with Kabern. "He was displeased by word of my ascension to Swordfather." She stared at the tallest flame in the candelabrum. A dollop of wax dribbled down the candle to the pan below. "He demanded to see the fang. Kardas's blood had barely dried. He looked at my name and then me. He spoke not a word." She pressed the tip of her finger hard against the palm of her hand. "When he gave it back to me, his hand was trembling. Then he stormed away."

She drank the dragon's share of her Kabern.

A warrior poured from a flagon until Andra's glass again brimmed with dark red wine.

A short and heavy man with more hair on his knuckles than his head sat to Andra's right. He had plump lips, a pudgy nose, and jowls that made it look as though he was holding his breath. The tremendous weight of his body made him seem soft as a pillow, though some strength remained. His shoulders were rounded, as if shouldering some great and unseen weight. "You're gonna have to win him back," the man said.

Andra faced him. "Grouss, don't worry." She patted the soft man on the back. The fat on his face jiggled each time her hand landed. "Berg was my greatest champion as I rose through the family. He'll accept me as Swordfather. It's only a matter of time." She took a long draw from her glass of Kabern. Rivulets of red sprang from the corners of her mouth.

"The way you said that...you tryin' to convince me or you?" Grouss asked.

"I'm sure of it."

Grouss drank from his tankard of brown ale. "I'll do muh best to help you with that. Sorry I wasn't at the Castle o' Towers when it mattered most. Muh body isn't what it was. These days, there's a lot more of it and it's all weak." The big, soft man sighed. "But I can help with this strike." His hand was on the table. Andra laid her hand on top of it. "Thunderin' gods, I miss the old dragon." His voice was tired.

"We all do," Andra replied, patting his hand.

Grouss cleared his throat and smacked his lips. "Young man, if you're goin' to do this thin' for us, you must know why. I'll tell you o' the Bleedin' Blade and why Raysk has chosen his dark path." He took a drink from the stone tankard. "For dragon's years, Swordfamilies were ruled by a Blade o' Blades. A Swordfather who led they own family and controlled all the rest, too. A man named Auzken was the last Swordfather who ruled them all." The wrinkles on his face grew deeper as he spoke. "He was a Heavy. When he died, he gave his power to the Council o' Sheathed

Swords. That's what we call all the Swordfathers agreein' on how to rule the realm together. Auzken knew that after he died, if one Blade tried to rule the families, there'd be more fightin'. He was strong and respected by all o' the families. If we warred after he died, everyone would o' suffered. There woulda been less coin for all.

"Methinks he made the council because he knew the Heavies woulda made more coin that way, too. Anyways, after he died he told the Swordfathers to bury him on top o' Mount Densmore. Can't say why he wanted to be up there, mighta thought the thunderin' gods woulda put him on their tallest gold mountain that way." Grouss screwed up his face, pondering the question for a moment. "His mind was gettin' rotten toward the end, so who knows. The families couldn't lay him atop no mountain, so instead they put him in a tomb with his sword. The Swordfather that has the Bleedin' Blade and keeps it from the other families is king o' the Swordfamilies. That's what Raysk is tryin' to do. If he gets the blade, he'll rule the families, includin' us."

"I doubt that he would be a kindly king," Mwizi added.

"Auzken was buried with the Bleeding Blade a long time ago. Maybe sixty eclipses," Andra added.

"Thirty years?" Mistahn asked.

His sister nodded.

"It's not just revenge the Fire Keepers seek. We must preserve the balance that Raysk means to destroy," Grouss said.

Mistahn did not speak, but his eyes blazed with eagerness.

Drumming her fingers hard against the table, Yutago sprang to her feet. "Why haven't we burned Xutsuh yet? And what of Kardas?" She punched her fist against her hip. "It's past time."

Anger flickered across Andra's face, but she quenched it like a torch.

"Their bodies are lying on the blue ice in the deep undercroft beneath the east tower. Kardas and Xutsuh are next to each other."

"They'd better not stay there as long as Fyur did," Yutago said.

Andra ignored her. "We're not burning them until Raysk is dead." More wine. "I don't want Kardas mounting the Cloud Dragon before this deed is done. If he does, fire is like to rain down on me from blue skies. When Raysk is gone, after we take that stone from my boot, that is the time for your husband and our late Swordfather to join the Keepers Beyond."

Mistahn sat to his sister's left. He revealed little trace of youth; his features were hard as the granite dragon in the room. None of the eyes directed at him looked at his face.

"Whether he lies upon a funeral pyre or bed of ice, Kardas will know what we're doing. The man will speak no more, but his last words must be said again," Mwizi growled. "Do not avenge me."

Pacing around the table, Yutago's footfalls sounded like war hammers pounding against the floor. She ground a fist in the palm of her hand. Then she leaned in close to Mwizi's ear. "Andra has thrown our dice. She is our Swordfather now. You will not speak to her with that tongue." She resumed her pacing, her steps no less thunderous. "Will Vasarox be at the parley? He must die for what he did to Xutsuh."

"Calm yourself, Yutago," Andra said in a whisper.

"Have you seen my husband's face? It's not enough to kill Darker Hands," Yutago said. "The disrespect! My hatred for that animal is hotter than dragon blood!"

With a small gesture, Andra directed Yutago to sit down. When the captain obeyed, the sound of her arse hitting the chair was louder than her stomping around the table.

"I say again, calm yourself. Hatred is the mortal enemy of reason." Andra frowned so hard that the skin at the corners of her mouth folded into crescents and her chin rumpled. "Our minds must be clear as a mountain lake if we are to right this terrible wrong."

Every Fire Keeper at the table fell silent. Glas, Ombran, and Tyv were among them. The three warriors sat rigid with obedient attention.

Andra plunged her hand into a pouch and produced a small wooden carving of a house. She placed the bauble on the table. After drawing a deep sigh, she slowly rose. Then she put her fingertips on the table and leaned forward.

"This thing we will do is not born of fury. It is not hatred burning hotter than a dragon's flame." As she spoke, her eyes went from Mistahn to every Fire Keeper. "It's our only chance to stop this war here and now. To return the Swordfamilies to the balance that made us strong for a good long time. This war dies while it's still young or it rages until our dragons' fire has gone out and our family is nothing but thin smoke.

"We only throw our dice when the odds are in our favor. Heavily." She paced around the table, her footfalls silent as the grave. "Raysk has called the parley between our families. It's our best chance to make a quick end to this bloody war."

Mistahn leaned back in his chair. "That's why I'm here with you all. If I can help the Fire Keepers, you have only to ask. My sister has asked and I will help." He looked his sister in the eye. "Before I met Kardas, I'd never seen a king bow. Hells, I didn't even know that kings had knees!"

Grouss laughed with the young man.

"Get this done and it'll be better than winning the Melee of the Risen Knight," Tyv said.

"You'd go from outside the family straight to captain," Glas chuckled. "And none of us warriors would breathe a word against it!"

"I thought we didn't mix blood with fire?" Mwizi asked coolly. "What about the Clouds of Flame? Those two brothers nearly burned our family to the ground. That's why kin can't join." The warrior's voice became deeper. "And let's not forget that I'm the next captain. After everything I've done for this family, I should *already* be a captain."

Andra ceased her pacing. She put her hands on her hips and glared at the warrior. "That was Kardas's rule, not the family's. When this is over and the war has ended, the Fire Keepers will owe Mistahn a great debt. Opening our family to him will begin to repay that debt," she said in a tone that would brook no argument. "Your place in the family is mine to decide."

For long moments, the only movement at the table was dancing candle flame and dripping wax.

Resuming her path, Andra clasped her hands behind her back. "When Raysk asked for a parley, I agreed. To avoid more bloodshed between our Swordfamilies, I told them my brother would represent the Fire Keepers." A smile flickered across Andra's lips. "I have no interest in the particulars of the surrender terms that Raysk will surely demand. Even if we agreed to whatever he proposes, there's no doubt our fallen kin aren't enough to satisfy him. He lusts for blood the way most men lust for Syrens."

Andra remained standing as she returned to her place at the table. Grouss pulled a deep draught from his tankard. Warriors scrambled to fill flagons as the Fire Keepers at the table tipped their cups.

"Swordbrother Glas, you've spoken to that Heavy you know?" Andra asked. "The one Kardas had you tell that we had the Bleeding Blade?"

"I have, my Swordfather," Glas said. His eyes were glassy. "Teska told me where they'll hold the parley. She's been tasked with driving the wain when the Heavies take Mistahn there. She told me they'll meet at a tavern called the Juggling Moons."

"You've done well, as always. Do you trust that her lips will remain tight?"

"I do. The Heavies will search the place carefully. To them, it doesn't matter if we know where the parley will happen. They'd hunt for hidden weapons even if we didn't know. A dragon attack won't happen because we agreed to the parley. To her mind, talking to me is naught, because Raysk's safety is certain."

Grouss slammed his tankard on the table. "The Jugglin' Moons! It's perfect for us!" He wiped the ale from his chin with the back of his hand. "It's away from the thoroughfares, down a narrow alley by the Satin Gate." He rubbed his hands together. "It's a small tavern, good food, tasty meat. It's usually empty, not sure how they managed to survive all o' these years. Me and Fyur used to go in there all the time for hot stew with hard bread and harder ale. Both burned about the same goin' down. Perfect." He clasped his hands together. "They got a privy that hangs out over a stream. Probably flows into the River o' Plenty."

Stroking her chin, Andra closed her eyes. "We might be

able to put the sword in there. Use something fine to hang it."

"Could work," Grouss agreed. "It's a privy so it's real dark in there. Just a little window up high that lets in some light. The shops and homes around it are tall." He pulled a single hair from the back of his hand and held it up. "We could use a horse hair. Maybe even a couple o' them. When it's done, the stream below probably won't move fast enough to sweep away the sword. But it will move anything that gets dropped from an arse. Heh! Shouldn't be hard to fish the sword out o' there."

His chair squeaked as Tyv leaned forward. "I don't care how dark it is. There's no sword in the realm that you can hide in a privy without someone seeing it. Glas said it, the Heavies are going to search the whole tavern before the parley."

"Do you have good eyes?" Andra asked.

"Yes."

"Do you see that knot in the wood? There on the table, near the candelabrum?" She pointed to a spot within arm's reach from where Tyv sat. A wood board had a dark circle near its edge.

"Yes."

"Touch it."

Tyv's eyes narrowed in suspicion, but he obeyed. He pointed at the knot but stopped short. He looked at Andra and she nodded for him to continue. He thrust his finger forward and yelped in pain. Quick as a bowstring that loosed its arrow, he snapped his hand back. A trail of blood drops followed. He clenched the wounded hand into a fist and pulled it tight against his chest.

"*Thu'gods what was that?*" he hissed through gritted teeth.

Reaching over the table, near where Tyv had just cut his finger, Andra wrapped her hand around something that couldn't be seen. She flicked her wrist and the top half of a candle toppled from the candelabrum. Hot wax pooled where it landed.

"Mistahn won't use a sword made of steel. He'll be wielding the Shard of the Specter."

She laid the sword on the table. The Fire Keepers who sat near where she set down the blade picked up their drinks.

"How?" Tyv asked breathlessly. He sucked on his bleeding finger.

"Metal or magic. Mayhaps both. I do not know."

Ombran reached his hand to where Andra had set down the hilt. He moved slowly and carefully, as if nearing hot coals. When he reached the sword's grip, his fingers curled around it. He gave the sword one hard squeeze and then released it from his grasp, not daring to raise the unseen blade.

"The sword that Hanngoh gifted you," Ombran said in a hushed tone. "Ha! Even if I still had two working eyes I wouldn't be able to see it. For once, the rumors were right."

"Aye, after Raysk tried to steal it from Dark Water, Hanngoh gave it to me," Andra said. "Now Raysk will get what he wants, as a gift from the Fire Keepers. Right in his rotten chest."

Grouss cleared his throat. "We could string it up over the privy. The folk crappin' in there will never know how much danger they were in. Even if someone looks at it, would be almost impossible to see a strand o' horse hair. If they do see it, it'll look like a strand o' spiderweb."

"I'll do it. If a hair doesn't work, I'll stab it into a wall up high. The privy's made of wood, right?" Yutago asked and Grouss nodded. "I'll put it where no one can knock into it."

"Thank you, Yutago. Find the best place and secrete it there," Andra said. "When you do it, move with haste, for time is more valuable than gold. After we're done here, go straight to Juggling Moons and hide the blade. The Heavies will soon put many eyes on that tavern." She put her hand on Glas's shoulder. "Tell them what we know."

He glanced at her hand before he spoke. "Raysk has asked for a parley and demanded that it happens on his terms. The Heavies will pick up Mistahn inside the Mages' Mist, near the bridge that spans the Wandering Waters." He locked eyes with Mistahn. "From there, they'll put you in a wain and take you to Juggling Moons."

As Glas spoke, Mistahn's skin adopted a lighter shade of white. As he paled, the streak of red that had graced his face since birth became more pronounced.

Andra approached her brother and put her hand on his shoulder, squeezing it tight. "The Heavies have given me their word that the Scabbards will protect you during the parley," she said. She moved the carving of their home sitting on the table closer to Mistahn. "But a Heavy's word is worth little more than an ugly Syren, so I talked to the Scabbards myself. It's true." She turned her attention to Glas. "Who will sup with my brother that night?"

"Raysk doesn't trust any of his underlings to speak for the Heavies, so he'll be there." Glas scratched at his neck hard enough to turn it red. "A Scabbard captain will be there as well."

"Anyone else?" Andra pressed.

"It's possible, but my girl didn't know with certainty." Glas shrugged.

Andra closed her eyes and rubbed her temples. "Thank

you, Glas. You've done well." She patted him on the back. "Between this and the heist that you helped pull off for Melyq, you could well make captain."

Glas beamed at his Swordfather and she beamed back at him.

Mwizi scowled.

"Why doesn't Raysk crush us?" Ombran asked. "If he's going to do it, now's the time."

"He'd rather cow us than kill us," Grouss replied dismissively.

"Seemed like t'other way around as he was slaughtering our family in the bailey," Ombran replied. He winced as he touched the sore wound on his forehead. "I saw what Vasarox did to Xutsuh with my own eyes. It was one of the last things I saw with both of them." He pressed his eye patch. "The thundering gods will trample that Heavy bastard when he's deep in the hells."

Yutago shook so much that her long black hair riffled like falling water.

"I wondered the same thing, Ombran. Then I realized that we have something the Heavies will never possess," Tyv said. He glanced at the carved red dragon. "Raysk would die in his bed of old age before his family could take our dragons and tame them. They'll always be loyal to us. If Raysk hopes to harness the power of our dragons, he needs us alive. Some of us, anyway."

Scooping up the tiny carved house, Andra returned to her chair. "Mistahn, two things will shield you before you kill Raysk. The Scabbard captain will be there. He'll be the one that doesn't talk much. No Swordfamily has ever committed an act of violence against another family in the presence of a Scabbard. Raysk, vile as he is, will respect the code of our Swordfamilies. He won't harm you because of

Sacred Kin. That's why I summoned you. Before you strike, you'll be protected by the Swordfamilies' sacred code and Raysk won't think you're a real threat."

The table shook as Grouss slammed down his tankard. Furwing scrambled to hide beneath Andra's chair.

"Surprise will be your lady companion for the night, and she's far better than any woman you could hope to bed. You must treat her right tenderly, because you won't have her for very long," Grouss said as he pointed at Andra's brother. "After you sit down and get Raysk to feel easy, say you have to use the privy. The Scabbard may pat you down before you go. Be calm. Panic is poison. Inside the privy, search for the sword. Take it from the spot where Yutago hides it. Heavies for sure won't find it. If you can't find it, get outta there. This is a golden opportunity, but we can get Raysk another time. There's more than one way to skin a dragon." Grouss grabbed someone else's glass of Kabern and drained it dry. "When you come back to the table, you can't hold the grip in your palm. If they payin' attention, they'll know somethin's amiss. Instead, you cradle the pommel between your fingers loose so it looks like you holdin' your hand like always. Try it."

With speed and certainty, Andra snatched the Shard of the Specter by its grip. She handed the sword to Mistahn with the blade pointing down. He took it from her slowly and gingerly felt the hilt. First the pommel, then the grip, and finally the cross guard.

After trying to walk naturally with the invisible sword hanging loosely in his fingers seven times, all the Fire Keepers agreed that he looked perfectly natural.

Andra forced him to practice his walk eleven more times. Then one last time because he scraped the point against the floor on the eleventh walk.

Grouss's jowls jiggled as he nodded to give his blessing. "Good. When you get back to the table, the first one you kill is Raysk. Run him through, right in the neck. If you can, hit them little bones in the back. Even if you don't, he'll be dead before he knows what happened. Remember this, it's important. Act like you're surprised when he starts bleedin'. Lean in close and yell, 'Are you all right?' Or somethin' like that." Grouss mimicked a stabbing motion while he looked confused. "That way the Scabbard won't think that you're killin' Raysk. That's key, because the Scabbard is next. If you can get him in the neck or head, do it. Just make sure you stick him before he gets his sword out of its leather." Grouss belched loud enough that the candle flames shook. "After that, if there's another Heavy there, stab 'em, hack 'em, tell 'em a scary story. Don't care what you do, just finish them real quick-like."

The Fire Keepers had filled sacks with potatoes as targets for Mistahn. He stabbed and slashed them with the Shard of the Specter, feeling the weight and judging the blade's distance.

Grouss pounded on his chest. "You can wield a blade, no doubt. But can you kill a man?"

"I've killed before," Mistahn said defensively. "I've much to do in the forest, so I only have time to dig them shallow graves. Scavengers get at the them, wanting the carrion and all." His eyes narrowed. "The men were all bandits or trappers who thought our home was easy prey. I don't doubt that what you've told me of Raysk is true. Not one of the men I felled was his size. But I tell you true when I say that when I've killed, I didn't hesitate." He stood, taller now than when he'd walked into the room. "I'll kill Raysk with a steady hand. Anyone else in the tavern will join him in the thundering hells before the gods have run roughshod over his cursed soul.”

“I like this one.” Yutago swept her hand from Andra to Mistahn and back again. “I can see the relation…he has the same fire.”

“You catch on real quick, but you gotta be even quicker with that sword.” Grouss clapped his meaty paws together. “Smear blood on the Scabbard’s sword and put that sword by Raysk. Then you gotta get rid o’ the Shard o’ the Specter. Run back to the privy and drop it down the hole. Run just as fast from the Jugglin’ Moons. You start screamin’ ‘bout murder and blood. Act like you almost been kill’t. Run like your life depends on it, ‘cause it does.”

The candles’ orange glow cast streaking shadows over Mistahn’s face. “I can do that.” The lines around his eyes and mouth deepened with each word. His birthmark was dark. “But what if I’m covered in blood? Outside the tavern, who will believe me?”

Mwizi tilted her chair and sighed. “I know a Kingdom Guard. Good friend of mine, a lad who’s loyal to me and not the crown. He’ll be in the alley outside the tavern and the only Kingdom Guard who happens to be there.” She scratched at her own throat and the backs of her hands. “He’ll take care of what needs to be taken care of.” Then she fell silent and stared at the tallest candle in the candelabrum.

Grouss grabbed someone else’s tankard and plodded around the table. He waved his hands as he spoke, spilling ale as if it were green sea pouring off the deck of a tall cog. “You run out screamin’ that Raysk is attackin’ the Scabbard and anyone else you killed. Then you fall on your knees and beg Mwizi’s Kingdom Guard to go in.”

Emboldened by the weak poison he’d been pouring

down his throat, Tyv stood. Somehow the light reflecting off his toothy grin shone brighter than the candle flames. "Let me guess. That guard will have a sword or three on him and he'll plant steel on the bodies if need be. Mwizi, I hope you reminded him to wipe the blood on the blades!"

Laughter erupted as Tyv wiped his hands all over himself, miming as if they were blades. His crotch and arse were wiped many times. His tongue wagged like a mongrel dog's tail for added effect.

The Swordfather calmed the room. "Remember, you must look terrified as you rush out." She patted him on the chest. "After this thing is done, you'll go away for a long time. A Scabbard dead. A Swordfather dead. The families will be wroth. After Mwizi's Kingdom Guard goes into the tavern, you run straight through the city to the docks." She held the carving of their house in her hand. "A Dark Water will be there waiting for you. Goes by the name of Faomen. He'll take you somewhere safe, across waters that even the sharks fear. After the furor has quieted, I'll summon you."

"Where will I go?"

"The only two people in the realm who know where you're going are me and the Dark Water who's taking you." She tousled his long red hair. "And you'll be the third to find out when you get there." Andra put her hand under her brother's chin. "With Raysk dead we get revenge for Kardas and the War of the Heavies ends as quick as it began. That's what Kardas wanted." She sighed. "Raysk's folly would rip the families apart like rotted cloth. Instead, we will restore balance and bounty to the families."

Grouss's cheeks rippled like waves of grain in strong winds. "Let's be clear. It's underhanded. Like somethin' the Lysnapi or Vycerow families would do. But after what the

Heavies did to us, the thunderin' hells aren't hot enough for those wretches!"

"Burn them all! Let the wind scatter their ashes!" Yutago yelled.

Now all the Fire Keepers stood around the table, drink in hand. They shouted and elbowed each other, their revelry a salve for the pain.

Furwing hissed from her spot beneath Andra's chair.

"We'll play Raysk like a fine lute!" Glas yelled.

"Wouldn't doubt that he killed Fyur! We'll get him for that, too!" Tyv screamed.

Grouss called, "THE TOAST!"

The drinks rose and Mwizi whispered to Andra. "If it doesn't go right, what happens to my man? Will he be safe from the other Kingdom Guards? Can he find quarter with the Fire Keepers?"

"Not if it puts our Swordfamily in danger." Andra gestured to the warriors to bring all the flagons and fill all the cups. "Family First."

Mwizi frowned.

A warrior poured Grouss fresh ale. As he raised his tankard, the drink sprayed. He raised a meaty paw to silence the family.

"Tonight, we drink our *fill*! Tomorrow, we savor the *kill*!"

CHAPTER TWENTY-SIX
EMERALD CROWN

"This peach is delicious," Melyq said as he ripped away a mouthful of its ripe flesh. The juices from the fruit dribbled down his chin, soaking the neck of his white jerkin. He wiped his plump lips with a small piece of cloth that was already moist with the fruit's sweet nectar. The cloth was dripping when he returned it to his lap. "I thank you for this unexpected invitation."

Across the table from Melyq, the queen smirked. Her eyes were only half-open. "The king is indisposed tonight."

Above them hung a candelabrum that held many burning candles. It was big as a wagon wheel and made of gold and silver fashioned in the same style as the crowns worn by the king and queen. Candles burned on each mountain peak that rose from this great crown. The primary difference between the candelabrum and the crowns worn by the king and queen were the jewels that adorned it. In this dining hall, the jewels were still emeralds.

The two were seated at a long table in the royal dining hall. Their places weren't at the ends of the table where they'd need to yell to hear each other. Instead, the couple sat in the middle, where their voices and secrets need only travel its width. This curious arrangement meant that their eastern and western flanks were besieged by long columns of serving platters armed with savory fare.

On either side of Queen Minacia and Counselor Melyq, the first line of dishes featured three different leafy greens picked that afternoon and rinsed in water clear as winter air. Past this verdant vanguard were plates of chicken roasted with garlic and rare beef piled high with sautéed morels.

At one end of the table were the serving girls' favorite dishes. Purposefully placed as far from the supping parties as possible, these delicacies were the girls' most cherished sweets. The luxuriant dishes were out of sight from the diners, and hopefully out of mind. Later, mice and scullions would be blamed when the succulent treats vanished from the kitchen. They included stacks of toasted bread topped with sweet ginger and honeyed wine, and thick strawberry pudding with currants.

To defend their saccharine treasures, the girls made good use of a dish that was seldom eaten. The royal chef's signature dish, which gave her a greater sense of pride than any of her seven children, was roast peacock. The chef insisted that the peacock was served on a bed of its own plumage.

The silver platter that held the peacock was so large that two serving girls were needed to carry it. One serving girl's hair was so feathery that it flowed like the bird's puffy feathers as she helped carry the dish. After setting it on the table, the girls took the feathers off the platter and stabbed them into the bird. Through the girls' efforts, the roast peacock spread its feathers one last time.

The peacock was positioned on the table between the girls' precious morsels and the royal diners. The feathers were a shield to deflect the wandering eyes of those who were served.

Arrayed on the table in front of Queen Minacia was an arc of delicate stemmed glasses brimming with the finest wines. The last glass on her left was filled with white. The last glass on her right was filled with red. Glasses arranged in the arc between the ends held wines that transitioned in color from white to red, light to dark. This peculiar arrangement reminded the queen of the stars that occasionally fell from the sky. It required a trusted serving girl to replenish the drinks properly.

Portraits of the princesses and princes hung from the dark stone walls. Beneath each was a brazier to ensure that light was cast on them day and night. As she chewed on a sundried grape from the greens, Minacia's eyes wandered amongst the paintings.

"Each time I birthed the children, my affection for my husband waned." She swallowed the bite and drank from a glass filled with a pink wine. "As they departed me, so did the warmth the king and I once treasured." She nodded at the portrait of the twins. "Before the twins were born, there was nothing left." She held an off-white wine in one hand and the darkest red in the other. "I suppose that's not true. There was more than nothing. There was rage."

"He still resents you for not allowing him to hold the twins as newborns," Melyq said.

Minacia smiled.

The serving girls were still as the empty suits of armor on pedestals in the corners.

Melyq sighed deeply and chose his words carefully.

"The twins are beautiful children and you are not responsible for your husband's...indiscretions."

The twins were depicted together in the middle of the five portraits. Princess Tajna sat on an oak settle with a cushioned back. Behind her stood Prince Tajnum, her slightly older twin brother. Their round, soft faces radiated youth with skin that was noticeably darker than the other children. Their eyes were brown and sparkled with mischief under crowns adorned with thick black hair. The twins were far bigger and stronger than their other siblings were at the same age.

"Certainly, I'm not to blame for my husband's weaknesses," Minacia said dryly, sniffing a glass of dark yellow wine. "Of which there are many."

"As the twins age, there is a risk that he questions their parentage."

Minacia sipped from the glass and shrugged. "There is also a risk that the Gods' Blade topples down on the castle. To my mind, both are equally possible."

"As your loyal counselor, I would observe that there may be consequences for what the king would consider an act of marital betrayal."

"In my experience, Fallov understands precious little of a woman's body. I doubt very much that he would understand the significance of differences in what we create." Minacia drained the wine glass that held the darkest red wine. "Voden is another matter entirely." She rubbed her hands together. "If all transpires as hoped, our noble king's reign may soon be at an end. He has no more hope of exacting revenge than he does sheathing his little sword in me." She snapped her fingers to summon a server.

A pale waif with feathery brown hair appeared at the

queen's side. She poured wine from the flagon with a well-practiced hand.

"Thank you, Belna," the queen said with appreciation.

The serving girl bowed deeply and disappeared from sight.

"With servants of such low cunning, I sometimes wonder if they can pour the right wine in the right glass, but they suffice. And it's certain that our secrets are safer if our words are not understood by those around us." The queen sliced the roast boar on her plate. The meat was so tender she could have cut it with a spoon.

Melyq poked at his liver of aurochs as he chewed. "Secrecy is paramount given the challenges ahead."

"Agreed. I thank you for all that you've done preparing my children for their forthcoming roles in the kingdom." Minacia raised a glass of white as Melyq did the same with his glass of water. The drinks chimed like a tiny bell when they met. "Oh, Melyq, I'd be lost without you. Your sage advice has helped to arrange all the pieces on the board, exactly where they belong." She took a deep draught of the wine. "I scarcely need to move them. I'll simply watch as everything plays out with the same certainty that water flows down a river."

Melyq grinned and sipped his water. "All good plans are conceived in the darkest shadows. Great plans remain there forever."

Flames in the candelabrum above flickered wildly.

"Tajna and Tajnum are too young to play a role in this, at least so far as I can see. Their time will come, many eclipses from now. My middle children remain merely children, but they have wisdom beyond their years. For that, I thank you." Minacia sliced off a bit of tasty meat from a dish she didn't recognize. "My children will be the foundation of a dynasty that shall outlive the Emerald Kingdom."

Melyq nodded.

The portrait of Princess Modawa hung to the left of her younger twin siblings. The middle princess had hair as white as sun-bleached bone. The healers summoned by the king and queen believed that her hair, which contrasted brilliantly with her light brown skin, was caused by the same affliction that paled half of Opvolk's body. Her face shined with youthful innocence, except for her eyes. The wrinkles under her eyes, and the crow's feet that spread from them, were like those of women who had seen far more eclipses than Modawa.

Prince Bruun was the middle prince. His portrait hung to the right of the twins. His square jaw and heavy brow gave Bruun a weightiness that had nothing to do with his body. A scar ran from the top of his forehead to the bridge of his nose and down a cheek. From there, it curved back to his ear. The scar was lighter than his olive skin and always attracted curious eyes at court. The boy who gave it to him would have been beheaded, were it not his older brother. Bruun used expensive ointments and jellies to wear his frilly black hair up, in the shape of a crown.

"The middle children vex me. Modawa and Bruun are of an age that is ripe for marriage and alliance. But to who, and when? The manner of their use eludes me." The queen briefly wondered what animal had died to produce the meat on her plate. She put a bite in her mouth and chewed thoroughly.

"My queen, I would suggest that you hold them in abeyance. You already control more than half the lords in the Emerald Kingdom, and all the houses with true power." Melyq gently set his fork and knife on the table. "With the coming changes in Fulccrum, the alliances necessary for absolute mastery of your queendom may need to be refashioned. If houses afar begin to slip away, the children could marry a lord or lady accordant with their appetites. If a seed sower or heir bearer should be necessary, adequate stock is readily available. The oldest and middle children could be the mortar that secures your realm. If, instead, we need to quiet potential foes within Fulccrum, they could marry or seduce a Swordfather."

"Seduce, you say?" Minacia finished a glass of rouge wine with relish. "Why, Melyq, have you been spending time in a Shrine of Solace?"

The counselor straightened his jerkin and picked up another peach. "I have not. Though from what I'm told, Opvolk has been, how shall we say, indulging himself."

Barely repressed laughter was the queen's response. "The eldest children are completely under my control, Opvolk and Silny both." The queen watched her counselor nibble at the peach. "Agreed that the middle two children may be my shields, but I intend to make the two oldest my swords. They are near and dear to my designs." She bit from a slab of beef and spit it out. "This meat is overdone. Take it from my sight and feed it to the hounds."

A servant quickly removed the plate that held the offending meat and scampered away.

Between his small bites Melyq said, "If the eldest children are to be your advisors, I must needs continue their teachings apace. They're not ignorant, but they have much to learn."

Prince Opvolk's portrait hung at one end of the five portraits, next to his younger brother Bruun. Princess Silny's portrait was at the other end, next to her younger sister Modawa.

Melyq reached forward and laid his hands on the table. The queen tapped her long fingernails against the hardwood.

"Advisors...then rulers." The queen fondled a wine glass. "After all, you're not the only one who's been teaching them. They've not yet mastered the Syrens' ways, but they're adept. When Opvolk visits a Shrine of Solace, the seducer becomes the seduced."

Blazing a trail through the forest of wine glasses before her, the queen placed her hands over those of her counselor's. Wrapped around Melyq's wrist was his bracelet styled as a green snake devouring its own tail. Minacia absently slid her fingers over the bracelet, spinning its head all the way around her advisor's wrist. She petted his hands tenderly.

Melyq blushed.

When Minacia withdrew her hands, she did so slowly. Her touch was light and warm, like the soft breath of a whispered invitation. Melyq's hands lingered. He pulled them away and wiped his sweaty palms on his thighs.

The counselor's first few words were unusually high pitched. "We must be mindful..." He coughed and gulped down some water. "We must be mindful of the Syrens' advances toward the Prince of the Eclipse. Doubtless their intentions are to control him and the throne upon which he will sit."

Another glass bid farewell to the better part of its wine before Minacia replied. "Silny and Opvolk are now the seducers. Or are you forgetting that I led the Syrens before I abdicated as their Swordfather? Had I succeeded in bringing the Heavies under my dominion, I might still be prancing around in those ridiculous dresses they wear."

"I haven't forgotten your time with the Syrens. Refusing

your beauty is to refuse a rare gift from the thundering horde of gods. Clearly all of Raysk's strength is in his body rather than his mind." Melyq pulled at the skin of a half-eaten peach lying on his plate. "What you did to his face was an improvement, like washing a layer of dirt off an urchin in the streets."

"I may still have some of his skin underneath my fingernails." The queen smiled as she tore away a piece of roast boar. "Probably some of his hair as well."

"It's hard to believe that you two were romantic. He's a brute."

"He once gouged out a man's eyes with his thumbs, then ripped the man's skull apart. At the same time."

Melyq stopped mid-chew.

Minacia shrugged. "I romanced the power, not the man."

"Raysk's gambit to escape your charms was extreme, though admittedly clever. I'll give him that much." Melyq dabbed a cloth at the corners of his mouth.

Pader Stones were piled high on a gilded platter. Minacia plucked the largest one she could find and popped it in her mouth. "There are vanishingly few ways to escape The Need. I had Raysk under my charms and the Heavies were nearly mine. He was a warrior at the time, but even back then I could sense he was destined to become Swordfather. His drive for power was without equal. Under my control, our two families could have crushed the rest." She masticated with moxie. "That's when he made Pametan do the unthinkable."

"How much of his heraldry did she take? The bend and the roundels? Or just the roundels?"

"Truthfully, I do not know. But I do know Raysk and I can't imagine he would be able to live without the bend.

The roundels are what drives a man to The Need. Most like, she only took the roundels."

"Then he took her hand."

"Yes, he crushed the one that held the knife. I'm told there was much blood. The Heavies had an excellent healer there for Raysk, who also saved Pametan. But the healer couldn't save her hand."

"So that's how Pametan came to be his consulary."

"She was his most promising captain before he lamed her. She cannot fight like a Heavy with one hand."

"Raysk ordered Pametan to do it?"

"He wouldn't do it to himself."

Melyq sat in stunned silence.

"Is there no other way to rid oneself of The Need?"

"I only know of one other."

"Which is?"

"Death."

Melyq eyed the mound of Pader Stones on the platter. "Most men would rather the headsman's blade fall on their neck than their manhood." He paused in a moment of thought. "That's when you left the Syrens."

The queen eyed a glass of pale wine, but she didn't take a drink. "Yes. My gambit failed. My leadership was undermined. It was my time, so I took my leave." She knocked over a glass of wine. "As I recall these things, it's strange. I wasn't angry with Raysk. Well, I wasn't angry after I tore his face to shreds and Pametan cut off his stones. Over time, I came to appreciate that he earned his escape from The Need. He was surprisingly forthright with me." Her eyes narrowed. "Unlike my lying, sniveling, pathetic husband who needs a throne with a high back because his rotted backbone isn't strong enough to hold him upright."

Melyq opened his mouth and then shut it without making a sound.

"I'm going to strangle the king with a length of rope so I don't have to feel the blood flowing from his black heart as he dies. The contemptible fool brought this doom on himself. He ruined our marriage, undermined his family, and weakened the crown." The queen's rage radiating from her like a bolt of lightning frozen between them. "The realm *must* be conquered because it *can* be conquered. King Fallov the Feckless has put our neck in an iron collar. The reds need only snap it closed and nail it shut. If it weren't their queendom, it would be one of the other crowns. Every link in the chains that would bind our realm is made of a terrible decision by our lowly king."

The queen paused to douse her rage with another glass of wine. She swallowed, then laughed and sobbed at the same time. She thought of Voden and Fallov.

"For her want of his nail the kingdom was lost," Minacia said.

Melyq cocked his head. "Does the king not have The Need?"

"The Need and love are entirely different things. I haven't used my Syren's charms on him. Men with The Need are boring. They are forever begging for affection. The Need is a powerful tool for collecting coin. But marriage to a man under The Need would be worse than the fieriest hell. Even worse than what I've suffered." She furrowed her brow. "Although, looking back, perhaps that was a misstep." She shrugged.

His glass of water shook as Melyq drank from it.

Minacia's temper cooled as quickly as it had risen. The lightning disappeared and with it the thunder of her rage.

She sighed. "The king forged the Emerald Crown's doom in the fires between the thighs of that harpy."

"You have enjoyed at least some measure of revenge against Fallov."

Minacia beamed with pride as she looked at the portrait of her children. "Indeed. Raysk, too. The thundering hells hath no wrath like a Syren scorned."

Mustering her courage, a serving girl cleaned the mess from the glass spilled by the queen and fled. Then Belna filled the glasses that had been emptied by the queen's thirst.

Summoning a plate of whitefish drenched in butter and surrounded by winkles, Melyq tucked a cloth into the neck of his jerkin. "We must be gracious hosts to the Crimson Crown. We have done all that we could to hasten their journey, but we can only do so much. I hope that the queens will understand that."

Seasoned pork sat on Minacia's plate. It was so tender that it could have been swallowed just as easily as the moat of thin gravy around it. A medley of vegetables was piled high on the meat.

"They are aware of our efforts. The greatest difficulty they face are the mountain passes. We've done what we can with our obliging lords and commanders in the field."

She swept the vegetables off the pork and sliced a chunk.

Minacia smacked her lips. "I must concede that I can't stop fretting over the future. What if the reds seek to chase my family from Fulccrum? What if they don't honor our agreement?"

"The Crimson Crown is ruled by two queens. They will have no heirs of their own," Melyq replied. "Like you, they need your children to thrive over generations. They must have royal blood for their legacy and their subjects."

"Surely the queens have a seed sower," Minacia said.

"Of course. Mayhaps dozens of them," the counselor replied. "If you can believe the Crimson Realm's poor folk, every man who's sired a child is welcome to try. It's said that there's been enough seed spilled inside those queens to harvest a bountiful crop of squalling babes. Yet, the queens have produced no heirs."

"Which queen has been unable to bear a child?"

"Both of them," Melyq said. "Therein lies the rub."

Minacia nodded. "What I love about you is that every side of the dice that you cast for me has a six on it. But this will take time. Fulccrum wasn't built in an eclipse. Neither will my children's dominance of kingdoms and families. After it has all come to fruition, they will rule without threat from the east. My successes as queen will at last eclipse my deeds as Swordfather." She liberated a wineglass from the table. "My children will rule realms and Sword-families alike."

Minacia locked eyes with her counselor.

"They will sit upon the throne with a scepter in one hand and the Bleeding Blade in the other."

The queen and her counselor raised their glasses in salute.

"I failed as Swordfather, but I will triumph as queen."

The glasses chimed merrily as they met.

"Still, in all schemes caution is the watchword. We must consider what other kingdoms may be of use in bringing the Crimson Crown to heel, if the queens should choose to see our agreement in a different light. They have many enemies." Melyq twirled a shrimp in a small bowl of oil and garlic.

"There are several possibilities should the need arise. The Kingdom of Bone, Land of White Nights, or Steel Oak Forest. The Castles of Vine or even the Seas Above may suffice."

"They've long been bitter rivals with the Realm of Rime," Minacia added.

"Yes, the Crimson Crown's enemies are many. I've doubled our loyal shadows watching the dovecote. If Fallov attempts to ally with one of the reds' enemies, he'll need to use messenger pigeons. If he does, we'll know."

"Good," Minacia said. "There's also the Amethyst Kingdom."

"Indeed," Melyq agreed. "The Kingdom of Kings, if you will. To my knowledge they've never been belligerent toward the Crimson Queendom. That type of relationship with the Crimson Crown could be beneficial if ever we need to strike the queens when their guard is down. They wouldn't expect harm from the kings. If the queens don't suit our needs, perhaps the kings could best fit your children's future."

"For all our dire talk, I expect the Crimson Crown will honor our arrangement," Minacia said, pursing her lips. "Although paranoia is the most valuable instinct."

"There are two kinds of people inside castle walls: the paranoid and the dead," Melyq growled.

The candles mounted on the giant crown above flickered.

Melyq tore the last bit of meat from a tiny leg of roast pigeon. The bone bounced when he dropped it on his silver plate.

"Our relations with the Crimson Crown are set for the nonce." He leaned back and patted his full stomach. "But we must consider the Swordfamilies as well."

Minacia took a deep breath and cracked each one of her knuckles individually.

"I'll rip their web of debts apart. The precious favors that they've spun will become worthless. Their threads will rot like cobwebs. After I've swept the debts and the families from the city, complete power will reside where it belongs. On the throne. *My throne.*"

"What of the other families in other realms? The families that reside in the Crimson Crown's capital delight in violence that would make the Swordfamilies in Fulccrum shudder."

"The families of Lysnap are singularly violent, but they don't concern me. During my time with the Syrens, not once did I hear of a Fulccrum Swordfamily allying them-selves with the Lysnapi. The families across realms respect territories." Minacia sighed. "We have an abundance of adversaries who are real; there's no need to imagine more."

"There are a great many enemies." Melyq rubbed his hands together. "Unfortunate that our ploy with the bones failed to achieve the desired effect. Driving a wedge of hatred between the Fire Keepers and the king, that would have been a masterstroke."

"Thundering gods alone know how Romlad fell into the Lava Sea. The boy was infatuated with flame, whether it roared from a dragon or flowed like water. I seem to recall that he would steal away to the kitchen and stare at the cooking fires. The scullions would bray about how the boy was always underfoot." The orange glow from a nearby candle reflected brightly in the lightest wine in Minacia's arsenal. "His charred bones were a generous gift from the gods. Mayhaps one of them is a salamander."

Melyq eyed the pigeon bone on his plate. "They were an even greater gift than the birds Lord Wrand sent that kept disappearing from the dovecote and reappearing in the kitchens without their messages. Pity that not all went to plan. I was certain that Fallov would order the Kingdom Guard to march on Kardas and his lot after the boy's charred bones were found on the dragon refuge."

"It was worth a throw of the dice." Minacia shrugged. "They remain allies, but both are weakened. That serves us well enough. I expect that another Swordfamily will soon recognize Kardas's weakness after his losses at Kellington's Pass and deliver a fatal blow to the Fire Keepers. As for the other Swordfamilies, we will contend with them after we greet the Crimson Crown."

"And the Syrens?"

"Despite our history, I despise them no more than any other family. Sinsasi was a warrior under me. I know her weaknesses. Their fate will simply follow that of the other Swordfamilies. Which will depend on how willingly they accept their fates." She picked up another wine glass. Reconsidering, she returned it to the arc on the table. "My husband has allowed those baseborn, lackwit criminals to lord over my city for too long. His failings have made the throne little more than a crude chair in a peasant's hovel."

Melyq placed his cloth by his silver plate. "Shall we indulge in dessert?"

"The desserts on the table do not interest me."

"I bought some dates at the Old Town Square Market today. A merchant there always has the sweetest dates. They're far sweeter than any I've tasted from our kitchens." Melyq produced a small silver box and opened it, revealing the tiny red fruits. "They're a splendid way to end a rich meal with flourish." He held the dates within the queen's reach.

"A kind offer, but my appetite for supper is sated."

Melyq shrugged and popped one of the dates in his mouth.

"Belna, bring me a great feather from that peacock down there."

Belna stumbled and almost fell as she started toward the bird. She yanked a feather from the roast peacock and returned to the queen.

The feather danced in the server's violently shaking hand. She gave it to the queen, who handed it to Melyq.

"Before she ruled the Crimson Realm, the younger Crimson Queen led the Lysnapi family that practices the same arts as my Syrens. In my experience, sharing flesh is the path to pure loyalty. You must not succumb to another queen's charms." Minacia gave him a tiny smile. "It's time that we retire to my bedchamber."

"Indeed, it is," Melyq said, grinning wide.

In unison, the queen and her counselor rose.

The queen left the room first. Melyq hustled close behind her, clutching the feather.

CHAPTER TWENTY-SEVEN

FIRE KEEPERS

Mistahn stood alone on a corner where two nameless streets crossed. Although he couldn't see it, a score of steps away from him a bridge spanned the Wandering Waters. One of his hands was curled around a walking staff topped with a sculpted bronze dragon head. Its mouth was open wide, revealing a burning candle inside.

Near total darkness enveloped Andra's brother. The early evening sun was still high above the horizon, but he saw no more than a dim yellow circle. Little light reached him after struggling through the eldritch darkness, as if the sky was matted with dark storm clouds. Mistahn kept reaching out his hand with the palm up, expecting to feel rain. None fell.

Candlelight shining from the windows of the homes around him was brighter than the veiled sun. The few people who walked past him carried two candles. They held one high and the other low to avoid stepping on the rats that covered the streets thick as scales on a dragon.

Mages' Mist was a blight on Fulccrum.

Wandering Waters flowed just to his north and its roar was loud. Heavy rains in the east had transformed its placid surface into a tempest of whitecaps. The swelled rivers in the capital city swept logs and branches ripped from trees down to the port.

Mistahn had stood in the same place long enough that his legs began to ache. He shifted more of his weight onto the staff with the bronze dragon head. The darkness shrouded passersby, and his imagination began to believe that the same people were circling him for some nefarious purpose.

Gazing into a lit window, he wondered why anyone would choose to dwell in a place the sun would never reach. There was a strong rime on everything around him. The frost was thickest on the ground. The air was so cold that even in the dark he could see his breath turn white.

The unrelenting darkness made gauging the passage of time impossible. He felt the Mages' Mist sapping his vigor. He blinked, but his eyes stayed shut and his head bowed.

He became aware of the sound of horse hooves and cart wheels, but they sounded very distant.

"You there!" a woman's voice called.

Mistahn jerked wide awake. "Y-yes," he replied.

"The breath on that dragon looks mighty hot," she said.

"This one has only been eating garlic and mustard seed," Mistahn replied, raising the staff. "If you think this is hot, you should see the dragons whose breath could turn this night to day." He brought the staff down with a thud. The flame inside the dragon head flickered.

The woman who drove the wain was shrouded in mist, but he heard her pound on a large wooden box. It sat in the wain behind her. The side of the box at the wain's rear dropped open. The sound of moving chainmail accompanied the large man inside the box who lumbered down the side that had become a ramp.

The man's silence told Mistahn everything he needed to know. The man was a Scabbard.

Meaty paws ran up and down Mistahn's arms, legs, and chest. Then the large man slapped the places that he hadn't already rubbed against. After he finished groping every nook and cranny of Mistahn's body, the Scabbard paused. He looked Mistahn straight in the eyes.

The two stared each other down so long that the horses hitched to the wain became agitated. Satisfied, the Scabbard nodded. In a swift movement, the silent man pulled a hood made of coarse cloth over Mistahn's head.

After being yanked up the ramp and inside the wooden box, Andra's brother sat on a bench. His back was pressed hard against the box. He was grateful for the hood that concealed his face when he felt a cold sweat beading on his upper lip.

A latch was jerked tight and creaking wheels below him began to turn. He couldn't be certain how fast they traveled, but he guessed that the horses pulled the wain at a brisk trot. The Scabbard's chainmail rattled when they rolled over large stones.

Pushing his back against the wood, Mistahn lost count of how many turns the driver made. The pace quickened and he gripped the bench as best he could. The horses moved in a straight path so long that his head began to ache. The wain slowed and Mistahn heard water splash as the wheels must have rolled through a stream. The horses resumed their fast gait and made a turn so sharp that he slid to the end of the bench, where his shoulder slammed into the box.

Hooves thundered over wood planks that Mistahn took to be a bridge.

"We must've crossed half the realm by now. Am I going to meet Raysk or the Crimson Crown's queens?" he sputtered. The Scabbard remained silent.

The horses slowed. The turns became fewer and farther between. Mistahn leaned forward and put his elbows on his knees. His head swayed in the same cadence as the wain.

If this keeps up I'll take my supper with a view of either the Pader Mountains or the bottom of the Angered Sea.

After a sharp turn to the right, the wain trundled down an alley at a leisurely pace. Mistahn judged that it must be narrow from the sounds made by the horses and cart echoing off the nearby buildings.

The horses came to a halt. An instant later, the wain shook as the Scabbard stood. The shrill scratch of metal against metal filled the box as a latch was undone. Warm air rushed in and with it came the scent of rich foods. Mistahn's mouth began to water.

A firm hand grabbed him under the arm and pulled him to his feet. His head slammed against the top of the box. The Scabbard guided him down the ramp. When he reached the cobblestone street, the short hairs of his beard caught on the coarse bag as the Scabbard yanked it off his head.

With the hood gone, Mistahn blinked hard and fast until his surroundings came into focus.

The door to the building before him was decorated with an ornate carving. There were no words inscribed on it. Instead, the etching depicted a jester. Clad in painted motley, the fool wore a cap 'n' bells. Bronze crotal bells were mounted to every point on its cap.

Arms splayed, the wooden jester held his palms up.

Three round objects were shown in an arc over his cap 'n' bells. After Mistahn blinked a few more times he could see that the objects weren't juggling balls.

Above the jester was a ball painted red and streaked with gray. Mistahn understood it to be Dragon Without Wings. Directly above one of the jester's hands was a dark circle speckled with dabs of white paint that was Rain Above Rain. The yellow moon's color above his other hand made it unmistakable as Night Scythe.

"Welcome to Juggling Moons," the driver said as she alighted from the wain. She was lean but imposing.

"The ride was a bit rough. Who do I have to thank for it?" Mistahn asked the driver.

"A Heavy," she replied as she tied the horses to a wooden post. She wore a white hood that concealed her face. It clung to her skin in spots where the cloth was yellow. "Now come, you won't keep Raysk waiting."

There's only one hole in that hood. How does she see with her other eye?

The Heavy took a step toward the front door to the tavern. Before she took the second step, she was stopped by the Scabbard's hand pressed hard against her chest.

"Stay here," the Scabbard growled at her. "Take this." He thrust the staff with the bronze dragon head against her shoulder. The candle inside the dragon's mouth had gone out. It was dark and cold.

The Heavy sneered at the Scabbard, but she obeyed.

"Raysk's orders," the Scabbard added. Then he pointed at the staff and said to Mistahn, "It could be a weapon. You'll get it back when you leave."

Torches in sconces burned next to the carved door. The sky was a warm blue as the sun lingered, unseen, somewhere over the Angered Sea.

The crotal bells on the jester's cap chimed as the door swung inward. The Scabbard stepped through and beckoned Mistahn to follow. After he did, the Scabbard closed and barred the door.

The tavern was a dark and confined space. The shadows here were black as spilled ink.

Small square tables were placed in no apparent pattern or order. On each table was a single large candle in a brass holder. No tables were below the iron candelabrum that hung in the middle of the room. On the floor below it was a circle of wax tall enough that it could stub a toe.

Statues of jesters adorned the walls and the bar. The candlelight cast shadows over their faces, turning their cheery jests into ghoulish jeers.

A man sat at a table away from the door. He was large as a knight clad in full plate armor, though he wore only simple clothes that stretched against his skin. On the plate in front of him lay a piece of meat the size of a ripe melon. Blood from the barely cooked meat spilled over the edge of the plate and onto the table. He cut off a large chunk and, after chewing thrice, swallowed.

Thu'gods his Swordfamily must be named after him. Ah, well, at least it's only him and no others.

The man looked up casually and smiled.

"Welcome," Raysk called. "Pat him."

"I already did," the Scabbard replied.

"I'm sure you did," Raysk said. "But you didn't do it in my presence."

Mistahn raised his arms and again the Scabbard methodically searched him for hidden weapons.

"Look for daggers. Fire Keepers used to hone small daggers from dragon fangs." He used the back of his hand to wipe away the blood on his chin. "Daggers are little swords for little people with little strength. But they can be lethal in skilled hands."

"There are none," the Scabbard said, having finished his task.

Mistahn straightened his jerkin. "Now check *him* for weapons," he said to the Scabbard in a voice of cool confidence. He pointed a steady finger at Raysk.

The Swordfather raised his eyebrows in surprise.

The Scabbard remained motionless.

Raysk stood and raised his arms.

Thu'gods, is he man or Pader Mountain?

The Scabbard followed Mistahn's order, slowly and deliberately. "The Heavy has no weapons," he reported brusquely. Finished with the task, he moved to a wall away from the table.

The second strike will require deft hands. Thank the horde that Scabbard wears no helm.

"Come, sit." Raysk gestured toward the empty chair at his table.

Mistahn rose to his full height and pushed out his chest. He felt a serenity born of singular dedication to his task.

The table was barely big enough for two men, particularly when one of them was Raysk. The candle in the middle flickered as Mistahn took his seat.

That meat is barely browned. Was it cooked using that candle?

"I'm Raysk, the Heavies' Swordfather. I understand that you're Andra's brother." He sawed off a hunk of meat and continued speaking as he chewed with his mouth open. "Welcome to Fulccrum, the city that's a realm unto itself."

Mistahn clasped his hands and put them in his lap. "I thank you, Swordfather. A pity that we're meeting this way."

Without realizing what he was doing, Andra's brother stared at the dark red scars covering Raysk's face.

"I can hear your thoughts," he said dully. "Most of the scars on my face are a token of affection from an old friend. The newest one is a scratch from Dark Water." Raysk raised a hand and gestured in a circle around his face. "Strange that you would look at me that way. I've no doubt that your own visage has attracted unwanted attention."

"For as long as I can remember," Mistahn replied, feeling the red streak across his face darken.

Blood dripped from Raysk's chin.

"The Fire Keepers have long been the crown's thralls. The king was the most important strand in that web of debt that Kardas spun." Raysk shrugged. "Or mayhaps the crown was the outhouse where Kardas hung the Fire Keepers' web." He lifted a flagon full of red wine and drank from it deeply. "You must understand that this had to happen. It wasn't my choice. The strong are destined to conquer the weak. It is our manifest destiny."

He slammed the flagon down on the table so hard the candle guttered. Mistahn didn't flinch.

"I only knew Swordfather Kardas for a brief time. But I did see the king bow before him."

"Hah! An empty gesture. Like two bumbling actors in a miserable play." Raysk again lifted the flagon from the table, revealing that the wood beneath had been marred when he slammed it down. "No matter how strong a web is woven, a Heavy can reach into its center and crush the spider." He swished the wine for a time before downing another drink. "That's how we throw our dice. With strength and certainty and without hesitation."

Mistahn glared at the Heavy.

"You're not part of a Swordfamily." Raysk eyed the

young man. "But you carry yourself well. If I didn't know you lived in that hovel in a miserable stretch of forest, I might think you a lord." He shook his head slowly. "But you're also small and weak. Hardly a threat. My family could make you strong."

"How?" Mistahn asked.

"We have friends who peddle things that grow muscles like they're weeds."

An elderly tavern keeper emerged from the kitchen. Her eyes were as gray as her hair. She hobbled over to the table with one hand on her back and the other on a simple cane.

"You want a cup for that wine?" she asked Raysk in a voice that was rougher than shark skin. He shook his head. She turned her attention to Mistahn and said, "What'll it be?"

"Try the lamb. It's the best in the realm," Raysk offered. He cut off a hunk of meat.

Mistahn eyed Raysk's plate. The meat was now half as big as it was when he'd entered the tavern.

"What're you having?"

The scars near Raysk's lips crumpled as he smiled. "I'm so glad that you asked. I'm supping on dragon meat." He twirled his fork around. Thick drops of blood fell from the meat stabbed on the tines. "This isn't the meat of just any dragon. It's from a dragon hatchling. They're even more tender than veal!"

Mistahn felt his stomach drop.

"Grown dragons are a better hunt, but worse meat. Stealing newborn dragons is boring, but the taste of their tender flesh is *divine*." With a grand flourish, he opened his mouth wide and placed the piece of meat on his tongue. Then clamped down and chewed, moaning as if he were in a Shrine of Solace. "Such fresh meat. I slaughtered this one today. Its blood is much cooler than a grown dragon's. And I brought enough for the kitchen to cook another plate. You're welcome to try it."

Blood mingled with spit flowed over Raysk's lips and poured from his chin. His teeth were red.

"I'll have the lamb," Mistahn said to the tavern keeper without looking at her. His voice was steady but his hands were curled into fists and trembling with rage.

The tavern keeper slowly turned and limped back to the kitchen.

"My sister sent me to put an end to your war."

Raysk swallowed the bite of meat and washed it down with the wine remaining in the flagon.

"She's their warrior of warriors now? The leader of the Fire Keepers' remains?" Raysk said with an air of indifference. "Mayhaps the family should address her as Daggerfather." He sawed at the dragon hatchling meat as he spoke. "I didn't even bother to look at whose name was on that fang before I plunged it into Kardas's chest. It really doesn't matter to me who's tasked with cleaning up the dragon dung."

"She wants to end the civil war between the families."

"There's nothing civil about this war."

He took another bite.

"Andra sent me here so that we could discuss peace without anger. I'm not a part of this war. I'm her blood family, not her Swordfamily. Let's end the fighting with our heads, not our hands."

Raysk put the fork and knife on his plate.

"I'm a reasonable man. When reasonable men talk through their differences, they will come to an agreement. How you respond to me will tell me whether you're a reasonable man, too." Raysk rubbed his hands together and smacked his lips. "The fighting will end. The Fire Keepers will train their dragons to obey my Heavies. If she knows, Andra will reveal to me which family holds the Bleeding Blade." Raysk flexed, stretching his jerkin so tight that some threads snapped. "The Fire Keepers are no longer a family. There are now only five great Swordfamilies. She leads nothing more than a band that answers to me. Those are my terms."

"No."

"I see that you are not a reasonable man."

Mistahn drew a deep breath. "Andra won't agree to that. Not after what you did to Kardas. How you killed him."

Folding his arms across his chest, Raysk frowned. "There was much confusion in the Castle of Towers. Smoke and bodies were everywhere. I wanted to make sure the next Swordfather could find the fang, so I put it in Kardas's chest for safekeeping." He looked at the ceiling. "It was raining hard during the battle. Tears are lost in rain and blood is lost in wine." He finished the last of the red wine. "The Fire Keepers' Swordfather died inside a dry tower, out of the rain. I've sent many a man to meet the thundering horde in far worse places." Raysk leaned forward. "Always remember, boy, the worst thing that *can* happen to you isn't the last thing that *does* happen to you."

"Your threats will not cow me," Mistahn whispered.

"Methinks you are a fool on a fool's errand," Raysk laughed, though he did not smile. "If Andra won't listen to reason, I'll wipe out her Swordfamily and the dragons. They'll fade into legend before they rot into myth. Scores of eclipses from now, mothers will tell their babes scary stories about flying lizards. They won't know that the stories are real."

Mistahn's throat felt very dry. "You would loose packs of wild dragons on the city?"

"Those dragons aren't as strong as Andra thinks. Kardas made the same mistake. It cost him his life. Don't let it be the end of your sister, too."

The elderly tavern keeper emerged from the kitchen once again. She set a plate of veal in front of Andra's brother.

"I need to make water. Where's the privy?" Mistahn asked the tavern keeper as he glared at Raysk.

"Past the bar where we serve the ale." She hobbled away on her fragile cane.

Scars folded as Raysk raised his eyebrows high. He snapped his fingers at the Scabbard, who neared the table. "Search him."

"I already searched him twice."

"And now you will search him a third time," Raysk growled. "Look for anything that can be used with a blade or bow."

This man is not dumb.

The Scabbard pressed hard on Mistahn. When his chest was searched, Andra's brother gasped for air.

"Nothing," the Scabbard said.

"You're certain?" Raysk shot back.

"Yes, there's nothing."

"Look under his chair."

The Scabbard turned Mistahn's chair upside down. He ran his hands along the wood. "Nothing."

"Very well. You may go, boy."

Mistahn turned and walked toward the bar at a deliberately slow pace.

"There's something that I should've mentioned earlier,"

Raysk called. He leaned back in his chair and cleared his throat.

"I only throw loaded dice."

Mistahn didn't look back.

Raysk shoved another hunk of bloody dragon meat into his mouth.

Down a dark hallway lined with candles, Mistahn found the privy. The door was quiet as he opened and closed it behind him. A small window let in enough light that he could see floating motes of dust. A dull roar sounded from below the hole. When he leaned over to search for the noise, he saw a swollen stream rough with tiny whitecaps.

Putting a foot on either side of the hole, Mistahn moved his hands over his head. He searched for the Shard of the Specter slowly, fearing that blood dripping from his hand would warn Raysk of impending danger. After he had reached high for long enough that his arms were tired, he pressed his fingers into the corners.

He felt no sword.

His heart began to beat faster.

Yutago said it was hung from the ceiling, but it's not there. She must've meant she jabbed it in a wall.

Beginning at the top of a wall, he ran his hands along the wood. He worked his way down to the floor where the smell stung his nostrils like an angry bee. Coarse wood rubbed against Mistahn's palms. He slid his hands across the walls more quickly than when he searched the ceiling. Where he touched the walls, his palms left behind streaks of sweat.

"Where in the thundering hells did Yutago put it?" he whispered.

Throwing his head back in frustration, his eyes fell on

the wood above the door. He spied a long, narrow hole in a board. To Mistahn, it looked nothing like a knot. The shape reminded him of how his knife would notch a piece of wood when he made a carving.

He swept his hand by the narrow hole but felt only cold air.

The blade must've fallen down the hole. There's more than one way to skin a dragon. I'll play the part, vowing to deliver Raysk's offer and counsel Andra to agree.

The door to the privy swung open, silent as a ghost.

Mistahn lurched backward, his calves now pressed tight against the privy seat.

Raysk stood in the doorway. His shoulders nearly touched the frame on both sides.

"Your lamb is getting cold."

Mistahn opened his mouth and began to stammer words that he, himself, didn't understand.

Raysk held up his index finger. Andra's brother fell silent.

"The Fire Keepers have profaned the code of Sacred Kin."

The breaths that Raysk drew were slow and deliberate.

"Let me offer you some advice. When you meet the thundering horde of gods, run faster than the horde."

Raysk raised a hand and slowly moved it toward Mistahn's chest. Andra's brother stood rooted in place, powerless and bewildered.

He felt something hot. When he looked down, Mistahn saw bright red blood trickling from a gaping hole in his chest. The blade felt like a flame made of ice, burning its way through his heart.

Raysk pushed the Shard of the Specter through Mistahn until the cross guard pressed hard against the young man's chest. Its point scratched against the privy's back wall.

White water below roared louder than an angry dragon. Raysk pulled the sword from Mistahn.

Blood spurted from the boy like Dancing Water. Raysk grabbed his arm and leg, lifting him into the air.

Before Mistahn's consciousness disappeared into the darkest of shadows, he felt himself turned upside down. His body was squeezed tight on all sides. Then he was falling and the whole world roared like a mother dragon mourning her young.

Blackness veiled his mind so quickly that he had scarcely enough time for one last thought.

Avenge me not.

CHAPTER TWENTY-EIGHT

FIRE KEEPERS

Kardas lay on the same scorched rocks that had borne Fyur's spirit to the Keepers Beyond. Next to the fallen Swordfather was the pyre for Xutsuh. On the other side of Kardas lay Mistahn. The three bodies were prepared according to Fire Keeper tradition. Each one had a dragon skull with the jaw open wide placed over their head.

A simple ceremony had been Kardas's wish. Fire Keepers silently poured the aged dragon blood into the departed. A dragon fang rested on each of their foreheads.

Near Kardas's feet, a brazier blazed.

Andra held a silent vigil before her fallen family of both sword and blood.

Yutago stood next to her husband's body. Her hand pressed on his chest. She made no effort to staunch her tears as she looked at his ruined face. She pulled their daughter tight.

To the west, the low sun was red as wine. Its warm light cast cold shadows. At this time of day, the Lye Tavern usually would have been bursting with the sounds of raucous merrymaking. Today it was silent and dark to honor the fallen Fire Keepers.

The Wandering Waters flowed near the pyres, smooth and quiet. Without any breeze, the flowers that festooned the riverbanks stood tall.

Grouss cradled a dragon egg in his arms as he approached Tyv, Mwizi, and Glas. He asked the warriors if Andra had spoken to anyone. When they replied that she had not, Grouss curled his lips into his mouth. He nodded with his head bowed. Then he approached his Swordfather.

"Andra?"

She didn't hear him.

"Andra," he said again, this time a little louder.

Silence. Grouss turned back to look at the Fire Keeper warriors. They quickly turned away.

Grouss trudged to a spot where Andra would see him. He said nothing as he handed the dragon egg to her.

"What's this?" she asked.

"It's from the Heavies," he replied.

"It's light." She shook the egg. "Something's rattling inside." She turned the egg over to find a small hole in the bottom.

Andra raised the egg over her head with both hands and slammed it against the ground.

The shell shattered into tiny pieces beyond count. It was dry and empty, except for the unborn dragon inside. The tiny, withered dragon came to rest against Kardas's funeral pyre.

The first frost of a deathly cold rage gathered in Andra's mind.

"It's an old Swordfamily message. It means Kardas Fire Keeper burns with the ashes," Grouss said.

"Another threat," Andra whispered. "Like that dragon bleeding into the Wandering Waters."

The Fire Keepers watched Andra intently.

"The Heavies are going to ice our dragons," Mwizi said.

"They're going to ice our family," Tyv added.

"We'll all be frozen in the cellar beneath the east tower," Glas agreed.

"At least we know how Kardas and Xutsuh met their end," Mwizi said, her voice full of sorrow. "We may never discover the answer to the riddle of Fyur's death."

Grouss shuffled away from Andra. The unseen weight on his round shoulders was impossibly heavy.

The three warriors neared their Swordfather.

"Raysk will pay the final price for what he did to Kardas," Tyv spat.

"But what happened to Mistahn?" Glas asked.

"My Kingdom Guard friend didn't see anyone go in or out of Juggling Moons until Raysk and the Scabbard left," Mwizi said.

"Raysk killed my brother with a single thrust," Andra said quietly. "I've no doubt."

"Mayhaps Raysk suspected danger when Mistahn searched for the Shard of the Specter," Tyv offered.

Andra maintained a strategic silence. *My heart tells me that I have been betrayed.*

Berg stood close enough to hear the warriors and Swordfather talk, but not so close that his presence was noticed. He glared at his Swordfather.

Mwizi shuffled away.

"We can hardly ask Raysk what happened," Glas groaned.

Lecata approached the funeral, ignoring the strangers

as she wove her way through them. She walked straight to Andra. A brief, silent embrace was their greeting.

"Sister," Andra said. She fought against her gathering tears. "I thank you for coming."

"How did our brother die?" Lecata asked.

Andra pondered the question for a moment. "Fighting the Fire Keepers' greatest enemy. He was braver than I could have hoped." She swallowed hard. "I am truly sorry for our brother's—"

The Swordfather's sister cut her short. "I lived with our brother. I understood Mistahn better than you. I know why he's here." Lecata managed a sorrowful smile. Then she moved to the head of Mistahn's funeral pyre. She picked up the dragon fang and rolled it between her fingers before returning it. She squeezed his hand tight.

A light breeze made the many-colored flowers on the riverbank sway.

Ombran grabbed Mwizi by the arm before she walked past.

"Thu'gods, if Mistahn went down the privy hole, how did we find him?" he whispered to her.

"Faomen, a Dark Water warrior," Mwizi replied in a hushed voice. "He fished Andra's brother from the port. Said the body was spinning around in a whirlpool. He brought Mistahn to Andra."

"How did he know it was Andra's brother?" Ombran pressed in a suspicious tone.

"You've seen his face." Mwizi shrugged. "A man doesn't need to see Mistahn to know his face. Probably nobody else in the Emerald Kingdom has one like it." She ripped off the tip of a fingernail with her teeth. "Body was still dripping wet when he arrived."

"I thought Dark Water left?" Ombran asked.

"Not all. Hanngoh left a few behind." Mwizi shrugged.

What little chatter lingered amongst the Fire Keepers quieted when Andra held up her hands.

"My family, no words can salve the loss that we honor here. But I must declare our enduring gratitude. These three men died for us. It is my hope that the Cloud Dragon will lessen the pain that we feel, but no word or deed of mine will halt it. We must hold tight to the cherished memories of our loved and lost. After the fires of anger yield to the ashes of acceptance, we will find great pride in the ultimate sacrifice laid by these men upon the altar of Swordfamily."

Andra wordlessly apprised Lecata of her task.

The Swordfather, her sister, and her captain silently lit small torches in the brazier. Then Yutago stood by her husband's funeral pyre. Lecata took her place near Mistahn.

Andra stood at Kardas's right hand. She was struck by the frailty of his body.

The three women dropped their torches into the mouths of the men lying on the pyres. Fire roared from the dead and the dragon skulls over their heads.

Andra said, "The Family Beyond will find our fallen."

The Fire Keepers responded by whispering only once: "Born to burn."

The fang still covered in Kardas's blood was nestled between Andra's breasts, close to her heart.

I will cleanse Kardas's fang in the blood that pools around Raysk's body after I send him to the thundering hells.

Andra watched as the man who'd made her the Fire Keepers' Swordfather became engulfed in flame. She moved to stand by Yutago's side for a time as the captain mourned her husband. Then she sighed and walked over to her sister, twisting the blade of her own grief.

The crowd of Fire Keeper captains and warriors stood in silence with their heads bowed.

"He begged me to join the Fire Keepers," she whispered to Lecata. "He said that if he failed, at least he would die as somebody rather than nobody." Her voice was tired.

Reaching into a pouch, Andra pulled out a tiny carving of her and Lecata's childhood home. Lecata looked at it and frowned.

Andra tossed the carving onto Mistahn's blazing funeral pyre. Then she returned to Kardas's flames.

Only half the sun remained in the sky.

Thu'gods, I despise sunsets. One day I will mount a dragon and fly into a sunrise.

Kardas's flames burned bright. The ashes of his body rose in the heat.

He was buried in the wind.

"Born to burn," she whispered. White plumes formed as she spoke each word.

Her eyes lingered on the clusters of pale blue flowers growing on the banks of the Wandering Waters. She ruefully remembered what the farmers called them.

Rage swept over Andra like an avalanche. The beads of sweat covering her body turned to flecks of ice. Lines of tears froze to her face.

Her breath was colder than hoarfrost on an ancient tombstone.

THANK YOU

Thank you for reading *Masters of Kings*. I sincerely appreciate your time and attention.

Honest reviews from readers are the most useful feedback for an author striving to improve their craft. I intend to read every review for *Masters of Kings* and learn from them. Please consider leaving a review on Amazon or Goodreads.

For updates on the next *Swordfathers* book, a full map of Fulccrum, and a newsletter sign-up that includes a free short story please visit:

swordfathers.com

Again, my heartfelt thanks.

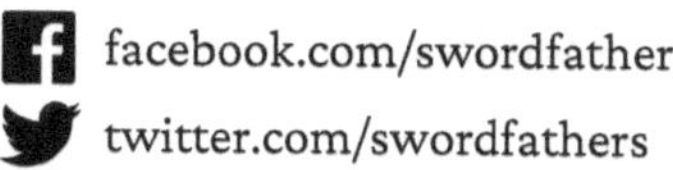

facebook.com/swordfathers

twitter.com/swordfathers

instagram.com/swordfathers

amazon.com/author/swordfathers

ABOUT THE AUTHOR

Dan Shields began writing *Swordfathers* when his muse made him an offer he couldn't refuse: either his internet browser history or his book would be published on Amazon. That's when Dan began typing the novel furiously.

He and his wife have four kids but—despite his fantasy writing inspired pleas—she wouldn't allow him to include a single apostrophe in any of their names. Dan holds degrees from Northwestern University, the University of Cincinnati, and New York University, a collection of schools that he refers to as an "academic sampler."

For updates on the next *Swordfathers* book, a full map of Fulccrum, and a newsletter sign-up that includes a free short story, please visit:

swordfathers.com

facebook.com/swordfathers

twitter.com/swordfathers

instagram.com/swordfathers

amazon.com/author/swordfathers

www.ingramcontent.com/pod-product-compliance
Lightning Source LLC
Chambersburg PA
CBHW022012300726
48970CB00003B/851